H16

Slough Library Services

Please return this book on or before the
date shown on your receipt.

To renew go to:
Website: **www.slough.gov.uk/libraries**
Phone: **03031 230035**

TELL ME IT'S NOT TRUE

1914. Mining engineer Tommy Birch goes off to war, leaving his new wife Rita behind in Pontefract. On the front line, Tommy is reported as missing, presumed deceased. But Tommy isn't dead. Found behind enemy lines, wearing only a pair of boots stolen from a dead German, Tommy is picked up by the enemy who believe him to be one of their own. He spends weeks recuperating in a German military hospital, where he meets, and quickly falls in love with, a nurse named Anna Kohler who tends him back to health. Meanwhile, back in Pontefract, Rita is destined to spend a lifetime wondering if her husband is still alive...

TELL ME IT'S NOT TRUE

TELL ME IT'S NOT TRUE

by

Ken McCoy

Magna Large Print Books
Long Preston, North Yorkshire,
BD23 4ND, England.

British Library Cataloguing in Publication Data.

A catalogue record of this book is
available from the British Library

ISBN   978-0-7505-4338-5

First published in Great Britain in 2017 by Piatkus

Copyright © 2017 by Ken McCoy

Cover illustration © Susan Fox by arrangement with
Arcangel Images

The moral right of the author has been asserted

Published in Large Print 2017 by arrangement with
Little, Brown Book Group Limited

Magna Large Print is an imprint of Library Magna Books Ltd.

Printed and bound in Great Britain by
T.J. (International) Ltd., Cornwall, PL28 8RW

To Val, who enriches my life
with her humour, wisdom,
patience and love.

Chapter 1

October 1914
'What's it all about, Dad?'
'What's what all about?'
'This flippin' war. It was supposed to be over by Christmas.'

Edith Birch looked up from the *Pontefract and Castleford Express* at her dad who was standing at the window, rubbing his shoulder and sucking on his dead pipe, trying to bring both muscle and pipe back to life as he looked out into the backyard, wondering if a couple of big pot plants might liven the place up a bit. He'd seen some in Castleford market, tanner a time including a half-decent plant pot. They'd blind the bin and be something more pleasant to look at through the back window. How to get them home on the bus, that might be a problem. He'd been thinking about making a trailer for his bike – now that would be really handy. The stuff he could cart about with a trailer. His tool-bass for a start.

Thursday was both payday and early finishing day in the building trade. It was twenty-five past five and Charlie Birch had been home ten minutes, after cycling from site on his boneshaker bicycle with his jute tool-bass slung over his shoulders and banging against his back every time he stood on the pedals to ride uphill. It was a difficult machine to ride at the best of times, never mind

11

having to carry a heavy bag which caused him to ride at a funny angle and which, he reckoned, had also caused him to pull a muscle in his right shoulder, the one he used for sawing timber. He decided that tomorrow he'd go on the bus, which was also something of a boneshaker but he wouldn't pull any muscles. Ha'penny there, ha'penny back – penny a day; a tanner for a six-day working week. Next to nothing really when you consider that a badly pulled muscle might cost him a day's pay, or maybe two or more days' pay – ten bob, maybe a pound, maybe more. Didn't bear thinking about.

Agnes, his wife, was keeping an eye on a pan of potatoes bubbling away on a gas ring. They were in the largest room in the house: combined living room, dining room and kitchen – better known as t'back room. It was a modest room in a modest home with an atmosphere of friendship, love, humour, pipe tobacco and boiled potatoes. The front room, better known as t'room, was kept for best and was permanently tidy. In t'back room there was a fire burning in the Yorkshire range, with a wooden clothes horse standing in front of it, investing most of its heat in drying young Stanley's steaming clothes which he'd got muddied falling in a puddle on his way home from school. He did a lot of falling did Stanley. His dad maintained that if he had as many ticks on his homework as he had scabs on his knees he'd be a genius. He was sitting at the table in his pyjamas, engrossed in *The Boy's Own Paper* – a comic for boys of Stanley's age – ten.

'I'd like to know which Christmas they're talking

about,' said Edith. 'It says here they've got recruiting people over at the Prince of Wales today. It says here that the West Riding Coal Owners' Association are raising a Miners Battalion for the King's Own Yorkshire Light Infantry.'

'It says that there, does it?'

'Yes, Dad, that's what I've just said.'

'Koylis eh?'

'That was your father's regiment,' said Agnes.

'I know,' said Edith. 'But what do they want miners for in the infantry? What're we going to do for coal if all the miners go to war?'

'Worried about your big brother are you?'

'I am, Dad, yes. I hope he hasn't gone and joined up.'

'Our Tommy? No, he's only just finished his apprenticeship. He's on man's money now.'

'He can be as daft as a brush when he tries, Dad.'

'I know, but he's still studying for his exams. This is his last year then he's fully qualified. He's not that daft, surely.'

'He's down the pit this week doing some surveying stuff and if the army turn up banging their drums and blowing their bugles, it might set him thinking.'

'No, he's a bright lad, our Tommy.'

'I hope he's too bright to have signed on.'

'He won't have signed on, love.'

'Anyway, I don't even know what it's about.'

Charlie Birch took a spill from the pot on the mantelpiece, lit it from the fire and reignited his pipe. He gave a few puffs on it, enough to envelop his head in smoke as he gathered his thoughts.

13

Edith sniffed it in. She liked the smell of her dad's pipe, which was just as well.

He stood up a lot did Charlie. In fact he spent much of his waking time on his feet. At work it was more or less necessary, at home it was to ease the discomfort that came from time to time. At such times he would curse Squinty McBride who had died within seconds of inflicting the accidental wound on his sergeant but in times of buttock discomfort it does no harm to have a genuine target for your venom. 'A bullet in the buttock is a wound for life,' was the medical assessment the army surgeon had given him, and you can't argue with experts.

'I'll tell you what it's about, Edith. It's about a bunch of damned bullies throwin' other people's weight about.'

'Right.'

She knew he'd need time to expand on his theory. She also knew his pipe might well go out again before this happened, but not this time.

'There's one thing fer sure,' he said, from somewhere within the blue cloud hovering around his head. 'It won't be their own weight they throw about. Never is in a war. It'll be the little man who gets killed, and at the end of it no bugger'll be better off.'

'So I take it you won't be signin' up.'

He gave a dry laugh. 'I wouldn't sign up again even if I were twenty years younger.'

'I've seen women giving white feathers to boys who aren't in uniform,' said Edith. 'It's to say they must be cowards. Ernie Clayborn came home with one yesterday and he's barely sixteen. It's not

14

as though he's big for his age. Some women need their heads testing.'

'Yer father's too old,' called out Agnes. 'He's forty-three next. War's a young man's game, eighteen to thirty-five, after that they slow down.'

'Will I have to go to war when I'm eighteen, Dad?' asked Stanley, without looking up from his comic.

'When you're eighteen, lad, this war'll be over and done with, and it's to be hoped them in charge'll have learned enough sense never to go to war ever again.'

'I'm glad you're too old, Dad,' said Stanley.

'Hey, I could give them young 'uns a run fer their money, lad. Any road, I did my bit fighting them damned Boers.'

'He got medals for that,' said her mother, 'and he got shot in his bum.'

'We know,' said Edith, who was grateful her father had never shown her his wound. He obviously had more respect for her than he had for his pals at the Pontefract Working Men's Club who had all been treated to many a viewing of Charlie Birch's heroic left buttock. Charlie was a foreman joiner for a local building contractor.

'Any woman shows me a white feather I'll show her me arse,' said Charlie, puffing on his pipe.

'Language, Charlie!' scolded his wife.

Charlie grinned. 'Trouble with me is I look young for me age.'

Edith looked in amazement at her mother who smiled and shook her head. Her daughter also smiled and looked down at her newspaper as her father expounded his unique knowledge of war.

15

'The last time we were invaded were nearly nine hundred years ago, and that were another King Billy. He conquered England but he never conquered Yorkshire. No, the Yorkshire lads back then took bugger-all notice of him and his foreign ways, and that made him as mad as hell.' He looked at Edith. 'Did you ever learn about the harrying of the north at school?'

She shook her head. 'Can't say I did.'

'That's when old King Billy the Conquerer decided to teach us Yorkshiremen a lesson for not behaving ourselves. He came up with his armies and burnt all the farms and villages but when they got to Pontefract they couldn't get across the river because our lads had knocked the bridge down. Stopped the buggers in their tracks it did. That's why it's called Pontefract – comes from the French for broken bridge.'

'So, what's this war all about, Dad?'

'This war? I'll tell yer what this war's about. It's to do with a load of damned treaties.'

'Treaties?'

'Yeah. You show me a treaty and I'll show you an idiot, in fact I'll show you a bunch of idiots.'

'Why's that?'

'I'll tell you why. You see, there's Austria and there's Hungary who've teamed up to form this big empire called the Austro-Hungarian Empire or some such thing, and they've got an emperor called Franz Joseph who's got a useless sod of a nephew called Fernando or Ferdinand or summat who he sends on a visit to Serbia, which is not a friendly country at the best of times. Now yon silly sod gets hisself shot dead swanning about in

16

the back of an open motor car which is probably why his uncle sent him there in the first place if the truth be told.'

'So his uncle wouldn't be all that bothered that his nephew had been shot?'

'No, not one bit. For a crown prince his nephew was as thick as two short planks. It's what they do, these kings and emperors. To them, having children's just a means to an end. Yer see, in this case, apart from getting rid of a useless crown prince it gives Austria and Hungary an excuse to attack the Serbians who they've never got on with, and what's more yon barmy German bugger Kaiser Bill was egging 'em on saying he'd help out, as and when necessary. He's been busting for a fight for years. Cut from the same cloth that lot.

'Anyway, what they weren't bargaining on was that Serbia has this treaty with Russia, who go to help Serbia, and this is where it really kicks off, because Germany attacks Russia.

'So now yer've got...' Charlie used the strong, gnarled fingers of his left hand to count countries, one by one ... 'yer've got Austria, Hungary, Serbia, Germany and Russia' he was now holding up all five fingers, 'all at it like silly sods, then bugger me, but it turns out Russia has a treaty with France who wake up one morning to find they're at war with half of Europe. Are yer getting me drift, Edith?'

'Sounds like a load o' daft lads ganging up on each other because they've nowt better to do. Not sure how we come into it, though.'

'Belgium, that how we come into it.'

'How does Belgium come into it?'

17

'Because we have a treaty with Belgium, so when Germany invade Belgium so they can get to northern France it brings us into the war.'

'Why would we need a treaty with Belgium?'

'No idea, love. Bugger Belgium, that's what I say. Lerrem all get on with it. We're an island. Best country in the world and we've got the world's best navy to protect us. Why should we send our lads ter get killed? War's a lot different now from when I fought in South Africa. This war'll be mechanised. Great big guns that can fire massive shells five miles, machine guns that can fire a thousand bullets a minute. They can drop bombs from aeroplanes and they've bombs they can just throw at each other. Wars used to be about cunning and strategy and bravery, this war'll be all loud noise, misery and hellfire. You mark my words. It'll be industrialised killing.'

'There must be more to it than you just said, Dad, surely to goodness.'

'That's the trouble, love, there isn't any more to it, except that Kaiser Bill's been busting to throw his weight about Europe for years and he took advantage of Austria to make a start. If it wasn't for that big silly sod there'd be no war.'

'It can't be right that one man can cause so much misery.'

'If that man's a German he can, and unless they wipe Germany off the map there'll be another war comes along. It's in their blood.'

'So there is a good reason for going to war – to wipe Germany out.'

'Yes, love, but our lot won't do that because when the war's over you get politicians taking over, and it'll be easier for them to make Germany pay for the damage, then leave them alone. It's a major job taking over a country that doesn't speak your language.'

'Supposing Germany wins. Will they do the same?'

'Not the Germans, love. They'll occupy every country and make us speak their flaming language even if it's at the point of a gun.'

'So it is a war worth winning.'

'Oh, it's a war worth winning all right but there's no need for us to be in it. This war'll be a right bugger. There'll be no honour in this war. Nowt'll come of it, other than pain, poverty, misery and death. Wars cost money and we live in a world that doesn't have much money.'

'So, why did you become a soldier?'

His pipe tilted upwards as he smiled. 'I could say it was travel and adventure. A young man in my position had only one way to see the world and that was to join the army or the navy. I joined up when I was twenty-five and got posted to South Africa. A year later we were at war with the Boers.' He looked at Edith and grinned. 'Hey, nothing to do with me – I didn't start it. Last year of the century that was.'

'So, you were already married to Mam when you joined up to see the world?'

'Well, there was actually a bit more than that to it, love. Our Tommy was four, you'd arrived, times were hard in the building trade. I kept getting laid off work as a joiner – I spent as much time laid off work as I did working. The army was a regular job and we were allocated married quarters straight away. When I got posted most of me money came straight home to yer mam. I signed on fer three years, after which was when the war finished, more or less.'

'Was I here then?' asked Stanley.

'Nay, lad,' said his father. 'You took us by surprise a bit later on.'

'Oh,' said Stanley.

'It was a pleasant surprise,' said his mother, quickly. 'Yer father spent ten months over there after the war, working at a diamond mine.'

'What? You worked down a diamond mine?'

Charlie laughed. 'No, yer wouldn't get me down one o' them holes. I helped to build accommo-dation blocks for the workers.'

'He was the boss,' added Agnes. 'Weren't you, Charlie?'

'Well there was a bit of a shortage of men who knew what they were doing out there, and with me being an apprentice-served joiner they put me in charge. Great money, and I was back to doing a job I was trained for. Stood me in good stead when I came home.'

'So, you didn't see us for nearly four years?' said Edith.

'Well, I came home for recuperation when I got shot, then I went back after three months and came home once the war were finished. We moved to a rented house and I went back to Africa to do the building job. The money was enough to put a decent deposit down on this place and make a few improvements to it.'

It was an end-of-terrace house and Charlie had spent some of his money knocking the wall through from the scullery to the outside lavatory, providing an inside bathroom. It was the only house in the row with such facilities.

'I'd have taken you three with me but it was a rough old place where I was working. Grand weather, though.'

Her mother added, 'It's easier to stand your husband being away from home when you know he's in no danger.'

'But you were glad to get me back for good, weren't you?'

'Aye, I suppose I was.'

He caught her eye. Edith looked up at them both and saw the mutual but silent love there, and she wondered if she'd ever know such love. She was fifteen and had never had a proper boyfriend unless you counted Tinley Bateson who once kissed her in Pontefract Park, but she hadn't kissed him back so it didn't count. She'd set her sights a lot higher than Tiny Tinley Bateson who was a bit vulgar, barely five feet two tall and a butcher's delivery boy who showed no promise of ever bettering himself. Her brother Tommy was her yardstick when choosing a boyfriend. Trouble was, there weren't too many lads around who could match Tommy, not that she'd ever tell him that.

The clock on the mantelpiece chimed six o'clock which meant it was twenty to six. It was a family tradition to keep it twenty minutes fast to ensure good time-keeping. This made no sense to Edith or Stanley but it wasn't their clock so they didn't argue.

'Tommy's late,' said Edith.

'He told me he was meeting Rita straight from

21

work,' said her mother. 'They're going to that new picture palace in Knottingley.'

'What's he gone to see?'

'Oh it's a cowboy picture, but Tommy's really gone to see them funny pictures that's on with it. He likes that little tramp feller with his bowler hat and moustache and walks with his feet at ten to two.'

'Charlie Chaplin?'

'That's him. Our Tommy thinks he's ever so funny. Never seen him myself. I think it's magic the way they have them photos moving about as if they're alive.'

'Next thing you know they'll have 'em talking,' said Charlie, still puffing away on his pipe. 'You mark my words.'

'Don't talk so daft, Dad. How can they do that?'

'Well they've got them phonograph things. Stands to reason if you ask me.'

'Blimey, Dad!' said Stanley. 'Talking photos. Did you hear that, Mam?'

'Nowt your dad says surprises me, love. Right, it's sausage and mash for tea. Extra sausage, with Tommy not being here. Who wants peas?'

Chapter 2

Prince of Wales Colliery, Pontefract. 1914
Tommy Birch walked out into the pit yard with Billy, his chainman. He was carrying his theodolite in its case while Billy was carrying the tripod and a staff. They both wore canvas mining caps with a leather brim, on which was a leather lampholder, onto which were clipped their carbide lamps. Billy was also carrying a hand-held lamp to help them in their work. Surveying work down a mine was a precision job and required a lot more light than was necessary to hack out coal. They both handed their lamps and identity tokens in at the lamp cabin and made their way to the washroom, a facility not available to the miners – pithead baths were still twenty years away. Despite neither of them doing any actual mining work their faces were blackened by the coal dust. Tommy was due to meet Rita at the bus stop in half an hour.

Washed and changed, Tommy made his way towards the pit gates, passing the manager's office on the way. Several of the pit yard workers were standing around the doorway. Tommy went over to see what was going on. Outside the manager's door was a big poster depicting a silhouette of a group of soldiers and a field gun, along with a quotation from Lord Kitchener:

Be honest with yourself.
Be certain that your
so-called reason is not
just a selfish excuse.

ENLIST TODAY

'They're recruiting for the army, Tommy,' said a passing miner. 'I've just signed up. It'll all be over by Christmas and we get paid to go to France – brilliant! Never thought I'd ever go abroad.'

A large man with a bushy moustache and three stripes on his khaki uniform was standing in the doorway. He called out to Tommy. 'You're just what we're looking for, big strapping lad. We're the King's Own Yorkshire Light Infantry. We're raising a Miners Battalion. Just suit you, lad.'

'I'm not a miner I'm an engineer, and I'm not all that strapping,' said Tommy, studying the poster.

The sergeant grinned. He had a face like a benevolent ogre. 'Better still. This is a pioneer battalion, we need engineers. Come on, lad, you don't want to be one of them who stays at home while there's all that going on in France. What'll everyone think? Come inside, let's have a chat. No obligation, lad. When that next shift comes off there'll be a queue a mile long.'

Signing on had crossed Tommy's mind several times. The KOYLI was his dad's old regiment and they had their garrison in Pontefract. A lot of his pals were already over in France. Some had been home on leave, swanning around in their uniforms, heroes already. He was beginning to feel a bit left out. He allowed himself to be ushered into

24

the manager's office which was full of excited young miners, all eager to sign up and go to France, as if it were some sort of free holiday. The manager wasn't looking too pleased. Tommy knew him well enough to seek advice.

'What do think, Mr Atkinson? I've only just finished my apprenticeship.'

'I'm not supposed to say one way or the other, Tommy. But the bosses say we're not to stand in the way of any under twenty-five year olds who want to go. Miners are needed as much as soldiers in this war.' He said the last bit loud enough for the recruiting officer, sitting at a table, to hear.

'Well, I'm only nineteen,' said Tommy, 'So I suppose I ought to sign up.'

Despite him being classed as 'management', Tommy was popular with all the young miners who gave a cheer when they heard him.

'Hey up, lads, Tommy's coming with us!'

Their enthusiasm and back-slapping left Tommy with no option but to sign on. He left the manager's office completely bewildered as to what he'd just done – turned his life upside down with no planning and no forethought. He was fifteen minutes late meeting Rita who wasn't too worried. There was another bus due and they'd still get there in time. It was the look on his face that worried her most.

'What is it, Tommy? There hasn't been an accident at the pit has there?'

Tommy looked at her and knew that what he said to her, and its repercussions, would have to be repeated again when he got home. He'd promised his mam he wouldn't sign on without talking it over with her and his dad ... and his sister Edith for that matter.

'Oh heck, Rita,' he said. 'I think you're gonna get cross with me.'

They sat through two Charlie Chaplins and a Fatty Arbuckle comedy without so much as a smile. Tommy was wishing he'd walked straight out of the pit yard without being nosey about what was happening at the manager's office, but he knew the recruiting people would be there to-morrow and the odds were that he'd have signed up at some time. That's what he told himself. The alternative would be to see the war through with every young man in Pontefract except him out there fighting the Hun, as the recruiting people called them. The main feature film came on, a Western called *The Bargain Hunters*. Tommy put his arm around Rita.

'What would you have thought of me if I'd been the only young man in Pontefract not fighting for the country? There'd have been women giving me white feathers.'

'I'd have given them black eyes,' said Rita, turn-ing to him. 'Tommy do you have to go? I mean, what about your exams?'

'Exams can wait, the war won't. Can't get out of it now, love. I've got two weeks before I'm off to Otley for training.'

'How long does that take?'

'Not sure. About three months I should think.'

'It could be that the war's over before you finish your training, and Otley's not so far away. I bet you can come home on a weekend.'

'Maybe,' he said, thinking this was something he could put to his mam when he told her the news. But 'Over by Christmas' was a possibility that was fading with the passage of time.

'I want to go home,' Rita said.

'What now? The big picture's just starting.'

'My dad's out and he won't be back until late. We'll have the house to ourselves.'

The prospect interested Tommy. Since he'd first met Rita the indoor opportunities for serious courting were few and far between. A house to themselves was an opportunity not to be missed.

'What time will he be back?'

'I don't know. He's out with his fancy woman. He might not even come back tonight. Not that I'm bothered.'

'Right. Off we go then.'

A man behind Tommy, who had heard the conversation, tapped him on the shoulder and wished him the 'best of luck tonight, lad'. The man's wife was still digging her husband in his ribs and telling him not to be so mucky as Rita and Tommy shuffled out along the row of seats.

They'd been courting five weeks. She was nineteen and worked as a cashier at the Yorkshire Penny Bank which was situated on Ropergate in Pontefract, a road known among the local young people as t'Bunny Run. It was a tradition that girls walked up and down the street in order to catch the young men's eyes. Rita had caught Tommy's eye just as she was leaving work late one evening. She wasn't meaning to catch anyone's eye. The only thing she intended catching was the bus home. It was her

27

long, flowing, dark, glossy hair that took his eye and had him following her to the bus stop. Tommy was a big admirer of beautiful hair on a woman but he hadn't yet got a proper look at her face. Quite often the face turned out to be something of a let-down. He knew that if this girl's face lived up to the promise of her hair she'd be a real beauty indeed and this was an excellent start in choosing a girlfriend. It was a shallow way to assess a potential girlfriend but Tommy was a young man and shallowness and young men go together like eggs and bacon. At the bus stop he stood by her side as if he was also waiting for the bus, and stole a glance at her profile. Her face did indeed match her hair; she was the prettiest girl he'd seen for a long time and he was now trying to think of something to open a conversation with her.

'I think you and me have got something in common,' he said, eventually, not yet certain how he was going to follow this opening remark. She turned and looked at him. He was a good-looking young man with an easy smile and lots of fair hair that needed a good comb.

'Oh, what's that?'

'Banks,' he said. It was the first word that came into his head. 'We've got banks in common.'

'Really?'

'That's right. You work in a bank. I plan on robbing a bank one day.'

Why he came out with that he didn't know. Sometimes his mouth worked a lot faster than his brain.

'How do you know I work in a bank?'

'I followed you.' No harm in telling her the truth

28

for a change. It gave him time to think of a follow-up line that might interest and amuse her. 'That's how we bank robbers work.'

'So, is that your job – a bank robber?'

'Not full time. It's more of a sideline at the moment. You and me should get together to work out my master plan. Then we can run away together and live the high life off the proceeds.'

'What's your plan if we get caught?'

She was going along with his nonsense. Beautiful, with a daft streak. He liked her style.

'Or we could just go dancing one night and forget all about robbing the bank. I take it you know how to dance?'

'Yes, I know how to dance.'

He was now on more solid ground, talking about something he knew. 'Well, there's a whist drive and dance on at the Ponte Welfare Club on Friday. Do you play whist?'

'Not really.'

'Then I need to teach you. The best way to do that is for us to go for a drink and get a table to ourselves and I'll bring a pack of cards, or are you one of these temperance ladies who hate the demon drink? If you are that's okay by me. Live and let live is what I say.'

Rita was smiling at his cheek and charm. 'I don't mind a small sherry now and again.'

'Sherry? Ah, as I thought, a lady of some style.'

'There is a bit of a problem, though.'

'What's that?'

'I have a boyfriend who takes me dancing.'

'Drat! I should have known a beautiful young lady such as yourself would have a boyfriend. I

29

might have to throw myself under the bus when it comes.'

'Or you could get on the bus with me and pay my fare to Featherstone.'

'I like your idea best.'

The bus arrived. They got on and sat together. Rita was quite amazed that she'd only known him for a few minutes and yet she liked him immensely.

'Where are you going?' she asked him.

'Same place as you, then I'm coming back. I live in Pontefract. I know of a ripping hotel just this side of Featherstone with a very nice cocktail lounge – suitable surroundings for a young lady of your obvious social standing. Perhaps you would accompany me there on Thursday evening to compensate me for my broken heart.'

'Perhaps I could.'

'My name's Tommy.'

'I'm Rita – and please don't tell me it's your favourite name.'

'My favourite name is Victoria after our late queen.'

'Oh no! That's my middle name – and they called me that because I was born on her 76th birthday – May 24th 1895.'

'That makes you a Gemini.' Tommy had memorised all the star signs, knowing it was a surefire conversational opening with girls. 'I'm a Virgo – Geminis are very compatible with Virgos.'

'You just made that up.'

'I got it from a respectable woman's magazine.'

'You buy women's magazines do you?'

'No, but my mother does – with her being a

respectable woman.'

'Hmm, next thing you'll be telling me is that fate has thrown us together.'

'Wouldn't dream of it. Tell me, Rita, this former boyfriend of yours. How will he take it when you tell him you've found someone else?'

When Tommy took Rita to the pictures on the night he joined up he hadn't yet been inside her house, although she'd been a welcome guest at the Birch home many times. Tommy knew the problem was with her father who had 'gone off the rails' to quote Rita when her mother had gone off with the coalman, leaving her alone with her dad.

'To be honest, I was never really close to either of them,' Rita had confessed to him. 'They weren't cruel to me or anything but they never had much time for me. I did really well at school and I realised that I was a lot brighter than both of them put together. When I left school at twelve I went to continuation classes in Castleford for three years while I worked for Robinson's clog makers in Featherstone. That's what got me the job at the bank.

'It was as though Mam and Dad couldn't cope with me reading books that didn't have pictures in. They never bought me any books. There wasn't a book in the house that wasn't mine. Thank God for the library. I spent hours in there. I was a bit surprised at how bad my dad took it when she left him. They weren't exactly Romeo and Juliet. Dad can't do anything for himself, not even his own laundry. He works down at the slaughter house. He's not on a big wage but he does pay the rent,

31

and chips in ten bob a week for food and stuff. I put the rest in.'

'Did you have to get a new coalman?' Tommy asked.

'Well, he came round to deliver, my dad took six bags off him and told him to get stuffed when he asked for his money so yes, we had to get a new coalman. Dad was going round telling people he'd sold my mother for six bags of coal.'

She took out a key and slipped it in the mortise lock. 'It'll be cold,' she warned him. 'There's been no fire since last night.'

The house was in darkness. She stepped into the middle of the room and pulled on a bobbin suspended on a string dangling from the ceiling. It worked a switch that lit a gas mantle light which gave gradual illumination to a frugally furnished room. There were two fireside armchairs, one worn, one almost new; a dining table; three dining chairs, and a dresser. The fireplace was a traditional Yorkshire range with an oven to one side. A brass fender enclosed a tiled hearth on which stood a fireside companion-set containing a poker, a dustpan and a brush that had seen better days.

It was a worn and tidy room, devoid of dust, decoration and colour. There were no pictures on the walls, no photographs, no ornaments, no books, no flowers, not even a casually discarded newspaper; nothing to take the interest of a visitor. The curtains were dark green and drab. On the floor was brown linoleum with two brown rugs, one in front of the fireplace, above which was a mantelpiece on which stood a large clock which had stopped earlier in the day, or earlier in some day past. Tommy looked at his pocket watch. It was seven forty-eight.

'Your clock seems to have stopped,' he mentioned, for want of something better to say.

'I know. It needs winding every day and it loses half an hour every twenty-four. I bought my own watch as soon as I could afford one, otherwise I'd never know the right time. So, what do you think of my humble homestead?'

'Well, it doesn't match you.'

'It's clean and tidy,' she said. 'I know that because I do all the cleaning and tidying.'

'In that case it's a credit to you.'

There was a small scullery to one side. Rita walked over to it. 'Would you like a cup of tea?'

'Yes, thanks. That'd be very nice.'

He sat down in the worn chair. It wasn't the most comfortable chair he'd ever sat in. 'Chair's comfy,' he lied, feeling he needed to say something complimentary about her home.

'No it's not. That's Dad's chair. Mine's the other one. I bought it myself from a neighbour whose husband got killed in a pit accident so he didn't need it any more. It's quite comfy.'

'Right.' He adjusted his position. 'Yeah, I er, I can feel the problem.'

'Grab a cushion from my chair, sit on that.'

He did as requested. 'Ah, much better. My bottom is most grateful.'

'That's what my dad says – only he doesn't say "bottom". I know it's not a palace, but it's the only home I've ever known. I do aspire to better things.'

'You deserve the best,' said Tommy.

33

'Well, I've made a start – I've got the best boy-friend.'

He sat there in deep thought as she made the tea, which she brought over to him. He took his cup and stared at her for a long moment, then blurted, 'I love you ... I think.' Tommy blushed with embarrassment that he should be so bold. Then he winced, awaiting her reaction, which was a surprised, 'What?'

Further emboldened he said, 'I think I love you. I was wondering if you love me.'

'You just *think* you love me?'

'All right then, I *do* love you.'

'Well, you've never said that before.'

'I've only known you a month.'

'Five weeks two days. How long have you known you love me?'

'I wasn't sure before today. Me joining up means I won't see you for a long time, and that's going to be hard for me. I've never felt like this about a girl before. It's a bit...' he searched for the word, 'it's a bit unsettling, to be honest.'

'I think love is a bit unsettling,' she said.

'Me and you, I think it's ... I don't know ... it just feels right ... and I don't want to be without you.'

'Well if you must know, Tommy Birch, I've known I love you for five weeks and two days but I never told you because I didn't want you to think I was being clingy. Now that was very unsettling.'

'Was it really?'

'Yes.'

'You can be as clingy as you like. I've never looked at another girl since I met you.'

'I bet you looked at a lot before you met me.'

He shook his head. 'Never looked at one like you. I'd ask you to marry me but, erm...'

She looked at him with raised eyebrows, encouraging him to finish, but he was pondering the implication of what he'd just said.

'But what?'

'To be honest, it never occurred to me that any girl would want me as an actual husband.'

'Why not?'

'Well, I tend to be a bit irresponsible at times. You know, not take stuff seriously and marriage is pretty serious.'

'So you think I should marry someone else, do you? How would you feel about that?'

'I wouldn't want that to happen.'

'Not ever?'

'Never.'

'Well, I'm not going to go through life as a spinster, Tommy Birch.'

He went quiet for a while, then he lit a cigarette that he handed to her before lighting one of his own. 'So, if I asked you to marry me, what would you say?'

She took a drag on her cigarette and exhaled slowly as Tommy watched her, suddenly realising the importance of this moment.

'I imagine we'd be happier than most,' she said. 'We get on, and we love each other. So, apart from you being irresponsible at times can you think of any reason why we shouldn't get married?'

'Well I can't actually, and it does pain me to think I won't see you for a long time when I join the army.'

'Tommy, it pains me to think I might *never* see you again when you join the army.'

'I won't be irresponsible over there, honest.'

'I do hope not, Tommy.'

'Do you want me to get down on one knee or something?'

'Tommy, are you serious? Because this isn't something you should joke about.'

'Rita, I don't think I've ever been more serious.'

'In that case, I think I would like you to get down on one knee. If you're going to do it you might as well do it properly.'

'Right.'

He put his teacup on the floor and flicked his cigarette into the empty fireplace, as did Rita. He knelt down and took her hand in his.

'Rita Victoria Clayton. Will you marry me?'

'Yes,' she said. 'I'd love to marry you.'

'Bloody hell! Honest?'

'Honest.'

He stood up and kissed her. She got up from her chair to make their embrace easier. They held each other in silence for a while, both enjoying the occasion. Then Tommy said, 'I'll get you a ring at the weekend. I've got a few bob saved.'

'Where will we live once we're married?' she asked.

'Well, with respect, I don't think we should live here.'

'No, nor me.'

'I'm sure we could live at our house until we get a place of our own,' said Tommy. 'I've got my own bedroom. Well our Stanley shares with me at the moment, but he can move up to the attic. It's a biggish room.'

'I'd really like that.'

She gave her next words some thought, then, 'Tommy, there is one nice room in this house. Would you like to see it?'

'Which room's that?'

'My bedroom. If we're going to get married I think we should get to know each other a bit better.'

'I like your thinking.'

Her bedroom might have been in a different house from the room downstairs. It was brightly decorated with floral wallpaper and had pictures on the wall, mainly prints by artists Tommy didn't recognise but he knew they'd be by important people that Rita would tell him all about one day. There were two wall shelves lined with books and a book called *Jane Eyre* on the bed that she must be reading at the moment. He liked the idea that she knew stuff she could teach him. He looked all around the room until his gaze settled on her. 'Do you like what you see?' she said.

'I do.'

'Would you like to see more?'

Their eyes met as the implication in her question sank in. He had never seen her naked, nor she him. They had never had proper sex, although neither of them had any religious or moral reason for not doing so. They simply obeyed the taboo of the time. Children born out of wedlock brought about too much shame to make the pleasure of their conception worthwhile.

'Yes please,' he said.

'You first.'

'Oh, right.'

Slowly they undressed, not taking their eyes off each other. Tommy was pleased he'd changed his underpants that day, in fact he was pleased he was even wearing any. They reached a stage where he was just wearing his underpants and she her brassiere and knickers.

'Your turn,' she said.

He slid down his pants and stepped out of them, aware of the stirring down there which had her full attention. She looked up at him. 'It's beautiful. I've never seen one before.'

'You've got stuff I've never seen before.'

'Okay.'

She unhooked her brassiere and allowed her breasts to fall out. They were full and firm and as beautiful as he knew they'd be. He had touched them outside her clothes and, in a few passionate moments, had felt their nakedness, but nothing more. This was a giant leap forward for them both. She was now taking her knickers down and stepping out of them. The sight of her brought him to a full erection, which seemed to impress her.

'Wow! Did I do that?'

He nodded.

'Can I touch it?'

Another nod.

She stepped forward and stroked him. He placed his arms around her and pulled her to him.

'I think we should get into bed,' she said.

She got into the single bed and positioned herself beneath him, saying, 'I've never done this before.'

'Nor me.'

'Liar.'

She said it in the hope he'd argue.

'Rita. I actually haven't. Honest... Anyway, what if you get er ... pregnant?

'I won't.'

'How do you know?'

She smiled up at him. 'Catholics call it the rhythm method. It's all to do with timing.'

'Right... Are you a Catholic or something?'

'Sort of.'

'Sort of? How come you never mentioned it?'

'Well I was born and bred into the faith but I became a bit disillusioned with religion of any kind.'

Tommy was in no mood to talk about religion. He placed himself just inside her, stroked her breasts and kissed her, gently. 'If I'm hurting, you'd better tell me.'

'Tommy, right now I think I want you to hurt me ... please.'

He thrust himself into her and she gave a squeal of pain, followed by, 'It's okay, Tommy. I'm okay, I'm okay ... keep doing it, please!'

He did as she asked until he was spent, then collapsed on top of her. She was still thrusting herself into him but he had no more to give. He just stayed there until she calmed down, then he rolled off her. They lay side by side for two full minutes before he spoke.

'What do you think?'

'Good grief, Tommy. That was ... whew! That took my breath away.'

'And me.' He left it a few seconds before adding, 'I don't think we were erm, properly ... er, synchronised ... were we?'

'Yes, I did notice. Maybe we should do it again and get our timing right.'

'Practice makes perfect, but I think I might need a few minutes to er, to refuel.'

'That's okay. Just, just hold me.'

'Tell you what, Rita. I really think we're doing the right thing getting married.'

Chapter 3

Charlie and Tommy were sitting in the front room. A tearful Agnes and Edith had left them to it. Charlie lit up his pipe and held out his match for Tommy to light a cigarette.

'Out of preference,' said Charlie, 'I'd sooner have had this conversation *before* you decided to enlist, but what's done's done and nowt I can do'll change that. I spent long enough in the army to know you can't change the rules to suit yourself.'

'I'm not sure I want to change the rules, Dad.'

'I know that, lad, and fair play to you, but I also know you, and that's what troubles me.' He took a few puffs of his pipe as he gathered his thoughts. Tommy knew not to interrupt his dad's thought-gathering ritual. 'Y'see, when you join the army in times of war you're expected to fight. They'll give you a gun and they'll expect you to shoot the enemy with it. Shoot 'em and kill 'em. Have you given this much thought, Tommy?'

'Dad, I thought you might be proud, with me

joining your old regiment.'

'I am proud, lad, it's just that ... well, you're not really soldier material.'

'Most of the lads who are joining up aren't exactly soldier material. I'm no different from them.'

'That's where I disagree with you, Tommy. Some of them'll be fighters, some won't. The ones who aren't natural fighters will do well to keep their heads down. Y'see, I spent some hard years fighting the Boers. I've shot em and bayonetted a few as well. I did well in the army, ended up with three stripes.'

'And a DCM, which you never talk about. The Prince of Wales presented it to you at Buckingham Palace. Mam went with you. Proudest day of her life she says, and yet you never talk about it. Blimey, Dad. It's only one down from a VC.'

'Aye, and I might have got one of them instead, only there were no senior officer left alive to certify what had happened, just a warrant officer and a few NCOs. The only senior officer involved got killed and he got a VC, which is fair enough I suppose. A VC would have been handy, though. You get a bit of a pension with a VC.'

'There's more to a VC than a pension, Dad.'

'Not a lot more, lad.'

'Okay, so, what did happen?'

'It's written down on a citation somewhere but it's a part of my life I'd sooner hadn't happened to be honest.'

'I don't know, Dad. You've got a DCM and a bullet hole in your bum and all you ever talk about is your bullet hole.'

'Hey, I wasn't running away when I got shot,

lad. It were one of our bullets that got me from behind. Not all of our lads could shoot straight.'

'I know. You think it was Squinty McBride, worst shot in the battalion.'

'I'd stake money on it. Aye, little Squinty. He got killed in the same action, so I mustn't think too badly of him. He went down side by side with me. I did ask him if he'd shot me, but he were dead so what can you do? You can't moan at a dead man for shooting you in the bum. Bad form that.'

'One of the rules of the Koylis is it?'

Charlie grinned and puffed on his pipe for a while. 'I'm going to tell you something now, lad, that you must never repeat to anyone, especially your mam or Edith.'

'What's that, Dad?'

'Well, back then some joker in our company made up a daft rhyme about me. They used to call it out when they were marching.'

'Go on.'

'I want you to promise you'll not say a word to your mam?'

'Promise.'

Charlie tapped out a marching rhythm on his knee as he called out the rhyme. Tommy roared with laughter. 'They actually marched to that?'

'Of course they did. When men are marching to war it does no harm to have a bit of fun on the way.'

'Aw, Dad,' Tommy said. 'You can't expect me to keep that a secret.'

Charlie had a wide grin on his face. 'I most certainly do, son. That's between me and you.'

His grin vanished and his face grew serious.

'Killing people scars you, Tommy. I still remember every man I shot and every one I bayonetted. I think about their families and I know I shouldn't and it pains me to think you might be burdened with the same thoughts, and I worry that your decent nature might not cope with it. I survived because I'm an aggressive man by nature, which is something I haven't passed on to you, thank God.'

'Aggressive? You're not aggressive, Dad. You've given me a few cracks now and again but nothing I didn't deserve.'

Charlie smiled and tapped his misshapen nose. 'Have you ever wondered why me nose is this shape?' He held up a huge right fist and added, 'And how me knuckles got so scarred? It's through fighting when I was a young man. I was very good at it and I'd never take no nonsense from anyone, no matter how big they were. The men at work know not to argue with me, which is probably why I was made up to foreman, although I am a damn good joiner. I was never aggressive to you because a proper man looks after his family, he doesn't hurt them. Them powder puff pats I gave you were nothing to what I could have done if I'd wanted to hurt you.'

'What are you telling me, Dad?'

Charlie looked at his son, then looked away to hide the mist in his eyes. He cleared his throat and took out a handkerchief, ostensibly to blow his nose but more to dry his eyes.

'You're a good lad, Tommy. Me and your mam are right proud of you, and we're scared to death of you going over there if you must know. I'd like to give you a piece of advice that might help you survive this damned war. I know you're competitive. I've seen you on the football field getting stuck in and in that sense you remind me of me. But you're also a gentle lad who never gets into fights, you never raise your voice, never talk back to me or your mam, everybody likes you because you're an amiable young man. Oh, I know you're a proper Smart-Alec – quick with witty remarks, and it's hard to better you in an argument but that's a good trait, a trait I wish I had. Better to talk your way out of a disagreement than fight it out like I used to do. What I'm trying to say is to know your own limitations out there. They won't expect you to work wonders. All you have to do is obey orders as best you can and look after yourself. Keep your head down and don't try anything above and beyond the call of duty.'

'What, like you did you mean?'

'I was that type, Tommy. I was warlike. I was good at being a soldier and that gave me the edge over the enemy who were probably more like you, and this is not an insult, Tommy. You're not warlike and if everyone was like you there wouldn't be any wars. You get back in one piece and I'll pin my medal on your shirt and never ask for it back because you'll deserve it more than I ever did.'

Tommy smiled. 'I have another reason to come back all in one piece, Dad. I asked Rita to marry me last night and she said "Yes".'

Charlie got to his feet and shook his son's hand. 'Well, I have to say this is damned good news. She's a bonny lass is Rita. Your mam'll be ever so pleased.'

'I've told Rita we could probably live here until

we find somewhere ourselves. I'd like us to get married before I go overseas so that she can stay and live here with you as a member of our family. Her dad's a bit of a dead loss.'

'We'd not have it any other way, Tommy. Our Stanley can move up to the attic. Come on, let's tell your mam and Edith. I might have to open a couple of bottles o' pale ale for this.'

It transpired that Tommy's regiment wasn't in a hurry to send him over to France but he was certainly in a hurry to marry Rita. The date was set for Saturday 12th December. Tommy had been given a week's leave which they intended spending in Scarborough for their honeymoon.

'The Grand Hotel always keeps a few rooms available during the winter,' said Charlie, 'and they practically let 'em out for nowt, so that's our wedding present to you both.'

'Hey, thanks, Dad,' said Tommy. 'I'm beginning to understand why Squinty McBride shot you where he did. If he'd shot you in the chest the bullet would have bounced off your wallet.'

Charlie laughed and Rita loved the camaraderie between father and son, in fact between the whole Birch family who all shared the same charm and cheek as her Tommy.

Chapter 4

Stanley was swinging on the backyard gate when his best pal, Eddie Butterfield, wandered over. Eddie was ten, the same age as Stanley.

'I bet your mam doesn't know you're swingin' on t'gate, else she'd come out and give you a right clatter.'

'No she wouldn't she'd just tell me to stop. Any road she's in t'room having a quiet half hour before me dad and our Tommy comes home.'

'Me mam says your Tommy's gerrin' married tomorrow.'

'He is, yeah. Then he's off to France to fight King Billy.'

'Me Uncle Walter got killed last week fightin' King Billy. Me mam's right upset.'

'I know. I hope that dunt happen to our Tommy.'

'It might.'

'It might not an' all,' said Stanley, still swinging.

'We'll have to join t'army when we're eighteen,' said Eddie. 'Don't fancy that, havin' flippin' Germans shootin' at me.'

'We won't,' Stanley said. 'Me dad says t'war'll be over by then and there won't be no more wars after that, if we kill King Billy.'

'Is that right?'

'Yeah, me dad knows all about wars. He got shot in his bum.'

'I know,' said Eddie.

There was a silence for a while, broken only by the squeaking of the swinging gate, and then by Eddie. 'If I were t'king,' he said, 'I wouldn't go round killin' people.'

'No, nor me, neither,' said Stanley.

'What would you do if you were t'king?' Eddie asked him.

'If I were t'king,' Stanley said, 'I'd swing on this gate and get me mam to make me dripping sand-wiches all day long. What would you do if you were t'king?'

'I don't know now – you've picked all t'best stuff.'

As his pal walked away, Stanley continued swinging, now wondering if he should push his luck and ask his mam for a dripping sandwich. Maybe not. She might just tell him to 'stop swinging on that damned gate or you'll have it off its hinges'. Better to be satisfied with what you've got and not be too greedy. That's what Tommy would have said. It made him sad that Tommy was going off to war and, like Eddie's Uncle Walter, might never come back. He got down off the gate and sat on the step, elbows on his knees, resting his chin in his hands, blinking away tears. The gate opened. Tommy came into the yard and looked down at his young brother.

'What's wrong with you, our kid? You look as though you've lost a shillin' and found a penny.'

'Aw, it's nowt,' said Stanley.

Chapter 5

Tommy chose not to wear his army uniform on his wedding day at St Joseph's Church in Ponte-fract. Rita was a Catholic but she made so little of the fact that Tommy wasn't sure what church they should get married in.

'I thought you were only *sort* of a Catholic.'

'I am, but once a Catholic always a Catholic I'm afraid. To be honest, I'm not all that devout since my mam ran off with our coalman. She was the devout one. My dad only converted so he could marry her, and she runs off with Herbert Potter and his nutty slack – I'm quoting my dad there. Nutty slack's a type of cheap coal.'

'I know what nutty slack is, I'm a mining engineer.'

'Of course you are. Anyway, it's all right, you don't have to convert. Father Mulvaney'll marry me to a prodidog. I've had a word.'

'That's good of him.'

'It is, actually. Catlikes and prodidogs aren't supposed to interbreed.'

'Hey,' said Tommy, 'with your beauty and my criminal mind we could produce a superior race of dangerous beings, maybe that's what they're scared of.' A disconcerting thought struck him. 'So, did you erm go to confession when we erm ... you know?'

'No, I didn't, nor have I any intention. If some-

48

thing as beautiful as that's a sin, then I'm a sinner, but I'll still get married in white.' She paused, then added, cheekily, 'I might wear red knickers, though.'

'You could wear no knickers.'

'Don't be so bold, Tommy Birch.'

Rita's father gave her away, although he wasn't entirely sober and was glad to sit down after he completed his parental duty. Her mother was at the back of the church crying her eyes out. Her coalman lover was nowhere to be seen. There was a crude joke being passed around the guests about him now delivering his nutty slack to a clog maker's wife in Ferry Fryston. Rita's mother was a woman in her forties whose good looks were rapidly fading, despite her lipstick, powder and paint battle against aging.

'Is that your mam?' Tommy asked as they walked back down the aisle.

'Yes, I'm glad she came.'

Tommy gave his new mother-in-law a broad smile, which seemed to increase the flow of tears. Outside, the winter sun shone, as if heralding a new dawn for them but they both knew that no new dawn would arrive until after Tommy had got home safely from the war. The bride and groom posed for a photographer who insisted on them keeping very still as he took the first of the three photographs he'd been booked to take.

Two young women stepped out of the crowd of guests and walked up to Tommy. He smiled, quizzically. One of them produced a white feather and stuck it in his breast pocket. Nonplussed, Tommy

49

took it out and looked at it. One of the women said, 'At your age you should be in uniform.'

Tommy's mother, stepped forward and gave the woman a vigorous slap that sent her spinning to the ground. She then stood over the prostrate woman, with her heel on her neck.

'My Tommy's got a uniform, and you've got an apology to make before I let you up.'

'Well done, Agnes,' called out one of the male guests. 'They should know better, these damned brainless women!'

The second woman was trying to get back into the crowd but Edith pushed her away. 'You too,' she said. 'That's my brother you're insulting. He'll be going to France to fight for idiots like you.'

'I didn't know.'

'Well you should know before you play stupid tricks like that!'

The photographer stuck in a spare plate intending to take a shot of the whole cameo, hoping it wouldn't come out blurred. Through force of habit he called out, 'Hold that pose!'

'What?' said Agnes, glaring at him.

'Oh, er, sorry, nothing.'

He stuck his head under the hood and took the exposure, hoping he might be able to sell it to the papers. The woman on the floor was saying she was sorry.

'I didn't hear you,' said Agnes.

The woman screamed, 'SORRY!'

Agnes took her foot away. 'Go on, clear off and take your idiot friend with you!'

To murmurs of disgust from the guests the two women slunk away. Tommy was grinning all over

50

his face. He saw the funny side of everything.

'Hey, I think I'll give Mam my uniform. She'll see Kaiser Bill off in ten minutes.'

The guests laughed. Rita smiled. It had been an awkward few moments but Tommy had alleviated the tension. It was what he did. Pity he couldn't alleviate the tension with the Germans, but he was now her Tommy, and nothing could spoil her day. Charlie walked over to the photographer. 'I'd like to buy that last photograph,' he said. 'Just me, nobody else.'

He could be an intimidating man, even at a wedding.

Chapter 6

By using his full title, Charles Birch DCM, on his letter, Charlie had secured the bridal suite at the Grand Hotel in Scarborough for his son and Rita at the knock-down cost of three pounds for the week. To Charlie this was a week's wages so he didn't think it was such a knock-down price. The weather was cold and wintry, all the amusements closed, and none of this bothered Tommy and his new wife who had plenty of amusements of their own to fill their time.

At eight o'clock on the Wednesday morning they were lying in bed, in each other's arms, early morning love-making over and done with until next time, having a comfortable conversation.

'What exactly will you be doing in the army?'

she asked him.

'Well, our job as a Pioneer battalion is to dig trenches, build roadways, bridges and stuff.'

'So, they'll have you digging?'

'Not me personally. My job is doing all the technical stuff, designing and setting out; knowing where to dig and how deep; how to build bridges over trenches, lay out barbed wire, even build wooden roads and railways to get stores and ammunition to the front lines. I'm told they'll make me a corporal to give me the authority to tell men what to do. I get a section of twelve men under me, plus an extra seven and six a week.'

'So, you don't do any actual fighting then?'

'Well, we give back-up to the front line troops after they've advanced into No Man's Land – which is the land between us and the Germans, but the only time we're really in the front line is when we're out there digging the trenches and stuff. In fact we're the first ones out there. That's why they call us The Pioneers.'

'So, all this stuff you've learned as a mining engineer will come in handy?'

'It will, especially as most of the men are miners who know how to dig. A lot of them are lads I know from Pontefract. What the hell was that?'

Their chat came to a premature end with a series of booms from out at sea. Tommy and Rita were wondering if it was something to do with the lifeboats. Then came a massive explosion immediately beneath their room, which vibrated violently. A mirror and various pictures dropped off the walls and fell to the floor, cracks appeared up the walls and ceiling. Tommy jumped out of bed and ran to the now broken window. Just outside, a cloud of dust was rising from below but beyond that he could just make out two large ships out at sea, less than half a mile offshore. Flashes coming from them. Flashes quickly followed by booms as the sound followed the flashes. A shell had obviously hit the hotel dining room immediately below them. He heard another, whistling overhead and landing in the town.

'Bloody hell, Rita! There's German ships firing on us!'

She was out of bed in a flash, standing beside her husband. 'Watch out for broken glass on the carpet,' he warned.

'Best get dressed, Tommy, and get out of here.'

Tommy had brought two sets of clothes. His civvies and his uniform which he thought might ward off the idiot women handing out their white feathers. He instinctively donned his uniform. Within two minutes they were both dressed and running down the wide, sweeping staircase. Staff were dashing about in a panic. The sight of Tommy's uniform had a group of them running over to him.

'What should we do?'

'Is there a cellar?' he said.

'There's a basement, yes.'

'I should get everyone down there as soon as you can.'

The sound of offshore guns and onshore destruction was becoming constant. Tommy turned to Rita. 'Look, love, you'd better go down with them. I'm gonna nip outside and see if I can help.'

'I'm staying with you, Tommy Birch.'

He expected no less and grabbed her hand. 'Just stay close by me, and do as you're told.'

'I'll stay close by you.'

They ran out of the front door and looked seawards to their left. Two German battle cruisers were steaming south and firing broadsides at the helpless holiday resort. Shells were landing in the town and throwing up flames and debris high above the rooftops.

'This way,' said Tommy, heading off to the right towards the town. It was where help would be needed. It was also where the danger was. He looked at Rita with concern, still uncertain that she should be going with him.

'If we go up in smoke, Tommy Birch,' she told him, 'we go together. You're not leaving me on my own in this world.'

He smiled and, hand in hand, they made to run into town when a shell hit a commercial hotel opposite, blowing a gaping hole in the front. People came staggering out of the door. One woman had her dress on fire. Tommy ran towards her and pulled her to the ground, smothering her and enveloping the flames with his uniform until they died out. He got to his feet and looked for Rita who was standing by the door helping people out.

One man was calling out. 'There's a man on the first landing, fallen over. I tried to help him but he was too heavy.'

Tommy ran inside, up two flights of stairs onto a landing where a large man was trying to get to his feet and failing. Flames were raging at the top of the next flight of stairs. The smoke was stifling, the heat overpowering, dust, damage and danger

54

everywhere. Tommy reached under the man's arms and tried to lift him, but he was much too heavy.

'Here. Let's grab an arm each and pull him down.'

Tommy looked round at Rita. 'You shouldn't be here,' he said.

She scolded him. 'Shut up Tommy, and you do as you're told. An arm each.'

They pulled the man, clumsily, down the stairs and out into the street where a policeman helped them pull him clear of the building onto a grass verge. Then he went back to shooing people away from the building.

'You shouldn't have gone in there, sir,' he said to Tommy, over his shoulder. 'Another hit and the whole place'll come down.'

An ambulance appeared, looking for casualties. The policeman waved it across. He then looked at Tommy. 'Is everybody out of there?'

'No idea.'

Just as he said it another shell hit the Grand, which was a prominent building where the Germans mistakenly thought the British might have a gun emplacement; at least that was their excuse when questioned about it after the war.

Then the front of the hotel they'd just been in suddenly collapsed. The man they'd just saved was being helped into the ambulance. He waved his thanks at them, realising they'd saved his life.

Tommy looked down at his singed uniform and at Rita's blackened face and he knew that whatever else he attempted to do now, she'd be by his side. She smiled at him and said, 'Okay, soldier, we seem to have saved one life, what now?'

'I think we should head for the station, love. See what we can do to help.'

The station was crowded with distressed and wounded people, and people simply trying to get out of town. Tommy and Rita helped where they could, until, exhausted, they sat down on a platform seat and enjoyed a cup of tea they were given by a Red Cross man.

'On leave are you, soldier?'

'We're actually on our honeymoon,' said Tommy. 'I was hoping they wouldn't start shooting at me until I got to France.'

'Nearly got you, did they?'

'Nah, they missed by miles.'

'They missed us by about three feet,' said Rita. 'It hit the room below us.'

'Right, I'll see if I can rustle you up a piece of cake.'

'Thank you.'

There was a lull in the firing as the two battle cruisers steamed too far south to be in range. Scarborough breathed a sigh of relief, short-lived because the two ships turned round and headed north to fire more broadsides at the town. The attack ended at 9.30 when the ships steamed north to attack Whitby. They had killed eighteen Scarborough citizens, including a fourteen-month-old baby boy, injured many more and had damaged or destroyed more than fifty buildings including the Scarborough Lighthouse.

The attack, which was carried out by the battle cruisers *Von der Tann* and *Derfflinger,* broke all rules of war, and aroused anger among the young men of the area that had them enlisting in droves. *The Scarborough Mercury,* the *Scarborough Pictorial* and many other newspapers ran this advert:

Avenge Scarborough. Up and at 'em now. The wholesale murder of innocent women and children demands vengeance. Men of England, the innocent victims of German brutality call upon you to avenge them. Show German barbarians that Britain's shores cannot be bombarded with impunity. Duty calls you now. Go today to the nearest recruiting depot and offer your services for king and country.

At one-thirty Tommy and Rita made their way back to the Grand Hotel. A lone fire engine was outside with a hose running through the front door. Other engines were tending to a dozen fires in other parts of the town. Tommy and Rita stepped over the hose and walked up to reception where a smartly dressed man smiled at them. There was a lot of dust in the air and firemen running up and down the staircase.

'I'm guessing you're closed,' said Tommy.

'Not to you, sir. I do hope this inconvenience isn't spoiling your honeymoon.'

'Not at all,' said Tommy. 'I was wondering if our room was still in one piece – we've left some of our belongings in there.'

The man checked a ledger. 'Let me see. You have our second floor honeymoon suite. I'm afraid it's out of action for the time being, so you might have to recover your belongings later.'

He noticed the disappointed look on Rita's face; her dress was in a terrible state. 'Tell you what,' he

57

said, 'I'll ask one of the firemen if he can retrieve the clothes from your room and we can offer you a standard room in an undamaged part of the hotel – that's if you want to stay here any longer of course.' He paused and added, 'I have the authority to offer you the standard room free of charge plus a refund of the whole cost of the honeymoon suite to make up for the inconvenience.'

Tommy and Rita looked at each other. 'Why not?' said Rita. 'It's been an exciting honeymoon so far. Thank you, that's very good of you.'

'We believe it was very good of you to pull that man out of the building opposite.'

'Oh.'

'Lots of us saw it. I think I'd like to shake both your hands.'

Chapter 7

In 1851 Helmut Müller, a butcher from Bremen in northern Germany, travelled to England on business where he met and fell in love with Beatrice Fox, a London dressmaker. Beatrice was reluctant to move with him to Germany so they got married in England, opened a butcher's shop in Camden Town and raised a family. Their eldest son was born in 1853 and called Michael, a name popular in both countries.

In 1878 Michael, an Englishman in all but his surname, married an Irish woman, Elspeth Brannigan, who gave birth to a son, George, in 1881.

Michael and Elspeth took over the family business on the death of Helmut in 1892. When George left school in 1893 he joined the family business, first as a butcher's boy, working up to be a fully trained and first class butcher.

In the first decade of the 20th century anti-German feeling was rife in Great Britain. Animosity was fuelled by such books as *The Invasion of 1910*, which had Germany invading and crushing Britain. Published in 1906 it became one of the bestselling books of that era. This and other publications combined with the factual knowledge that Germany was indeed building up its armaments and made no secret of their aim to become a world power. But at whose expense?

In 1909 George took the decision, unpopular with his parents, to officially change his surname from Müller to Miller and advised his parents not only to do likewise but to move their business premises to another side of town, or preferably to a new city where no one knew of their German ancestry.

'Dad, I'm as English as anyone. I've never been to Germany, I can't speak a word of German but the name's becoming a problem. We're an English family, we speak English with English accents, we should have an English name. A German name's inviting trouble, and I think it's losing us business.'

His father shook his head. 'The English people are a reasonable people. Look at your mother, even the king has a German name. Are the king's sons asking him to change the family name? You go ahead and change your name, but to me you

59

will always be my son, George Michael Müller.'

So George changed his name to George Michael Miller and moved into lodgings a mile away from his father's shop.

On May 7th 1915 the world's largest passenger steamer, *Lusitania,* was sunk off the coast of Ireland by a German submarine at the cost of almost twelve hundred lives including a hundred and twenty-eight Americans. This sparked anti-German riots first in Liverpool where the ship was based, then in London and then in Britain's major towns and cities. On the night of May 13th five thousand protesters, infiltrated by the usual hooligans who, since time immemorial, had never missed an opportunity to escalate a protest into a violent riot, attacked and looted many German businesses in north and east London. Camden Town was as badly hit as anywhere and Müller's Butchers on Camden High Street was an obvious target. Every window was broken, all the stock stolen, all the interior fixtures and fittings smashed to pieces and the place set on fire. The police did little to restore order and very few rioters were arrested.

Michael and Elspeth initially escaped with a few cuts and bruises but Elspeth, who was jostled in the street, fell and banged her head.

A shocked George turned up for work the following morning to find a policeman guarding the burned-out shop. This was the first he knew about it.

'Where are my parents, Mr and Mrs Müller? What the hell's happened?'

'A riot happened, sir, with this being a German shop.'

'German? They're no more German than you are.'

'Mr and Mrs Müller are in St Pancras Hospital. Mr Müller's okay, Mrs Müller had a nasty fall.'

A group of people saw his concern and gathered to jeer. Men, women and children. George stormed across to confront them.

'What the hell are you lot jeering about?'

'Bloody Germans deserve all they get,' sneered a woman. Face full of hatred, clad in a shawl.

'My parents aren't Germans, they're as English as you,' retorted George angrily, 'which you'd know if you ever bought meat off them.'

'They've got a German name,' shouted a man.

'So has the king. Are you going to attack him as well? You're idiots, all of you. If you want to fight Germans, do it like men and join up!'

'Why haven't you joined up?'

'I'm in civvies, home on leave. I've been fighting in France for the past six months and I come home to this. I'd rather shoot you than the Germans. You're worse than the Germans, all of you.'

George was hoping none of them actually used the shop because this was a lie intended to make them feel ashamed. It seemed to have the desired effect.

His mother never recovered and died in hospital two days later. His father's unbridled rage at everyone and everything about him became a problem and he was interned as an enemy alien on the Isle of Man where he died of a heart attack in August.

In October 1915 George Miller inherited the

remnants of his father's business which was well covered by insurance, and moved to Yorkshire where he opened a butcher's shop in a town he'd never heard of called Pontefract – he rather hoped London people hadn't heard of it either. It wasn't far from the Birch household. Rita was one of his first customers.

Chapter 8

It was late afternoon and Rita was sitting at her desk in the bank when a young messenger boy stopped beside her. He'd taken a shine to Rita and had been most disappointed when she got married, but he saw no harm in endearing himself to her, with her husband being away at war. There might come a time when she needed a bit of sympathetic male company and he was just the lad to provide it.

'George Miller's just had a meat delivery. I should get in there quick before word gets round and they start queueing.'

'Oh, right, thanks, Edward.'

She went over to the chief cashier, her immediate boss. 'Apparently the butcher's just had a delivery. I wouldn't mind nipping out for five minutes.'

He looked at his watch. 'Five minutes, then I'm out there as well. Ask him to put a nice piece of topside away for me if he has any, or anything he thinks I might like.'

'Will do.'

With the German blockade of the Atlantic, the lack of imported food was beginning to get serious. Bread, fruit, vegetables, meat of all kinds was in short supply, to the extent that all arable land including gardens and allotments were being used to grow food. Rita knew that once word got round that Miller the butcher had taken a new delivery there'd be a queue the full length of Ropergate.

The butcher's was just two doors down from the bank. George Miller smiled at her when she came in. Rita had a beauty that would light up the dullest of days. He wouldn't have minded her lighting up his house with it, but she was married. Although her husband was away at war, so you never know. He knew he shouldn't think like that but Rita's charm and beauty was enough to prejudice any man's mind against her husband, no matter how good a man he was.

'Do you have any topside of beef, George?'

'I've topside of something, can't guarantee it's beef. The supplier didn't seem so sure. If it's not I'm paying him for horse, which isn't so bad. I'll take a good look at it.' He had a London accent which sounded quite posh when set against the broad Yorkshire accents of Pontefract. Although Rita had polished the rough edges off her own Yorkshire accent, mainly because she didn't want to end up talking like her father, who had more thees and thys in his vocabulary than the Bible.

He went round the back and in the minute he'd been away four more customers had arrived, forming an orderly queue behind Rita. George came back carrying a slab of meat on a large plate.

'Yes, it's definitely cow,' he said.

'Could you let me have a pound?'

'I can, but that's about the limit. I need to share my supplies out as fairly as I can. Heard from your husband lately?'

'I have. He's well, thank you.'

'I'm very pleased to hear it.'

She then said in a low voice, 'Mr Gibson asked if you could put some aside for him. He'll be here in a few minutes.'

In an equally low voice he said, 'I can let you have a half pound of pork sausages as well.'

Rita thanked him and said she'd take them. She looked around as he was cutting the beef. The shop was full and spilling out into the street. Mr Gibson was already in the queue, alerted no doubt by the messenger boy. Rita left the shop with her meat, happy in the knowledge that the Birch family would have its first nourishing meal in weeks.

Oranges, lemons and bananas hadn't been seen in greengrocers' shops for over a year. The last fruit pie she'd had was a blackberry pie made from wild blackberries that Stanley and Edith had picked from the country lanes around Pontefract. That had been a real family treat. Bread and margarine was the staple diet of many families, or bread and scrape as it was known; bread and dripping was a luxury. But even the bread was beginning to taste different, with other grains such as maize and barley being mixed in with the wheat – it made the limited supplies go further. They were called war loaves and were more nutritious than the normal ones but the taste was bordering on unpleasant, which made them unpopular.

Agnes was peeling potatoes when Rita got back. 'I've got us beef topside and pork sausages for tea,' Rita announced.

'What? From proper cows and pigs?'

'Proper cows and pigs.'

'By heck, that butcher must fancy you. Do you flirt with him?'

'Of course not, but a pleasant smile goes a long way, don't you think?'

'I think I do if it's one of your smiles. I think that meat we had on Sunday were running at Doncaster Races on Saturday. Charlie reckoned he had a tanner each way on it with your dad.'

'Oh, my dad's not still a bookie's runner is he? He only makes ten bob a week at it and if he gets caught they'll fine him ten times that – and Dad'll have to pay it, not the bookie.'

'I don't know – Charlie reckons he picks up bets from the cop shop, so they're not gonna pinch him for it. I see no harm in a man having a flutter on the horses now and again. Better than 'em spending it on booze and coming home knocking their wives about.'

'Better to spend it on their wives,' said Rita.

'I can't argue with that. Charlie does all right by me, I have to admit. So it'll do no harm to spoil him with a nice bit o' topside.'

Chapter 9

December 1915

A year had passed since Tommy joined up and still he hadn't seen a shot fired in anger. The Miners Battalion had been stationed in Otley, then in Burton Leonard near Ripon and then down at Fovant in Wiltshire for final training prior to setting sail for Egypt to guard the Suez Canal in early January.

But before they went they'd been brought back to Yorkshire for a ceremonial march down Bondgate in Pontefract in two hundred and fifty rows of four, heading for Purston Park in Featherstone. They marched behind the regimental band of the King's Own Yorkshire Light Infantry which was playing 'The Keel Row', one of the three regimental marches. This one had the men marching at the double. The road was packed three deep with spectators, all there to wish their menfolk, sons and brothers goodbye before they went off to war. The way the war was going they knew it might be the last they saw of them.

Charlie was there with Agnes, Edith, Stanley and Rita. As the band approached, Charlie stepped out into the road. He was wearing his KOYLI beret and he instinctively touched the badge, a French horn wrapped around the white rose of York. Pinned to his coat were his five war medals, the first time he'd ever felt the need to wear them. He waved at the band master and shouted above the noise of the band.

'Play something slower – "Minden March", we want to say goodbye to our lads.'

The bandmaster glanced across at him. Charlie pointed to his medals, in particular the dark blue and maroon stripes of the medal he'd been awarded for gallantry in the field. He was hoping it might carry a bit of weight. The unique medal identified its wearer.

'Are you Sergeant Charlie Birch DCM?' called out the bandmaster without breaking step.

'Er, I am, yes.'

'This is from the regiment, sergeant.'

The bandmaster was now passing Charlie who ran to keep up with him.

'What is?'

The bandmaster raised his baton high in the air. The band stopped playing. Charlie returned to his place next to Agnes. All the crowd could now hear was the marching of a thousand pairs of boots, tramp, tramp, tramp, to the rhythm of the big bass drum which now thumped out a slow beat. After six strides a thousand men's voices raised in unison to chant this marching rhyme.

Our sergeant wears his wound with pride,
Shot up the arse by Squinty McBride.
What did he do with the medal he won?
He used it to plug up the hole in his bum...

Tramp, tramp, tramp, tramp...
Tramp, tramp, tramp, tramp...

67

Our sergeant wears his wound with pride,
Shot up the arse by Squinty McBride...

The liberal and public use of a naughty swear-word had the children screeching with laughter. A few of the women felt obliged to appear disapproving, albeit briefly. Most people went along with the fun of the moment. Charlie smiled and pretended it was nothing to do with him.

'Here comes Tommy,' called out Edith.

He was at their end of his row, matching smartly along, rifle over his shoulder, big grin on his face, chanting the rude rhyme like the rest of them, perhaps louder. The rhyme caught on quickly and, by the time Tommy arrived alongside, everybody in the crowd was chanting it.

'Nothing to do with me, they already knew it, Dad!' he called out. 'You're a legend in the Koylis.'

Edith threw him an apple. Rita rushed out and kissed him on the cheek, walking alongside him, as were many children, wives and girlfriends.

'You come back to me, Tommy Birch,' she shouted as she had to give way to other people wanting to walk beside their boys. It was a social occasion and the army had no intention of being overly strict, as the marching chant suggested.

Rita stopped and stood there with tears streaming down her face until she could see him no more. She went back to where Charlie and her new family were, all of them equally red-eyed.

As they headed back home, Agnes, Edith and Stanley, walking in front of Charlie and Rita, began to march in step and chant the marching rhyme. Rita caught up with them and joined in.

Charlie fell into step behind them but kept his mouth shut. No point encouraging them. Legend in the Koylis eh? Wouldn't do any harm to go to a reunion.

Chapter 10

In Egypt in early 1916 Tommy had his first taste of battle, albeit fighting off minor attacks on the Suez Canal by the German/Turkish-backed Senussi tribe. On various occasions he fired his rifle in their general direction and experienced being fired upon. He took his dad's advice to keep his head down for five months before he was sent to France where there were real battles being waged.

France. July 1st 1916
As dawn broke Tommy was in a trench less than 300 yards west of the German lines in a tiny hamlet called Serre in northern France, an area named the Somme, after the river running to the south of it. Ironically the name is a Celtic word meaning Tranquillity. Tommy was soon to witness the Somme becoming the least tranquil place on the face of the Earth. Ever.

The trenches had been dug under his supervision in castellated lines with a right-angle corner every seven yards so that the shrapnel from any shell landing in a trench would only travel as far as the next corner. Tommy's trenches had many corners.

He and his section were in the fourth line of trenches, part of a platoon commanded by Lieutenant Peter Walker, a civil engineer in civilian life. For three days the British and French heavy artillery had kept up a sporadic barrage, firing all along the German lines. They were at the top end of eleven divisions of the British Fourth Army. Each division had several regiments and each regiment was split up into battalions comprising around 1,000 men. Tommy was in the 12th Battalion KOYLI, known as T'Owd 12th. The Fourth Army formed a front stretching twenty miles north of the Somme. The idea was to soften the Hun to a degree that all the fight had been knocked out of him and to destroy the lines of barbed wire in front of the German trenches. The constant firing had been deafening, reducing some men to tears.

It was a terrible bombardment that should have left nothing alive in the German trenches. Unfortunately the British artillery lacked the quality and calibre of the shells needed to destroy the reinforced shelters deep below the German lines where the enemy took refuge, shaken but largely unharmed, waiting for the bombardment to lift. The men who had originally made the shells back in England were now serving in the army and had been replaced by women who now worked in the munitions factories, and for all they worked heroically, they simply lacked the expertise of the men who had trained for years to do this dangerous job.

The shrapnel from the shells also proved ineffective in clearing the barbed wire entanglements, long stretches of which survived intact in front of the German lines. Tommy knew nothing of this. In front of him were the frontline assault battalions in deep trenches, ready to go over the top as and when ordered. Beyond that was No Man's Land, a truly God-forsaken stark grey wilderness of mud, blood, danger and death where shell craters occupied every square foot of muddy ground not occupied by shell-shattered, skeletal trees.

They'd been told it would be a 'cake walk' against an already beaten and demoralised enemy. All around Tommy were infantry battalions in reserve trenches and behind them a company of Indian cavalry ordered there by General Haig who was a cavalry man. His idea was to break the German lines and send the cavalry through. The big guns, sited behind the cavalry, had fallen suddenly silent just before the dawn.

The silence was eerie. A prelude to what was to come. What that was, none of the men really knew, except it would be something they'd never known before. Those who spoke did so in whispers. Then suddenly the British guns opened up again with a barrage of colossal power and intensity. Never before had so many guns been amassed behind any battle front. There was a rolling roar of shellfire, the earth spewed flame and the sky was ablaze with exploding shells. To Tommy, nothing could survive such a stupendous artillery storm. The bombardment lasted an hour and a half then, just after seven, it stopped and the men knew that their time had come.

Tommy was standing on a firing step, looking over the top towards the British front line trench.

A platoon officer blew his whistle and was first up the scaling ladder with a revolver in one hand and a cigarette in the other, shouting encouragement.

'Come on, lads.'

Men swarmed out of the trenches all along the line. The infantry behind were climbing out and running forward across the trench bridges. Tommy and his men formed a queue to get to a communication trench. Then they heard the German machine guns open fire. Tommy peered through the smoke and could see little then, as he moved down towards the second line of trenches, he saw wounded men staggering back. The German machine guns' raking volley fire was ear-splitting and continuous but still the British kept disappearing into the smoke. He and his men eventually arrived at the front line trench as returning wounded were falling on top of them. The noise was deafening. He heard his platoon commander, Lieutenant Walker, blow his whistle and saw him climb up the ladder. Tommy followed behind him, fairly certain that this would probably be the last ladder he would ever climb, but like all the other men he was carried along with the thrill and enormity of the occasion. He was part of a great battle and he was determined to remain a part as long as he could. He carried his Lee Enfield with bayonet fixed, not firing lest he do a Squinty McBride on Lieutenant Walker. The machine guns rattled mercilessly; men around him dropped but his officer, immediately in front of him, kept going, so did Tommy. He saw splashes of mud kicking up on the ground around him and he wondered what they were. Then he realised they were bullets that weren't hitting him.

He now saw the barbed wire about thirty yards away. Walker turned to Tommy and indicated they go over to the right. Tommy followed him, not sure what to expect, hopefully a break in the wire. But there was no break in the wire, which looked to be around thirty to forty yards deep. Completely impenetrable. It seemed that he and his officer were the only two to have got this far. Then Walker went down and rolled into a shell crater. Tommy saw no reason to carry on forward and jumped in the crater himself.

'Are you hit sir?'

'Yes, in the leg. Can't walk. This is a bad do, Tommy.'

'It's not what I expected, sir.'

'We're taking a bad beating. Our heavy guns didn't do the job they were supposed to. We're practically at their trenches and there's no break in the damned wire. There's nothing you can do on your own out here. You try to get back to our lines. I'll have to surrender.'

'I think I'd better stay with you, sir.'

He crawled to the lip of the crater, then went back to Walker. 'We're not far from a machine gun, sir. I think I can get them from here.'

'How far?'

'About forty yards. It's in a gap in the wire.'

Walker, wincing at the pain in his leg, looked at the crossed rifles on Tommy's sleeve.

'Marksman eh?'

'Yessir.'

'Do you have any Mills bombs?'

'Two, sir.'

'Could you reach them?'

'Easily, sir.'

'Excellent. Give it a go. If it doesn't work give 'em hell with your rifle before they toss a bomb in here.'

Tommy took the two hand grenades from his pouch, an innovation in British weaponry. He'd been trained in their use but didn't have complete faith in them not to explode as soon as he pulled the pin out. He took a deep breath, pulled the pin and threw the bomb as quickly as he could. It landed near the machine gun before exploding but didn't quite do the job, as he could hear the gunners shouting. But he now had more faith in his second grenade. He pulled out the pin, took careful aim and landed it right among them. Boom! He waited until the smoke had cleared then popped his head up again. The machine gun was twisted and pointing skyward and there was no movement from the gunners. He rolled back down to the officer.

'I got them, sir.'

A German soldier appeared at the edge of the crater, pointing his Mauser rifle at them.

'Bugger! Best surrender, Tommy,' said Lieutenant Walker. 'Get your hands in the air, quickly, man!'

Tommy dropped his rifle and held up both his hands. The German pointed his Mauser at him and pulled the trigger. Tommy knew he was going to die right up to the point where the Mauser misfired – apparently a common fault with this particular make. The German looked down and was struggling with the firing mechanism when Tommy picked up his Lee Enfield and shot him through the chest. The German hovered there long enough for Tommy to see he couldn't have been much more than seventeen. He fell in the crater, still alive, but only just. His eyes were open. Tommy shouted at him.

'Why did you fire at me? I'd surrendered, you bloody idiot!'

Then the young man died.

'Bloody hell!' said Walker. 'How the hell did he get this side of the wire? There must be a break somewhere near.'

Tommy wasn't interested in breaks in the wire. The thought of killing such a young man sickened him. He looked down at his officer. 'What's up with these people? There was no need for him to die.'

'Oh bugger him. Well done, Corporal. I don't suppose you could get me back to our lines, could you?'

Tommy looked around him. The smoke limited his vision, so it would do the same for the Germans, but the machine gun fire hadn't abated and the shell crater was giving them ample cover.

'I could give it a go, sir, but I think we should wait a while. Will you be okay?'

'You're the boss right now, Corporal.'

Tommy looked down at the dead German who was wearing soft leather, calf-length boots. 'Do you think it'd be in order to nick his boots, sir?'

'Perfectly in order. Although I don't know what the Hun will think if you're captured wearing a pair of their boots.'

'Never thought of that, but these boots of mine are crippling me and his look just about my size.'

'Well I wouldn't want you to carry me back wearing uncomfortable boots.'

Tommy had his own boots off and the German's on in two minutes.

'Do they fit all right?'

'Perfect fit, sir,' said Tommy, tying the laces of his own boots together and slinging them around his neck.

The machine gun fire was slackening but the smoke cover was still there. Tommy was glad his officer wasn't a big man. His year of training had toughened him up to the extent that he could easily hoist the lieutenant onto his shoulder. He climbed out of the crater and stumbled back towards the British trenches. The officer called out to him, 'How are the boots, Corporal Birch?'

'First class, sir. Worth every penny.'

'Carry on.'

'Sir.'

The few minutes it took to get back to his own trench were the longest minutes of his life. For the whole of the journey the air was thick with smoke and bullets and fire and noise. He passed dozens of fallen men, some dead, some dying, some weeping, convulsed with pain and asking for his help, but he couldn't stop. One man ran past them screaming with fear, flinging his rifle away. It was all too much for him. Tommy knew how he felt but had no sympathy for him. It would have been good if the man had stopped to give him a helping hand. The lieutenant was getting really heavy, as was the ground underfoot. Tommy was looking around for stretcher bearers but couldn't see any. This part of No Man's Land was a complete hell-hole and he knew his luck wouldn't hold out forever. He jumped into a crater and slid the officer from his shoulder just as a violent salvo of bullets swept over where they'd just been.

'Bloody hell! We seem to be riding on your luck, Tommy.'

'I've always been lucky, sir.'

'Good show so far. How far away are we?'

'About fifty yards, sir. Half a minute's run – when we get going again. It's getting a bit warm out there.'

'Yes, I noticed.'

'How's the leg?'

'Hurts like hell. I hope I don't lose it, but it should be enough to get me back to Blighty. Right now I'll be happy to get back to our lines.'

There was a lull in the firing. Tommy hoisted the officer onto his back, climbed out of the crater and set off at a stumbling, tripping, shuffling run. As he ran, a strange thought struck him. His new boots were really comfortable and made this terrifying journey that much easier. If he got back in one piece they'd make his time in the army that much easier. All the more reason to get back. A bullet hit Walker's sidearm and whined off into the smoke, another put a hole through Tommy's water bottle and another pinged off his helmet. It took him a full half-minute of near misses, mumbling curses and a racing heart to get back. He just threw himself and his officer into the trench.

'Much obliged, Tommy,' said Walker from his upside-down position.

'Oh, sorry, sir.'

'No, I meant it. You saved my life. That silly bugger would have shot me if you hadn't been there.'

Chapter 11

On Saturday 16th September Tommy's battalion had been moved ten miles south and had made an advance of around four miles up to a village called Longueval where they'd commandeered billets and erected tents. They were resting in an encampment prior to more action. Tommy's platoon, under constant fire, were in the process of digging trenches 500 yards west of the village and had already built wooden roadways to ease the burden of the horses pulling supplies and ammunition wagons up to the front. He was sitting on an empty shell box, scratching his head with a pencil and perusing a plan of proposed trench bridges when a sergeant came up to him.

'Corporal Birch.'

'Sarge.'

'I want you ready and up bright and early in the morning. Half an hour before dawn.'

'Ready for what, Sarge?

'Firing squad duties. There'll be twelve of you. One firing blanks as usual.'

Tommy lit a cigarette as the sergeant walked off. He knew what this was about. There'd been a court martial that week. Back at the Somme a man had been seen throwing his weapon away and running from the enemy. Tommy was pretty certain it must have been the man who passed him when he was staggering back with Lieutenant Walker. The offender had run straight into an MP who put him under arrest for cowardice in the face of the enemy.

Tommy made further enquiries. The condemned man was a private in the Bradford Pals Regiment – his part of the world, and the action was indeed the battle where he'd saved Lieutenant Walker's life. Tommy knew that the colossal noise of that day had been enough to drive anybody mad, in fact he was amazed he hadn't gone mad himself. But death was always the punishment for cowardice in the face of the enemy. No exceptions and all the men knew it. This was the deterrent that stopped them running away. It was a deterrent that had made heroes out of frightened men. Running away meant certain and ignominious death by firing squad, going forward gave a man at least a fifty/fifty chance of heroic survival.

They'd been told that the July 1st offensive had been a success, but no mention made of the cost in human lives. History would record that the British took around four hundred yards of German territory that day, at massive expense. Sixty thousand British casualties including over nineteen thousand killed. Almost fifty dead men per yard of gain. The most ever killed in any British war in a day, ever.

As the day wore on Tommy began to feel sick at the prospect of shooting the boy. An image of the young German he'd shot kept coming to mind. He had a look of surprise and indignation on his face, as if Tommy had no right to shoot him. The Germans in the machine gun emplacement didn't trouble his thoughts, he hadn't seen their faces. He was reminded of his dad's words:

I still remember every man I shot and every one I bayonetted. I think about their families and I know I shouldn't and it pains me to think you might be burdened with the same thoughts.

He then found out that the condemned soldier was only seventeen years old, too young to be even on active service. Despite this, General Haig had approved his execution. As the day drew to a close Tommy sought out the sergeant who had ordered him to be in the firing squad.

'It's my birthday tomorrow, sarge. I'll be twenty-one. This firing squad – I don't want to be shooting anyone on my birthday.'

'Corporal. I've got five volunteers and six men on punishment in the squad. I'm looking to you, as an NCO, to be the twelfth man. Afterwards the men on punishment will have their offences rescinded and the volunteers, which now include you, will be excused duties for the rest of the day.'

Tommy knew that he couldn't take the day off. He was too important a part of the Pioneer team, but there was no point telling the sergeant that.

'The lad's seventeen, Sarge. I shot a lad about that age back at Serre.'

'I know. I'm told you're up for a medal. Don't try and take advantage of that, Corporal.'

'I'm not, Sarge – didn't even know.'

'Corporal, I've been in a firing squad myself on two occasions. It's not a good experience but it's a necessary evil. In war it's the ultimate punishment that keeps men in line. If we lose the ultimate deterrent we lose the war. Simple as that.'

'How come we're shooting a seventeen-year-old boy?'

'He turned and ran and threw his rifle away. If we all did that we'd lose the war in a week.'

'He was probably just shocked, Sarge. I've heard it called shell shock.'

'Yes, and I've heard it called cowardice.'

'I know but–'

'I've been patient with you, Corporal. One hour before dawn.'

'Sarge.'

Tommy went back to his billet to write a letter to Rita. It would be his last letter to her, but he had no way of knowing that.

Chapter 12

Tommy had had about three hours troubled sleep when he was awakened by the sergeant, who was unusually civil.

'It's that time, Corporal, the squad's waiting.'

Minutes later Tommy went out of the tent, carrying his Lee Enfield. The dawn was half an hour away and the sergeant was standing across the road by a churchyard, along with eleven men who were all chatting and smoking as if they were simply off to do a normal day's work. When he joined them he realised they were talking about football and the sergeant was purposely goading them into an argument.

'Bradford City? Rubbish team nowadays. The best team in Yorkshire's Barnsley. FA Cup winners 1912 and still goin' strong.'

Tommy listened as the argument swayed back and forth and he knew it was simply to take their minds off the job in hand. The execution was to take place in a field behind the village church. An officer arrived with two privates to collect their weapons and have them loaded with one round each. Tommy would know if his round was a blank from the strength of the recoil. He'd fired enough blanks in training to know the difference.

He lit a cigarette and stood there as the subject changed from football to the relative merits of Music Hall star Ada Reeve who, Private Barraclough claimed, was his cousin from Dewsbury.

As grey dawn began to light up the sky the condemned man was being taken around the other side of the church so that he couldn't hear the execution squad and they couldn't see him. He was taken, with his eyes bandaged and his hands tied behind his back, to a stake in the field to which he was securely tied. A chaplain, who had spent the night with the young man, stood beside him, reading from a prayer book. Also in the field was a doctor and an army captain who would give the order to fire by raising and bringing down his ceremonial sword. The order came for the men to march in line to the field.

'Now listen, lads,' said the sergeant, quietly, as he walked alongside them. 'This job has to be done quickly and cleanly for the prisoner's sake. So do not aim to miss. You'll be doing him no favours.'

'Sarge,' murmured some of them.

The rising sun lit up the day from behind grey clouds as they marched in silence, led by the sergeant, then by Tommy who took his place at the end of the line just seven yards from the target. It was an unmissable distance, close enough to see the silent tears escaping down pale cheeks from bandaged eyes. But for all this the lad didn't cry out in fear or protest. He stood erect, with his chin up, as if to say, "Do I look like a coward?" The sergeant stepped up to him and pinned a white cloth over his heart – the target. The captain, standing to Tommy's right, raised his sword and called out.

'Take aim...!'

'Mother!'

The word came from the prisoner just as the sword fell. It caused Tommy to adjust his aim to miss by so little it shouldn't be noticed. All twelve guns fired at once. The young man slumped forward but his bonds still held him. The doctor went up to him, knelt beside him and pronounced him dead; the chaplain stood over him and blessed his body. Two stretcher bearers arrived to take the boy away.

'Squad dismiss!' called out the sergeant.

The squad trooped away without a backward glance and not a word exchanged. They'd been cursed with a memory they could do without. It was later found that eleven bullets had hit the body. Tommy knew he'd been given the blank. Had his been a live round, only ten would have hit the body. No way was he going to celebrate his 21st birthday by shooting a boy in cold blood.

Chapter 13

Longueval, France.
Tuesday 19th September 1916

It was raining, as it had been all night. At 7.20 am whistles blew along the British front line signalling the first wave of battalions to move into No Man's Land. The German machine guns laid down a withering spray of deadly fire. Usually the first ones to fall were the junior officers who almost always led the advance with great bravado.

Tommy was in one of the rear trenches and therefore not among the early casualties. He was normally a fast runner but the muddy ground slowed him down a lot. Halfway across No Man's Land he took a bullet in the leg and went down. He rolled over onto his back and raised an arm to signal the stretcher bearers, who spotted him but he was only one of many needing their help. He rolled into one of the myriad shell craters to allow the sweeping machine gun fire to pass over his head. He'd been hit in his right thigh and his leg was dead from the waist down. The pain was bad, as was the noise of constant shellfire and bullets whining within inches of him. He rolled over a couple more times until he was lying in the puddle at the bottom of the trench. Wetter but safer.

He'd grown used to the shellfire over the past weeks but he wasn't entirely sure that he was out of the machine gun's line-of-fire. All he could do was hope and pray and think of Rita and hold his Lee Enfield at the ready, still remembering the appearance of a German soldier the last time he'd taken cover in a crater.

What he didn't know about was that while his men had been digging trenches along the British front line the German sappers had dug a tunnel into No Man's Land and placed a twenty thousand kilogram mine there. It was sixty feet beneath the crater where Tommy was sheltering.

He would never know anything about the explosion that sent him hurtling through the air towards the German line. He was unconscious even as he took off. Apart from his socks and boots, every stitch of clothing, plus his dog tags, were blasted from his body and he landed in a naked, broken heap amongst the German barbed wire entanglements.

The stretcher bearers who had spotted him earlier were blown over by the blast despite being a quarter of a mile away. They waited until the filth and smoke had settled before they checked to see what had happened to him. They saw no sign of him. No sign of any living thing. None was expected, no way could anything have survived such a colossal explosion. Their ears were ringing, and would be for quite some time. They had to shout at one another.

'What the hell was that?'

'A mine.'

'Jesus! I thought the world was coming to an end.'

'Biggest one I've ever known.'

85

'And me.'

'This war's a right bloody mess.'

These were men of the Royal Army Medical Corps who wore Red Cross arm-bands which, under the Geneva Convention, gave them certain protection from enemy fire, but not random machine gun fire. They dropped to the ground and crawled to a shell hole where they took shelter until a lull in the firing enabled them to make their way to a fallen man who was crying with pain. His body had been ripped open by bullets. He died within seconds of them reaching him. They moved on, passing arms and legs and decapitated heads. Then they arrived at the gigantic hole created by the mine. A hundred feet in diameter and sixty feet deep. It would still be there in a hundred years. One of them picked up Tommy's dog tags from the mud and read the name:

'Birch ... Thomas, do you know him?'

'Tommy Birch, yeah. Pioneer Corporal. Pontefract lad. I reckon he's the one who was waving. Poor sod.'

'Well he's out of it now. God knows where.'

'Bits of him everywhere I should think.'

The call came to withdraw to their trenches which they did with some alacrity. They handed the dog tags to a lieutenant who pulled a face when he saw Tommy's tags.

'This man is dead?'

'Yessir. We only found Corporal Birch's tags. He went up with the mine, sir. Bits of him all over the place I should imagine.'

'Corporal Birch is definitely dead?'

'Yessir. He was waving for help when that mine

went off, right underneath him. After that he'd gone.'

'Bloody hell! Why we send engineers out with the infantry beats me. He was much more valuable as an engineer than as an infantryman. How the hell are we supposed to win this bloody war? It'd make more sense if we sent the generals out in front.'

The lieutenant held up a white flag to ask the enemy for a truce to recover dead and wounded. The truce was agreed by the other side who had many dead and injured of their own. A stretcher bearer asked an important question.

'There's lots of body parts out there. What shall we do, sir?'

'Just bring back those who are in one piece, dead or alive. I doubt if the Hun'll hold off long enough for us to be ferreting about for body parts and we need to keep pushing forward. We can pick up the remains once we've taken their positions. Do either of you know what Corporal Birch looks like?'

'I do, sir.'

'Right, well if you find anything of him that you er ... that you might recognise I want it brought back here. If he's dead I want to know for certain.'

It would be three days before they pushed the Germans back. Three days of fierce fighting and constant rain that saw No Man's Land turned into a quagmire. No chance of collecting any recognisable remains.

Chapter 14

A week later there was a loud knock on the Birch front door, indicating that the postman had left an important letter. Agnes went through to the front room and stared down at the envelope on the doormat. It was buff coloured and had OHMS printed on the outside. Charlie had gone to work. Rita was about to leave for the bank and Edith for her job at Wilkinsons cabinet works where she was a French polisher, making quite good money for a seventeen-year-old. Stanley was getting ready for school. Agnes turned round and went into the back room without picking up the envelope.

'Was that a letter, Mam?' Stanley asked.

Agnes couldn't speak. Her face had gone pale. Her hands were shaking. Edith said nothing and walked past her mother into the front room. She came back holding the envelope in her hand, making no attempt to open it. She put it on the table and looked at her mother who was in tears.

'I daren't open it, Edith.'

Edith made no reply. Rita stared down at it and looked up at Agnes, asking, 'What do you think it is?'

'It's addressed to you, Rita,' said Stanley, taking a look at the address on the envelope.

'Me?'

'You're Tommy's immediate next-of-kin, now,'

said Edith, quietly.

'Tommy? Is it from Tommy?'

'I don't think so.'

Rita gasped, 'Oh no! Is he wounded?'

'He might be,' said Edith. 'That's probably what it is.'

Agnes was panting for breath. Stanley was worried about her. 'Do you want me to open it?' he asked.

The three women looked at each other. Edith gave a slight nod. Stanley picked up the envelope and opened it under three terrified gazes. He took out the contents and looked up at them before he read it. Then he realised that this might be very bad news indeed.

'Oh heck!' he said, giving the letter to Rita. 'You should prob'ly read it, with it being addressed to you.'

Rita took it in a shaking hand and read it, with Agnes and Edith watching her face, trying to gauge her reaction. Rita read it and stared at it in complete disbelief, unable to move a muscle. She then looked up, over everyone's heads with glazed eyes. Agnes took the letter from her and read it. She collapsed to the floor. Stanley picked it up and read it. It was an army form B.104-82 with the details filled in by hand:

It is my painful duty to inform you that a report has this day been received from the War Office notifying the death of...

Name... *Thomas Birch*

Regiment... *King's Own Yorkshire Light Infantry*

which occurred at... *Longueval France*

on the... *19th September 1916*
and I am to express the sympathy and regret of
the Army Council at your loss.
The cause of death was... *Killed in Action*

Stanley didn't read all this out loud. He just
looked at his sister and said, 'Our Tommy's dead.'

Edith squeezed her eyes together and hung her
head for a long moment, then she kneeled on the
floor beside her weeping mother. She looked up
at Stanley. 'I think you'd better stay off school,
Stanley. Go to Dad's work and tell him to come
home.'

Her mother dripped silent tears onto the rug,
shoulders heaving in anguish. Edith put her arm
around her but knew no words of comfort.
Losing her beloved brother was like an arrow in
her heart as well. It was a torture far too much
for Rita to endure so she refused to believe it. She
didn't have the emotional capacity to believe it.

'I'll get your father,' she said, in a voice devoid
of emotion. 'I'll tell him there's been a mistake.
He'll know what to do.'

'Mistake?' said Stanley. 'You mean Tommy's
not dead?'

'No, no, he won't be dead,' said Rita reaching for
her coat. 'They shouldn't make mistakes like that.'

She went out of the house. Stanley looked at
Edith. 'Does she know where Dad works?'

Edith, her eyes red with grief, was stroking her
prostrate mother's hair and patting her face. She
gathered herself together enough to tell him, 'I
don't think so. Look, nip next door to fetch Mrs
Morley. Tell her Mam's poorly and can she come

and keep an eye on her while I go get Dad.'
'Okay. Shall I tell her about this letter?'
'No.'

Chapter 15

Charlie was high on the scaffolding fixing roof trusses when he heard his name called from below by the site manager. He turned and looked down at Edith's distressed face. She was standing beside the manager, holding the letter in her hand. He stared down at her with an expression asking, *'What?'*

Edith shook her head and held the letter a little higher. It was still in the buff envelope. Several men saw it and recognised it for what it was. A buff envelope was the last thing anyone wanted coming through the letterbox. There was a stillness in the air as they all looked up at Charlie. Ralph, his workmate, seemed to get the message a little quicker, or maybe Charlie simply didn't *want* to get any such message.

'Oh no,' Charlie said, eventually.

Ralph put his hand on Charlie's shoulder. 'Take it steady on that ladder, mate.'

Ralph watched from on high as Charlie climbed slowly down the ladder and went over to his daughter. The men looked on. Many of them had sons and young brothers fighting overseas and never a day went by without them dreading getting a letter from the War Office. A letter in a buff envelope.

Edith gave him the letter and took a step back. Charlie read it and his whole body slumped to the point of collapse. Edith stepped forward and held him as he was now obviously weeping on her shoulder. Ralph climbed down the ladder, not sure how he could help, but Charlie was his pal and if he needed anything... He walked up to the father and daughter. Edith, in tears, looked at him from over her father's shoulder.

'Is it your Tommy?'

Nod.

'Is he...?'

Another nod.

Everybody on the site was now watching, some of them in tears of their own. Charlie was a popular man and many of them knew and liked Tommy. The site manager, standing a few feet away from the weeping pair, looked at the men, shook his head, solemnly, and held a finger to his lips.

All the residual noise of the building site now ceased. The concrete mixer was switched off, men stopped talking and shouting, hammering and sawing; those indoors came out and stood with caps removed and arms by their sides out of respect. Charlie looked up and gave a brief nod in appreciation, then he went off in wretched silence, holding onto his daughter.

Charlie was home when Rita got back from walking around Pontefract in a daze. She vaguely knew she needed to find him but had no idea where, so she just stopped by various building sites and looked to see if he was there. She didn't speak to anyone, her mind was in too much of a turmoil. The news that Tommy was dead simply would not register as the truth. It was news she simply couldn't accept without seeing his dead body. In her heart Tommy was still alive. For her to think he was dead was betraying him because he'd know he was alive. He'd know they'd got it wrong – that's if he even knew that such terrible news had been conveyed to her.

All the family were in the back room. Charlie in his usual chair, Agnes in hers, Stanley and Edith sitting at the table, no one speaking, all of them staring into space. All had been crying – everyone in the room except Rita who saw nothing to cry about because her Tommy was alive. She paused and looked at them but they didn't look up at her. It was as if they weren't aware of her arrival.

'I'm going up,' she said.

Edith acknowledged this with a brief nod. No one else seemed to hear. Rita went quietly upstairs to her room, not daring to cry because crying would be admitting she believed all this rubbish. She couldn't believe it. Her heart wouldn't stand the strain of such belief. She had his living, breathing baby inside her womb. She couldn't afford to believe he was dead.

Chapter 16

The following Sunday Rita waited until St Joseph's had emptied before she made her way down the aisle to the sacristy where Father Mulvaney would be. She tapped on the door. He had already divested himself of his liturgical garments and came to the door in a black shirt, black trousers and his dog collar.

'Why, Rita. I thought I saw you at the back. Haven't seen much of you since your wedding day.' He was Irish and his years in England had scarcely diluted his Mayo accent. Rita didn't want to get involved in giving excuses for her non-attendance at Mass. She came straight to the point.

'I've had a letter telling me that Tommy's been killed, Father.'

'Oh, my dear child. Come in and sit down.'

Rita went in and sat down on the only chair.

'Well, this must be a bad time for all your family.'

'It is, Father, only...'

'Only what, my child?'

She took a deep breath. 'Only I don't believe he's dead, Father.'

'In the eyes of the Lord he's not dead, Rita. His living soul has just passed on to a better place.'

'No, Father, it's not that. I feel as if I'd know if he were dead and I don't.' She tapped her chest. 'In here I know he's still alive.'

'And so he might be, my child. We live in confused times.'

'Am I foolish in believing this, Father?'

'Some people think it's foolish to believe the sacred host I give out at communion is the true body of Jesus Christ. But I truly believe that, so you're no more foolish than I.'

Tears came to Rita for the first time since she'd heard the news. The old priest took her hands. 'Rita, why have you come to me?'

Her words tumbled out through the tears. 'Father, I want you to tell me it's not true. I want you to say it's a mistake. I want you to tell me the army get things wrong. I want you to say my Tommy's coming home to me.'

He closed his eyes for a few seconds then released her hands and walked across the room. She looked up at him and, through the mist of her tears, she saw the back of his head silhouetted against a stained-glass window illuminated in red, blue and yellow by the winter sun. He turned.

'My child, all I can ask you to do is have faith in your feelings.' He tapped his own chest. 'I too believe in an inner truth that defies all logic. If you have a belief that Tommy is alive then it's not a belief to be dismissed lightly. There is a living, breathing bond between the two of you that has been blessed by God Almighty, and if that bond is broken ... why wouldn't you be aware of it?'

'So, you think it's God who's saying it isn't true?'

'My child. I'm not here to give you false hope, but nor will I advise you to give up hope, which is the most blessed and human of all the theological virtues. Was his death witnessed? Has his body been found?'

'I don't know any of that, Father, just that he was killed in action in France. Tommy's dad thinks we'll get a letter from an officer giving us more details of Tommy's death.'

'His family are non-Catholic, I believe.'

'They are, Father, but they're the best of people.'

'I believe you, my child, and some Catholics are the worst of people. We don't have a monopoly on the good people of this world.'

He sat down on the edge of a table and rubbed his chin. 'The only way I can help you, Rita, is to encourage you to keep on believing what you feel inside you. I have a sense that you are a spiritual person.'

'I'm a sinner, Father.'

He smiled. 'And didn't the Lord create a whole human race of sinners? Then he set himself the task of reforming us all.'

'Tommy and I had sex outside marriage, Father.'

The priest allowed himself time to formulate an answer. 'And did you think it was a sin at the time?'

'Not at all, Father. It was a wonderful act of love.'

'Well, I will absolve you of that and all the other sins that you cannot now remember. Now go into the church and say five Hail Marys. Not as a penance but as supplication to Our Lady to be on your side in the hope that Tommy is still with us. If it's any consolation at all, I believe you could be right.'

'Thank you, Father.'

Chapter 17

Dear Mrs. Birch,

My name is Lieutenant Peter Walker. I wish to offer you my sincerest condolences at the death of your husband. I was Thomas's platoon commander in the Somme area of France. His gallantry at the first battle of the Somme included him saving my life, almost at the cost of his own, so his death came as a great sadness to me personally as well as all of the men in my platoon. He has been recommended for a Military Medal.

Thomas was an excellent engineer who made the work of the Pioneers much easier with his imaginative ideas and skill. As well as this I knew him to be a fine man and a brave soldier who saw the humorous side of many a difficult situation, which helped with morale.

Your husband's death was witnessed by two stretcher bearers, he died instantly when a huge enemy mine was detonated underneath him. The explosion was quite massive and took the lives of Corporal Birch and several others. Unfortunately because of the enormity of the explosion your husband's body could not be recovered but now we have cleared the area of enemy a suitable stone will be placed in his memory and you will be notified of its location in due course.

Thomas was truly a man to be proud of but I suspect I don't need to tell you that.

Yours sincerely,
Peter Walker

Rita looked up at Charlie after she'd read it out to him. 'I already knew they hadn't found him, Mr Birch.'

'How did you know that, Rita?'

'Because he's not dead. I knew he wasn't dead when I read the first letter.'

'I see.'

'Do you think he's dead?'

'Rita, I'd love to think he isn't but the army don't make mistakes like that.'

'But they do, Mr Birch. I've read about it. I read about a woman who was notified of her husband's death when it turned out it was another man with the same name.'

'But this isn't like that, Rita.'

'I know but it proves that the army sometimes get things wrong.'

Charlie sighed. 'True but...'

He hadn't the mental strength to argue with her. He just wished she'd accept things as they obviously were. Her refusal to believe Tommy was dead wasn't helping matters. It was over a week since they'd heard of Tommy's death. Charlie hadn't been back to work and Agnes had scarcely been out of bed. Edith had stayed off work to look after her parents despite being bereft at her brother's death. Stanley had cried a lot and had gone back to school after a couple of days. He shared his sorrow with his pal, Eddie, who had now lost another uncle to the war.

Chapter 18

Monday 27th November 1916. 10.15 pm

A stone clattered against Stanley's bedroom window, waking him up. He slid up the sliding sash and looked out. In the backyard was Eddie, pointing upwards. 'Hey up, Stan, it's a Zepp! Look.'

Stanley looked up but could see nothing. 'I can't see nowt.'

'Yer could if yer were down here. It's right over your roof. Come on down, it might drop a bomb on yer!' Charlie, who had heard the commotion, went to the door. 'Eddie, what're you doing out at this time of night?'

'It's a Zepp, Mister Birch. Up there, look.'

Charlie stepped out and looked upwards. Above him was a huge dark shape, like a gigantic silver shark nosing its way across the sky, picked out by three searchlight beams. Anti-aircraft fire was being directed at it but the shells were exploding much too low. It droned on westwards, seemingly unassailable.

'Bloody hell!' said Charlie. 'How are we supposed to fight that?'

'Charlie,' shouted Agnes. 'You'd best come in. It might be dropping bombs any minute.'

But curiosity overcame any fear Charlie might have had of any bombs. He went out into the street which was by now full of people watching the slow progress of this German giant droning across the sky above them. Agnes, Edith, Rita and Stanley joined him within minutes.

They could see the lights from the gondola slung below its belly. A light flashed from its middle. A brief light caused by the opening and closing of a bomb door.

'Hey up!' shouted Charlie. 'That could be a bomb they've let go.'

He was still ushering his wife and family into the house when they saw a flash over distant roofs, followed by an explosion, followed by another flash and another explosion like the boom of a muffled bass drum. Then the crack of heavy ground artillery firing into the sky and the sound of angry women screaming at the tops of their voices.

'I think we're okay here,' called out Charlie, looking around the sky. 'He's on his own and heading away from us.'

Those who had been heading for cover returned to the street as more bombs fell on distant people who they might well know tomorrow, but not tonight.

'Where are they landing, Charlie?' asked Agnes.

'I reckon they landed in the Ponte Park,' guessed Charlie. 'Can't do too much harm in Ponte Park this time o' night.'

One man said, 'There'll be a few courtin' couples out there.' Murmurs of agreement to this.

'Aye, we did a bit o' courtin' there, didn't we, Mavis?'

Mavis, whose eldest had been conceived in Pontefract Park, didn't answer. She just dug her husband in the ribs with a sharp elbow. The fainter sounds of two more bombs. 'I reckon they dropped on Ackton,' said Charlie. 'Bloody hell! I didn't reckon them damned beasts'd be able to reach Yorkshire. They've been shootin' 'em down in London. God, I wish I had the means to shoot the bastards down!'

'Charlie! Watch your language.'

'Agnes, them bastards killed our Tommy!'

'I know they did, Charlie, but–'

'I know they didn't,' said Rita.

It was the wrong moment for her to say this. Charlie turned on her. 'And I wish you'd stop banging on about him being alive! It's hard enough having to cope with his death without us having to cope with your fantasies! Just give it a bloody rest, Rita!'

He stormed back into the house followed by his family, leaving Rita standing in the street, white-faced. Charlie had always been so pleasant to her.

Back in the house Agnes went straight up to bed, ushering Stanley up in front of her. Edith looked at her father. 'You were a bit sharp with Rita, Dad.'

'It's what was needed, love. To stop this non-sense.'

'Maybe it's her way of coping with Tommy dying.'

'That's just it, she isn't coping. She hasn't even begun to cope, and in the meantime it's holding back the rest of us, especially your mam. When all's said and done it's your mam who suffers the most in the long run.'

'But we all miss him, Dad.'

'We do, love.' He picked up his son's MM dis-

101

played in its open case on the mantelpiece. It was a source of pride to Charlie because he alone knew what a man had to go through to be awarded a gallantry medal. The whole family had been to the KOYLI headquarters to see it presented to Rita by the Regimental Colonel. Charlie had wondered why the colonel was over here in the barracks and not out there with his regiment but he knew better than to ask.

He clicked his fingers. 'God knows I'd swap places with him like that if it'd bring him back to this family.'

'But he was Rita's future, she's lost all that.'

'Rita's a beautiful young woman. A war widow. Once she accepts he's not coming back she'll get down to grieving properly, and when she finishes grieving she'll realise she's still young and still beautiful.'

'You mean she'll find someone else?'

'To be honest, I imagine she will, yes. Okay, she'll not find another Tommy, I grant you, especially with all the likely lads out there in France and many of them not coming back, but a girl like Rita'll always have the pick of the crop, as and when she's ready.'

'Is that what our Tommy was?'

'Our Tommy was the best of the best, Edith.' He thought for a while, then said, 'When our Tommy came into a room it got warmer, did you ever notice that?'

'I think I did, yes. It got warmer and it got brighter and it got more friendly. We smiled more when Tommy was in the room.'

Charlie blinked away a tear, picked up his pipe

and lit it by poking a spill into the fire embers. 'Rita'll get through this. It's your mam I'm concerned about.'

'Why just Mam?'

'Because a mother's love for her child is a special love that can't be matched. Not by the dad, or brothers or sisters. For nine months the child is a living, breathing part of the mother, then she has to go through the horrible pain of birth, sending her child out into the world. This gives the two of them this magical bond. Tommy will have left a big hole in your mam's heart that'll never be healed.'

'We've all got one of those, Dad.'

'Yes, but we'll learn to live with it because we have to. His mam'll think she's betraying her boy if she ever stops grieving. That's the way mothers think. As for me, our Tommy died a soldier's death which makes me proud of the way he died. It's a pride I'll always carry with me, along with the sorrow. It's how you and Stanley'll remember him eventually, with pride and sorrow and great affection. We'll always have his photo and his medal up on the mantelpiece and when people ask who that handsome young man is we'll tell them he's our Tommy who fought and died for us in the war.'

'But all Mam'll have is a hole in her heart?'

'She'll have that, and she'll have his memory and she'll have us. What she won't have is his grave – a place where she can go and talk to him. That would have been a great help. She'll have a hatred of Germans all her life. She'll want to kill any one she sees. I'm not so struck on them myself, but I know your mam better than anyone, and I know that's the way she sees things. She's

103

not been the same since Tommy died, but I suppose you've noticed that.'

'There's something I *have* noticed, Dad.'

'What's that?'

'I think Rita might be pregnant with our Tommy's baby.'

The pipe dropped out of Charlie's mouth onto the floor. He picked it up and stamped out the spilled ashes burning on the hearth rug.

'What?'

'I'm surprised no one else has noticed.'

'But—'

There was a timid knock on the door. They both turned as Rita came in. There was an awkward silence before she said, 'I'm sorry for upsetting you, Mr Birch. I won't do it again.'

Charlie smiled at her, glancing at her bulging stomach and realised Edith might well be right. He knew he hadn't noticed because he had other things on his mind, as had Agnes.

'You can start by calling me Charlie,' he said. 'I think you've known me long enough to cut out the formalities, and I know Mrs Birch would like you to call her Agnes.'

'I'd like that. It's just that...' she hesitated. 'It's just that with Tommy not around I'm wondering what right I have to go on living here. I do have a home with my dad if I want to go back there.'

'Do you want to go back there?'

'Not really. I feel that this is my home. I feel Tommy's presence here, even though he's ... he's not here. Is it okay for me to say that?'

'More than okay,' said Edith. 'Because we all feel the same way.'

'And we all look upon you as part of the Birch family,' Charlie said.

'Which you are ... you being Rita Birch,' added Edith.

There was a silence before Charlie broached the subject. 'Rita,' he said, 'are you er ... are you with child by any chance?'

Rita stood there, taken by surprise, saying nothing, her silence providing enough of an answer.

'It would be wonderful if you are,' Charlie added.

'I am,' said Rita. 'I just wanted Tommy to be the first to know, which is why I didn't tell yo–'

'Hey, you don't have to give us excuses,' Charlie told her. 'These are not normal times.'

'It er, it happened on Tommy's last home leave in August.'

'So, you're about three months erm ... pregnant?' said Edith.

'Yes.'

'With my grandchild.'

'With Tommy's child,' said Rita. 'Look, if I'm living with you I'd like to pay my way a bit better. I've got my army pension award through at last and I'll be getting one pound three and eightpence a week. I'm okay for money with my wage so I think you should have all of that. Plus I'll be getting some accrued back pension I can let you have.'

'Hey, the usual ten bob a week for your board'll be plenty,' said Charlie. 'It'll go up when Agnes says so and not before. We're not here to make a profit out of you so never you mind giving us your accrued pension. You owe us nothing and you'll have to give up work before long. No matter what, we'll all manage. By heck this really is a bit of good news. Do you mind if I tell Agnes?'

'Not at all.'

Rita thought of her own father and how he'd have insisted she pay him all her pension on top of ten bob a week board. Not that she'd have ever told him about her pension.

'You're a kind man ... Charlie. I'll put my pension away for family emergencies ... my family – our family.'

'Right, I'll go and pass on the good news,' said Charlie, making his way to the stairs.

After he'd left them Rita looked at Edith, saying, 'I can't help the way I feel about Tommy, but I will keep my mouth shut from now on. I don't want to upset your dad.'

'Rita, there's only one golden rule about how not to upset Dad,' said Edith.

'What's that?'

'Don't upset Mam.'

Miraculously, out of eight bombs dropped on Pontefract that night no one was hurt or even injured, nor was any damage of any significance done, only a few holes in the ground that needed filling.

Chapter 19

City Hospital, Mannheim, Germany. December 1916

Nurse Anna Kohler looked down at the man in bed 9. Above him was the name *Unbekannter Soldat* ... Unknown Soldier. He had been brought in the day before by train from a field hospital 400 miles to the west where he had lain in a coma for ten weeks. He had spoken to no one which was not unusual for coma patients whose road to full awareness always tends to be piecemeal. It was a worry that he might have lost his mind but until he had a proper psychological examination this could not be ascertained. A doctor came to stand beside her.

'And we have still no idea who he is?' she asked him.

'Not a clue, and all this hospital reorganisation has not helped. Thousands of patient notes have been lost, but I doubt if that made any difference in this man's case. What we know is that he was blown up by one of our own mines. The blast broke sixteen of his bones and he had contusions over practically every square inch of his body. He had a bullet in his leg but in general the blast only broke his skin where bones came through. He was cushioned by at least twenty metres of earth between him and the mine. It ripped off every piece of his clothing except his boots. His identification was gone, everything. He was probably thrown thirty metres into the air, landing in our barbed wire.'

'I would have thought the fall would have killed him.'

'The theory is that the shock waves were still heading upwards as he was falling downwards, slowing him down considerably. Strangely enough the barbed wire would have made a softer landing than hard ground. He landed on his back as you'll see from all the laceration scars. It was evidently a dangerous job just disentangling him and bringing him to safety, although what he was doing on that side of the wire hasn't been explained. Some of the younger ones took it upon themselves to go through the gaps and engage the enemy who had dodged all our bullets and got through to our lines – in close combat.'

'Why would they do that?'

'Youthful bravado, most probably. Trying to prove themselves to their older comrades. This one's certainly young enough to have been up for something like that.'

'If this man was naked with no identification and he hasn't spoken, how do we know he's even one of ours?'

'I'm told he was naked apart from his boots. He was wearing fine German boots, not clumsy British boots.'

'And he has blue eyes and fair hair,' she observed. 'I had a brother who looked very much like him.'

'You *had* a brother?'

'Yes, he was killed in France seven months ago.

108

He was twenty years old, his name was Paul.'

'I'm sorry, I did not know. This is not a good war.'

'What war ever was? I cannot get over the stupidity of it all. The horrible waste of young men's lives. We are killing off a whole generation of young men. Quite possibly a good man I might have married one day. We'll end up with a whole generation of spinsters, including me.'

'I never actually thought of it like that, although I doubt if you'll remain a spinster for long.'

'I don't see why not.'

'Anna, we have to forget the stupidity and get on with the work it brings us.'

'Take this man,' said Anna. 'Why should I have even *wondered* if he was German? Had he been English it would make him no less of a human being; an injured man, forced into a war, no doubt against his better judgement. If he had been English he'd have been no less deserving of our care than my brother, but that wouldn't have happened, would it? He'd have still been taking up a much-needed bed in a Clearing Station in France with the staff giving him minimum care and hoping he'd do them a favour by dying. I bet him surviving this long would have annoyed the hell out of them.'

'The staff at the aid stations are all Red Cross the same as us, the same as the British Red Cross. He'd have been given proper care, and you know it.'

'I'm not sure I do know it. I know if this man had turned out to be British he wouldn't be here, in the high dependency unit.'

'We have scarcely enough of these units to serve our own soldiers, much less the enemy.'

'My point exactly. He's only in here because he was wearing German boots – his passport back to life.'

The doctor knew she was right, but he chose not to be drawn. He'd taken the Hippocratic Oath and was doing his best to abide by it, but in this outrageous war it wasn't easy.

Anna said, 'How has he survived this long by the way?'

'Well, for a start he is something of a miracle. We believe he was blown up by a huge mine that normally would only leave tiny splinters of human remains. Normally you would not find as much as a foot inside a boot, but this soldier survived more or less intact apart from many broken bones, bruises and lacerations. Maybe he was standing on some more solid block of ground that protected him from the main force of the blast that took off with him on it like a passenger. Who knows how he survived.'

'A miracle indeed. Is he aware of what's going on around him?' Anna asked.

'Possibly, but it's also quite possible that he has no memory, no ability to speak or to understand what's being said to him.'

Anna gave Tommy a long look and said, 'He's smiling at me. Surely he has awareness.'

'Well he's regaining the use of his limbs so he might regain the use of his mind in time.'

'And no one knows who he is?'

'Apparently not. After he was taken to a field hospital his battalion suffered heavy losses. There was no one left alive who could identify him. Whoever he really is will have been listed as missing presumed dead, along with many others who got blown to bits. We can only hope that one day he might be able to identify himself.'

'Good grief.'

'It's war, Anna. Such things happen in war.'

'Stupid things.'

'Be very careful how you speak, Anna,' said the doctor moving on down the ward.

Tommy had heard them but hadn't understood a word. He wasn't aware of the many weeks he'd spent in the field hospital being fed on a drip leading up his nose, down his oesophagus and into his stomach. All he could remember was being in a lot of pain and waving to the stretcher bearers to come for him. Then he woke up in a bed different from this, after which his memory was patchy but he did remember being on a train. He could see the world passing past the window and the distinctive sound that train wheels made when they ran over the joints in the track. And now he was here. Where *here* was he had no idea. With him now being awake they'd propped him up on a pillow so his previous recumbent view of the hospital ceiling was now a view of the bed opposite and the two people looking down at him, a man and a woman.

The woman was pale and pretty and was wearing a full-length white pinafore uniform with a red cross on the front. On her head she wore a white linen headscarf affair, tied at the back and revealing strands of blonde hair escaping down to her forehead. Her sleeves were that of a blue shirt with long white linen cuffs extending up to her elbows. Even in his confused mind he knew she was a nurse, so presumably the man was a doctor. He was dressed in a white coat buttoned up to his neck. He wore a moustache, a centre parting in his thick black hair and stared at Tommy through a pince-nez. Tommy avoided his gaze as he didn't much like the look of him but the nurse looked okay. He looked at her instead.

Their voices began to enter his consciousness and he worked out that he was among foreigners, most probably German. Why German? Because they sounded like Germans. These German medics were taking care of him. That can't be right. Why not? He didn't know why not. Surely he wasn't German. He had no knowledge of being a German, nor any inclination to be one. His brain wasn't working so well that he knew how things worked in this world currently enveloped in a fog too thick for him to see anything clearly. He didn't know who he was, or that he was married, or that he was a Yorkshire mining engineer, or how he'd been injured. But every so often another piece of the five-hundred-piece jigsaw that was his memory fell into place.

He now had no pain in his leg but his body didn't feel too great. Generally he felt numb all over. He could just about move his head and his arms and legs but not to the extent that he might be able to get out of this bed without falling over. He was aware of the tube up his nose but wasn't sure what purpose it served, then it occurred to him that he couldn't remember the last time he went for a pee; or when he'd felt the need to have one. Surely that wasn't right. He didn't know much but he knew the basic human functions. He checked his nether regions and located the narrow tube leading from his penis and out of his bed. Bloody hell! What was that? Tommy had never been in a hospital before, he knew nothing about catheters.

He was tempted to pull the tube out of his nose until he realised that this was probably feeding him. He'd somehow heard of this method of feeding unconscious patients and he wasn't hungry and he didn't need a pee so probably this was all to his advantage. He was a bit worried about his bowel movements. Surely this couldn't be dealt with by a tube? Bloody hell! He was in a right state. What had happened to him?

He had tried to speak on a few occasions but nothing came out. He had the words inside his head but not the ability to turn them into sounds. Then it occurred to him that with his language being different from theirs it was maybe a good idea not to let them know that *he* was different. Why he thought this he didn't know, but instinct told him it was the right thing to do. Button it, Tommy, until you figure out what's what.

Tommy! That was his name! He remembered now. He had a name and it was definitely Tommy. He looked up at the nurse and smiled as he felt a surge of elation. She smiled back and said something to him in German. He opened his mouth and tried to speak but he knew that he couldn't and that it would do no harm for her to realise he couldn't. He needed to know a lot more

113

than his name before he worked out how or if to speak to anybody. He needed to know who Tommy was and why he was here.

Anna found herself suddenly beguiled by the smile of this young mystery man whose visible skin was largely unbroken despite the horrendous explosion that had blown him here. All his cuts were on his back where he'd landed on the barbed wire, and they'd all healed by now. His face was unscathed, his teeth were all intact, he'd just been clean shaven by one of the Red Cross auxiliaries and many of his bandages had been removed. He was a handsome young man. His limbs were no longer encased in plaster-casts and his skull injury had been repaired by an expert surgeon. Whatever injuries lay within his skull were yet to be assessed. His lack of a voice was hampering progress in that direction. She thought she'd give it a try by asking him how he was today.

'Wie geht es Ihnen heute?'

Tommy continued to smile as if he simply hadn't heard. Anna tried again with a simpler question.

'Wie heisst du? Dein Name?'

He was sure he understood this, but for him to answer, even with a made-up German name such as Herman, would blow his cover as a man who had no voice. So he continued with his beguiling smile. Human instinct told him there was some value to this but he wasn't sure why ... just a sense that to smile was good.

She smiled back at him and he realised one thing if he realised nothing else – she was very pretty and he liked pretty girls. So, there it was. His name was Tommy, he liked pretty girls and he knew a smile

114

would do him no harm. Such was the extent of his progress on his first full day of consciousness in ten weeks; although as far as Tommy knew it might have been two days. Anna stuck a thermometer in his mouth, as much as an excuse to be near him as anything else. She checked the reading.

'*Es ist normal.*'

He nodded, thinking it would do no harm for her to think he understood German, despite the phrase being almost English. His eyes were alive with humour and understanding and she suddenly wondered if he was mute through choice for some reason. If he was she would keep his secret *for the time being*. He was a young man she wanted to share something with, if only the secret of his silence. His very existence was a mystery to everyone, so perhaps he was not all he appeared to be?

She took a small writing pad from her pocket and handed it to him along with a pencil. He took it and, anticipating what she was after, held it lightly, just balancing it between his fingers. She asked him who he was.

'*Wer bist du?*'

Who are you?

He stared at her for several seconds as if absorbing her question. Luck had him translating it correctly. He shrugged, as if to say, *I don't know.*

He held the pad very lightly in his left hand and pressed the tip of the pencil onto it. The light pressure he applied by pushing from his arm, slid the pencil back through his grip. This told her he hadn't the hand strength to grip a pencil properly. It did occur to him that this subterfuge might be difficult to maintain when it came to eating and

115

drinking. Now he was awake surely they'd take his nose tube away. He shook the pencil forward and tried again, ensuring the same result.

This time he allowed the pad to slip from his grip. She picked both it and the pencil up and stuck them back in her pocket, saying, '*Vielleicht, wenn du stärker bist.*'

Maybe when you are stronger.

He nodded again, assuming this to be the correct response. Anna went off to make her rounds of the wards, not entirely convinced. She knew when a patient was pretending, but he'd been at death's door for over two months, why should he pretend anything? And why was she thinking the worst of him? She hated this war! Not only that but she knew full well who had started it – that brainless bastard Kaiser Wilhelm who wanted to rule the whole of Europe. Her parents hated him and she shared that hatred.

It was a hatred she was wise to keep to herself. She suspected that others at the hospital agreed with her but she had never asked anyone openly about it. One young nurse, who had just lost an eighteen-year-old soldier patient who had been expected to live had cursed the Kaiser's very existence and the stupidity of war and how she never saw any of their great leaders lying wounded in the beds or dead in the morgue. She was hurried away and never seen or heard of again. Anna didn't want to suffer the same fate.

Her mother had gone back to England at her doctor father's behest when various European countries began to declare war on each other. England's eventual involvement was inevitable, he'd told her, and he couldn't guarantee her safety if Germany and Britain went to war. He would have gone with her, but the German authorities were keeping a watchful eye on professional Germans, trained in Germany and now fleeing to Britain and America. If he'd tried to go with her obstacles would have been put in their way, ending up with neither of them being allowed to go. Anna herself had lived with her mother's family in England where she'd studied medicine at the London Free Hospital for Women. She came back to Germany the week before her mother made the same journey in the opposite direction. This was six years ago in 1910. The plan was that at least one of the family's women should be around to look after the father who, they thought, might be prone to self-neglect if left to his own devices.

Tommy's mind was still on the pencil and pad problem. At some stage he'd have to show them he could hold a knife and fork so why not a pencil? Then his solution arrived. He knew he could write but did they? Flashes of memory were returning all the time but only he knew what was going on inside his head, which was to his advantage. Yes, he'd be able to hold a pencil but his brain hadn't yet remembered how to write. He would write squiggles, strange hieroglyphics, nothing that constituted a recognisable word, or even a letter.

A dead man passed by, wheeled on a gurney by two orderlies, his head covered by a white sheet on which sat a *Pickelhaube* – a black lacquered leather helmet with an intricately detailed gilded brass spike – presumably to honour this man's ultimate sacrifice for his Kaiser and country. The nurse and the doctor fell silent in respect, as did every man in the ward. The buzz of conversation resumed as soon as the dead man passed through the door. Tommy looked on, first in curiosity that turned, eventually, to realisation.

This set him wondering if this was a place where they brought you just before you died. He certainly wasn't feeling his best. He now remembered Rita and he began to cry because as far as he knew he might never see her again, and not seeing her again was as bad as his life could get. He knew that if he knew nothing else. The clouds in his memory were clearing but not to the extent that he knew where he was or how he'd got here, or even what day it was. The man in the bed to his left had just finished reading a newspaper. Tommy signalled as best he could that he would like to have a read. The man puzzled over his efforts then nodded his understanding. He swung his legs out of the bed and gave the newspaper to Tommy who read the date at the top. Fortunately, German dates were pretty similar to English ... *Montag 4.Dezember 1916.* He tried to remember the last date he'd been aware of but that was too much of a challenge. Then he remembered the firing squad and looking down the barrel of his Lee Enfield at the weeping boy tied to the stake. It was an unspeakable, unforgettable sight, branded on the dark part of his memory. He remembered aiming to miss because no way was he going to kill anyone on his birthday – September 17th. Bloody buggery hell! His name was Tommy, and he now remembered his birthday and how to swear. Progress.

But that was three months ago. What had happened in those months? He struggled to think. Not much. Just flashes of memory. None of it good. In deep trenches, crowded with soldiers, scared faces, mostly friends. Rain, mud, water, duck boards. The smell of cordite, sweat and cigarettes. The whistle – he didn't much like the whistle. No one liked to hear the whistle. The whistle was bad. Up a ladder; over the top; hold rifle straight forward, do not drop it and do not shoot your comrade in front, especially up the arse! Fixed bayonet, running, shouting, scared, expecting to die any second. Noise of death all around. Bullets cracking past, explosions, men falling, crying, prepared for death, hoping it won't hurt. How am I still alive? Aaagh, me leg! Spoke too soon. Down now, horrible pain in leg, stranded out here, helpless, with every square inch of air filled with screeching, hurtling metal trying to finish him off. Then lots of nothing.

Nothing? Sleep? Was it just sleep? Then being on a train and being in bed. Three months of memories in half a minute.

He looked to his right and to his left and saw he was in a ward of perhaps thirty beds. Some patients were lying recumbent, sleeping; some were sitting up reading, some smoking pipes or cigarettes, some sitting on others' beds talking in German. There were names above beds: Heinrich Friedmann, Boris Krueger, Franz Gottlieb – not a Bill or a Ben among them. He was wondering what name was on the wall behind him but he didn't have sufficient movement to turn around

119

and see. He looked at the man who had passed him the paper and mimed that his brain was so scrambled he didn't understand the words. Maybe the man would pass the message on to the nurse. The man smiled and took the paper from him. When Anna returned, the man called her across and whispered, confidentially. 'He borrowed my paper but I don't think he understands a word. Gone in the head, poor chap.'

'Has he now?' said Anna, thinking, *or has he just got no ability to read German?* What would she do if he turned out not to be a German soldier? What if he was a naked enemy soldier just wearing stolen German boots? Is that even feasible? Come on, Anna, in war anything's feasible! His convalescence would take a serious turn for the worse, no doubt about that. But could she do that to him? It might be worth having a word with her father about him.

At that very moment Tommy was thinking about his own father, and his mother and his sister and brother. He remembered them all now. Not in any detail, just their existence and that he loved them dearly. Where in this world were they? *That* he didn't know yet. What he did know was that his memory was coming back without any effort from him. He felt tired now. Staying awake had exhausted him. He closed his eyes and slept, dreaming about being deep underground and quite happy to be there.

Anna looked down at him and knew he was sleeping now, no longer in a coma. He was mentally fragile but she was confident he'd regained his awareness and she felt happy for this mystery man and suspected he might cause her problems in time to come. Maybe even a problem of the heart. Stop that, Anna! You hardly know him. As she stared down at him she knew she wanted to get to know this handsome, smiling young man a lot better. If her suspicions were correct he'd need a confidante and she spoke fluent English. If he wasn't German she was hoping he might be English rather than French or Belgian or any of the other enemy nationalities. The English weren't her enemies.

With her mind full of this problem and all possible solutions she made her way back to the nurses' station. If he needed her on his side it had better be sooner rather than later. If she suspected him it wouldn't be long before someone less sympathetic did. She grimaced at the worst case scenario. If Dr Lehmann found him to be an imposter he'd be out of this hospital and on his way to some primitive POW camp hospital within seconds. That's if they thought he qualified for hospital treatment. Most likely he'd become just another prisoner of war, no matter what the state of his mental health.

Senior Physician Dr Ingrid Lehmann had sexual leanings towards her own sex, to the extent that she didn't like men one bit – a problem the patients had to endure as best they could, as she was a highly skilled doctor. The prettiest nurse under her wing was Anna, who had rebuffed her as politely as she dare after Lehmann found out that Anna's boyfriend had been declared Missing In Action. Anna had been saddened but not bereft – more guilty than bereft. It hadn't been a relationship with a future and it had saved her the problem of telling a man fighting on the western front that his girlfriend was splitting with him. It had been a letter she'd begun several times but she hadn't the heart to finish. If he turned up alive then she'd tell him how relieved she was, but that they were over. So sorry, Dietrich.

The more she turned this problem over in her mind the more she hoped this mystery man was English, like her mother. A plan formed in her mind.

Tommy was due for a check-up at eight that evening and Anna would be doing it. Just his temperature and pulse. He would need to be awake for that. She also needed to check for speech function.

At eight o'clock she gently shook his shoulder until his eyes half-opened. Before he was fully awake she said, 'What would you like for breakfast?'

'What?'

'Bacon and eggs or cereal?'

'Bacon and eggs?'

His voice was low and slightly slurred. It was a voice that hadn't been used in over three months, activated by a brain that wasn't yet fully awake. It was a voice speaking English, the same language Anna had been speaking. She was now smiling, almost in triumph.

'Do not raise your voice,' she whispered.

'What? Oh bugger!'

'A fine English expletive. Never used by Germans, not even German soldiers.'

Tommy was now as awake as he could manage.

Awake enough to know she'd rumbled him. They kept their voices low.

'What are you going to do?'

'Nothing. It's you who has to do something.'

'Do what?

'You need to keep up the pretence of being German. Pretend you cannot speak.'

'How long for?'

'For as long as it takes. I will help.'

'Why? You don't know me.'

'It's my job to help people who are ill.'

'How did I end up here anyway?'

'You were in an explosion that stripped you completely naked apart from your German boots. It's a miracle you are even alive never mind more or less in one piece.'

'So I'm more or less in one piece am I.'

'You've broken a lot of bones but you haven't lost any of your limbs. You were in a coma for over ten weeks. No identification, nothing. Your boots led us to believe you're German. Plus you have fair hair and blue eyes.'

'How did I come to be wearing German boots?'

'You probably stole them from a dead German.'

'I'm assuming that we're at war with Germany.'

'You assume correctly.'

'Why are we at war?'

'No one really knows, but our countries have been at war for over two years. Hundreds of thousands of men have died.'

'Surely someone must know why we're at war.'

'War is what soldiers do from time to time, otherwise there would be no reason for their existence.'

'I see. So I'm a British soldier.'

'I believe you are. What exactly do you remember?'

'Not much. I scarcely know who I am except that I'm not German. I'm obviously English but I don't know where I come from.'

Anna sensed the man in the next bed was looking at them. She stood up straight and smiled at him, then flapped her fingers in the manner of a moving mouth.

'Gibberish,' she said. 'I thought I'd get him talking before he woke up properly.'

'No luck eh?'

'Well I've got him talking but what's coming out of his brain isn't coming out of his mouth.'

She leaned over Tommy again and whispered in English, 'You need to learn to talk gibberish. I will now speak to you a bit louder, in German ... *Was wünschen Sie für das Frühstück morgen?*'

'Zeee grinckeen berrberrisshnish habbishenish.'

Tommy's gibberish was audible to the man in the next bed. Anna turned to the man and spread her arms as if to say, 'See what I mean?'

The man nodded sympathetically, then closed his eyes and fell immediately asleep. Anna leaned down to Tommy again, whispering, 'I asked you what you wanted for breakfast in the morning.'

'And I told you bacon and eggs.'

'I'm going to check you out, then you go to sleep. We must hope you don't talk in your sleep.'

'I don't think I do.'

As Anna did her routine checks Doctor Lehmann stopped by Tommy's bed and asked her, 'Is he making progress?'

'He was awake for a short time today and he has some voice but it all comes out in gibberish.'

'Time might improve that.'

Anna nodded, took the thermometer out of Tommy's mouth and looked at the reading: 37°C. She called out the reading to Lehmann.

'Normal,' said Lehmann, smiling at Anna.

'Yes,' said Anna, putting the thermometer back in her pocket without looking at the doctor. Lehmann moved on. Anna leaned over Tommy once more and whispered.

'She's my boss and she is attracted to me.'

'So am I. Why are you helping me?'

'My mother is English and this war is stupid.' She placed a hand on his cheek and said, *'Gute Nacht!'*

'Gute Nacht,' imitated Tommy, accurately.

'Very good. Maybe I should teach you some German phrases,' she whispered. 'By the way, do you know your name?'

'Tommy is all I remember.'

'Hello, Tommy, my name is Anna. Thomas will be the common German name that I have decided to call our unknown soldier.'

'Is that what I am?'

'That is what is written above your bed – *Unbekannter Soldat.'*

Tommy gave her his version of this, she smiled and went on her way, leaving him somewhat confused but relieved that he had her on his side. He remembered so little about this war, just the violent images in his brain. He would ask Anna to tell him about it. Then another image dredged itself up in his memory – an image that had only ever appeared in dreams he'd forgotten. He was deep underground, working with a technical instrument rather like a camera on a large tripod. He was looking through it and everything was upside down. In saner moments he would have known it was the prisms within the theodolite that caused this inversion but his mind didn't grasp that, nor did it grasp what a theodolite was, despite him working with them for five years. To him it seemed that his memory was upside down – no change there. Then he thought about Rita once again and tears arrived. How he needed a hug from Rita right now. But he didn't really know who or where she was, only that he missed her. He had her face now. Beautiful, but much too far away.

'Rita, who are you?'

'Where are you?'

Chapter 20

Pontefract. December 1916

'Do you have any beef in this morning?'

'You mean cow meat?'

'I do, yes.'

George Miller had a twinkle in his eye. He was thirty-five years old, thirteen years older than Rita, but he had an honest and friendly face, a full head of dark hair and a mouthful of gleaming white teeth, none of them false. Girlfriends for George had come and gone, none of them having met the standard he expected from a wife. But, with Rita, his standards went out of the window. She was the woman he wanted, and to hell with his stupid standards. He'd been hoping she'd come in, as he'd been saving her a nice piece of topside in the cold store. Of his favoured customers she was at the top of his list. She was the only one in his shop.

'No news of Tommy?' he said. The concern in his voice earned him a bleak smile from her.

'Not so far, no.'

'I'm sure he'll turn up. You read about such things every week. A man declared dead turns up out of the blue.'

He was secretly hoping that Tommy wouldn't turn up. Not that he wished Rita any unhappiness, but he felt he might one day fill the hole left in her heart by Tommy.

'Mr Miller, you're the only person who believes that,' she said.

'George, please.'

'George ... everyone's given upon him, as if the war office never make mistakes.'

'Well, I'm an optimist who likes to think that good things happen to good people.'

'Did good things happen to you?'

He frowned at the memory of his parents' deaths. 'Actually no, they didn't,' he said, wondering if he should elaborate.

'Oh?'

'I've got a nice piece of topside if you want it.'

'Yes please. So, what happened to you?'

He hesitated a while, studying her face. If he told her his story and she told someone else he might end up getting the same treatment as his parents. On the other hand, such a terrible secret shared might bring them closer together.

'Something I really don't want people to know about.'

'Oh, okay.'

'Unless you promise to keep it a secret.'

His attraction to Rita was greater than his need to keep himself safe.

She shrugged. 'I can keep a secret.'

Another customer came into the shop and asked for half a pound of pork dripping. George served her as Rita waited.

'Well?' she said, after the woman had left.

He came around the counter and went to the door, looking up and down the street before turning to face her.

'I'm of German descent,' he said.

'Oh ... you don't look German.'

'I've never been to Germany, nor had my father and mother. It was my dad's father who was German. Our real family name is Müller. I changed my name before war broke out – Mum and Dad didn't – something to do with the king having a German name. They had their shop burnt out by a mob in London. Mum was killed and Dad was sent to an alien civilian internment camp on the Isle of Man. That was in May 1915, he died there in August – of a broken heart probably.'

'Close, were they?'

George held a up a hand with crossed fingers and said, sadly, 'Very ... he wasn't much good without Mum. I couldn't get over there to see him – I couldn't even get to his funeral, what with the war and all that. All I have is a short note that he wrote to me just before he passed away.'

He touched his chest with an open palm as he quoted his late father: 'May God damn in hell the people who started this war, for it means that you and I, my dear son, will never meet again.'

He could see the sympathy pouring from her beautiful eyes and how he wished he could take her in his arms.

'Oh you poor man! Is that why you came up here?'

'Yes. Up here I'm George Miller, English butcher. As a third generation German the authorities don't regard me as an undesirable alien but they don't want me as a soldier either. I'm apparently of more use as a qualified butcher, which suits me, although I do have quite a collection of white feathers.'

'Not from customers, I hope.'

'I recognised one woman in my shop who had given me one in the street. I took a feather out of my drawer and gave it her.'

'What did she say?'

'Well, I told her that the last time we met she gave me this and did she want to take it back?'

'And did she?'

'No, she went red in the face and went out of the shop without any meat. Never seen her since.'

'Well, you're the best butcher around here. I bet she regrets what she did. A silly woman gave one to my Tommy on our wedding day. His mother knocked her flying.'

'What about you? After what happened to Tommy do you think these women should be handing out white feathers?'

'No, I don't. I think this war is stupid and will do

no one any good. I think we should have let the countries in Europe fight themselves to a standstill if they wanted but leave us out of it. There won't be any winners, just a lot of dead men.'

'Well, someone might win a pyrrhic victory.'

'You mean a victory not worth winning,' said Rita.

George nodded and smiled and went to bring her meat. 'Like I said, this alien thing is something I need you to keep to yourself. You're the only person I've ever told about it.'

'I understand – my lips are sealed.' She looked him up and down. Like his father before him he wore a straw boater and a long apron with black and white vertical stripes. 'You couldn't look more English if you tried,' she said. 'All you need now is a Yorkshire accent.'

'Thanks, I'll try that.'

Happy that he'd established a secret bond with her he wrapped and weighed her meat. Rita saw the scales move to ten ounces.

'Half a pound,' he said.

'Since when were there twenty ounces in a pound?'

'I need to keep my special customers happy, and you're one of them – that'll be sixpence please.'

'Shilling a pound? That's your price for stewing beef, not best topside.'

George grinned as another woman came into the shop. 'Madam, do you want to buy this eight ounces of thoroughbred horsemeat or not?'

'Yes, please.'

He was wondering if he should take this opportunity to ask her out, but was it too soon? Maybe once she'd had time to think about this secret bond they had, and wanted to hear more of his story. They'd each been deeply troubled by the war so they had much in common, certainly enough to talk about during a night out. He smiled to himself as he served his next customer half a pound of best carthorse.

Chapter 21

December 1916

'Agnes?

'Yes.'

Rita had just got in from work, having called in at George's shop on the way home. He was keeping the Birch household well supplied with meat, courtesy of his affection for Rita who had just given Agnes half a pound of pork sausages for tonight's meal of sausage and mash.

'George has asked me out for a Christmas drink. I don't know what to do.'

'You mean George Miller the butcher?'

'Yes.'

'How do you mean, you don't know what to do?'

'Well, I'm pregnant with Tommy's baby. It doesn't seem right to me.'

Agnes was at the sink, peeling potatoes. She stopped and spoke without looking round at Rita. 'Tommy's gone, Rita, we all know that.'

'You know what I think about that, Agnes. I know you all think I'm daft bu–'

'No one thinks you're daft, Rita. We just think you're clinging on to the impossible.'

'How do you know it's impossible? If he came walking through that door, would you think he was a ghost or something?'

'Well, of course not but–'

'Exactly. You'd know it wasn't a ghost because his body was never found, nor any bits of it. I know that because I wrote to Lieutenant Walker and asked him. All they found were his identity tags.'

'Look, Charlie knows about war, love. He doesn't think it's unusual for him to disappear without trace. The stuff they blow each other up with over there is nobody's business. If one landed on this house there'd probably be neither hide nor hair left of us.'

'Agnes, can we beg to differ on this without falling out? I have a very strong feeling that Tommy is still alive somewhere.'

'Okay, love, we beg to differ.'

'So, what do you think about me going out with George Miller?'

'Just for a drink? No harm in that, he seems a nice enough chap and it does no harm to keep in with the butcher.'

'I wonder what Charlie might think?'

'He won't think anything, love.'

'I hope them Zepps don't come here again, Agnes.'

'Charlie reckons they won't, love. We're too far inland. All they have to do is fly up the North Sea then turn inland to bomb the coastal towns.'

'Well, I know what that feels like,' said Rita, remembering her honeymoon in Scarborough.

132

'Of course you do, love. Our Tommy reckoned you were a bit of a hero that day.'

'All I did was follow him round.'

'Followed him into danger I'll be bound. I wonder if that's what happened to him. I know Charlie told him to keep his head down but our Tommy had a tendency not to listen to good advice at times.'

'I told him the same thing myself.'

'But did he listen to you?'

'I hope so, Agnes.'

Agnes shook her head, as it seemed they were getting back to the argument as to whether Tommy was alive or dead so she changed the subject.

'Can't understand why that George Miller hasn't been called up. They're conscripting men from 18 to 41 now, which means you join up whether you like it or not. Charlie'll just miss it, thank God.'

Rita thought quickly then said, 'With him being a properly trained butcher he was made exempt with it being a reserved occupation.'

'Well I never knew that. Still, it makes sense. It would never do to have just anyone chopping our meat up for us.'

Rita put her hands on her pregnant bulge. 'I suppose I could have an orange juice with him or something. I don't want to be drinking wine or beer with this little one on the way. I've heard pregnant mothers drinking alcohol is bad for babies.'

'I've heard the same about smoking. There's always someone spouting rubbish. Still, you must do what you think's right for the bairn. How old is this butcher?'

'Dunno. I'd say he's in his thirties.'

'At least,' said Agnes. 'And he'll be well placed for money. I never met a poor butcher.'

'Agnes, I'm going out for a Christmas drink with him, I don't plan on marrying him – Tommy wouldn't like that.'

'I wish Tommy had the choice whether to like it or not,' said Agnes, chopping up the potatoes and putting them in a saucepan. 'Mrs Harrison lost her son, did you know?'

'No, I didn't. I'm sorry to hear it though.'

'Including Tommy that's two in this street alone,' said Agnes, 'plus another with a leg blown off and one blinded. Rachel Witherspoon's son, Ernest, died of them chlorine gas bombs. Terrible things. They got him back over here and she went to see him in hospital in Birmingham. He died on the day she got there. Apparently his face was bright red, his ears and fingernails were blue and he was gasping for breath all the time. His skin was bitter cold, his pulse was racing and he was gasping and coughing up God knows what. All the time, cough, cough, gasp, gasp, cough. Terrible pain he was in, poor lad. Rachel said it was a blessing when he died. No mother should have to watch her son die like that. Pity it can't happen to the people who started this damned war. At least our Tommy died quick.'

Rita didn't comment because she believed her Tommy wasn't dead, although this belief was fading with every passing day. If he was alive he'd have been taken prisoner and would have sent word. Most women whose men were prisoners of war got to know about it before long; it was one of the few civilised things about this war. To reassure herself she caressed her bump and the child it was concealing. No, she felt only life there. The baby's life and her husband's life. The feeling was too strong for him not to be on this Earth somewhere. For God's sake, Tommy, I know you're out there, make your existence known to the people who love you. And be alive, Tommy Birch, please tell me I'm not going mad.

Charlie looked across the site at the van which had just arrived. On the side it said, Jack Scurfield and Son, Builders. It meant that the boss's son, Victor, had arrived on site and Charlie didn't get on with Victor. He climbed a ladder to the top lift of scaffold to keep out of the way and was just stepping off onto the boards when a shout came from below.

'Birch, I want a word please.'

The use of his surname annoyed Charlie. He was a man not a schoolboy. Even Victor's dad called him by his first name. Charlie was in charge of the site and knew that to get the best out of the men you had to treat them with respect. Victor had yet to learn this basic rule of man-management.

'What for?'

The other men looked at each other sensing a confrontation and a confrontation with Charlie could only have one outcome.

'If you come down here I'll tell you.'

'Gimme a minute.'

Watched by Victor, Charlie walked across the

scaffolding then ducked through a window opening into a room decked out with floor joists but no floorboards yet. Now out of sight he sat down on one of the joists and lit a cigarette. Men underneath looked up and wondered if he was pushing Victor too far. Victor was a director of the company but in reality he was of much less use than was Charlie, who finished his cigarette then climbed back onto the scaffold and strolled to the ladder, stopping on the way to give an unnecessary instruction to one of the men. Then he climbed down and walked slowly over to Victor.

'I'm a bit pressed at the moment, what is it, lad?'

Victor scowled at being called 'lad'. 'I want you to go to Hull. We've got a contract repairing bomb damage.'

'When?'

'Starting tomorrow. You'll be there for about three months, Monday to Saturday.'

'You mean you want me to lodge in Hull?'

'That's right.'

'Sorry, lad. No can do. I don't want to go there. Besides, you need me here to do this roof truss.'

'No man's indispensable – I'm passing on my father's instructions, although I'm in charge of all the labour.'

'Well, I'd like you to pass my instructions back to your father. I'm not going to Hull. I work for your dad because he's a local builder and a good man to work for. Hull isn't local and you're not a good man to work for.'

'It's part of the war effort,' snapped Victor. 'All building firms have to do their bit if we want to tender for government contracts.'

'I've done more than my bit. I've lost a son to this damned war and I'm wondering why you haven't been called up yet.'

Victor reddened with a mixture of embarrassment and anger. 'As a matter of fact I have been called up. I'm due to leave for officer training next week.'

'You, an officer? Bloody hell!'

Charlie knew that Victor's university degree would have qualified him for an officers' course and he wondered how on Earth it could be possible to win this war with lads like Victor in charge.

'I'm telling you to go to Hull.'

Charlie couldn't resist this one.

'And I'm telling you to go to hell!'

'Right. You work here 'til Friday, then you're fired!'

'I'll just pick up me bass and I'll be off now,' said Charlie. He looked up at the building he'd just left and added, 'You'll need someone who knows how to make them trusses. Complicated job, that – dual pitch and all them hips and valleys. It had me beat for ages but I'd just got it figured – best of luck with that, lad.'

'Hey, you can't walk off site halfway through the week.'

'Don't be silly, lad. You can't just sack a man and expect him to keep on working. I'll call in the office for me money then I've another job to find. Shouldn't be too hard.'

As Charlie walked off to pick up his tools another joiner came to stand beside Victor who was staring up at the roof Charlie had been talking about.

'I hope your dad knows how to make it. I'm blessed if I know how to start. Charlie had it worked out.'

'Dad was a brickie not a joiner.'

'Aye, more's the pity. I reckon this job's come to a stop now yer've sacked Charlie.'

'You carry on talking to me like that and you'll join him.'

The joiner stood there for a few seconds, pondering his options. Without a word he walked back to the job he was doing. He knew Victor would have a major problem with his father and he had no need to join in the fight. Let the bosses sort it out.

Chapter 22

Nurse Anna Kohler was standing on a chair fixing one end of a string of brightly coloured Christmas decorations to the wall behind Tommy. She stepped down and viewed her work with some satisfaction and said, *'Frohe Weihnachten'* to Tommy. Then she leaned nearer and whispered, 'Merry Christmas.'

'And you!' whispered Tommy, who wasn't supposed to have any voice back yet, neither German nor English. He'd resigned himself to remaining mute for the duration.

On a table at the end of the ward was a small Christmas tree, devoid of any coloured lights, but decorated with the same home-made decorations that Anna had just strung across the ward. Other patients were receiving Christmas cards and Tommy was wondering how things were back in Pontefract. During the two weeks since he regained consciousness his memory bank had refilled above the halfway mark. He now knew who he was and he remembered his family and Rita in particular but, oddly enough, he only had flashes of memory of being in the army, including the firing squad but nothing at all about the action that had blown him to oblivion. It was a mental disability which gave him a genuine air of confusion and this helped him maintain his subterfuge in the face of the examining doctors. His friendship with Anna was key to him maintaining this subterfuge insofar as she kept him informed of the doctors' opinions of him. This helped him play the part they expected of him.

His main problem now was to keep it from all the staff, bar Anna of course, that he'd got back this memory. As far as they were concerned his mind was as blank as it had been when he first woke up. The most difficult part was not speaking. He'd perfected a thin smile and a look of perplexity and uncertainty.

He figured it would be okay to make noises in order attract attention when he needed help or medication but these occasions were now few and far between. He could now walk more or less unaided although his left arm was still in a sling. Apparently he'd sustained multiple fractures in that arm and it had been a work of art putting it back together again.

'I doubt if your English surgeons could have

done such a good job,' she'd whispered to him.

'Well, it was a German who did this to me. It's only fair that a German should put it right.'

She'd made arrangements to accompany him on occasional walks outside the hospital building where there were extensive gardens and, more importantly, privacy to talk unheard. It was during one of these walks that she suggested he escape and make his way over to the Allied lines which were about two hundred and fifty miles away to the west.

'That's a long way.'

'You could walk it in ten days.'

'It's still a long way for a man who can't speak, trying to avoid German soldiers.'

'We could supply you with food enough for ten days and maybe a map, maybe even a compass.'

He thought about Rita. 'I'm very tempted,' he said.

'And I'd come with you.'

'Would you?'

'Yes. Still tempted?'

'Very tempted now.'

'And I think my father would too. It's the only way he'll ever get to see my mother. Once we get to British lines you can vouch for us and my father will get to see my mother again, and so will I.'

'You'll see each other when the war's over, surely?'

'Who knows what's going to happen in the future? If the battle lines reach here we might be killed by British guns, and what happens to us Germans if we lose the war?'

'Dunno – nor do I know what I'll do.'

'If we escape you'll be better off in England no matter what, and my family will be together again. My father is of the opinion that there will be no winners in this war, only losers. There'll be lots of dead people, poverty and broken buildings in Germany, France and Belgium. I believe England has hardly been touched in comparison.'

'I believe you're right, although me and my wife had our honeymoon disturbed by German ships shelling our hotel in Scarborough.'

'Yes, I read about it in the papers. It was described as a great victory for the German navy.'

'They were shelling civilians in an undefended seaside town. I'd hardly call it a victory.'

'Is your wife very pretty?'

Tommy smiled as her question brought up a picture of Rita in his mind. 'Pretty doesn't do her justice. She's actually very beautiful.'

'She's a lucky woman having you for a husband.'

'But she hasn't got me, has she? She probably thinks I'm dead. Maybe she'll get another feller. I could hardly blame her.' He looked at Anna as an idea struck him. 'I don't suppose you could get word to her, could you?'

'I've already thought about that but my father says it's too big a risk to take. The only way is to somehow get a letter from here to the French underground movement and hope they can get it to Spain and hope the Spanish can get it to England.'

'Are there people in Mannheim who would help get a letter to the French?'

'I believe so. Our people are suffering greatly from this war. There is a terrible food shortage as you must know. I believe it is because the British navy is blockading our ports.'

'I have noticed a lot of turnips on the menu recently.'

'I know. People are beginning to call it the turnip winter. It was our Kaiser who started the war, we ask ourselves why and no one knows. It certainly wasn't for our benefit.'

'It seems to me that there's a lot of hope involved in getting a letter to England. Too much, do you think?'

'Too much danger for the people carrying the letter. Anyone caught with such a letter on them would be tortured by the police to find out who sent it. Such a letter might well lead them back to us.'

'So, we'll be better off just escaping eh?'

'I think so.'

Chapter 23

Charlie walked in the house and dropped his tool-bass on the floor with a rattling clump. Agnes, standing at the stove, turned round in surprise.

'You're home early.'

'I've been sacked.'

'What? Jack's sacked you?'

'Victor sacked me.'

'Victor's not Jack.'

'Well Jack put Victor in charge of labour,' said Charlie. 'He told me to go to Hull tomorrow and lodge there for three months. I told him to go to hell.'

Agnes returned her attention to her frying pan. 'Rita brought us some nice pork sausages from that butcher friend of hers.'

'I thought I could smell summat tasty,' said Charlie. 'I'll have a scout round for work tomorrow.'

'Is there much about?'

'There's a couple of builders who know about me. I should think I'll get a start somewhere. Trouble is I might end up having to go to Hull or somewhere that's been bombed by them damned Zepps. The government's tightening up on who they award contracts to.'

'Damn war!' said Agnes. 'There's people going on strike down south and the miners up here aren't happy with working conditions.'

'They won't strike up here, love. What right do men have to strike when there's good men dying out there?'

'Our Edith's got herself a job as a land girl on a farm near Ferry Bridge – Fox's Farm, have you heard of it?'

'Can't say I have.'

'She says she's doing her bit as part of the war effort.'

'Which is why I was supposed to go to Hull.'

'You've done your bit for the country, Charlie.'

'Is she getting more money?'

'Less, I think.'

'Not a good time for me to get the sack then.'

'I'd tell you to go back cap-in-hand,' said Agnes, 'but I know better than to waste me breath. Do you want roast spuds as well as mashed?'

'I do that. By heck, talk about the condemned man eating a hearty breakfast. Seems like I'm eating a hearty tea.'

'I know you'll always put food on the table, Charlie Birch.'

'Well, we won't go on the parish. I can promise yer that.'

'That butcher's invited Rita out for a drink.'

'Is she going?'

'She's asking me what I think, with her still being married to Tommy.'

'Good God. Will this nonsense never end?'

'She'll be asking you when she comes down. It's only a Christmas drink.'

'She's the best looking lass in Pontefract,' Charlie said, than added, hurriedly, '...apart from you and our Edith.'

Agnes smiled. 'She turns a few heads and no mistake. And now she's three months gone she's got a real glow to her. By heck I wish our Tommy could see her ... now.' Her head went down and she stopped what she was doing. 'Oh, why did he have to die, Charlie?'

'I don't know, love.'

She had her back to Charlie but he knew she was crying. He went up behind her and put his arms around her, saying words of comfort he never thought he'd say. 'Y'know love, there might be something in what Rita says. I've heard that pregnant women have some sort of sixth sense about the father, and Rita's so sure he's still alive – happen she's right, Agnes.'

She straightened her shoulders and turned

round. 'There's something she said the other day that had me beat,' she said, tearfully.

'What was that?'

'She said, "If Tommy came walking through that door, would I think he was a ghost or something?" and I honestly have to admit I wouldn't because his body was never found nor any trace of it. So it wouldn't be impossible for him to be still alive, would it?'

Charlie, who was still trying to stem her tears, went along with this. 'There you are, you see. Maybe we're all wrong. Maybe he's alive and kicking somewhere and he's just lost his memory. I know that happens. I had a bloke in my mob who got blown up and didn't get his memory back for months, and then only a bit at a time.'

'Charlie, will it do any harm for us to believe that?'

Charlie wiped a tear from her cheek with a thumb still dirty from the building site, leaving a grey smudge where the tear had been. 'Do you know,' he said, thoughtfully, 'I think it might do us the world of good to believe that.'

'Can we, Charlie? Can we believe that?'

He kissed her and said, 'Agnes Birch, it's now, official. Thomas Birch is still alive and well and won't be home until he's got his memory back.'

'Can I tell Rita?'

'Bring her down, love. Where's our Stanley? Let's tell him and Edith as well. I tell you what, love. Our Tommy won't be so pleased when he finds out we thought he was dead. Good God! What have we been thinking of?'

Agnes was smiling through drying tears. 'I'll get

Rita,' she said.

The meal was over when someone knocked on the door. Stanley asked permission to leave the table.

'Yes, unless you want to take it with you.'

It was the traditional family response to this request, and it raised a traditional smile from Stanley. 'One day I will do,' he said, walking to the door, assuming it was his pal Eddie; Agnes was assuming differently; Charlie was devoting his full attention to the remnants of his delicious sausages. He placed his knife and fork down on his empty plate and sat back, saying, 'My compliments to the chef – that was a meal and a half.'

His daughter and daughter-in-law were concurring with this when Stanley called out from the door, 'It's Mister Scurfield for you, Dad.'

'Which Mister Scurfield?'

'This one,' said Jack Scurfield, stepping in through the door.

Agnes got to her feet. 'Cup of tea, Jack? The kettle's on the boil.'

'I'll sup a cup of your tea anytime, Agnes. By the heck, summat smells good. What have you been having?'

'Pork sausages,' said Charlie, 'and mash and roast and fried onions and peas.'

'Proper pig meat sausages?'

'I hope so.'

'Good grief! I'll be having sawdust sausages and I'm your boss.'

'Not any more, Jack.'

'Well, that's what I've come about,' said Jack, now looking at Agnes. He was in a family home now and the manager of the family home was always the wife. 'Would er, would it be all right if me and Charlie went through to t'room to have a bit of a talk?'

'It would,' said Agnes. 'I'll bring your teas through.'

Charlie got up from the table and followed Jack through to the front room. It was a room kept spotless by Agnes for special occasions such as Charlie's boss begging him to come back. She'd fully anticipated this happening the second Charlie told her that he'd been sacked by Victor. Charlie was almost as valuable to Jack Scurfield as he was to her.

The room had a three-piece suite in light and dark brown moquette which looked new despite it being second-hand when Charlie bought it in a house-clearance sale three years ago. The exposed floorboards had been sanded down by Charlie, then stained dark brown and polished by Edith using French polish from her work. The floor was mainly covered by a carpet square ten feet by twelve. It had a tiled fireplace with a grate that had been set with paper, wood and coal in readiness for a fire; fires were only lit when the room was in use. Above the fireplace was a mantelpiece replete with photographs of Tommy surrounding his Military Medal on display in its box. Jack went straight to it and, being an old army man himself, threw a casual salute.

'You have to be proud of this boy, Charlie.'

'I am. I'll put a light to the fire.'

'No need. I hope this won't take long. You know my lad's been called up?'

'He told me.'

'I'm worried about him, Charlie. They think he'll make an officer.'

'From what I've seen of *some* officers I think he might,' said Charlie.

'Aye, some of them are pillocks right enough and I reckon that's the best he can set his sights on... Second Lieutenant Victor Pillock. He's not cut out for soldiering isn't my lad.'

'There's not many men cut out to be soldiers,' said Charlie. 'To be honest I never thought my lad was and I told him that in this very room. Looking at that medal I should have kept me big mouth shut.'

Jack turned round to face Charlie. 'My lad made a mistake telling you to go to Hull.'

'He did a bit more than that Jack. Sacking a man at Christmas, even he should know better.'

'I know. He overstepped the mark sacking you, but as from next week he won't be here. He'll be in the army.'

'So you say.'

'I'm asking you to come back, Charlie. I've given Victor a proper bollocking and I've told him I'm coming here to try and get you back. I'm thinking that after the war's over, and assuming we win, I'll talk him into staying on as a regular. It could be the making of him – or the breaking.'

'He should make a good peacetime soldier,' said Charlie, *'and* he'll have a war record, which won't do him any harm.'

'He might not survive the war, Charlie. Junior officers are more likely to get killed than the enlisted men who're following the officers over the top. I'm hoping they get the measure of him and they don't stick him on the front line. If they do he won't last two minutes.'

Despite his low opinion of Victor, Charlie felt sympathy with Jack. No one knew better than he what it was like to lose a son. A son's a son, no matter how big a pillock he is. Jack continued:

'What the lad doesn't know is that a building firm relies very heavily on the good men it employs and you don't sack good men, you treat them with kid gloves.'

'Is that how you've treated me, with kid gloves?'

'No, I've treated you as a friend ... and as a friend I want to make you an offer.'

'What sort of offer?'

'Well, I'm knocking on for sixty now and I was hoping to hand the business over to Victor, but today's fiasco showed how much sense that made. Plus he's going in the army so he wouldn't be around even if he was any good.'

Charlie was interested now. 'What's this offer, Jack?'

Jack rubbed his chin, ruminatively, before saying: 'Well, I want you to be my building manager.'

'Building manager? I haven't been a site manager yet.'

'That's only because up to now you've been more use to me as a foreman joiner. I'm not an idiot, Charlie. I can see your potential. I've seen how you deal with people and how well you know the job. Effectively I want you to take charge of the building work on all the sites. You'll be in sole charge of labour, ordering materials, liaising with customers, architects, local authorities and services; in fact you'll be dealing with all aspects of building. You can work with me for a few months learning the ropes, after which you'll be doing my job in all but getting the work, chasing the money and paying the bills. All the site foremen and site managers will report to you; after me you'll be the boss, and I can tell you now, Charlie, after this war's over there's going to be a lot of work about.'

Charlie strode over to the window, thinking. 'This sounds like a well-paid job, Jack.'

Jack smiled and spoke to Charlie's broad back. 'It'll be regular money, right enough. Same every week. No being laid off for bad weather or lack of work, and you'll get a firm's motor vehicle. Can you drive?'

'Don't know, never tried.'

'It's not difficult. If Victor can drive, anyone can. I'm swapping the van for a new pickup truck – an Albion. Very smart. We can move materials around the sites double quick with it. Plus people will sit up and take notice when they see that going around Airedale with the firm's name on it. We'll be a firm to be reckoned with. What do you think, Charlie?'

'I'm thinking four pounds a week for a five day week.'

'I want you working six days as usual.'

Charlie did a quick mental calculation. 'Time and a half on Saturdays, that's nearer five pounds.'

'I'll make it four pound ten, which is thirty bob more than you make on average right now.'

'Four pounds fifteen and shake me hand.'

'Oh for God's sake, Charlie. You've got me over

150

a barrel with this bloody roof truss and you know it.'

'Am I still expected to make the truss?' Charlie said. 'I thought I was management.'

'You are, and you're expected to supervise all the tricky joinery jobs to the extent that I'll expect you to do them yourself if no one else can.'

'I'd best have a scout round for a couple of joiners who know what they're doing, and we wouldn't need to if it wasn't for this damned war. We've got three apprentice-trained joiners over in France.'

'Two,' said Charlie. 'Young Albert Evershed's been reported killed.'

'Aw no! Bloody hell, Jack! He was only nineteen, just come out of his time. Big pal of our Tommy's.'

'His mam came round to tell me this morning. She was in a right state. That's three of my younger lads killed and another three wounded.'

'I'd best have a scout round for a couple of older joiners who know what they're doing.'

'I'd appreciate that, Charlie.'

'So, are we agreed on four pounds fifteen for six days?'

'Oh, I bloody suppose so.'

Jack shook Charlie's hand.

'And can I use the pickup to get to and from work every day?'

'You can.'

'And can I have it on a Sunday to take Agnes out for a ride in the country?'

'Bloody hell, Charlie! It's a work vehicle not a bloody charabanc!'

'Maybe not every week, just now and again.'

'Once a month maybe, certainly not every damn week – and you pay for your own petrol. It costs a fortune nowadays with this damned war – nearly three bob a gallon and that pickup'll only do twenty-five miles to a gallon. You get seven gallons for a pound which is more than two days' wages for a working man.'

'I'll not fiddle you out of a penny, Jack, and you know that.'

'I do know that, Charlie.'

Agnes arrived with the tea. She smiled at Jack, saying, 'I like the sound of the ride in the country.'

'How much have you heard?' asked Jack.

'All of it. I'm sorry to hear about young Albert. Our Tommy'll be sad to hear of it.'

Jack was bemused at this, knowing Tommy to be dead, but he said nothing. Grieving mothers aren't always rational.

'So you heard about the job I've offered Charlie.'

'I have. And it's my business as Charlie's wife to know what he's agreeing to.'

'And do you agree to all this?'

'I think I'd have asked for five pounds a week. It's a lot of responsibility you've given him, and you know the men'll pull out all the stops for Charlie.'

'I think I might be changing my mind about this,' said Jack.

'What?'

Charlie was now dismayed that this plum job was about to be whisked away from him. He gave Agnes a dark look. She smiled because she knew he'd got nothing to worry about.

'I think,' Jack said, 'that I might be better off

giving the job to Agnes. She's certainly got her business head screwed on right.'

'So, it's five pounds?' said Agnes.

Jack shook his head. 'Nay, we've shook hands on four pounds fifteen, Agnes.'

'I'd like to think that when Charlie gets the hang of the job you'll be shaking hands on five pounds.'

Charlie looked at his boss with amused and interested eyes. 'Let's see how things pan out,' said Jack.

Agnes winked at her husband who had almost doubled his average wages. What with Tommy's resurrection this was turning out to be not such a bad day at all for the Birch family.

Chapter 24

Pontefract. Wednesday 20th December 1916
'How long are you taking off for Christmas?' Agnes asked, in general.

'Well we haven't got much to do, with it being winter,' said Edith. 'We're learning how to do stuff mainly. We're having the full week off.'

'So come spring you'll be a proper farmer's lass,' Charlie said, grinning.

'Something like that. How about you, Dad?'

'Christmas Day and Boxing Day as usual, although with Christmas Eve being Sunday we're taking Saturday off as well, so we have four clear days. Finish Friday, go back Wednesday.'

'Was that your idea,' Agnes enquired, 'with you being management now?'

'It was. The men need a decent break.'

'I wonder what sort of break Tommy's having?' said Rita.

Four pairs of eyes looked at her, remembering the agreement they all had, to declare Tommy alive but missing. Rita had been a more than willing party to this and she took full advantage of it.

'I think he must have lost his memory,' declared Stanley.

'It's just one of many reasons we haven't heard from him,' said Charlie.

Rita smiled at this and said, 'Oh, I forgot to tell you all. George is getting us a turkey for Christmas.'

'Getting *you* a turkey more like,' said Edith. 'I think he fancies you.'

Rita blushed and retorted, 'He's just a nice man. We get on very well.'

'I wonder what Tommy would say?' Edith went on. 'You walking out with the butcher?'

'I'm not walking out with him. We've been to the pictures a few times that's all. I like the pictures and I don't want to go on my own.'

'Why hasn't he been called up?' asked Agnes.

'I've told you. He's a butcher and the country needs butchers.'

'The country needs mining engineers and builders but they've all been called up. What's so special about George? Has he got flat feet or summat?'

Rita went quiet, wondering whether or not to tell them about his past. She looked from one to

154

the other, knowing them to be good and decent people who would honour George's secret.

'George has a problem,' she said. 'He came up here because his father's shop was burnt down in a riot in London. His mother was killed in the riot and his father died not long after that.'

'Aye, I heard about them riots,' said Charlie, 'mostly against Germans living over here.'

'So, how come Michael's mother was killed?' asked Agnes.

'And what happened to his dad?' asked Charlie.

Rita gritted her teeth, knowing she had to tell all. 'George had a German grandfather,' she said. 'His father was called Michael Müller and he was sent to an alien civilian internment camp on the Isle of Man, which is where he died, probably of a broken heart, according to George.'

'So, his dad was a German?' said Agnes.

'He was a German who didn't speak a word of the language, nor had he ever been there. Born and bred in London and lived there all his life. George's mother was Irish.'

'Why did George change his name to Miller?' asked Edith, sharply.

Rita answered her heatedly. 'Well, I'd have thought that was obvious. For the same reason they want the king to change his German name from Saxe-Coburg-Gotha to something not German. Michael didn't want his shop burning down.' She looked at them, assuming this to be an unassailable argument, then added, 'The king's just as German as George.'

'He could have volunteered for the army,' said Charlie.

'He did, but he was turned down.'

'Because they thought he might be a traitor,' said Agnes.

'I don't know what they thought. I don't imagine they think the king's a traitor for all his German ancestry.' Rita was becoming annoyed at this aggressive questioning of her innocent friendship with the butcher. 'Look, if you don't want the blasted turkey, just say so!'

'I don't want his bloody turkey,' said Agnes. 'His lot killed our Tommy.'

'Right, I'll start getting our meat somewhere else, although God knows where.'

'*I'll* get the meat in future,' said Agnes.

'I thought you'd all decided Tommy wasn't dead,' said Rita.

'That was before we knew you were consorting with the enemy!' Agnes was practically snarling now. Her grief about Tommy had resurfaced and had found a target in this woman, this wife of Tommy, who was defending the people who had killed him.

'Steady on, girls,' said Charlie, trying to calm the situation. Edith opened her mouth to say something but was stopped by his wagging finger. 'This is all getting a bit silly.'

Agnes screamed at him. 'A bit silly? Do you think our Tommy'll think it's a bit silly, with his wife going out with a bloody German? He'd never have anything to do with a German woman in a million years.'

'No, love. I don't suppose he would but–'

'I bet she's dropped her knickers for him already.'

'What?'

Rita took a step forward and slapped Agnes hard across her face. 'You horrible bloody woman! I'm pregnant with Tommy's baby. Who the hell do you think you are, talking about me like that?'

Agnes sat down and collapsed into tears. Rita headed for the stairs, calling out over her shoulder. 'I'm packing my bags, and I'm out of here. When Tommy comes home he'll come back to me, not to you lot. If he wants to know why, I'll tell him what you just said.'

The room fell into a silence broken only by Agnes's sobbing. Charlie put a hand on her shoulder. 'Yer gonna have to apologise for that, love,' he said.

Agnes shook her head. 'I can't, Charlie. Them Germans are an evil race. The evil won't have been bred out of that butcher in two generations. He's a German – that's why our army wouldn't take him. He'll be no better than his granddad. I'll not apologise, Charlie.'

'In that case we've lost her, and if our Tommy doesn't come home we've lost his child as well.'

'I don't care. Let her go. Good riddance.'

'Good God, Agnes! This isn't like you.'

'Yes it is like me, Charlie. When they took my boy from me it was like having my heart ripped out. You'll never get me to like any man with a drop of German blood in him as long as I live, and that includes the king, if you must know.'

Charlie knelt beside her and put an arm around her shoulders, hugging her to him. 'Losing Tommy was hard, love, and we'll never get over it ... never. But we will learn to live with it.'

'How on Earth can we know a thing like that?'

'Because we have to, love, and because other people do it all the time. The world keeps on turning, our loved ones sometimes die before their time and we don't know who's going to be taken next. Our lad died a good death, a quick and painless death – a hero's death. The best we can do for him is to always remember him and to always be proud of him.'

Agnes sobbed on. Edith was now in tears. Stanley looked up at her, muttered, 'Blimey, Edie! This is a lot o' bloomin' fuss over a turkey,' and went out to play.

Charlie stood up and lit his pipe, wondering if he should go up and have a word with Rita. But what use would that be if his wife didn't change her tune? And, knowing Agnes, there was no chance of that.

Benny Clayton was shovelling coal onto the fire. He didn't bother to turn around when he heard the door open and shut behind him. The front door opened straight into the living room and he assumed it would be Horace Tattersall from next-door-but-one coming to lay a bet on with him. Benny was a part-time bookie's runner. It was illegal but the police never bothered chasing any-one for it because they laid as many bets as any-one.

Whilst most professional sports had been sus-pended for the duration, horse-racing was allowed and Benny earned up to ten shillings a week from his illicit job, although most of it went on horses he himself backed. He lived frugally, keeping one

158

week behind with the rent and a month behind with the gas, which was frequently cut off, denying him both light and cooking.

'Stick yer stake on t'table, Horace. I'll take it round later.'

'I'm not Horace, I'm Rita.'

He turned, slowly, to see his daughter standing there, lowering her suitcases to the floor. It was the first time he'd seen her since the news of Tommy's death. And he hadn't been round to see her then, not even to offer words of comfort. For all he was her father, Benny was a simple man who was no good at offering words of comfort.

'Oh,' he said.

'Remember me, Dad?'

'What? Don't be daft, our Rita.'

'I've come back to stay.'

She looked around the dismal room which was in stark contrast to the warm, welcoming front room of the Birch household. The gas mantel flickered above her head, normally a prelude to the gas being cut off. The two of them looked at it until it stopped flickering and resumed its steady light, as if to say, *pay the bill, or next time I don't come back on.*

'Have you paid the gas bill, Dad?'

'It just needs a new mantel. That one's buggered.'

'The gas company's near where I work. I'll go round in the morning and pay the bill.'

'Well, that'll do no harm.'

'I need proper heat and light.'

'Why has thee come back?'

'Well, with Tommy gone I didn't want to im-

159

pose myself on his family for too long.' She didn't think her disagreement with the Birches was any of his business.

'So, yer thought yer'd impose theself on me, did thee?'

Her dander was still up after her confrontation with Agnes, especially the remark about her dropping her knickers. That was an awful thing to say. There was still anger in her voice when she said, 'Not if you don't want me here. I can easily find somewhere myself, but I thought you might need the money.'

'What money?'

'The ten bob a week I give Charlie Birch. I might as well use it to pay the rent and gas here.'

'Ten bob's not enough – fifteen bob more like.'

'I'll pay whatever it costs. At least I'll know we won't get cut off and kicked out at Christmas.'

'I pay me way, allus have.'

'No you haven't. So, what you'll pay for is coal and food. You give me fifteen bob a week and I'll pay the coalman and buy all the food and do most of the cooking. I've got a great connection with a butcher.'

'I'm er, I'm sorry to have heard about young Tommy,' he said, awkwardly.

It was the first time he'd expressed any sympathy at Tommy's death. He looked at her stomach, which was beginning to bulge.

'I reckon he's left thee with a babby,' he added. 'How soon is it due ter drop?'

'Don't be so crude. It's due to be *born* at the end of April. Is my room tidy?'

'It's how thee left it.'

'Except it'll have four months' dust on it by now.'

'I expect so. Someone's upset thee, lass. Is it them Birches?'

'None of your damned business! Have you eaten?'

'I was thinking of havin' fish 'n' chips.'

'Good. I'll have some as well.' She took out her purse and handed her father a shilling. 'Here, fish and chips twice. I'll have some scraps as well. I'll put the kettle on and get the table ready.'

He stood there, looking at the silver coin in his hand as he assessed the sudden change in his circumstances. Was it good or bad? Having the rent and gas paid and cooking done for him was good, and fifteen bob was little enough for him to fork out. Living would be cheaper and she was a nice bit of company for him. He'd never acknowledged that in the past. His daughter was a pleasant person to have around when she wasn't in a strop, and there wasn't too much pleasantness in his life. He went off of to the fish shop with a smile on his face. For him at least, life had got better.

After he had gone Rita sat down in her chair and cried her heart out. Christmas 1916 would be the most unhappy Christmas of her life.

Chapter 25

Pontefract. February 1917

When Stuart Gooding learned of his brother's death in France he was eighteen years old and four years into his apprenticeship with Jack Scurfield Builders Ltd. Charlie had high hopes for the young man and was a little concerned that Stuart's 18th birthday had just been and gone and that his call-up papers would soon be landing on his door mat. Stuart was fighting away tears when Charlie said good morning to him. The site foreman took Charlie to one side.

'The lad's brother's been killed, Charlie. He's neither use nor bloody ornament today, but I can't just send him home. He's not right in his head.'

Charlie shook his head in sorrow at the latest in this list of dead friends and workmates that was growing by the day. 'D'yer know, Wilf, I'm sick to death of all this. Our lads are dying for nowt. All this king and country stuff is bollocks. Let them bloody continentals fight it out among themselves is what I say. It's nowt to do with us isn't this war. My lad's lying out there as well, and our Edith's just got a job at a munitions factory in Leeds, filling shells.'

'Whereabouts?'

'Barnbow.'

'Bloody hell, Charlie. There was a massive explosion there just before Christmas. Loads of

162

women killed. It were never in any papers cos they don't want the publicity but it's right.'

'Thirty-five killed to be precise, Wilf, including a woman from Pontefract, but our Edith's got this notion that she has to do her bit, what with our Tommy giving his life. Plus it's well-paid work. With her bonus she can earn more than me.'

'She'll end up bein' one o' them canary girls. It's all that cordite that does it, yer know that don't yer, Charlie?'

'I know everything there is to know, Wilf, and I'm not so suited. Yellow skin, yellow hair, and it makes yer poorly. Lack of ventilation, that's what causes it all. Them bloody Germans! I hope they all rot in hell. My missis hates their guts for what they did to Tommy and I'm not far behind her.'

'Word's going round that there's a German butcher in Ropergate. I'm amazed he's still open for business.'

'Aye, well that's my fault, Wilf. I shot me big mouth off about him when we had a bust up with our Tommy's wife, Rita, who's a friend of his. She reckons his granddad was a German and my Agnes thinks that makes him a German as well. Anyroad it's caused a right bloody rift in the family. She's gone off to live with her dad in Featherstone, and her six months pregnant.'

'There's a lot who'll think the same as your missis, Charlie. Word is that there's a few who's boycotting his shop.'

'Us among 'em,' said Charlie. 'It's daft, but what can I do without upsetting Agnes? The feller's prob'ly as right as rain. It's not his fault his granddad was a bloody kraut. My father came

163

from Wigan but no one holds that against me.'

'If I were him I'd shut up shop until the war's over,' said Wilf.

'Yer prob'ly right, Wilf, but a man's got to make a living. Even a man with a kraut granddad.'

George was a worried man. It would seem that people had got wind of him being of German descent. It was Mrs Farnsworth who first mentioned it to him, and she wasn't the most tactful of people.

'I've heard our lads are winning the war over there, which must be a bit rough on you.'

'Why would us winning be rough on me, Mrs Farnsworth?'

'Well, with you being a German.'

'I'm not a German.'

'Oh. Why would people say you are?'

'I don't know. You should ask them. I've never been anywhere near Germany. My father was English and my mother was Irish. Neither of them had ever been to Germany. I don't speak a word of German and I dearly hope we British win the war.'

'I'm sorry, I'm sure, but people are saying you're German.'

'Then I must be the only German with a cockney accent.'

'Yes, I did wonder about that.'

'I'd really appreciate it, Mrs Farnsworth, if you would go round telling people that just because I'm not from Yorkshire, it doesn't make me a German.'

He had been wondering why his custom had dropped off over the past few days and he had decided to put a notice in the shop window telling people he was as British as anyone around. He might have to lie about his family name and about his paternal grandfather but he'd be telling the basic truth, and if he offered to knock 25% off all meat orders for a week it might bring his lost trade back. His notice would read thus:

George Miller born in London 1881. Lived in England all my life.
Father: Michael Miller, butcher. Born London 1853.
Mother: Elspeth Miller, née Brannigan. Born Cork, Ireland1854.
Grandfather: Herbert Miller, butcher, born London 1830: Grandmother, Beatrice Miller, née Fox, born London 1832.
Please note:
Despite the rumours I am not a damned GERMAN! In the interest of goodwill to my customers my prices will be reduced by 25% for one week only.

However it was all to no avail. The notice never made it to his window. In fact he was on his way back to the shop to do just this when he encountered the mob. He stood on the perimeter for a while, listening to the bile and venom issuing from the mouths of the rioters and the sound of his shop being destroyed before it all got too much for him and he forced his way through the crowd.

That same evening Stuart Gooding was on his way home from work. A journey that took him past the end of Ropergate. He saw a crowd of people outside what looked to be Miller's butchers. Stuart

165

was carrying his joiner's bass, full of tools. He took out a lump hammer, with no specific intention in mind, and went over to the crowd who were virtually baying for blood. The shop had closed at six o'clock, twenty minutes ago and someone had painted *Hun Bastard* on the window in red paint. As Stuart joined the back of the crowd he heard a crashing sound as the door was kicked open and the crowd swarmed inside. Stuart joined them. Once inside he swung his hammer, intent on doing as much damage as he could to avenge his brother's death. People had broken into the cold store round the back and were coming out with joints of meat, plucked birds, strings of sausages and the like. Stuart wasn't interested in looting. He was only interested in doing as much damage to this German shop as he could. His brother was dead and this German bastard who owned the shop was alive and that wasn't right. He smashed the scales, the marble counter, the shelves, anything he could see and then, above all the melee, he heard the angry shout of George Miller.

'What the hell are you all doing? Get out of my shop. I will call the police!'

He was grabbing people and pushing them towards the door but the people were fighting him back. George grabbed at Stuart trying to wrest his hammer from his hand, but Stuart was a strong young man who did a physical job and was more than a match for George. He pulled the hammer free of the butcher's grasp and swung it around his head in an attempt to make George keep his distance. The hammer struck George at the side of the temple with considerable force. Two women watching through the broken window gasped and clutched their hands to their mouths as they saw George drop to the floor. Stuart, unaware of what he'd done, moved deeper into the marauding crowd, screaming angry anti-German slogans at the top of his voice. A police car arrived, two uniformed officers got out and stood at the door, most reluctant to try and contain this angry mob who outnumbered them at least ten to one. A woman came over to them, saying, 'Mr Miller's on the floor badly hurt.'

'Who's Mr Miller?'

'It's his shop, love. They're all saying he's a German but he's not. He's from London. Them barmy beggars don't know the difference between a Londoner and a German!'

The two officers forced their way over to where George was lying on the floor, unconscious, with blood pouring from his head and onto the notice intended for his shop window. One of the policemen picked it up and read it whilst the other set to work on the unruly crowd with his truncheon, forcing most of them out of the shop. Stuart was still around the back shouting his slogans. He emerged and looked around for his bass that he'd put down but couldn't remember where. The woman who had spoken to the policeman came into the shop and pointed at Stuart.

'It was that lad what hit him. I saw him do it with me own eyes. Me friend Nellie Brigshawe saw it as well. He did it with that hammer he's holding. Shocking it was.'

More police arrived. One of the original two policemen went over to where Stuart was putting the hammer back in his bass. 'I'll take that, lad. And you'll come with me.'

'What? I haven't done nowt.'

'Hasn't done nowt?' said the woman. 'He were bloody wrecking the place wi' that hammer. He clattered Mr Miller on his head with it. The lad's a bloody lunatic!'

Stuart stared down at George as realisation set in. 'He came for me,' he protested. 'I was only protecting meself. He started it.'

'It's his bloody shop,' shouted the woman, 'and you were smashing it ter pieces! I make no damned wonder he came for you!'

Stuart was now in handcuffs and being marched out to a newly-arrived police van. His blood-spattered hammer was in an evidence sack and his tool-bass in the back of a police car. George was being carried to an ambulance. The two women were being interviewed by a police sergeant. One of them was blaming it all on this bloody war and saying it was a crying shame that the best butcher in Pontefract was out of bloody business and the police should stop this stuff from happening.

'How's Mr Miller?' asked the other woman.

'I don't rightly know, madam,' said the sergeant. 'But it might well be that you've both witnessed a murder.'

The two women looked at each other, excited at this wonderful twist in their humdrum lives. Stuart was weeping profusely as the black van took him to the police station. In the ambulance George hadn't regained consciousness as a nurse held a wad of bandage to his head to try and stem the flow of blood. His shop had now been cleared of rioters, a few of whom had objected to police interference and had been arrested for charges ranging from disorderly conduct to looting and criminal damage, to assaulting a police officer. They were taken away in two horse-drawn vans. It was the first and last incident of its kind in Pontefract during the war. The next morning, as Stuart was being taken before the Pontefract magistrates' court which would determine his immediate future, his call-up papers arrived.

Chapter 26

Charlie knew nothing of this until he arrived at the builder's yard the next morning. Jack was already there, standing in his office doorway as Charlie climbed out of the pickup.

'Poor do this, Charlie.'

'What is?'

'Young Stuart. Have yer not heard? There was a riot at that German butcher's. He's in a bad way in hospital.'

'Who is? Young Stuart?'

'No, the butcher. Young Stuart's been arrested for hitting him with a hammer.'

Charlie closed his eyes as he thought about the implications and his part in it all.

'Bloody hell, Jack. It could be my fault all this, opening me big mouth on site about the feller. Up to then nobody knew who or what he was, apart from a damn good butcher.' He looked up at Jack. 'Is he going to be all right?'

'No idea. If he's not, then Stuart's had it. There are witnesses to say he did it.'

'Bloody hell! Not young Stuart. Good a lad as you could come across. It's all because he lost his brother is this. He took it badly, that.'

'You lost a son, Charlie, and you didn't go round attacking people.'

'No, all I did was shoot me big mouth off and cause other people to do it.'

Rita had passed George's shop on her way to work. She stopped in horror as she saw the devastation and read the words written in red paint on the window. A policeman was guarding the broken door.

'What happened?' she asked.

'There was a riot, madam. Word got around that the proprietor was a German national and people didn't take too kindly to it.'

'I know him well. He's not German. He's as English as I am.'

'So I'm told, but there's no accounting for idiots, madam. There's a lad taken into custody for assaulting him.'

'What? Is Mr Miller all right?'

'I don't know. He's in Pontefract Infirmary.'

'Oh no. I must go there.'

'He'll be under police guard, madam.'

'Will he? Perhaps I can telephone them. I don't suppose too many other people will be enquiring after his welfare.'

She hurried into the bank and went into the manager's office. 'I wonder if I might use the tele-

170

phone, sir. It's about Mr Miller the butcher. He was badly injured in the riot and I'd like to know how he is.'

'Of course you must. He's one of our valued customers.'

'He's in the infirmary, sir.'

'Pontefract Infirmary? I have the number on my list I believe. It's always good practice to be in telephonic contact with doctors and hospitals. I'll ring them myself, shall I? A man's voice sometimes carries more authority in these situations.' He picked up the earpiece from its cradle and spoke into the mouthpiece to an operator.

'Hello, could you put me through to Pontefract Hospital please, I have the number. It is Pontefract 368 ... thank you...'

'Pontefract Infirmary. Which department do you want?'

'Oh, hello. My name is Mr Barnes, I'm the manager of the Yorkshire Bank on Ropergate and one of my customers was brought in injured in a fracas last evening. I wonder if you might find out for me how he's doing? His name is George Miller. I imagine he'll be in the emergency department.'

'One moment please.'

He smiled at Rita and tapped his fingers on his desk as he waited for the information to arrive. She watched his face as a voice came back through the receiver.

'Emergency Ward.'

'I'm enquiring about Mr George Miller. He was brought in injured last evening.'

'Are you a relative, sir?'

'What? Er, no I'm not a relative... I'm his bank

171

manager, but he is a valued customer.' Barnes frowned in exasperation at all these damned stupid questions. Rita held out her hand, offering to take the handset. Perhaps a woman's voice might be more persuasive after all. He saw the sense in this unspoken suggestion and passed it to her.

'Hello. My name is Rita Birch. I was a particular friend of Mr Miller's. I'm afraid he has no relations at all. His parents are both dead and I may well be the nearest person to him. Could you tell me how he is, please?'

There was a silence as the person she was talking to excused herself and went off in search of a doctor. Rita whispered to her boss, 'She's bringing a doctor to the phone.'

Barnes nodded his approval. A man's voice came through the earpiece. 'Hello, who is this?'

'My name is Mrs Rita Birch. I'm a good friend of Mr George Miller who was brought in injured yesterday evening, in fact I may well be the closest person to him, with him having no relatives in this country.'

'I see ... and the gentleman who first came on the telephone?'

'Oh, that's Mr Barnes. He's the manager of the Yorkshire Bank on Ropergate, which is where I work. We're just up the road from Mr Miller's shop. He's a valued customer of the bank.'

'I see.' There was a long pause before he spoke again. 'I'm afraid Mr Miller passed away in theatre. We did everything we could, but his injury was too severe.'

Rita froze in shock. The earpiece dropped from her grasp. Barnes picked it up and spoke to the doctor. 'Yes, Mr Barnes here ... oh no, oh dear! Yes, we have a lot of Mr Miller's details at the bank. Would you like them?... Yes ... of course, I'll have someone bring them to you. If you need anything at all please don't hesitate to contact me. My number is Pontefract 774.'

He put the phone down and looked at Rita. 'I think you should go home, Mrs Birch.'

She shook her head. 'No, I'm better off here than at home. I have friends here. I have no one at home.'

As the day wore on, pieces of information filtered through to the bank via its customers, the main piece being that the person arrested for attacking George was a young apprentice joiner called Stuart Gooding, who worked for Jack Scurfield. Rita had even heard Charlie talk about him. Charlie, one of the few people who knew about George's unfortunate ancestry. It didn't take much to figure out how Stuart Gooding got to know about him. The lad would be hanged for this, and all because she'd been stupid enough to tell the Birches about George.

But why shouldn't she? Resentment began to mount within her. Resentment that she should have been able to tell them about George in confidence without any of this happening. The chief cashier had a telephone on his desk. She went over to it and asked for Scurfield's number. Charlie replied.

'Scurfield's Builders.'

'Charlie?'

'That's me. Who are you?'

'I made a big mistake telling you about George.

173

He's dead because of what I told you, and now Stuart Gooding is going to hang.'

She hung up the earpiece before he could reply and marched back to her position at the counter with a pale face and a fixed frown.

Charlie stared at the earpiece for half a minute before replacing it. His mind was full of self-recrimination, and a certain amount of resentment towards Agnes whose warped opinion of George Miller had led to all this. Young Stuart hanged for murder? Bloody hell! It'd happen too, in this day and age when they shot good men for cowardice.

Tommy had told him, in a letter before he was killed, about how awful it had been to be a member of a firing squad. It had been allowed by the censor as a story that might get around back home and illustrate the extreme sacrifices their soldiers were making on the country's behalf. Jack came into the office.

'George Miller died,' said Charlie.

'Oh, dear God!' said Jack.

Rita was sitting on her stool with her hands clasped around the back of her neck, swaying to and fro with a pale, tear-damp face. Her colleagues looked at each other, wondering if they might say something helpful, but none of them could think of anything. One of them tapped on the manager's door and spoke a few quiet words to him. He emerged, went over to her and placed a *Position Closed* sign on the counter in front of her.

'Go and sit in my office, Rita. I'll have some tea

sent through to you.'

She slid, zombie-like, from her stool and did his bidding in silence, watched by her colleagues who had just heard her side of the phone call and who weren't quite sure why she was acting like this. The bank hadn't opened for business yet, which gave the girls an opportunity to chat about the events unfolding around them.

'What was that about? Has she lost someone else?'

'It's something to do with George Miller. I think he's dead from that riot. Something to do with him being a German. If he was, Rita would probably know.'

'Who's this Stuart Gooding?'

'I heard he was arrested for attacking George – so if George's dead he's in big trouble. I think Stuart works at Tommy's dad's firm. It's his dad she was talking to.'

Lots of 'ohs' from all around as the meaning of the phone call made more sense.

'Why should Rita be so bothered?' said one girl. 'Was she going out with George or something?'

'Not really. She went to the pictures with him now and again. She's due a bit of company after what happened to Tommy.'

'I don't think George'd ever make up for Tommy.'

'He were lovely were Tommy.'

'I don't suppose any feller'd make up for Tommy.'

'I don't think she'll ever get over him.'

'Nor me. I think her and George were quite friendly that's all. He probably fancied her a lot

175

more than she fancied him.'

'Every feller in Pontefract fancies Rita – including my Harold, if the truth be told.'

'I liked George meself. He didn't sound German to me. I always called him Cockney George. He used to laugh at that.'

'Poor old Rita. I know she's had a fall-out with her in-laws and she's back with her dad.'

'Right flipping dead-beat he is. How he came to have a daughter as lovely as Rita beats me.'

'Best treat her with kid gloves when she comes back out. Best not talk about George Miller or the riot or anything that might upset her.'

'We should talk about what rise we'll be getting in April.'

'Hmm, that'll be a short conversation.'

More remarks about this as the doors were opened for business. Rita was sitting silently in Barnes's office pondering why her life had suddenly crumbled to ashes. If only she knew for certain that Tommy was alive. She put a hand on her bump. Surely she'd know if he was dead.

The *Pontefract and Castleford Express* beat Charlie home by five full minutes. By the time he got in, Agnes had read the front page.

'Blimey, Charlie! Did you know about this riot on Ropergate?'

'The one where they ransacked George Miller's shop?'

'Is that what it is? Oh yes. Well, I'm not surprised. It was only a question of time before people found out about him.'

'It was nothing to do with time, it was all to do

176

with me opening my big mouth at work. George Miller's dead – murdered.'

'Dead? Oh dear. I never wished him dead.'

'The person who killed him's young Stuart Gooding. That's one man dead and a young man due to be hanged.'

'Young Stuart? Florence's youngest?'

'Florence's one and only after her Alfie got killed.'

'He's a good lad,' Agnes said. 'They won't hang a good lad like that for killing a German surely.'

'George Miller was no more a German than the king, Agnes. Of course they'll hang Stuart, and it's my fault for listening to your damned stupidity about the butcher. It's split this family and caused the deaths of two good men.'

Agnes's bottom lip quivered from his sharp tone. 'So, you're blaming me for all this?

'No – I blame meself for listening to you. I got a phone call from Rita. She made it plain that she blames me.'

Such unfriendly talk between his mam and dad was too much for Stanley who went outside to find his pal, Eddie, who was shinning up a lamp post in the street. It was one of Eddie's favourite pastimes. The post had a cross bar where the lamp-lighter rested his ladder. Eddie would swing from this and then attempt to jump down without falling over, so far without success. Stanley called out to him.

'Hey up, Eddie. What d'yer know?'

Eddie made a grab for the cross bar, swung backwards and forwards then dropped to the ground, falling over and adding another rip to his tattered trousers.

'Hey up, Stan. What d'*you* know?' It was their latest form of greeting. It would be followed by a competition about who knew the best stuff.

'I'll tell yer what I know,' said Stanley. 'I know this war's buggerin' everythin' up. Me mam and dad are having a right set-to. What do *you* know?

'I know me cousin Alf's been killed in action.'

Normally this would have been an outright winner, but Stanley had something better up his sleeve.

'Oh heck! Isn't he the one who's Stuart Gooding's brother?

'Yeah. Me Auntie Florence came round yesterday to tell me mam. She were in a right state.'

'Well,' said Stanley, 'I know they're gonna hang your Stuart for murderin' our butcher.'

'Give over!'

'It's right. He's been arrested. It's what me mam and dad were arguing about. Me dad's Stuart's boss. Me mam thinks it's all right to murder German butchers.'

'Blimey!' said Eddie, still on the ground. 'I didn't know that. Oh flippin' heck! I'll have to tell me mam. I'll have no cousins left at this rate. Me Auntie Florence won't be so pleased.' Then he added, gruffly, 'He's all right is our Stuart. He's never murdered no one before, I know that much.'

Tears appeared in his eyes as he got to his feet. Stanley put a friendly arm around him. Sorry now that he'd won their stupid competition with such sad news for his best pal.

Chapter 27

Barnbow Munitions Factory, Crossgates, Leeds. 21st March 1917

At ten minutes to six in the morning Edith Birch was in the women's changing room, stripped down to her underwear before getting dressed in a buttonless smock and cap and, like all the other women, she wore rubber-soled shoes. Hairpins, combs, cigarettes and matches were all strictly forbidden. Hours were strict, conditions poor and holidays non-existent. All over the country food rationing was severe, but because of the nature of their work, the employees were allowed to drink as much milk and barley water as they wanted. Barnbow even had its own farm, complete with 120 cows producing 300 gallons of milk a day. Working with cordite, a propellant for the shells, for long periods caused the skin of the operatives to turn yellow, the cure for which was to drink plenty of milk.

Five hours later, Edith and two of her workmates were hard at work in Room 40. It was time for their second, fifteen-minute break which would be taken in the canteen. Most of the women had already left, but the three of them weren't ready to go just yet; they were still packing the last of a batch of six-inch shells which were already filled with high explosive. Edith had inserted the last fuse by hand, screwed it down and placed it into a machine that revolved the shell and screwed the fuse down tightly. She was walking away from it when her world went dark with noise and pain. No one would ever know what caused the explosion.

In Room 40 it caused death and destruction but it didn't stop production in the rest of Barnbow where sixteen thousand workers were kept hard at it, producing shells for use at the front. War is a merciless task master.

That same evening Charlie looked at the clock on the mantelpiece. It said half past six.

'Ten past six, our Edith's late tonight.'

Agnes was standing by the gas rings, watching over her boiling vegetables. 'If she's not home soon her tea'll be going cold.'

'Hope she's all right.'

'What do you mean?' asked Agnes.

'Well, it's not the safest job in the world is it?'

'I wish you wouldn't talk like that, Charlie. It's bad enough her coming home looking like a daffodil without me worrying about her getting blown up like our Tommy.' She paused for thought then added, 'I hate that place.'

'Barnbow?'

'Yes. I've hated seeing our lovely daughter turn yellow from all that gunpowder stuff. Even her hair's going yellow. People in the street call her Canary Girl, did you know that?'

'That's what they call them all,' said Charlie.

Another hour went by with no sign of Edith. The meal was eaten in a worried silence with all three of then constantly glancing at the clock.

Eventually Charlie put his knife and fork down.

'Something's happened to her. She's never this late.'

'Maybe she's had to work overtime,' said Agnes. 'I've had to keep your dinner in the oven plenty of times when you've been held back working overtime.'

Charlie picked up his fork and stabbed it into one of the two remaining potatoes. 'Yeah, I suppose that's possible, but I never worked in an armaments factory.'

There was the rattle of a noisy engine outside in the street. Stanley slid out of his chair and went to the window. Outside was a large van with a red cross painted on the side, and the words: BRITISH RED CROSS AMBULANCE.

'Hey, Mam! There's an ambulance stopped outside. It's one of them new Sunbeams. I saw one before, outside our school when that bloke got knocked down by old Lenny Barraclough's horse.'

'Don't stare, Stanley!' scolded his mother. 'It's hardly come for us. None of us need an ambulance. It's probably for old Mrs McGinty across the street. I hope she's all right.'

'She's hardly all right if she needs an ambulance,' remarked Charlie. 'She's been on her last legs for a while, poor old lass.'

Stanley was now giving a running commentary on events outside. 'Hey, there's someone gettin' out of it, Mam. It's a woman. She's all covered in bandages. Her arm's in a sling thing. She's limping. She's wearing a green coat like our– Hey Mam! I think it's our Edie. She's all bandaged up!'

181

Charlie was at the door in an instant, helping his daughter into the house. She had a bandage around her head, her left arm was in a sling, her face was badly bruised, her eyes swollen and almost shut and he could smell smoke on her clothes.

'They tried to persuade her to stay in the hospital,' said the ambulance man, 'but she's a very determined young lady.'

'What's happened?' said Agnes, taking over from Charlie and leading her daughter to a chair.

'There was an explosion at the factory,' said the man. 'She was one of the lucky ones. Two dead, quite a few badly injured. Edith's injuries are pretty superficial by comparison. Cuts and bruises and a broken arm when she was thrown by the blast. She wanted to come home on the bus, believe it or nor.'

'Oh, I believe you,' said Charlie, leaning over his daughter to take a closer look at her face. 'Edie, love. I'm sorry but you're never going back to that damned place, my girl. It's back to your proper job for you when you're better.'

'Oh, Dad, Elsie and Flo are both dead. I was talking to them when that, er ... w ... when it happened. It was awful. They landed on top of me. I th ... thought I was dead as well.' Her voice was badly distorted.

'It's a miracle she's alive,' said the ambulance man. 'I'm told Edith was just walking off for a tea-break. She was apparently shielded from the blast by two other girls behind her who took the full brunt of it. It's the second time we've been called out to that place in the past few months.

182

The last time was a lot worse, but this was bad enough. She really is a lucky young lady.'

'Our Tommy will have been looking after her,' said Agnes. 'He always did.'

The bemused ambulance man managed to smile as though he knew who Tommy was and he therefore fully understood. Satisfied that his sister was alive and reasonably well, Stanley went outside to examine the ambulance.

The man handed Charlie a buff folder. 'This is from the Leeds Infirmary for her to give to the people at Pontefract Infirmary. It's got her x-rays and some notes. She needs to go there in the morning. We can arrange for an ambulance to take her if you like.'

'I'll take her myself,' said Charlie. 'I've got transport.'

The man handed Charlie a small jar of pills. 'These are for the pain. She's to take them in accordance with the instructions on the label.'

Chapter 28

Doctor Lehmann came to her office door and called out to Anna. 'Nurse Kohler. I would like to speak with you please. In here.'

'Yes, doctor.'

Anna went into the office and stood in front of Lehmann's desk like an obedient schoolgirl in front of the head mistress. She didn't want to convey any feeling of affection towards the doctor, who made her feel uncomfortable. Lehmann looked up at her and smiled.

'Are you feeling all right, nurse?'

'Yes, thank you.'

'Good. I want to talk to you about the patient you call Thomas. I've some misgivings about him.'

'Misgivings?'

Anna now had misgivings of her own. A shiver of fear shot up her back. Had someone heard him say something in English – a light curse, perhaps? It had always been a danger. It was known that she was a fluent English speaker.

'Are you sure you are all right, Nurse Kohler?'

'Yes, doctor.' Anna tried to keep any fear from her voice.

'I am thinking the time has come for us to send him on his way. He is taking up a valuable bed and our influx of patients is increasing by the day.'

'Where will we send him?' asked a concerned Anna.

'That is the problem. His communication skills are almost non-existent, although physically he seems to have made a full recovery.'

'But his injuries were quite serious, Dr Lehmann. What if he has a relapse?'

'I am aware of that problem. He will have to be placed under hospital care but outside the hospital and not too far away.'

'In a convalescent facility?'

'Ideally, but there is nothing suitable in the whole of Mannheim.' Lehmann was looking down at her notes. She looked up and smiled again at Anna. 'In view of the fact that you are the only person able to communicate with him in any way, and that you have made yourself his principal carer, I hope that you might be able to help us with this problem.'

'Doctor Lehmann, if you are suggesting that I have developed an emotional attachment to Thomas you are wrong. I believe him to be quite disturbed by his disability and I feel that I might be able to help him overcome it. My feelings towards him are that of a nurse, nothing else.'

'Quite. I never suspected anything else. Perhaps men do not interest you as much as they do other women.'

Anna saw a light go on in Lehmann's eyes that said *I hope this is true.* 'Well, my last boyfriend didn't, that's for sure.'

'Ah, you and your soldier boyfriend are no longer together?'

'He was reported missing in action. I believe he is dead, doctor.'

'Ah yes, I remember, my condolences once again. Anyway, my question to you is this. I know you live with your father, Dr Kohler, in a large house not far away. I would like you to suggest to him that you take Thomas in as a convalescent patient in your home.'

There was a long moment of silence between them as Anna took this is in. Thomas living with her? That might well turn out to be a dream come true.

'Would this mean I look after Thomas full time at home? I'm not sure I would like that, Dr Lehmann.' Of course this was a lie but she didn't want to appear too eager.

'Not at all. Thomas is mentally capable, apart

185

from his vocal disability is he not?'

'I wouldn't say that. He cannot speak nor can he understand anyone else's speech, nor can he read or write.'

'But you seem to be able to communicate with him?'

'After a fashion, yes.'

'The ideal solution would be to send him to a mental institution which specialises in his unique disability and such institutions no longer exist, as far as I know. This war has deprived us of so much.'

Anna felt it was time to seem more positive about Lehmann's suggestion. 'Well we certainly have room for Thomas and I think he might be able to cope on his own for part of the day while I am at work here. It will really be up to my father.'

'With him being a doctor, your father is key to this whole idea. If he agrees to this I will have your hospital hours adjusted to suit your time caring for Thomas and your father will receive remuneration to cover the cost of his care.'

'I will ask my father tonight. Conveying the idea to Thomas, without confusing him, might not be quite so easy.'

'I'm sure you will manage.'

The doctor gave her a wolf smile and Anna thought that if her own romantic preferences were for women, Lehmann wouldn't be her first choice of partner.

'That will be all. I expect to hear from you to-morrow.'

'Yes, Dr Lehmann.'

Tommy was still occupying a bed in the ward. Even he felt a trifle guilty for taking up a bed under false pretences. Anna went straight to him from Lehmann's office and did a pretend mime for him to come outside with her. It was a common occurrence and a much-used mime. He signalled that he understood and went with her. Once in the hospital garden she spoke under her breath with her back to anyone who might be watching.

'I have some remarkably good news for you. To free your bed you're to come and live with me and my father at Dr Lehmann's request. I haven't finalised the arrangements yet, in fact she only asked a few minutes ago. Anyway, pretend you understand this. I think she might be watching us.'

She went into a mime routine which, to a distant onlooker, might well be her telling Tommy he was to leave the hospital and go with her. Or possibly not, it didn't matter, their method of silent communication was a mystery to most at the hospital, including Tommy at times. Lehmann was indeed watching from an upper floor window. She nodded her approval when Tommy smiled his understanding, stuck up a thumb and went into a mime routine of his own, which had Anna sticking up her thumb. They walked away with their backs to the hospital windows, still miming as they spoke in English.

'My father doesn't know about this yet and Lehmann believes I have to clear it with him, so it will be tomorrow when I take you home. But it will do no harm for you to get your things ready.'

Tommy looked down at the clothes he was

187

wearing. 'You mean my dead man's uniform?'

His trousers were in heavy quality grey serge wool, fully lined, with red piping and a long mend in one leg where the previous owner had been shot. Cleaning hadn't quite taken all the bloodstains out. Ideal for winter wear but not for the fine weather they were having today and the oncoming summer.

His tunic was in the same material, probably from the same soldier, who had obviously been much sturdier than Tommy. It buttoned up to the neck with eight brass buttons and had red piping which matched the trousers.

'I can't go round in public wearing this stuff, surely? It only fits where it touches. What are people going to think I am? Certainly not a German soldier. More likely a grave robber.'

'I can get you some civilian clothes that will fit you.'

'Really? We don't get many civilians come to die here.'

'My father is roughly your build. I'm sure he can spare you something ... and I have a nice surprise for you.'

'What's that?'

'I found your boots in the clothes locker yesterday.'

'My German boots?'

'Yes. The ones that saved your life, most probably.'

'I seem to remember that they were really comfortable. Yes, I think I'd like them back.'

'Well you can wear them tomorrow, along with your civilian clothes.'

Chapter 29

Mannheim. April 1st 1917

Anna was walking with Tommy in a park near her home. It was a fine day and he was wearing a pair of dark brown striped trousers that might have been tailored for him and a matching waistcoat above a khaki, open-necked shirt. Most of his boots were concealed by his trousers but they didn't look out of place. It was the most comfortable form of dress he'd had since he emerged from his bed and his pyjamas some three months previously. His physical wounds had largely healed and his bogus mental condition and lack of identity had a major advantage insofar as it kept him from being called "back" into the German army. Anna had important news for him.

'It says in the paper that Americans have come into the war.'

'Have they? Whose side are they on?'

'Your side of course. Father says it will be over by Christmas.'

'I've heard that one before. Are they over here already?'

'I'm not sure.'

'Do you know how far away the front line is?'

'According to my father the German troops have withdrawn to the Hindenburg Line.'

'Where's that?'

'I believe it's about four hundred kilometres to

the west.'

'How does your father know all this?'

'I'm not supposed to tell you.'

'What? In case I turn out to be a spy?'

'Don't be silly.'

She hesitated for a while as they walked on in silence.

'Anna,' he said, 'I'm a British soldier impersonating a German soldier. All I want to do is go home. Any secret your father has couldn't be safer than with me.'

'Yes, I know that. My father is in contact with a chain of people who are not sympathetic to the Kaiser. He has secret information passed to him. It worries me just how much he does know at times.'

'Such as?'

'Well, he knows what eventually brought the Americans into the war.'

'I always thought the sinking of the *Lusitania* would do that. Lots of Americans aboard that ship.'

'No, it wasn't just that. Apparently the Germans sent a telegram to the Mexican government saying that if the Americans entered the war against Germany it would be a good time for the Mexicans to declare war on America and reclaim Texas or something, and that if they did, Germany would help them. It was all done in code but the British got their hands on it, decoded it and showed it to the Americans. President Wilson was most angry, as were the American people. It swung American public opinion in favour of entering the war.'

190

'And have the Mexicans declared war on America?'

'No. Father says they have more sense.'

'Massive cock-up on the part of the Kaiser, then. Is this man playing with a full deck?'

'What does that mean?'

'It means, is an important part of the Kaiser's brain missing?'

'You must hope so.'

Tommy only spoke to her when he was sure no one was within earshot and even then he kept his voice so low that Anna could barely hear him at times. Her news gave credibility to a plan he'd been forming for some time.

'Four hundred kilometres, that's about what, two hundred and fifty miles? If we could get hold of a couple of bikes we could be there in a week. You in your nurse's uniform, I'll be your deaf and dumb patient.'

'Tommy, I've been thinking about that. Even if we got to the front line there'll be thousands of German soldiers wondering what we're doing there.'

'If your dad could come with us he could use his credentials that show him to be a doctor. Doctors are needed at the front line, so are nurses. We could do it in stages so that we're not linked. I've supposedly wandered off in one of my dazes, only I'm hiding in the attic. Who cares about me? I'll be no great loss to anybody. You report my disappearance and all that'll happen is the local police will be asked to keep an eye out for me. The following day you'll make some excuse for claiming a couple of days off work, and off we go with no one chasing us.'

'Well I do get three days off every two weeks, but I don't always take them. My dad could do the same.'

'Good, you could wear your nurse's uniform. I'll wear some hospital patient stuff. Let's face it, I couldn't look more like a patient if I tried.'

'And why would a deaf and dumb patient be needed at the front line?'

'We'll baffle 'em with bullshit.'

'You must teach me this bullshit.'

'No problem, I'm very good at bullshit.'

'Or,' suggested Anna, 'you could just sit out the war in our house and wait for the British to come to you.'

'I could, but I'm not sure I'll be still in one piece when they get here. I think I've been lucky getting away with being a dumb German soldier for seven months. I'm not sure my luck's going to hold out for another seven months, even living in your house, something could go wrong. If I'm found out they'll treat me as a spy and shoot me.' He put an imaginary gun to his head, then added, 'And then they'll come for you.'

'Like they came for Nurse Edith Cavell?'

'Yeah, what happened to her? I heard she'd been arrested for helping British and French soldiers to escape.'

'She was executed by firing squad ... last October, I think.'

'Really? Shooting a nurse? That's barbaric. I wouldn't want that to happen to you.'

She saw the affection in his eyes and smiled. 'Why wouldn't you, Thomas?'

'I think you know why.'

'Me too,' she said, kissing him, lightly, on his lips.

At that moment Tommy was wondering whom he preferred, the wife he dearly loved and missed but hadn't seen for many months and who might have justifiably written him out of her life, or Anna, with whom he was also in love. Bloody hell, Tommy! As if your life isn't complicated enough. Time to change the subject.

'So, are we going to make a run for it?' he asked her. 'Bearing in mind what they did to Edith Cavell? I'll fully understand if you say no.'

'I'll see what my father says.' She looked around to check that no one was looking, then added, 'Would er, would you like another kiss – a proper one?'

'I'm still married,' he said.

'I know that, Thomas, but your wife will think she is a widow.'

'Yeah, I know. It worries me does that, I hope she hasn't found anyone else.'

'I'd be happy to take her place.'

Tommy turned to face her. Her silky blonde hair caught the morning sunlight, her blue eyes twinkled and lit up her pretty face. It was a face telling him she loved him and he'd been short of a woman's love for a long time. Maybe Rita had written him out of her life, he could hardly blame her. Given his miraculous survival he had no right even to be alive, and here was someone else he loved, inviting him to love her back, and Tommy Birch was only human.

'Well, after all I've been through, a proper kiss would be quite therapeutic.'

'There's no one in the house, you know. Father will be out all day at work and I am not due back until after lunch.'

'Are you intending to seduce me, Nurse Kohler?'

'Of course I am. It's all part of your convalescence.'

Fifteen minutes later they were in Tommy's bed, both of them naked. Anna was the first naked woman Tom had seen for many months and it was a sight much appreciated. But it was also a sight mingled with a similar memory of Rita. A sight that aroused unwanted guilt as well as passion. She sensed that he wasn't putting his heart and soul into their love-making.

'Thomas, are you all right?'

'Not really. I'm being unfaithful to my wife.'

'Not completely unfaithful. We haven't, er, we haven't quite got there yet.'

'Anna, I'm not sure I want to go there.'

'That is not a problem Thomas. You are a good man who loves his wife and I am a bad woman who loves you.'

She reached down beneath the bedclothes and took him in her hand. 'Ah, you seem to be quite excited by what we are doing.'

'Blimey, Anna! I'm not made of stone. You're a very beautiful woman, lying naked beside me.'

They kissed, passionately, and she thrust herself towards him, enticing him to place himself inside her but his passion exploded in a ferocious climax stimulated by eight months of celibacy. He lay back and breathed out a long sigh of satisfaction. Anna was sighing in frustration. After several minutes of silence he said, 'Sorry.'

'Sorry? What for?'

'Well, I know it wasn't quite what you wanted.'

'Lying with you is enough for me, Thomas. Are you still feeling guilty?'

'Right now I'm actually feeling quite rotten.'

'Then I should feel guilty.'

'No, you shouldn't,' he said. 'You didn't exactly force me here. I'm here because I fancy you like mad.'

'Fancy me like mad? What a strange collection of words.'

'Oh, it's an English thing. It means I'm very attracted to you. I can't help feeling bad. I love my wife like mad and here I am with you.'

'And me?'

'If I wasn't married I'd love you like mad as well. In fact maybe I do. I'm very confused. Is it possible to love two women at the same time?'

'Of course it is. Frenchmen do it all the time. They call the one who is not their wife their mistress.'

'So I've heard.'

'I am happy to be your mistress, Thomas.'

'I'm not French, Anna, and I'd be very worried about you becoming pregnant.'

'I have thought of that myself and I can acquire prophylactics if necessary.'

'Really? Er ... what's a prophylactic?'

'I believe it is what you English soldiers call a Rubber Johnnie.'

'Ah.'

She giggled.

'What are you giggling at?'

'I am teaching you your own language.'

'I've led a sheltered life.'

'Maybe you want to talk about escaping back to your own people.'

'And putting your life at risk? I think it's better that I go alone. If I get caught I don't want you involved in any way.'

'I'm already involved. If you get caught, with or without me, word will get back to the hospital and they will interrogate you very brutally and soon find out you were never a German soldier, and if you are not German, based on where you were found, you can only be an enemy soldier.'

Tommy gave this careful thought, then said, 'Yes, I take your point, but what about you? Where would you fit into this? You could swear you thought I was German. Everyone else at the hospital did.'

'Yes, but not everyone else at the hospital has an English mother. I would also have to explain why we were both heading in the direction of the British lines. They will also know that I speak English fluently and that I may well be a British sympathiser who is helping a British soldier escape back to his own people. It will be more than enough for our military courts. Enough to put me in front of a firing squad.'

'In other words I've already put you in danger.'

'I put myself in danger, Thomas, because I was foolish enough to fall in love with you.'

'Anna, if you escape with me I'll be going back to my wife.'

'Maybe, maybe not. Who knows in wartime? If

there is a chance of me being with you, I wish to take that chance.'

'Blimey, Anna! What am I supposed to say about that? If we get caught I'm responsible for your death and possibly your father's, if he comes with us. And, as I said, if I make it home I will go back to my wife.'

'I have a mother over there,' said Anna. 'My father and I will live with her. I will be very sad that I have lost you but I will be happy that I have shown my true colours and chosen to live with the people who have fought and won an honourable war.'

'You seem sure Germany will lose. Why is this?'

'Well, in a nutshell as you English say, and according to my father, industrial output in Germany is collapsing; we don't have enough food to the extent that our people are eating dogs and crows; in our factories machinery is becoming obsolete and our workforce is not physically fit enough to work the machinery because they are starving; too many of our men have been killed and the ones who are still alive are living on meagre rations of horse meat. We are fighting the Great British Empire, Russia, France, Italy and now America, the richest country in the world.'

'That's a pretty big nutshell.'

'It is. Thomas, if you want to run I will run with you.'

'We're kind of overlooking the hardest part of all this.'

'What's that?'

'Getting from the German front line to the Allied front line. We have to get through the

German defences and across No Man's Land. We've as much chance of being shot by the British as by the Germans.'

'White flag?' suggested Anna.

'Probably, we make sure we've got one they can't miss, and run like hell.'

'I'll pack a white bed sheet and a broom handle.'

'You wave the flag, I'll sing "Pack Up Your Troubles".'

'I know that song. My father sings it sometimes.'

'Not in public I hope.'

She put her arms around him and kissed him, pressing her naked body into his. Tommy felt his passion rekindling. This time some of his guilt had left him – as Anna hoped it might.

He was thinking that if he did manage to get back home in one piece Rita might forgive this infidelity in compensation for the joyous news that he was still alive. On the other hand that might be pushing it, so better not mention it to her. No point upsetting her unduly. In fact the odds were that he'd never make it home. So, what the hell?

Chapter 30

Benjamin Kohler tapped his pipe on the edge of a large glass ashtray into which the ashes of his tobacco fell. It brought a smile to Tommy's face.

'Why do you smile?' Anna asked him.

'Oh, my dad does that. You remind me of my father, Dr Kohler.'

198

'Do I indeed? Is he tall, dark and handsome?'

'He smokes a pipe.'

'I was joking, Thomas. I know we Germans are not supposed to have a sense of humour but I spent some time in your country and maybe it has, how do you say it ... rubbed off?'

'So is he?' asked Anna.

'Is who what?'

'Is your father tall, dark and handsome?'

'Never thought about it. He's fairly tall and he's got dark hair but I'm not sure if he's handsome. He's all right I suppose.'

'Maybe you get your good looks from your mother.'

They were in the living room of the Kohler household, gathered there to discuss their escape to the Allied lines. Doctor Kohler was all for it, having considered the repercussions of the Allies arriving in Mannheim.

'Our soldiers will fight to the death and take us with them if necessary.'

'If our guns open up on Mannheim there won't be much left of the place,' said Tommy.

'They wouldn't shoot at civilians, surely,' Anna said.

'They would if German soldiers are hiding among them,' Tommy told her.

'We might well lose this house,' said Benjamin.

'Better than losing your lives,' said Tommy. 'You can always build a house again.'

'I have already lost more than this house to the war,' said Benjamin. 'I have lost my son.'

'I'm sorry, I didn't know.'

'He was killed a year ago now, but he is still in

our hearts.'

'I didn't tell him, Father. He had enough grief without having to share ours.' Anna looked at Tommy. 'My brother Paul had a look of you and he will have been around your age.'

'Is this why you decided to help me?'

'Possibly.'

'You took a big risk. You must have been close to your brother.'

'I was.'

'I have a brother who'll think I'm dead. He'll be twelve now. I have a sister as well.'

'I'm sure they will be overjoyed when you get home,' said Anna.

'*If* I get home.'

'I will take all the house deeds and papers with me,' said Benjamin, 'to prove that at least the ruins are mine.'

'I'm sure the British won't begrudge you a few ruins,' said Tommy, 'especially when I give you a letter saying how much help you've been to a British soldier.'

'That would be good to have,' said Benjamin. 'I know where I can acquire three military bicycles. They were abandoned as useless by the army but I know a man who fixes them and sells them. I will get them tomorrow.'

'Tomorrow? Wow!' said Tommy. Their day of departure seemed to be approaching at high speed. 'We'll need a map of where we're going.'

'No one has any maps. People who have cars sometimes have road maps but I'm not one of them. Can you drive, Thomas?'

'I've driven army trucks now and again so I

imagine I can drive a car if necessary.'

'It is a skill which may become helpful. Anyway, I do not have maps but I do have friends who have a very good knowledge of this part of the country. I know for a start we must head in a north, north westerly direction towards a town called Rockenhausen which is about fifty kilometres from here. From there we will travel sixty kilometres to Idar-Oberstein and then another sixty to Bitburg and then we travel another sixty to Bastogne in Belgium. To get there we will have to travel through Luxembourg which is supposed to be a neutral country but the people are not to be trusted. When we get to Bastogne I have an address of a man who will shelter us and help us in the next part of our journey which involves us going through the Forest of Ardennes.

'Our ultimate destination is the French town of Arras which is behind the British lines. The whole journey is one of perhaps five hundred very dangerous kilometres.'

'About three hundred and twenty miles,' said Tommy to himself, then, 'Sorry I always do that.'

Benjamin continued: 'I think we should travel by day, as to travel by night might arouse suspicion. I have enough money to pay for our needs. I have a large tent and some old camping equipment in the attic, including a compass and a stove. We can carry everything on our bicycles. My credentials as a German doctor should help with anyone checking who we are, as will Anna's. Doctors and nurses are needed at the front which is where we're headed.' He looked at Tommy. 'You should say nothing. We will say you are a patient who has been shocked into silence. Nothing more can be done for you, so we're taking you back to your military unit. The reason being that you don't need a voice to fire a gun. The German military mind will understand such logic.'

'Do your contacts know you are leaving?'

'I only have two contacts. We are all part of an information chain. We often ask strange questions of each other without giving a reason and no one asks for a reason.'

'Do you have a gun?' asked Tommy.

Benjamin hesitated, Tommy said, 'Just in case we need one as a last resort.'

'I have a revolver,' said Benjamin, 'once owned by my father but I have never used it.'

'Do you have ammunition?'

'Yes. There are three boxes of bullets.'

'Twenty in a box?' guessed Tommy.

'About that, yes.'

'I'd like to take a look at the revolver to make sure it's in working order.'

'I believe it is. My father kept it wrapped in an oily cloth. We still have some of the oil he used on it. It is an American weapon, a Colt 45, about thirty years old.'

'Wow! That's what the cowboys used in cowboy pictures,' said Tommy. 'I'd love to see it.'

'Cowboy pictures?' said Benjamin.

'He means the moving films, Father.'

'Ah, the moving films. I have only ever been twice. It is more of a French and Italian thing.'

'It's fairly popular in England,' Tommy told him. 'Me and my wife used to go every week.'

'I will bring you the gun,' said Benjamin, aware

that his daughter wouldn't want the conversation to move to Tommy's wife. He had warned her that her affection for him might lead to unhappiness, but he couldn't say for certain that it would. Her theory that Tommy's wife might well have remarried by the time he got back had some value to it, especially if she was very pretty, and he liked this young man immensely.

Ten minutes later Tommy had dismantled the Colt into fifteen different pieces and laid them out on the table. He picked up each piece individually and scrutinised it. The ones that needed oiling he set to one side.

'You seem to know what you're doing,' commented Anna.

'Weapon maintenance was part of my army training,' explained Tommy, 'although I've never taken one of these to bits before.' He looked at Benjamin. 'This is a very well-made gun, far better than our standard army issue. I imagine it's pretty accurate as well.'

'My father said he could hit a wine bottle from fifty metres, even after drinking all of the wine himself.'

Tommy grinned. 'Well I hope to be sober if I have to use it.'

'Pray to God you don't have to,' Anna said.

'Amen to that. Trouble is, I won't be able to practise anywhere without drawing attention. I'll just have to assume it works okay.'

'Maybe when we reach an area where there is gunfire,' said Benjamin. 'A few practice shots wouldn't draw any attention.'

'It's a thought,' said Tommy, thinking back to

the last time he heard gunfire. It wasn't a fond memory.

'Are you a good shot?'

'I'm pretty good with a rifle, and not too bad with a handgun.'

'I have a gun belt and holster,' said Benjamin, 'but I wouldn't recommend you cycling across Germany wearing it around you.'

'No, but we can take it with us.'

'Of course.'

'When do we go?' Tommy asked.

'Today is Monday, we go on Saturday. Anna is due three days' leave starting Saturday.'

'If she's taking leave who's supposed to be looking after me here?'

'I am,' said Anna. 'I've agreed to look after you here during my leave time. I get paid extra – not that I'll be around to collect it.'

Her father added, 'I will request the same with the reason that I need a break from my work and wish to spend the time with my daughter. That way we will not be missed until Tuesday and if we are known to be together no one will worry unduly for maybe another day or two by which time we should have reached our destination.'

'Five days to do three hundred and twenty miles?' said Tommy.

'On bicycles it should be quite possible. If not, we take as long as it takes.'

Tommy shrugged, saying, 'I imagine our progress might be quite slow at times.'

'We will not travel along any main roads, just minor roads which should be free of military vehicles taking supplies to the western front. It

204

may be difficult without a map and we may have to rely on my compass.'

'What about road signs?' said Tommy.

'Some have been taken down fearing the Allied advance, but not all of them.'

'A map would be really handy,' Tommy said.

'There is a map on a wall in the hospital,' remembered Anna. 'It is a big old map, more for decoration than for information but it shows all the roads for miles around here.'

'I know it,' said Benjamin. 'It would be useful, old as it is. It shows the countryside to the west of here, exactly where we're going.'

'I know it as well,' said Tommy. 'It's in a frame on the wall next to the patients' lavatory. Look, I'm due to spend a night back in hospital tomorrow for my monthly check-up.' He paused for thought as they both looked at him, then he said, 'All I do is take it off the wall in the middle of the night as I'm going to the lavatory, then I take it into the lavatory and into a cubicle where I can take the map out of the frame. Then I check the corridor's clear and hang the empty frame back on the wall and back to bed with the map inside my pyjamas.'

'What if you're caught?'

'Okay, if I am, I just act dumb, which is what I'm supposed to be.'

'I'll be in the corridor checking it's all clear,' said Anna. 'I'm doing an early morning split shift tomorrow. I start at five, finish at nine. I'll wake you up and I'll be in the vicinity while you're taking the map. There'll be no one else around.'

Anna and her father looked at Tommy, weighing up whether or not he should be the one to steal the map.

'It'll be really quiet at night,' Tommy assured them, 'I'll fold it up and stick it in my pyjamas and give it to Anna before I go back to my bed.'

Anna took it from there. 'I finish my shift at nine and bring Thomas and the map back here. I doubt if anyone will miss the map for ages. It's one of those things you hardly look at. The staff will think it's been taken down to be replaced with something else.'

'That's if they notice it at all,' said her father. 'Okay, we'll have that map.'

Chapter 31

April 1917

A tap on his shoulder awoke Tommy. He'd been away from his hospital bed long enough for it to become unfamiliar. He opened his eyes and, for a couple of seconds, he was disorientated. Anna was leaning over him with a finger to her lips, whispering in his ear, 'It is five o'clock ... ready?'

They had an agreement that the slightest hint of English spoken within the hospital confines was dangerous. He gathered sufficient wit to whisper, *'Jawohl.'*

Anna moved off silently. Tommy lay there for several minutes listening to the various snoring sounds, including those coming from the beds either side of him, then he slipped out of bed and headed for the Men's lavatory – a trip he'd made many times before during the night. He was bare-foot so he made no sound. There was a single, dim light in the ward on the ward nurse's desk – a table lamp on Anna's desk – and she wasn't there. He went into the corridor which was deserted, and headed for the framed map. He'd studied it during the previous day and had ascertained that it was hung on a single cord and could be unhooked easily. What he didn't yet know was how to get it out of the frame with just the pair of pliers he'd brought from Anna's house, now in his pyjama pocket. He went into the lavatory, which was unlit, indicating that it was unoccupied. He turned on the lights and checked the toilet cubicles – all vacant. Then he came back and saw Anna was at the end of the corridor. She stuck up a thumb, the universal signal that all was okay from her end. He did the same and positioned himself in front of the map. The frame was quite large – three feet by two feet, and heavy. He held it by its sides and lifted it up, watched only by Anna, until he was satisfied that the cord was off its hook. Then he set it on the floor and leaned it against the wall as he reopened the lavatory door which had closed of its own accord, as German hospital doors did. He picked up the map and backed into the lavatory as the door started to close again, pushing it open with his backside. He then carried the framed map into the nearest cubicle, turned it facing the wall and closed himself in the cubicle with it. If anyone came in he was simply a patient using the toilet, not a British soldier removing a wall map from its frame.

It was backed with a sheet of thin plywood, held

in place with eight metal fasteners, which could be moved clockwise to release the picture. Aided by the pliers he moved all of these in quick time and took out the backboard, behind which was the map. He fixed the board back in the frame and laid the map on the floor. With three straight folds he reduced its size to twelve inches by nine and stuck it inside his pyjamas, tightening the pyjama cord to hold it in place. Then he winced as he heard a noise outside in the corridor. A man was wheezing heavily and the noise grew louder and louder still upon the opening and closing of the main lavatory door. Now the wheezing man was directly at the other side of his cubicle door. The wheeze turned into a shout of pain as the man staggered into the cubicle next to Tommy and fell down, retching and wheezing and shouting in pain. He now heard footsteps that he hoped might just be Anna's but there was more than just one person coming to help. Three voices at least, two female, one male and none of them Anna. The sound coming from the unwell man became more and more feeble. He had no idea what was being said, but from the tone it sounded as though the man was on his last legs. Jesus! If the man pegged it in here surely he'd be found with the empty frame and the map stuck down his pyjamas. It occurred to him to replace the map but he'd make too much noise doing that. He could hear the unwell man's rattling breathing now as the medics tried to resuscitate him. Then the breathing slowed down and stopped. There was a silence all round then the words, *'Ich glaube, er ist tot.'*

Tommy had spent enough time in this hospital

to know that the last three words meant, 'he is dead'. His heart sank, not so much in pity for the dead man but in trepidation for what was yet to come. More hospital staff, one of whom was sure to try his cubicle door and shout out to whoever was inside. What then? All he could think of was to play his usual dumb act, but this time he'd be subject to much more scrutiny. Possibly enough scrutiny to discover he wasn't even a German soldier. And how would that affect Anna? Not too well. She'd become a suspect, with her English connections, her dad as well. Maybe he could flush the map down the toilet and act dumb about the frame. Let them think it was there when he came in. Anna would become involved at some stage and would translate his hand signals to this effect. That might be his only chance.

He was about to rip the map up into flushable pieces when he heard Anna's voice. It was the voice of authority; the voice of the nurse in charge of this ward. The other voices obviously belonged to staff subordinate to Anna. She entered the lavatory and delivered what sounded like commands. People answered in an obedient fashion and Tommy stood poised, with his hands still on the map, ready to rip it up. He guessed that Anna was standing right outside his cubicle door, allaying any notion that it might be occupied. The conversations continued in German with Anna obviously in charge. Sounds of the dead body being lifted and taken out of the cubicle, under Anna's firm instructions. Then the sounds moved outside the lavatory into the corridor and Tommy was assuming that the body was being taken away in the opposite direction to his bed. After a short time all was quiet. He came out of the lavatory and looked out into the corridor. Deserted.

Within a minute the empty frame was back on the wall and Tommy was walking back to his bed with the map stuck down his pyjamas. He lay in the dark for half an hour until Anna arrived and stood over him, saying nothing. In the dim light he could make out that she was miming that it had been a close shave. He took out the map and gave it to her. She stuck it inside her uniform which was already unbuttoned to receive it. Tommy slept no more that night as he pondered on what might have been had Anna not come to his rescue. He wouldn't be lying in a warm and comfortable bed, that's for sure. In fact his life had been very much in Anna's hands ever since he'd regained consciousness. Taking the map had seemed so simple back in her house. Even her father had thought it would be simple. But they weren't out of the woods yet.

At eight-thirty Dr Lehmann came to the ward nurse's desk where Anna was reading a folder of patient's notes. Lehmann had a security guard in army uniform with her. Anna's heart gave a lurch, which she hid by looking up then back down to her work immediately.

'A map has been stolen,' said Lehmann. Anna closed the file she was working on and looked up with studied disinterest on her face, as if to say, *this is a hospital why should I be interested in a missing map?*

'Map?'

'It was on the wall in a frame. It has been stolen.'

Anna shook her head and gave the matter some thought, as if trying to remember the map. 'Oh, that,' she said, eventually. 'Who would steal that?'

'Enemy agents,' said the security guard.

Anna said, sarcastically, 'I do not think we have any enemy agents here, with it being a hospital. Or do you think enemy agents are deliberately getting themselves seriously wounded to come and spy on all the other wounded men?'

'Do not try to be clever, nurse,' the soldier snarled. 'The enemy will try to get their hands on any map they can.'

'I'd have thought the enemy would have enough maps of their own,' retorted Anna, heatedly. 'A lot more up-to-date than that old thing. Are you sure the maintenance people haven't taken it for some reason? Maybe to change it for a more interesting picture.'

'I have asked the maintenance people,' said the guard.

'All of them?' said Anna. 'There are quite a few – mostly doing nothing useful. There was a death in the men's toilets earlier, which left a real mess in one of the cubicles. I assume it's their job to clean it up, so far nothing's been done.'

'There are two on duty at any one time,' said the guard, 'and we've asked the two who are on duty now. They know nothing about it. It is they who brought it to our attention.'

'I wish someone would bring the mess in the toilets to their attention,' said Anna. 'Come to think of it, wasn't that map on the wall right out-

211

side the toilets?'

'Yes it was,' said Lehmann. 'It's not there now. We are now obliged to search the patients and their beds,' sighed Lehmann. 'As if we haven't enough to do.'

'If it was me I'd ask the maintenance workers on the other shifts,' said Anna, 'before I disturb the staff and patients.'

'We might as well start with you,' said the guard.

'What? You're searching me for an old map in a big frame?' Anna stood up and held her arms out. 'Search my pockets if you must or do you think I've hidden it my underwear?'

'The frame is still there but the map isn't in it,' said Lehmann.

'What? It's been taken out of the frame and they've only just noticed? It could have been taken days ago. This is ridiculous!'

The guard stepped forward to search Anna. She put out a hand to stop him. 'I'm not having your hands all over me. If you must do this stupid search I want Dr Lehmann to do it and without you watching.'

'It will have to be a strip search,' said the guard.

'Really? You do surprise me. I can see why a pervert like you would be so keen to do it. Will you be searching Doctor Lehmann or any of the other senior people?'

'My office, nurse,' said Lehmann.

The excited gleam in the doctor's eyes didn't escape Anna's notice. She followed Lehmann to her office, knowing that if she tried anything there'd be more than a gleam in her eye, there'd be a fist. Anna's main concern was the neatly folded

212

map which was on her desk, hidden in plain view within the pages of a thick folder marked: *Military Patients Notes, Strictly Confidential.*

When Lehmann closed her office door behind them both, Anna turned to face her. 'I assume you think this is ridiculous as well?'

'I do, but we are governed by the military and we must obey their rules.'

'Will all the senior doctors and surgical staff be searched?'

'I don't know. Just unbutton your uniform then I can at least say I've searched you without lying to the man.'

Anna unbuttoned her white uniform from the neck to the waist and held it open, showing a white, cotton slip. Lehmann gazed at it for two seconds. Anna lifted up her slip and showed her naked stomach up as far as her brassiere.

'Do you need to see any more?' she asked.

'No. I hardly expected to find anything anyway. If the maintenance people have taken it there'll be hell to pay for that damned soldier.'

'To be honest, doctor, that old map could have been missing for days and I wouldn't have noticed it had gone.'

'No, nor I.'

Anna buttoned her uniform up and followed the doctor back to her desk where the guard was waiting. She made a conscious effort not to look down at the incriminating folder, just the guard's face. He obviously hadn't looked inside. She turned her attention to Lehmann.

'If the patients are to be searched could you start with Thomas, as I will be taking him back with me at nine o'clock?'

'Very good, Nurse Kohler.'

Anna took the guard to Tommy's bed, winking at Tommy when they got there and saying to the guard, 'We are treating this soldier with cognitive behaviour therapy. He was seriously injured and does not understand the written or spoken word. He most certainly wouldn't understand a map or why you think he might have stolen it.'

'Would you ask him to get out of his bed?'

Anna went through an elaborate mime that Tommy studied, then stuck up a thumb to say he understood. As he got out of bed his pyjama bottoms fell down, with the cord being unfastened. He made no move to pull them up as any normal person would. Anna mimed him to unbutton his pyjama jacket which he did and took it off, standing there in his vest and cotton underpants, with his pyjama bottoms around his ankles. Anna forced back a smile as the guard searched through the bedclothes and under the mattress for a map that had been under his nose only minutes ago.

'Do you wish to search inside his underpants?' she asked the guard, insolently. 'To see what he's hiding in there? It doesn't look as if he's got much down there to me.'

'No, I do not.'

'Good.'

She mimed to Tommy to get dressed in his day clothes as she packed his pyjamas in a small case. Then, followed by Tommy and the guard, she made her way back to her desk where Lehmann was waiting.

'It's still a mystery, Doctor Lehmann,' Anna

214

said. 'Tommy doesn't have the map.'

As Anna took herself into an office to sign out, Lehmann addressed herself to the guard. 'Will you be searching us all?'

'Yes.'

'In that case you will need a female guard to assist you and if this map has been removed for innocent reasons I intend reporting this stupidity to your superiors.'

Anna returned and said to Lehmann, 'I have signed off my split shift, Doctor Lehmann. As you know I will be taking three days' leave.'

'Along with your father.'

'Yes.'

'Well, give my regards to your father and have a good rest.'

'Thank you, doctor.'

Anna turned to go, along with Tommy, and was almost out of the door when the guard called out for them to stop. They turned round to see that he had picked up the patients file.

'I would like to examine this before you leave,' he said.

'That is a highly confidential file,' said Lehmann. 'Full of patients' private notes.'

'I will not be looking at the notes, just to see if there is a map hidden in there.'

'Oh, very well, but be warned this will be added to my complaint.'

As Lehmann, Anna and Tommy looked on, the guard flicked through the pages of the folder. Several pages dropped out and fell to the floor. Anna protested, loudly.

'You idiot! I had everything filed in date order.'

'Have you finished annoying us?' said Lehmann to the now hapless guard.

'Yes.'

As Anna and Tommy walked out of the hospital to the street he murmured, 'Jesus, Anna! When I saw that soldier I nearly had a heart attack. What the hell was it all about?'

'They were looking for the map.'

'They've missed it already? Blimey, that was quick.'

'I know. I insisted on Lehmann searching me instead of him doing it, but I didn't have it on me.'

'Where was it?'

'In the folder the guard was just looking through.'

'Why didn't he find it?'

'When I went into the office to sign out I took the folder with me, then brought it back out, minus the map.'

'Clever girl. I didn't notice.'

'More to the point, nor did the guard. I kept Lehmann between me and him all the time. He did not see me take it.'

'Hey, what was all that about?' he said, indignantly. 'You asking that guard if he wanted to see what I've got in my underpants? And saying it doesn't look as if he's got much down there?'

Anna laughed. 'Well, you dropped your pyjamas for him without being asked. I didn't think you'd mind. He'll be searching everyone's underpants today.'

'Including Dr Lehmann's?'

'Everyone's.'

'Well, rather him than me with that. Where is

the map by the way?'

'Inside my uniform.'

'Lucky old map eh?'

'Luckier than the man in the next toilet to you.'

'Is he dead?'

'Yes he is, poor man. He had just about recovered from severe wounds he sustained many months ago then he was diagnosed with terminal colorectal cancer. He was only thirty-four.'

'Poor sod. He was dying two feet away from me and all I was worried about was getting caught.'

'Thomas, if you had been caught your own life would have been at risk.'

'And yours.'

'Thank you.'

'What for?'

She linked his arm and pulled him to her. 'For showing concern about me.'

Tommy smiled. Because of her he was as happy as he could be, *under the circumstances.* Tomorrow his life would enter a new phase. He just hoped he could remember how to ride a bike. He'd never actually owned one. The only bicycle he'd ever ridden was that old boneshaker of his dad's – and he hadn't ridden that too often. Bloody hell, Tommy, you never thought of that! Best not mention it to Anna, who was no doubt an excellent bicyclist.

That thought of his dad's bike triggered a longing for home, and that triggered an even greater longing for his beloved Rita. What to do about that? Oh hell! This wonderful woman clinging onto his arm had no doubt saved his life simply by befriending him and falling in love with him and helping him in so many ways. Without her he certainly wouldn't be going back to Rita. He wouldn't be going anywhere. How could he repay such a debt? Was it right for him to just dump her and go back to his wife?

For a fleeting moment he wondered if Rita might be so grateful to Anna that she would allow her into their lives to live as man and two wives. But reality hit him almost as quickly as this bad idea had. Men having more than one wife might be the custom in certain faraway countries but not in England, and especially not in Pontefract. He grimaced at the prospect of his father's reaction to such an arrangement, not to mention Rita's. Anna looked up at him and caught this expression.

'Oh dear, Thomas, what is the problem?'

'I was thinking … actually, I was er … I was hoping I still knew how to ride a bicycle. I probably need to practise a bit before we set off.'

'You think your injury might have affected you?'

'I think the fact that I never had a bicycle of my own might have affected me. And now I'm planning to ride halfway across Europe with people maybe shooting at me. On top of which I've done no proper exercise for months. I hope I don't keep falling off.'

Chapter 32

Leeds Town Hall. April 1917

Stuart Gooding's trial was being held at Leeds Assizes in the Town Hall. In view of the weight of evidence against him Stuart had been advised to plead guilty and allow his barrister to plead in mitigation on his behalf for a life sentence rather than a death sentence. His barrister, Quentin Cutler KC, made the mistake of bringing George's German nationality into his mitigation plea.

'My Lord, my client is a young, impressionable man taken up in a red hot fervour of nationalistic anger against a German who was living among us, plying his trade as a butcher in perfect safety and hundreds of miles away from where his fellow countrymen were slaughtering our own men, including Mr Gooding's brother, to whom he was very close, and who had been killed that very week. It's not unreasonable to say, My Lord, that his hatred of the Germans is most probably mirrored by the same hatred engendered into our armed forces by their leaders to enable them to fight with greater fury–' The judge held up a hand, to stay the counsel's speech.

'I must stop you there because I have a difficulty with this line of mitigation, Mr Cutler. You see, Mr Miller's nearest German relative was his paternal grandfather. His paternal grandmother was English; his father was born and raised in

England and his mother was Irish. Neither of them had ever lived in Germany, nor even spoke the language. Mr Miller himself had been born and raised in London and had already lost his Irish mother to a rampaging mob in that city. His English born-and-bred father subsequently died in an alien internment camp in the Isle of Man.

'Now, our own King George also had a German grandfather – Prince Albert of Saxe-Coburg-Gotha; his grandmother was Queen Victoria; his parents, King Edward the Seventh and Queen Alexandra, are both considered to be English, as is our present king. So, if I am to suppose Mr Miller is of German nationality and therefore a natural target for civic unrest then I must also suppose that King George V of the United Kingdom is also of German nationality. If this is the main basis of your plea, Mr Cutler, I'm afraid I have great difficulty with the precedents it may create. I have sympathy with your client for losing his brother to the war but this is happening to countless families all over the country, without them resorting to murder. The courts must never condone such crimes in any way. Do you have anything else on which to base your plea in mitigation, Mr Cutler?'

'I do not, My Lord.'

'Then I will retire to consider the sentence.'

A confused Stuart, in handcuffs, looked to Cutler to tell him what to do now, but the barrister had his back to him. A policeman took Stuart's arm and led him from the dock, down the stone stairway back to the cells under Leeds Town Hall to await his fate. Stuart sought advice from the policeman.

'What do you think will happen to me?'

'I don't know, son.'

'Do you think they'll hang me? I didn't mean to kill anyone. I was off me head. Everybody else was just as mad as me. Trouble is I had me tool bag with me, with a bloody hammer in it. I won't get hung will I? I'm only eighteen. Our kid were killed in France and me dad died when I were five so if they kill me, me mam'll have no one left. They might as well kill her.'

'I shouldn't think they'd hang you, lad.'

'I hope not, for me mam's sake.'

The court had reassembled. Stuart's head gradually emerged in the dock as he mounted the steps, then all eyes were on the door to the judge's room. He came out, clad in his red robes and long, horsehair wig, face set in no particular expression, giving away, no clues as to Stuart's fate. He sat down and faced the court as he composed himself. In front of him, hitherto unseen by anyone in the court, was a small square of black silk. He slowly picked it up and placed it on his head. Then he turned to address Stuart:

'Stuart Gooding, the jury have convicted you of murder... You will suffer death by hanging.'

Stuart stared at him, disbelievingly, wide-eyed and now having difficulty catching his breath. His mother, also in court and hoping for the best, gave out a long, anguished scream. Stuart collapsed and was held up by two sturdy policemen, both ready for this eventuality. They took him back down the steps to the cells, the only sound in court still coming from Stuart's mother.

Charlie, who had come to hear the verdict and, like Mrs Gooding, was hoping for the best, shook his head in deep sorrow. As the court cleared he went over to the weeping mother and placed a strong hand on each of her shoulders.

'I expect his barrister'll appeal against the sentence, Florence.'

She looked up at him with streaming eyes as she heard this unexpected ray of hope.

'So, they might not hang him, Charlie?'

'All I know is it's not over and done with yet. There's plenty of call for hope.'

'If they hang my Stuart I swear I'll hang meself, Charlie.'

'No need for talk like that, Florence. By the way, I don't condemn Stuart for what he did. I condemn the bloody war. Stuart's a good lad who got caught up in a daft situation and got carried away. If anyone's needed to speak up for him at the appeal I'll be glad to help, and so will a lot of others.'

'Thank you, Charlie.'

Cutler came over to them. 'I was hoping the judge wouldn't come up with all that royal family stuff. It's long been a bone of contention. I think we've got grounds for appeal on that basis alone.'

'There you are, Florence,' said Charlie, 'the lad's gonna be all right.'

'Er, there's no actual guarantee of that,' said Cutler.

'I know,' said Charlie. 'I know yer've got to say that. But there's a good chance isn't there?'

'Yes, I'd say there is. I believe the judge passed the maximum sentence knowing I'd seek an appeal, which means he's leaving the final decision to others.'

After speaking to Florence for a few seconds Charlie caught up with Cutler as he headed for the barristers' robing room.

'Mr Cutler, you sounded optimistic about Stuart's chances back there.'

'I always sound optimistic, even when I'm not.'

'So, what are his chances of a reprieve?'

'I'm not sure who you are, Mr...?'

'Birch, Charlie Birch. I was Stuart's boss at work.'

'Ah.'

'So, what are his chances?'

'Well, I'd say our chances of getting appeal are probably four to one in our favour. The chances of getting Stuart a reprieve from hanging are about even money, so the odds are slightly against him.'

'Bad as that eh?'

'Better than most I'd say. Not many murderers are getting reprieved during this war. The authorities are dealing harshly with all breeds of criminal. The country has enough on its plate dealing with that damned criminal in Germany.'

'Right.'

Chapter 33

Featherstone. April 1917

Rita was sitting in her chair by the fire. Spring had arrived in England but not in Featherstone. She was wearing a full length maternity gown in pale blue cotton but it failed to hide her eight-month bump. There was a yappy dog barking in the street. She recognised it as the bark of an unlovely animal that didn't even live in their street. It was a small mongrel which came round every day just to annoy them. It was almost drowning the noise of the boys playing cricket in the street, using some-one's dustbin as a wicket. The yapping turned to yelping when one of the boys threw the ball at it. The shot was accurate and earned him shouts of approval from his pals. Rita didn't see this but guessed what had happened and was grateful to the hotshot who had thrown the ball.

She looked up from her newspaper through the window at gathering rain clouds and hoped they'd hurry up and arrive to wash the boys away as well. This street was so much noisier than the Birches' street. There was a brief knock on the door, which opened before Rita could prise herself up from her chair.

'Only me.'

'Hello, Edith.'

'I've just been for an interview to get me old job back at Wilkie's.'

'Definitely not going back to Barnbow then?'

'Rita, I'm lucky to be alive to have that choice – that's what me dad says.'

'How is Charlie?'

'He's okay.'

A horse came clattering across the cobbles, pulling a cart loaded with junk. Its driver shouted the traditional ragman's call, 'Raaagbone, any old rags?'

'How much am I worth, mister?' called out one of the skinnier boys.

'Why do they always shout that?' said Rita.

'Shout what?'

'Ragbone. They don't collect bones do they?'

'Not that I know of. It doesn't make sense I suppose. Are ragmen supposed to make sense?'

'Probably not. Nothing in this world makes sense, Edith,' said Rita, returning her attention to her newspaper. She was reading about Stuart Gooding's conviction and sentencing for the murder of George Miller with mixed feelings. Was it her fault for telling the Birch family about George? If so, was she responsible for George's murder and Stuart Gooding's death sentence? Apart from her brief outburst to him on the phone she hadn't spoken to Charlie since she left their house just before Christmas. The banner headline said, simply:

GOODING TO HANG FOR GERMAN
BUTCHER'S MURDER

The very words 'German Butcher' made this an inflammatory headline. The paper had an

225

editorial about how Stuart Gooding had received his call-up papers on the very day of the killing and how his brother had been killed in France. The story was bound to arouse anger among the people of Pontefract. Young Stuart Gooding was a good lad, one of their own who'd simply lost his rag and killed a kraut after the krauts had killed his brother. Better for the lad to go to France to kill krauts serving king and country than be hanged for killing one over here. How little sense this war made was the sentiment of the article.

How little sense anything made, Rita was thinking. She was feeling guilty about the fate of Stuart, whom she vaguely knew through her father-in-law. Had she not blurted out that George was a German he'd still be alive and Stuart wouldn't be in prison awaiting the hangman's noose – and she'd still be living with the Birch family where she'd been happy, or as happy as she could be without her Tommy around. The longer time went on with no news of him the more despondent she began to feel. The slim strand of hope she was clinging to got slimmer by the day. She placed her hands on her bump and she could still feel Tommy's presence in the world. In a month his child would be born.

She looked around the sparse living room of her father's house. The brightest thing about the place was the coal fire burning in the grate, illuminating Rita's face with its dancing light. She was saddened that her child should be born into such squalor, but it was all she could offer it. No help at all had come from the Birch family, whose only contribution to Rita's welfare was Edith calling in to see her now and again. Edith felt bad about the way she'd been treated, especially after George had been murdered as an indirect result of that same family altercation. She often called in to see Rita and help out in any way that her one arm would allow.

'I'll make us a cup of tea, shall I?'

'That'll be nice. Did you get your job back?' Rita asked her.

'I did, yes. They're happy to have me back, and I'll be happy to go. I always enjoyed working there ... and I won't get blown up. Mind you, the money's nowhere near as good. With me bonus my last wage packet was nearly eleven pounds – that's nearly five times what I'll be getting at Wilkinsons.'

'It's not much good if you're not alive to spend it.'

'Like Elsie and Flo you mean?'

'I do, yeah, and I'm really glad you didn't get killed, Edith. Will you get compensation?'

'I should think so. I'm on sick pay right now, but that expires when this pot comes off. We all pay into an insurance fund.' Edith was filling the kettle from the tap when she threw this question over her shoulder. 'Rita, do you think Stuart found out about George from Dad?'

'It wasn't just Stuart, Edith, dozens of people knew. I think Charlie mentioned it at work and it spread around Pontefract like wildfire. And, let's face it, there are some right idiots in Pontefract.'

'Yeah, I know. Before the war I tried to find a boyfriend who matches up to our Tommy. Back then it was a struggle, right now I've got no chance. Any lad not in the army is either too old or has flat feet or some such ailment. It could be that all the good ones fighting in the war will be dead before they come home.'

Rita was mightily relieved that Edith hadn't been killed in the Barnbow explosion. She liked Edith. The trouble was she liked both Charlie and Stanley as well – and Agnes for that matter. She missed being part of Tommy's family but, after what Agnes had said to her, the Birch family had broken a link that mere words couldn't mend.

'There aren't any young men around here who match up to Tommy, that's for sure,' Rita said.

'So, what will you do?'

'I'll wait until Tommy gets home, what else can I do?'

'But...'

Edith kept forgetting that Tommy wasn't dead in Rita's mind. It had been like that at home for á short while, until the family's bust-up with Rita.

'Oh Rita, if Tommy comes home won't that be the most wonderful day ever?'

'It'll be one of them.' Rita patted her stomach. 'The day this feller pops out'll be a great day for me. At least I'll have part of Tommy with me.'

'This feller? You think it's a boy?'

'When I talk to him I do it as if he's a boy.'

'Talk to him a lot, do you?'

'All the time. I call him Benjamin after my father.'

'If you called him Benjamin Charles it might soften Dad up a bit, Mam as well – and it'd definitely suit our Tommy.'

'I might just do that, Edith.'

'I hope it's a boy, then. When he's born can we come and see him ... or her?'

'I don't know. Who's we?'

'Me and Stanley.' Then she hesitated before adding... 'And maybe Dad.'

'I'm not sure, Edith. They both turned on me that day, which is why I'm having to live in this awful dump.'

'Dad didn't turn on you. He wanted Mam to apologise.'

'He's never been to see me, to see how I'm going on.'

'He doesn't need to, Rita. I tell him.'

'He knows this place is a dump because I told him. He also knows my dad's a bit of a waste of space.' Then she thought about what she'd said, and added, 'But having said that, he does his best for me and his future grandchild, which is more than Charlie ever does. What do you think Tommy would say if he knew about all this nonsense that's gone on between us?'

'It's not all that bad here, Rita.'

'It *is* bad, Edith. When it was just me and Dad living here I could manage, but not with a baby. I lived most of my life here but I never imagined I'd be stuck here with a baby and a missing husband ... and a missing mother for that matter.'

'What about your mam?' asked Edith. 'Where does she live?'

'Don't know. I haven't seen her since the day I married Tommy, and I was amazed she turned up then. In fact I never even got to speak to her. She shot off straight after the church service. You don't know how lucky you are with your family.'

'Except that you hate our mam.'

'I don't hate her. I hate the fact that she somehow thinks I betrayed Tommy by going to the pictures with George, and that horrible remark about me dropping my knickers for him was unforgivable, Edith. She should be ashamed of herself but I don't suppose she is.'

Edith was looking embarrassed. Rita put a hand on her arm. 'Oh I'm sorry. I shouldn't talk that way about your mam.'

Edith said nothing. She picked up her bag with her good arm and headed for the door.

'Edith, I'm sorry.'

'Rita, I don't think you are, and nor would I be if anyone said that about me.'

'Are we still friends? Please don't stop coming to see me.'

Edith raised a bleak smile and said, 'I won't ... bye.'

Chapter 34

Mannheim. April 1917

When Anna and Tommy arrived home with the stolen map Benjamin was sitting at the breakfast table looking quite thoughtful.

'I spoke to my contact last night,' he said, 'about the route we intend to take and have been informed that we would have no chance of success.'

'Ah,' said Tommy, suddenly disappointed. 'So we're not going then?'

'On the contrary. All I am saying is that I didn't know about the obstructions created by the German forces when, last month, they carried out a strategic withdrawal known as Operation Alberich. They evacuated their forces from the Somme to the Hindenburg Line some forty kilometres nearer to us, leaving behind complete devastation to hinder the advancing Allies, not to mention us.

'Many miles of the very ground across which we were planning to travel has been destroyed. Villages have been flattened, wells poisoned, trees cut down, massive craters blown in roads and crossroads, and booby-traps left in ruins and dugouts. This was country across which the three of us would have needed to travel before reaching the Allied lines, and that was after we'd got through the massive German fortifications at the Hindenburg Line. It would have been a hard journey to make in a tank, much less on a bicycle.'

This brought a grin from Tommy, who was listening intently as Benjamin went on: 'Our only hope comes from the intelligence I am receiving from the people who sympathise with my hatred of this war and of this ridiculous Kaiser who has led us into it. I have people we can go to for help in places from here to Nancy in France which is now our ultimate destination.'

'So we head for Nancy?' said Tommy. 'As opposed to Arras?'

'We do. That way we do not have to cross the German fortifications that Mr Hindenburg has erected. We will be travelling south of them. My contact tells me that Arras would be an impossible route. Do you have the map?'

'We do,' said Anna, taking it out of her tunic and handing it to him.

'Excellent,' said Benjamin, spreading it out on the table for the three of them to pore over. He ran a finger over it.

'If we travel south along this road,' he said, pointing to a minor road out of Mannheim, 'and follow the Rhine ... well, more or less, using minor roads all the time, the terrain will be reasonably flat and good for bicycles. Then we turn west here, towards Nancy.' He pointed to the town. 'And we eventually cross the western front near a small town called Arracourt – and here it is.' He tapped a finger on the name Arracourt, a few miles east of Nancy. 'Hmm, this map is not too bad at all. The journey is a lot shorter than heading for Arras and of course we will not have to cross the Hindenburg fortifications.'

'How much shorter?'

'Total distance, three hundred kilometres – about two hundred of your miles.'

'You make it sound easy,' commented Tommy. 'Crossing the two front lines'll be quite tricky. I know, I've tried to do it from the other side a couple of times. The last time I didn't wake up for nearly three months, and even then I ended up on the wrong side.'

'If there is a problem at all,' Benjamin said, 'it is that we will be running into French Allies, not British.'

'That won't be a problem,' said Tommy. 'I just hope they've forgiven us for Waterloo.'

'I am more than aware that will not be easy,' said Benjamin. 'Both front lines will be well fortified with guns, wire and trenches and we will need guile, courage and good luck to get through, but I am thinking that our reward at the other side will be enough to justify the danger we are putting ourselv–'

'Benjamin,' interrupted Tommy. 'I get the feeling that, if it wasn't for me, you two wouldn't be attempting this at all. I don't feel comfortable about putting you into such danger.'

'You are wrong, Thomas. You see, I am becoming increasingly worried that the anti-war group I am associated with may fall foul of the German Secret Service police who have already arrested the members of many such groups, and once these people are arrested they are shot without trial after a period of torture. I personally think, and Anna agrees with me, that making a run for the Allied lines is our safest option.'

Tommy looked at him, trying to detect a lie in his eyes, but he saw only an honest man smiling back at him.

'What about the people we are relying on to help us? What if they've been arrested?'

'We have a very efficient grapevine that tells us if anyone's been arrested. So far my chain of contacts has not been broken, which means they are all safe.'

'*Chain* of contacts?' said Tommy, puzzled.

'Don't ask me about it,' said Benjamin.

'Right, have you got our bikes yet?' asked Tommy.

'I have.'

They were military bicycles, of solid construction, quite heavy and no more than a year old. Anna's father had ensured they all had new tyres and a tool kit along with a pump, a good-sized saddle bag and a puncture outfit. Tommy looked at the machines approvingly as they stood in a line, with their pedals propped on a stone kerb in the doctor's garden.

'They're a lot more modern than my dad's old bike,' said Tommy. 'Do the brakes work and everything?'

'They do,' said Benjamin. 'New brake pads front and rear. Everything that needs oiling has been oiled. All worn nuts and bolts replaced, new bearing rings on the wheels. They're all as good as new. Try yours out.'

'Which one's mine?'

'The one at the front. I have set the saddle to suit me and we are about the same height.'

Tommy went to the bicycle and cocked his leg over the substantial saddle, which seemed the right height for him.

'Yeah, that seems fine,' he said.

He moved it away from the kerb and balanced with one foot on the ground and the other on a pedal, ready to move off.

'Off you go,' said Benjamin.

Tommy didn't move. To set off and fall straight over would have been too embarrassing.

'He hasn't ridden bicycles very often,' said Anna.

'Oh, right. I tell you what, Thomas. I will hold onto the saddle while you set off. If you have ridden one before you will not have forgotten.'

'Yeah, so I've heard.'

Benjamin took hold of the saddle, as he had for

his daughter many years ago, and walked alongside Tommy as he wobbled off. He let go without telling Tommy, in the manner of all fathers teaching their children how to ride, and watched as Tommy rode off down the drive and out into the road with growing confidence. His father's bicycle had been much more cumbersome, with poor brakes and a chain that had a habit of jumping off the cogs. This, if nothing else, was a highly efficient German bicycle that ran smoothly without a squeak or a rattle. Yes, given decent roads, they could travel perhaps fifty to sixty miles in a day on transport such as this. He travelled a hundred yards down the road before slowing down and turning in its width, then riding back to his two friends who were now standing in the gateway, admiring his proficiency.

'This is much easier to ride than my dad's,' he reported. 'I reckon we can average around fifteen miles an hour on these.'

'I agree,' concurred Benjamin. 'Slower uphill, faster downhill. The first part of our journey is quite flat.'

'We'll have to take into account my lack of fitness,' Tommy pointed out.

'We'll let you set the pace,' said Benjamin. 'Any time you want to stop, we stop. Our first destination is a small town called Freckenfeld which is only fifty kilometres from here. I have people there who will give us food and a bed for our first night.'

'Do these friends know where we're going?' Tommy asked.

'No,' said Benjamin. 'They know to expect us when they see us – it is the only way in our dangerous circumstances but I assure you they can be trusted. One of them is my sister, who is a contact in my chain. Her husband was a soldier, killed in the first year of the war. She bears the British no grudges. They did not start this war. We are to be passed from contact to contact until we reach Nancy.'

'Who else is in Freckenfeld besides your sister?'

'My two nieces – fourteen and twelve years old, and my mother. My father is dead. If a stranger asks, our story will be that we are on a short bicycling holiday to get away from the constant rigours of the hospital. You are who you say you are – a wounded German soldier who is in our care, but who has lost the power of communication. That way I do not get my family into any trouble with enquiring Germans after we disappear.'

'True,' said Tommy. 'Why should anyone even suspect you're running west to join the enemy?'

'No reason. I am not sure the Mannheim police will even trouble themselves to track down three missing civilians. The German military has too many other things to worry about, and we might well be at our destination by the time our disappearance is even reported.'

Tommy remembered the danger and terrible devastation at the front lines and he knew that the last two or three miles, and the crossing of No Man's Land, would be the most dangerous part of their journey, but he said nothing. The trick was to get there first and then worry about getting across. The nearer he was to the western front, the nearer he was to his beloved Rita. But what the hell was he going to do about his beloved Anna? It seemed to Tommy that getting across the western front wasn't the biggest problem he was facing. What the hell was he worrying about? He would most likely get himself killed before he got to the Allied lines.

'Right,' he said. 'Are we ready for the off?'

'You need to pack all your belongings,' said Benjamin.

'Belongings?' said Tommy. 'Apart from the clothes you lent me I don't have any actual belongings – apart from a very nice pair of boots and I nicked them off a dead German soldier.'

'I have a spare rucksack you can pack your things in,' said Benjamin. 'I wish to set off before noon tomorrow so we arrive in Freckenfeld at a reasonable hour and so I can gauge what sort of progress we can expect to be making for the rest of our journey.'

'Right,' said Tommy. 'I do appreciate having you two organise all this. Left to my own devices, and without Anna's help, I'd be in a prisoner of war camp by now.'

'Or maybe worse,' said Benjamin, pointedly.

Tommy nodded, having got his point.

Benjamin knew the roads to Freckenfeld quite well, although the route he took was not the most direct one. The fifty kilometre journey was probably nearer sixty-five with all the meanderings they took along minor roads past farms that looked to have been untended for years. The roads were flat and mostly devoid of traffic apart from the odd horse-drawn cart. No motorised vehicles on these roads. They had ridden for two hours non-stop and Tommy was finding he could cope with the effort with reasonable ease. To facilitate conversation, wherever they could, they rode three abreast with Benjamin in the middle.

'No wonder there's a food shortage,' Benjamin said, looking at the implanted fields on either side. 'All the farm workers are no doubt at war.'

'It's the same in England,' said Tommy, 'only our farms are being worked by women. It's called the Women's Land Army. My sister was thinking about joining. I wonder if she ever did?'

'I do not think German women support the war effort with such zeal,' said Benjamin. 'We have them working in factories but I do not think they go about their work with much enthusiasm. It's the difference between the aggressors and the defenders. When a woman is defending her home and her family she will do anything within her power. Our women were not supposed to be defending anything, just to wait at home while their men fight and win a war which their leaders started.'

'I sometimes find it hard to do my work with enthusiasm,' called out Anna. 'I sometimes think that every wounded man who comes in has only himself to blame for what happened to him. I know it's wrong but someone's to blame and we can hardly blame the people we invaded.'

'You didn't actually invade England,' said Tommy, remembering his dad's attitude to the war.

'We invaded Belgium knowing they had a treaty with the British,' said Benjamin.

'My dad thinks we should have reneged on that treaty,' said Tommy. 'And he was a hero of the Boer War.'

'Many a country would have reneged,' said Benjamin, 'but not Britain. They are among the most honourable people in the world.'

'Very costly thing, honour,' commented Tommy. 'It's certainly costing a lot of lives.'

'I have no argument with that,' said Benjamin. To their right was an unfenced field beside a small lake – an ideal spot for a picnic. 'I think we're about halfway there. Does anyone wish to stop for a rest and something to eat? We have apples, cheese and cold bratwurst sandwiches. All stolen from the hospital kitchen by my darling daughter. We also have beer, brewed by me.'

Tommy was already slowing down with a big grin on his face. He was having a moment that he hadn't had for many months. All suddenly seemed well with the world. He'd had a few glasses of Benjamin's beer in the past and it was quite palatable. Anna was looking more beautiful than ever, maybe it was the exercise that had brought a bloom to her cheeks; the day was bright and warm; the war seemed a million miles away, and he loved bratwurst sandwiches.

Gefreiter Heinrich Brinkerhoff cursed his bad luck as he rode his creaking bicycle along the same road that Tommy and his companions had travelled ten minutes earlier. He had a Luger pistol in a holster strapped to his waist and across his shoulder was a belt holding a message pouch with a letter for that useless Kapitänleutnant Glöckner.

239

He knew that the Kapitänleutnant was a joke officer who had been promoted into a job where he could do the least harm and he would never be trusted with a message of any great importance, nor the leadership of men in battle. But of course Brinkerhoff was a mere Gefreiter, a lowly private soldier, whose whole day was of less importance than wasting two minutes on a field telephone. It was only two days since he'd come off a three month stretch on the western front, holding back the Allied advance from the Somme. He had known death, terror, and the loss of good friends, not idiots like Kapitänleutnant Glöckner who had never been near the front line. Brinkerhoff was a man with a grudge against the war and the German army in particular. He was also hungry, with his unit being on half rations so that the men at the front didn't go without food. That was the story, but he didn't remember eating well on the front lines. He remembered men shooting crows and dogs to supplement their rations.

When Brinkerhoff arrived at where three bicycles were lying in the grass at the side of the road he dismounted from his own cycle and examined them. Three perfectly good military bicycles, all of them much better machines than the one he was riding. Then he heard laughter from the field beyond. He unclipped the strap over his sidearm holster and walked over to where Tommy and his two companions were enjoying what looked like a delicious al fresco meal, complete with beer.

The scene and their hilarity annoyed the hell out of Brinkerhoff, who saw nothing to laugh at that day. Where did these civilians get their food from to enjoy a picnic? And what right did they have to be on bicycles superior to his? No right at all was the answer. They were military bicycles. These people had to be thieves, stealing food and bicycles. He pulled out his weapon and pointed it at them as he approached. 'Are you the thieves who have stolen those military bicycles?' he shouted. 'And where did you get all that food?'

'Put your weapon down, soldier,' said Benjamin, calmly. 'We are not thieves. I bought those bicycles.'

'They are military bicycles and military property is not for sale,' snarled Brinkerhoff.

'Why are you still pointing your gun at us?' enquired Anna, hotly.

'I am pointing my gun at you because you are thieves.'

'As my father explained, we are not thieves. Stop pointing that gun at us.'

There was a madness in Brinkerhoff's eyes that Benjamin found disconcerting. He saw a problem here and held up a calming hand. 'The bicycles are army surplus. I bought them from an army surplus shop in Mannheim.'

Brinkerhoff aimed his Luger at Benjamin. This angered Anna who hadn't spotted that the soldier looked mentally unbalanced. 'Shouldn't you have asked to see our identity papers or something?' she enquired.

'Do not tell me what to do.'

'I think someone ought to. You're certainly not behaving like a normal soldier.'

'Careful, Anna,' said Benjamin.

Tommy didn't understand what was being said,

241

but he caught the gist of it and he had sufficient presence of mind to keep his English words to himself.

'Yes, careful, Anna,' said Brinkerhoff. 'Do not speak to a German soldier like that or I will have to kill you.'

'I do not think the German army will thank you for murdering a German citizen,' said Benjamin, trying to make the soldier see the lack of logic in what he was saying. But logic was way beyond Heinrich Brinkerhoff, who was going red in the face with annoyance.

'You are thieves, not citizens!' he shrieked.

'Oh, don't be so ridiculous!' said Anna scathingly. 'You are not a soldier, you are an idiot!'

'Oh shit!' murmured Tommy under his breath. He didn't understand her words but it was pretty clear to him that she was insulting this unbalanced, enemy soldier.

Brinkerhoff had been subjected to plenty of such insults from superior officers. He certainly wasn't going to take this from this thieving civilian woman. Up to very recently he had been shooting at his adversaries and this woman was no different from them. He waved his gun back in her direction and pulled the trigger. The bullet missed her, but not by much. She sprang to her feet and instinctively began to run away from this madman. Benjamin was screaming at Brinkerhoff to put his gun down, but the German was taking careful aim at the fleeing Anna. He fired again and this time Anna fell to the ground about thirty yards away from them. Brinkerhoff laughed and strode towards her as she lay on the ground, writing in agony. He stood over her and pointed his Luger at her head to finish her off. She found herself, mute with terror, looking down the barrel of his Luger, behind which was his deranged face. There was another gunshot and Brinkerhoff fell to the ground. Anna had closed her eyes, awaiting her death, but it wasn't to be. She had heard the gun go off but that was all, she still felt alive. She opened one of her eyes to see Brinkerhoff lying on the ground in front of her. Tommy was running over to where she was cowering on the ground, holding her arm, which was bleeding profusely.

'Are you okay?' he asked.

She couldn't find a voice to answer him. Her breath was coming in short gasps.

'Anna, are you okay?'

Her pent-up distress released itself in a hoarse scream of pain. 'Oooh ... m ... my arm hurts!'

'Just your arm?'

'Yes.'

'When you fell I thought...'

'No, I ... I tripped!' She was sobbing now.

She noticed Tommy was holding her father's pistol and also that her father was kneeling over the soldier. Tommy followed her gaze.

'Is he ...?' Tommy asked.

Benjamin nodded. 'He's dead. Good shot, Tommy. If you hadn't shot him he'd have killed Anna for sure. He looked quite mad.'

Tommy was looking all around him to see if the incident had been witnessed by anyone. No one. Just a couple of ancient horses looking at him from over a fence.

They all looked down at the dead German who

had two bullet holes in his head. A small one at the back and a larger one at the front where the single bullet had gone clean through.

'Do you have anything to fix Anna's arm?' Tommy asked Benjamin.

'Yes, I do.' Benjamin went back to where he'd left his rucksack, took out a small doctor's bag and went back to tend to his daughter.

Tommy walked over to a nearby hedge, which was overhanging a deep, water-filled ditch. He went back to where the dead soldier was lying, took him by the feet, dragged him over to the ditch and rolled him into the muddy water where he sank, out of sight. Then he had a disconcerting thought and walked back to Benjamin.

'He was definitely dead, wasn't he?'

'He had a bullet clean through his head, Tommy.'

'Right, just checking.'

Tommy went over to the road and brought the soldier's bicycle back with him. He pushed it into the stream next to the dead soldier. Just the handlebars were sticking above the water. To the casual observer it was just an old bike whose owner had dumped it in the stream. In fact it was out of sight to anyone more than six feet away and even then they'd have to be looking for it. He looked around to see if he'd removed all traces of the German, then saw the Luger lying in the grass. He dropped it into the ditch. Satisfied that his work was done he went over to where Benjamin was bandaging his daughter's arm.

'How is she?'

Anna was silent now but shaking violently and

squeezing her eyes together to hold back tears and failing in this. Benjamin tied off the final fold of the bandage and looked into his daughter's eyes. Then he turned to Tommy. 'Physically she's not too bad, under the circumstances. The bullet just creased her arm. I had some of the latest antiseptic ointment which should help a lot and I've given her a mild opiate for the pain which means she won't be able to ride any further today. If she does she'll keep falling off.

'Right now she's in shock,' he added. 'A few minutes ago she thought she had just two seconds to live.'

'I know that feeling,' said Tommy, remembering the young German soldier whose gun misfired as he aimed it at him.

'I doubt that, Thomas,' said Benjamin. 'If it happened to you in the heat of battle you will have been mentally prepared for the eventuality of death and capable of keeping your wits about you ... well, to a certain extent.'

Tommy nodded as he remembered thinking quickly enough to pick up his own gun and shoot the German.

'Anna went straight from a moment of happiness to a moment of imminent death at the hands of a madman. What she needs now,' said Benjamin, 'is a hug from someone she loves.'

Tommy looked at Benjamin as the most likely candidate for this, but Benjamin inclined his head back at Tommy, selecting him for the job.

Tommy knelt beside Anna and took her in his arms, hugging her to him as she held her father's hand. The three of them stayed like that for several minutes until Anna's body stopped shaking. Tommy relaxed his hold on her, kissed her forehead and ran his fingers through her hair. She wiped away her tears with the heel of her hand and gave Tommy a fractured smile, still unable to speak.

'What was all that about?' Tommy said to Benjamin. 'I could see he was a madman but I didn't understand a word of what he was saying.'

'It was about the German army putting a uniform on a deranged man and giving him a gun,' said Benjamin. 'He accused us of stealing the bicycles. Called us all thieves, which he seemed to think gave him the right to shoot us. Sometimes the war gets to men and sends them over the edge, even when they're safely behind the lines. They see the enemy where no enemy exists. I'm guessing he wasn't a long time away from the front. The horror of war doesn't leave the mind when the man leaves the battle lines.'

'I suspect Anna wound him up a bit,' said Tommy.

'Yes, she did indeed. She called him an idiot. Did you see it coming, Thomas?'

'When he waved the gun at you I expected something, so I took our gun out of my rucksack while he wasn't looking. If I hadn't, I wouldn't have been ready to shoot him.'

'Anna owes you her life.'

'I owe her about six lives.'

Benjamin got to his feet. 'We must make camp in this field,' he said. 'I have brought two tents, one for Anna and myself, and one for you.'

Tommy winked at the look of disappointment

that Anna pulled behind her father's back. 'I suggest we pitch the tents and put the bikes where they can't be seen from the road,' Tommy added. 'No point inviting any more curious visitors.'

'Good idea,' said Benjamin. 'Is the erm, corpse out of sight?'

'I doubt if anyone will find him for a while, but if he's missed today someone might come looking for him.'

'If they do we must have a story to tell them upon which we're all agreed,' said Benjamin. 'I suggest we keep it simple, and just say we didn't see him.'

'What about the bandage on Anna's arm?'

'She must wear her coat and keep it on at all times. We were lucky today, Tommy.'

'I know. I hope it's not going to be like this all the way to Nancy.'

'I think the nearer we get the worse it will get,' said Benjamin. 'How do you feel, by the way?'

'You mean after killing a man?'

'Yes.'

'I feel as though I've gone against one of the principal rules of nature. I've killed the enemy at close range before, it's what I'm trained to do, but I'm told that taking another man's life always gets to you ... if you're normal.'

'I'd say you are perfectly normal.'

'I need to keep telling myself what would have happened if I hadn't shot him.'

Anna found her voice. 'I'd be ... d ... dead is what would have happened, Tommy.'

Tommy put his arm around her once more. 'Well, you keep saving my life. Today it was my turn to save yours.'

Benjamin closed his eyes as the reality of what had happened hit him. He had been so close to losing his darling daughter. He took the two of them in a silent bear hug and held them until they had to forcibly escape his grip.

Shielding the field from the road was a row of redcurrant bushes, some up to six feet tall. It was in the shade of these bushes that Tommy and Benjamin erected the two tents. An intruder would have to walk several yards into the field and look over to his left to be able to see the tents, which were themselves in camouflage colours so not immediately obvious to the casual eye. They spent the rest of the afternoon and evening talking and eating the rest of their food and drink in the hope that the people in Freckenfeld would be able to replenish their supplies.

'If not there are shops in the town and I have brought plenty of money with me,' said Benjamin. 'In fact I have brought every mark I have in the world, without selling my house, and believe me I would have done that if I could have found a buyer.'

'Maybe you should share some of it with us,' said Anna. 'In case we get split up for any reason.'

'Good thinking. I will give you two hundred marks each, which is equivalent to twenty English pounds.'

'Or four months' army pay,' said Tommy.

'Canned food would be a good idea,' suggested Anna, who had regained much of her composure. Tommy was inwardly comparing her favourably to Rita on the day the German ships fired on

Scarborough. Both girls were made of the same steel but, if and when the time came, he would have to choose Rita, who was his wife. A man must always choose his wife – unless she was a bad wife, and Rita was far from that.

Every time they heard anyone coming along the road, be it in a motor vehicle or horse or just footsteps their conversation ceased, as they all listened in the hope that the passers-by would do just that. They all did, but this only happened six times in four hours. At around seven o'clock the sun went down over the western hills and Benjamin suggested they take to their beds.

'I will wake at dawn which will be around six-thirty,' he said. Anna nodded her confirmation to Tommy that her dad would indeed awake at this time. Tommy waved a hand to say he was impressed and said goodnight to them both.

'And don't lie on your arm, Anna.'

'Thomas, I am a nurse. I know these things.'

He grinned and took to his tent. For an hour he lay there, first listening to the sounds of Anna and her father talking quietly. Then the talking stopped and the only sound he heard was that of someone walking along the road, whistling, but not very well. Tommy could have taught this man a thing or two about whistling, or maybe it was a woman. No, he didn't know any women who were good at whistling. His dad now, his dad could whistle for England. He never needed a whistle to blow for tea-break on site, he just stuck two fingers in his mouth and let out a whistle loud enough to stop work on all the building sites in Pontefract – at least that was his, boast.

His dad often boasted about silly things, but never the things he was entitled to boast about, such as his DCM which might well have been a VC had there been an officer around to witness what he did. Tommy smiled in the dark as he remembered his dad's face when the Koylis marched through Pontefract calling out the Squinty McBride marching chant. Then he remembered his first visit to Rita's house which ended in her bedroom. That was a night he'd never forget. She had left him with so many memories, that girl. That beautiful girl.

Snoring from the next tent. He knew it wasn't Anna. He definitely knew that Anna didn't snore. He was now hoping that no one else would come along and investigate where this noise was coming from. Perhaps they should have pitched their tents at the far side of the field. Should he warn Benjamin of this? His tent flap opened and Anna came in. She was just a shadow but he knew it was her.

'Move over,' she said. 'I'm sleeping with you.'

'What if your dad wakes up?'

'He won't. He's a creature of habit is my dad, and he's not in the habit of waking up in the middle of the night.'

She snuggled up to him and put her arm around him nuzzling his neck as her father snored on, seemingly louder. There was an approaching engine noise in the distance. Probably a motor cycle, Tommy thought. It seemed to be slowing down, stopping now with the engine just ticking over. Tommy went over to the tent flap and peeped out. A strong beam of light, no doubt from the machine's headlight, was sweeping across the field as the rider moved the handlebars from side to side.

The sound of the engine ticking over was just obscuring Benjamin's snoring but not by much. Tommy reached into his knapsack for the pistol and held it at the ready. Anna said nothing, she knew exactly what was happening.

The rider switched his engine off and shouted, 'Gefreiter Brinkerhoff! Gefreiter Brinkerhoff!' Then he went quiet, to listen for any response.

By this time Tommy was in Benjamin's tent, with his hand over the older man's nose, whispering urgently in his ear.

'You're snoring and we've got a visit–!'

He was interrupted by another shout.

'Brinkerhoff... Gefreiter Heinrich Brinkerhoff!'

Tommy crept out of the tent and lay flat on the ground with his gun aimed steadily at the man on the motor bike whose silhouette stood out clearly against the moonlit sky. No doubt the man would be armed. If he dismounted and came their way Tommy would shoot him dead. The only thought in his mind was to protect Anna and her father against the enemy. There were four bullets in his gun and he was hoping to get the job done with just one, to keep the noise down to a minimum. He was confident he could do it. The man on the motor cycle shouted again.

'Brinkerhoff... Gefreiter Heinrich Brinkerhoff. *Bist du da?*'

All was quiet. The two men heard the motor cycle being kicked back into life and the machine roared away with the rider not realising how close

251

he'd just come to death.

'What was he saying?' Tommy asked.

'He was asking Corporal Heinrich Brinkerhoff if he was there.' Heinrich Brinkerhoff. Tommy now knew the name of the man he'd killed. He would try and forget it. Not knowing names was easier to handle.

'I wonder what made him look in this field?' Benjamin asked.

'He's probably stopping at all the likely places the man might have bedded down for the night.'

Benjamin looked around his tent, asking, 'Where's Anna?'

'She's in my tent. Couldn't sleep with you snoring. She's perfectly safe with me.'

Benjamin paused before saying. 'Hmm, under the circumstances I suppose it makes sense for her to share with you.'

'Perfect sense,' said Tommy, who was still holding the gun. 'At least she'll get a good night's sleep.'

'We must hope so,' said Benjamin. 'We must let her sleep late tomorrow to regain her strength.'

The major part of Anna and Tommy's night was devoted to sleep.

But not all of it.

At eleven-thirty the following morning they had been riding for two hours and were almost at Freckenfeld when they came across two mounted soldiers heading their way. They wore smart grey uniforms and helmets surmounted by steel spikes. Tommy noticed mainly their leather knee-length boots which were identical to the ones he

252

was wearing. One of them pointed at his boots and said something to him in German.

Benjamin answered for him and the soldiers seemed satisfied. They asked for identification which was provided. Tommy had been given a form of identification provided by Mannheim Hospital which identified him as unknown soldier patient Thomas Schmidt, currently undergoing treatment. A further conversation went on between the soldiers and Benjamin, who were now impressed that they were talking to a senior doctor, whose rank, had he been a soldier, would have been much higher than theirs. They parted company on friendly terms and, when they were out of earshot, Tommy asked what had been said.

'When they found out we were doctor, nurse and patient they became respectful. Even respectful of you, as your treatment involved taking fresh air and exercise to restore your sanity.'

'Sanity? You told them I was insane?'

'I gave them a technical term for it which they wouldn't understand.'

'He baffled them with bullshit,' Anna explained.

'Bullshit baffles brains,' said Tommy.

Benjamin continued: 'They asked how long we had been riding and I said since dawn. Then they asked if we had seen a soldier on a bicycle and I said we hadn't. They asked about our bicycles and I told them I had bought them from a shop which deals in such things in Mannheim. They said something about the soldier going AWOL yesterday, but it would be a pleasant horse ride over to Mannheim where they would spend the night and return tomorrow, having conducted a thorough search for the deserter. I wished them a good journey.'

'How's the arm bearing up, Anna?' Tommy asked.

'Not too bad. I'll be glad of a rest in Freckenfeld.'

'I suggest we have a two-hour break to rest and replenish our supplies, then we head out again this afternoon,' said Benjamin.

'Head where?' Tommy asked.

'Further south to Betschdorf. We have a friend there.'

'How far?'

'Twenty-five kilometres.'

Tommy looked at Anna. 'If the road's flat and we don't have to shoot any soldiers we could do it in two hours.'

Anna treated him to one of her whitest smiles and said, 'I could do it in an hour and a half.'

'So, it's a race is it?'

'Could be. If I lose, I sleep with dad and his snoring.'

'What if I lose? Do I sleep with him?'

'No, if you lose you sleep with me.'

'Then I accept the challenge, knowing that I will be magnificent in defeat.'

Benjamin was pretending he couldn't hear this conversation but he was happy enough for his daughter to have taken a liking to this young man who had already saved her life, probably his as well. He was also happy to be able to inform them that his friend in Betschdorf would be able to give them a room each.

254

In Freckenfeld, Carla, Benjamin's sister, cooked them a chicken that had been running round the garden that morning, after which, Anna put herself straight to bed.

They lived in a small farmhouse on the edge of the village, a suitable distance away from the gossiping patriots who might suspect their hatred of the Kaiser. With her husband now dead and she unable to do the work as well as raise a family, the farm was now untended, like many farms all over Germany. Carla was vociferous in her condemnation of the Kaiser.

'Did it not occur to the idiot that taking our men away from us would destroy our country a lot quicker than any enemy could? That idiot's the country's biggest enemy.'

'How are you all managing?' Benjamin asked.

'We have just ten chickens left that we save for eggs and emergencies,' Carla told him. 'Our people are starving. They are eating dogs and crows.'

'So I've heard,' said Benjamin. 'The good news is that Germany is losing this war, which is why we are heading for the Allied lines.'

'I wish you well, my brother. But your journey from here will be dangerous, not just from the German army but from the Allied aeroplanes that are no longer just used for reconnaissance, they are now dropping bombs and shooting guns this side of the western front. Especially on the approaches to Nancy in France. They even shot down a Zeppelin returning from a bombing raid on England.'

'I can hardly blame them for that. Where will I

255

be able to buy supplies?'

'If you have money I can point you to the right man. His name is Bruno. I despise him because he is a crook and a black marketeer, but he will be able to give you what you need for the right price. You must not tell him who you are and definitely not where you are going. He will sell that information to the Germans as quickly as he will sell you a loaf of bread.'

'War tends to spew up types like that,' said Benjamin. 'Anna has been wounded in her arm. I will need to put a clean dressing on her.'

'Then I suggest we keep her here tonight at least until she gets stronger.'

'Thank you. A good rest will do her arm the world of good.'

He told her the story of the dead German soldier which shocked her into wanting to help somehow. 'If you wish, I will visit Bruno myself and purchase your supplies for you.'

'Thank you, and you must purchase some for yourself,' he said. 'As much as you need. I have plenty of money which will be useless once we cross the lines.'

'You may need it between here and Nancy. I hear that bribery is working with some soldiers and who can blame them, having to fight and die for an overblown shit like the Kaiser?'

'You have a way with words, Carla. It would be wise to keep most of them to yourself.'

After a night's comfortable rest and a good lunch, Benjamin and Anna bade tearful farewells to their family in Freckenfeld. Their supplies

256

were replenished, as were Carla's, and Anna's wound had been properly cleaned and dressed. They had spread their map out on the kitchen table and plotted a route to Betschdorf across the border in France, where an elderly Frenchman called Sébastien would help them.

'Do you know this man?' Benjamin had asked Carla.

'He was a friend of my husband and I first met him when he came here to express his condolences about Hugo's death. When he has anything of importance to tell me he comes to Freckenfeld on his horse and trap and stops at the gate for me to take him some refreshment and exchange information. He is a strange and eccentric character and the last man the secret police would suspect. They are brutal but not terribly well organised and would not believe in a million years that he has information of any use to our movement. Where he gets his information from I do not know.'

'Is he your only contact?'

'Apart from you he is. I am just a link in a chain... You?'

'Same chain. I too only have one contact apart from you. A priest in Mannheim.'

'Ah, let me guess. He passes to you the secrets of the confessional.'

'Exactly,' said Benjamin. 'He's a real mine of valuable information. There are more than just me going to his confessional and all our collective information is shared without any of us knowing who the other ones are. In fact not even the priest is supposed to know who we all are.'

'So, how does he know *what* you are?'

'You mean against the war?'

'Yes.'

'Well, from my demeanour I imagine. I go to confession once a month to confess my pathetic sins and I suppose he got to recognise my voice and one day I found myself in conversation with him about the war. I expressed my misgivings about the Kaiser and his ridiculous war in no uncertain terms, knowing that even if he suspected my identity I was protected by the seal of the Sacrament of Penance.

'He told me he was of like mind and that there were others who came to his confessional of like mind. He also mentioned that although our sins would always be kept an absolute secret there was no Catholic law against him giving out advice based on information he received in the confessional. I did have an item of information for him which I know was passed on and acted upon.'

'About one of your patients?'

'As it happens, yes.'

'But aren't you also bound by an oath?'

'I am, but I am also bound by a sense of duty to humanity as a whole which, in dire times such as this, must be balanced against professional integrity.'

'You always did believe in fighting fire with fire.'

'Right now it is the only way, Carla. Thomas fought fire with fire back there on the road. If he hadn't, my darling Anna would be dead.'

'Sébastien is a devout Catholic,' said Carla. 'I wonder if we have solved the mystery of where he gets his information from? Maybe there are priests all through the chain, collecting and dispensing secret information in their confessionals.'

'That is not as stupid as it sounds,' said Benjamin. 'No secret meeting places for the secret police to find. No messages in hidden places. Just one brave and trusted man collecting information and spreading it around in the most secret of all places by word of mouth to people he has learned to trust but whose identity he does not know.'

'Put like that, what can possibly go wrong?' said Carla.

'In war anything can go wrong. All we can do is use the brains God has given us to outwit them.'

Carla's two daughters were sad to see Tommy come and go so quickly. 'Can't you leave him with us?' they asked their cousin, Anna, only half-jokingly.

'He comes with us, and you never speak about him to anyone,' Anna warned them, sternly. 'Or about any of us.'

Both girls mimed locking their mouths shut. They knew all about keeping quiet for fear of reprisal. It was a way of life for them – better than a way of death.

Chapter 35

April 30th 1917

'According to my reckoning,' said Benjamin, 'we are now in France. I think we crossed the border five kilometres back.'

'Are we?' said Tommy. 'Not sure I feel any safer.'

It was early evening and they had ridden at a leisurely pace that day to allow Anna time to recover and had stopped cycling for a breather. They were eating cheese and tomato sandwiches by the side of a small road. Benjamin was perusing the stolen wall map.

'How do you know?' asked Anna.

'We have just passed a sign saying Trimbach, which is here.' He stabbed a finger on the map, then moved it an inch forward and added, 'I believe we are here.'

The three of then stared at the narrow, country road; just two thin, black lines amid a tracery of others. Tommy pointed to Betschdorf, not too far away.

'How far would you say we are from here?' he asked Benjamin.

The doctor looked at his pocket watch. 'It is five-thirty, if we travel non-stop we should be there before six. First we need to get on the main road ... here,' he pointed to a road drawn in thicker lines, 'or we will miss Betschdorf altogether. I have the directions to Sébastien's house in my head.

When we enter the village this road becomes the main street with a school on the left where we turn right. About one kilometre up this road there is a stone house in an orchard to our right. There will be an old white horse in the orchard. This is Sébastien's house.'

He moved his finger across the map and said, 'His house is about here.'

Ten minutes later they arrived on the main road, which was barely busier than the roads they'd been travelling on. In fact Tommy was beginning to think they'd have been better off using such roads from the start as it was a more direct route. It was then that he heard the noise of traffic coming from behind. He looked around and saw a column of military vehicles approaching them. Up until then most of the vehicles they had come across had been horse-drawn, or even just horses with people mounted upon them. This was a column of mainly motorised vehicles.

Captain Eustace Gibbons of the Royal Flying Corps leaned sideways from the cockpit of his Armstrong Whitworth FK8 biplane and looked down at the ground three thousand feet below. He was a hundred miles beyond the western front, almost at the France/Germany border and he'd seen no action. Behind him sat Sergeant Mick Heller, fingers drumming on the Lewis gun mounted on the edge of his cockpit. Suddenly he tapped Gibbons on the shoulder and yelled into his ear. 'Down there. Road at three o'clock.'

Gibbons glanced down to his right where a road ran from the north east. Maybe two miles away and heading their way was a column of moving vehicles, some probably horse-drawn – hard to make out from this distance. What he did know was that it would be a supply column heading for the front; a bona-fide target. He stuck up a thumb for his sergeant to ready his weapon. Gibbons had a front-firing Vickers machine gun of his own but he preferred giving flying his full attention when they were in action. It was how he had won the tag Flying Ace; along with his sergeant they had forty-three victories.

As well as the guns the aircraft was armed with four 29 kg bombs on underwing racks. The enemy column was an ideal target for these. Gibbons pointed to the wings, indicating he was planning a bombing run. He swung the aircraft round in a slow arc then straightened up as he lined himself up with the road below and increased the revs for a high-speed dive. He stuck two fingers up indicating that they were to drop just two bombs, the other two he'd save for a return attack. Heller tapped him once on his leather helmet to say he understood. Half a minute later he had dropped from three thousand to one thousand feet and was flying straight and level at the aircraft's maximum speed of 95 mph. The column approached him rapidly; Heller's hand was on the lever that worked the bomb rack; enemy rifle fire was coming their way, the odd bullet passing through the plane's canvas covering. They were passing over the front vehicles when a bullet came though the bottom of the plane right beneath where Heller was sitting.

'Aaah! Jesus!'

The shock jerked his hand on the lever. Two

bombs fell and took out three vehicles which were now behind the plane. Heller was howling in pain.

Soon they were being overtaken. The three of them pulled up to allow this to happen. At the head of the column were two private cars, each carrying four officers of high rank. Benjamin and Anna waved at them, shouting words of encouragement. Tommy simply smiled the smile of the simpleton he might have to claim to be, but the column moved on and, not being checked by the officers, the rest of the column saw no reason to question them. Behind these were four personnel carriers, each carrying around twenty men and their rifles. Then ten trucks passed them, most with canvas canopies which Tommy took to be ammunition trucks; others carried men; others pulled trailers carrying field guns; others had open backs, carrying wooden boxes, possibly tinned food Tommy guessed. There were motor cycles, many with sidecars, each carrying an armed soldier with rifle at the ready; several horse boxes, a cattle truck and, at the end of the line, what Tommy took to be an armoured car with two machine guns mounted on the back.

The line had almost passed them when Tommy saw the biplane hurtling towards them. Above the roar of the traffic he knew his English words would never carry to the Germans.

'It's one of ours, Benjamin. Quick, into the ditch!'

Right beside them was a deep ditch. Tommy grabbed Anna and pushed her in just as the first bombs dropped, near the head of the column.

The blast passed over the tops of their heads but the noise was deafening. All three of them pressed themselves into the bottom of the ditch and held their hands to their ears as bushes and trees were blasted away, vehicle parts flew through the air. Tommy saw the remains of a soldier fall into the ditch only feet away from where they were cowering. Then an arm, then a head. He looked at Anna and, to his consternation, saw splashes of blood on her. He was about to ask if she was all right when he realised that he too was being splashed with dead men's blood. He was too shocked to feel the nausea this would normally have caused.

The noise subsided until all that could be heard were various engine noises, orders being shouted and men screaming with pain. Benjamin looked at Tommy and said, 'It's gone.'

'It might come back,' said Tommy, who knew a little about aerial bombardment. He looked up from the ditch and saw the plane turning for another run. 'He's coming back,' he reported.

Benjamin and Anna flattened themselves into the bottom of the ditch once again. Tommy did the same.

Gibbons gained height and looked back at his colleague whose face was white and drained with pain.

'Where?' he asked.

'Arse,' grunted Heller.

'Ouch! I'd like to drop the other two.'

'Hhggghh.'

Gibbons took this as a "Yes" and turned the plane round for another bombing run. Heller

264

managed to pull the lever at the right time, destroying two more trucks. Gibbons gained height and headed back for the Allied line at top speed, appreciating the pain his sergeant must be in.

Benjamin climbed out of the ditch and, carrying his medical bag, he ran to where several German soldiers were lying in the road, dead and dying. Anna and Tommy were close on his heels. Benjamin was calling out for any first aid supplies the column might be carrying, telling anyone who cared to listen that he was a doctor. Not far away was a fiercely burning truck. A German soldier appeared, carrying a first aid kit. Benjamin took it from him and called out to Anna.

'Take this and go to the head of the column. Just do what you can.'

'What about me?' Tommy asked him, quietly. 'Do you want me here or with Anna?'

'It's up to you, Thomas,' murmured Benjamin in English. Both of them were still wary of being overheard speaking the enemy's language, although most of the men around them had no interest in what language they were speaking.

Anna took the kit and raced the other way, now closely followed by Tommy, whose main aim was to protect her. The carnage awaiting them made Tommy wonder what the hell they were supposed to do. Two trucks were ablaze, a third completely destroyed, one of the cars was upside down in a field and also burning. Men and bits of men were all around. Tommy wouldn't have known where to start.

'We can only work on one at a time,' Anna was

265

saying. 'This man here. Let's take a look at him.'

The man in question was lying on his back, his uniform soaked in blood. Anna managed to unbutton it until his intestines fell out. She put two fingers to his neck and said, 'He's dead. Let's try him over there.'

The second man had lost an arm and most of his face. Anna looked in the kit and found a syringe, which she filled from a bottle marked morphine. She injected the full syringe into his shoulder and looked at Tommy, whispering, 'It's all I can do for him. He needs surgery right now.'

A third man had a single wound to his side. Anna now spoke only in German but Tommy pretty much understood that she was saying she could help this man. She gave him morphine and dressed his wound. Tommy looked around and saw they could only attend to maybe one in twenty of those needing attention, but it was this one who was the lucky one. Why deprive him of his luck? A man needed luck in times of war and Tommy had had his fair share. She was looking at him now.

'What?' he said.

'My arm hurts like hell. I'm not sure I can do much more.'

'Let me have a look.'

She took off her coat and revealed her bandaged arm. The bandage was soaked in blood.

'Maybe if I gave myself an injection of morphine and showed you how to dress it,' she suggested.

'No, maybe we should let your dad take a look at it.'

'My father has enough to do.'

'We'll let him decide that, shall w–?'

His last word was cut off by a tremendous explosion. They looked back to where Benjamin was working but he was out of sight around a bend in the road, which was why the blast from the explosion didn't affect Tommy and Anna as much as it might have. It came from the blazing ammunition truck that was stopped just a few feet away from where Benjamin was working. The explosion lasted several seconds as box after box detonated. The last ten boxes all went off at once with a colossal bang that could easily be heard five miles away in Betschdorf and way beyond. Just the fringe of the blast flung Anna and Tommy to the ground where they lay for ten seconds before Anna got to her feet and set off running to where she'd last seen her father. Tommy followed her. They both stopped short of the scene of total devastation. Benjamin was nowhere to be seen, nor were the men he'd been working on. On the ground and still hanging in the air were minuscule bits of man and machine, nothing bigger than a man's toe, such was the force of the explosion. There was a hole in the road ten feet deep, inside which was nothing; around which was nothing – nothing alive anyway.

Anna looked at Tommy. 'Where is my father?'

Tommy knew exactly where he was. The answer was, "all around us", but he wasn't going to say it. He put his arm around her shoulder but he knew she took no comfort from it. The only arm she wanted right then was in a thousand pieces. He felt her collapsing and took her weight.

A German officer appeared behind them and said something that Tommy didn't understand. Without looking at the man he just shrugged, mutely, hoping that might be the correct reaction to what the man had said.

'*Mein Vater ist tot,*' said Anna.

Tommy understood this and tried to think of a sympathetic phrase in German for the benefit of the officer.

'*Es tut mir Leid,* Anna,' he murmured, eventually – *I am sorry, Anna.*

The officer moved away without saying a word to them.

The British plane had gone, having dropped all its bombs. Tommy was wondering how Anna might feel about this Englishman holding on to her – the same nationality as those who had just killed her father.

'Your father isn't here any more and we need to go.'

'I cannot just leave him.'

'Anna, he's no longer here for you to leave, and the longer we stay here the more dangerous it becomes for us. Your dad would want us to leave.'

'Would he?'

'Rita, he died in the blink of an eye, doing the job he loved and he'd want you to be safe. Wherever we go now he'll be with us.'

'Will he?'

'Yes.'

Tommy was now becoming quite agitated at her reluctance to get a move on. 'Rita, we need to move. I need to get you safe and it isn't safe here with all these burning trucks. Another could go

268

up any bloody second.'

'My name is Anna, not Rita,' she mumbled.

She put up no resistance as he led her away to where their bicycles were. He was still holding her coat which he put around her shoulders as she mounted the bicycle, wobbled off and immediately fell to the ground.

'Just walk with it until we get clear,' Tommy said. 'Quick as you can.'

She did as he asked, with him walking beside her past burning vehicles and dying men. Another ammunition truck exploded behind them, adjacent to the very ground they'd just left. Anna looked round, then at Tommy.

'I think you just saved my life, Tommy.'

'Just keep moving, Anna.'

'At least you remember my name now.'

'Sorry about that.'

When they were clear he helped her to mount and held the saddle as she set off, running beside her until he was confident she'd be okay. Then he went back for his own machine and caught her up. Before they reached Betschdorf she'd fallen off four more times, but each time she remounted herself without saying a word. Her stoicism and courage had Tommy marvelling at her.

'Do you know the way to Sébastien's house?' she asked, eventually.

Tommy was remembering Benjamin's words when he said he had the directions in his head. *When we enter the village this road becomes the main street with a school on the left where we turn right. About one kilometre up this road there is a stone house in an orchard to our right. There will be an old white horse in the orchard. This is Sébastien's house.*

'Yes,' he said. 'Your father gave me the directions.'

He took the lead and led her to Sébastien's house where an old white horse was looking at them from over the fence. Under other circumstances Anna would have abandoned her bike and run across to it to pat it on its nose but today she gave it scarcely a glance as Tommy opened the gate and both of them walked through, pushing their bicycles. As they approached the door it was as though a floodgate of tears had been opened. They streamed down her pale cheeks, soundlessly. He stood with his arm around her and knocked on the door.

Sébastien answered the door and stood there amazed at the sight before him. 'Carla from Freckenfeld sent us,' Tommy explained, hoping he understood English. 'This is Anna, her niece. Her father was just killed back on the road.'

'Yes. I heard the explosions. It was an aeroplane dropping bombs, I assume?'

Sébastien spoke English quite fluently, which would prove to be handy. He was a wizened old man with a grey beard and startling blue eyes. His teeth were much too white and even for them to be his own but his grey hair was most definitely genuine and quite luxuriant for a man of his advanced years.

'Please come in, my dears. Carla's niece, you say? And her father is dead?'

'Yes. He was killed by an exploding German truck.'

'And why were you with him?'

270

'It's a long story, and we really need to get Anna inside.'

'Of course, I am so sorry, but I tend to be far too talkative when I have visitors which is almost never nowadays. I seem to have outlived most of my visitors.'

He walked with a stoop but his steps were lively enough. Like a trained dancer whose spine had let him down a bit. Tommy wheeled both bicycles into a small hallway and, holding Anna by the hand, he followed Sébastien into a large living room, furnished mainly in wood except for a large, leather settee.

'Would you like a drink of coffee or cognac or some such thing?'

Tommy looked at Anna whose eyes were still streaming. She shook her head.

'I'll have a coffee, nothing for Anna. She's still suffering from shock. It all happened less than an hour ago.'

'Oh the poor girl! British plane I assume?'

'Yes. It bombed a German supply convoy which just happened to be passing us.'

'And you were heading for me?'

'Yes. I'm a British soldier and the three of us are heading for the Allied lines. I'll explain how I came to know them later. My immediate problem is how to deal with Anna and her grief. I have no experience in such matters.'

Sébastien sighed. 'Ah, the only cure for grief is time. I have known my share of it in my lifetime. Grief and talking and having another reason for living.' He looked at Tommy quizzically. 'Dare I ask if you might be a good reason for her living?'

271

'Anna and I are lovers,' said Tommy, amazed at his openness with this old man whom he'd only known for a few minutes. 'But I am married to a wonderful woman in England.'

'Really? A wife and a mistress? Perhaps you have French blood in you somewhere.'

'It's all undiluted Yorkshire as far as I know.'

'Ah, a Yorkshireman. I am told you never have to ask a Yorkshireman where he comes from because if he is from Yorkshire he will have already told you – and if he is not from Yorkshire why embarrass him?'

Tommy smiled. 'You've got that right.'

'And it is to England and Yorkshire that you are headed?'

'Hopefully, yes.'

Sébastien looked at Anna, who was perched on the edge of the settee, as if ready to get up again any second. Sébastien was unsure if she was listening to them or not. 'I will make you that coffee,' he said eventually.

After he left the room Tommy sat beside her and took her hand. 'Would it help if I told you I loved you?'

Her eyes, which had been flickering around the wooden room, suddenly fixed themselves on him as she said, 'You told him we were lovers.'

'I did. I'm sorry if you think I've betrayed a secret.'

Her eyes were still moist. She shook her head and said, simply, 'You told him the truth. Thomas, I will never love anyone as much as I love you, but I cannot have you ... can I?' The last two words were phrased as a question.

'I don't know the answer to that, Anna – other than to say, I love you.'

'You ... you said my father will be travelling with us.'

'I did, and I genuinely believe that to be true. He set out with us on this journey and I'm sure he'll want to finish it with us.'

'Will he know how the journey ends – for me, I mean?'

Tommy knew exactly what she meant. 'I would think so. I'd like to think he was watching over me as well.'

'So he'll be watching over us both?'

Tommy nodded, realising just how powerful his love was for this remarkable woman. He took her in his arms.

'Every step of the way, my darling.'

'And we will take all of these steps together?'

'We will,' he said.

Rita was a million miles away from his thoughts as he said those words but, with Anna in a state of deep grief over just losing her father, she needed such conviction from Tommy. It would help them both get through the most dangerous part of their journey.

'Your father was a brave man, Anna. He will have known the burning truck contained explosives, but his work was more important than his safety.'

'He should have taken his patient to a place of safety.'

'Maybe he needed to finish an urgent procedure before he moved the patient.'

'That is possible,' she conceded.

'And that means he died bravely. Giving up his life for his fellow man. Even if that man was his enemy.'

'Nothing makes sense, Tommy. Not my father's death, not you and me ... nothing.'

'How's the arm?' Tommy asked.

He helped her off with her coat and saw that the bandage was completely saturated with blood.

'I'll see if Sébastien has any first aid stuff.' A thought struck him. 'It's a good job your father told us exactly where Sébastien lived.'

'My father allowed for all eventualities.'

'If he hadn't told us we'd be up the creek without a paddle.'

'What is this creek?' asked Anna.

Tommy smiled. She was coming round enough to ask questions.

'Just one of my daft sayings. I mean we'd have been struggling had we not known how to get here. We've got no map, nothing, just an old man called Sébastien who we don't know from Adam.'

'My father always looked after me.'

'He looked after you until the end, Anna.'

'*And after the end* ... will you look after me?'

'I will.'

Sébastien was returning with Tommy's coffee. He had overheard the tail-end of their conversation.

'I have a suggestion to make,' he said, handing Tommy the cup. 'I suspect Anna will turn it down but I need to throw it into the mix of what you do from here. And I do this because your journey from here will be most dangerous.'

'It hasn't exactly been plain-sailing up to here,'

said Tommy.

'Ah, plain sailing, another of your English phrases. I understand that one. Do you understand it, Anna?'

He was trying to distract her grief by engaging her in light conversation but she was having none of it.

'What is your suggestion?' she asked him.

He sat down on a wooden dining chair directly opposite her and Tommy. 'My suggestion is this: You, Anna, are wounded both physically and emotionally and to succeed in the next part of your journey you need to be at your very best.'

'Are you saying we should give up?'

'No, I am first asking if the people at Mannheim will be wondering where you are?'

'Not yet,' said Anna.

'She's supposed to be taking three days' leave,' said Tommy. 'She's not due back until tomorrow.'

'So, if you returned tomorrow no suspicion will be attached to you, or even if you returned one day late having experienced severe trauma.'

'What are you getting at, Sébastien?' Anna asked.

'Well, it seems to me that Thomas will have more chance of succeeding if he goes on from here on his own. I take you back to Mannheim on my horse and trap and you explain that your father and Tommy were both killed when the plane attacked the convoy.'

'But the people there saw us both ride off.'

'No matter. You both rode off, then you kept falling off your bicycle and sent Thomas for help. Thomas did not return and I happened upon you. You have no idea where Thomas is, but with him having mental problems it is hardly surprising that he got himself lost.'

Tommy took up the story. 'It's an idea, Anna. That way you can go back to Mannheim and carry on with your life with no repercussions. If you stick with me the odds are that we'll get caught and both of us will be shot. If I get caught on my own I'll tell them absolutely nothing. They'll have no reason to associate me with the missing German soldier Thomas Schmidt.'

'But, Thomas, you definitely will get caught if I'm not with you. You don't speak German, or French for that matter. At least if I'm with you I can do all the talking. I speak both languages.'

'Maybe we should both go back, then,' said Tommy.

The room went quiet for ten full minutes as Anna and Tommy thought about this. Sébastien decided to contribute nothing further. He'd done enough.

'My father would be most disappointed,' said Anna, eventually.

They both looked at her but made no comment. There was none to make. She was right. Two minutes later she spoke again.

'It means he would have died for nothing.'

Neither man could argue with this.

'My father gave his life helping us to escape and now we're talking about giving up.'

'Perhaps if Sébastien is kind enough to let us stay here until you are feeling stronger,' suggested Tommy. 'Then we can decide what to do.'

They both looked at the old man who gave a

Gallic shrug and said, '*Mes amis,* you are both most welcome to stay here as long as you wish.'

The following morning Tommy woke up in a small bed in a small room, knowing that Anna was in the much larger bedroom next to his – and in a much larger bed for that matter. He had slept badly with his head a mass of confused thoughts; none of them about his chances of getting home alive. He didn't fancy those chances one bit.

He could go back to Mannheim with Anna and continue to play the mentally confused German soldier, but he felt deep down that this subterfuge had run its course. A man is entitled to a limited amount of luck and he'd already exceeded that limit by some way. Not being blown up alongside Benjamin was an incredible stroke of luck. Had he not chosen to help Anna he wouldn't be alive now.

So what to do? Should he take Anna with him as he tried to find a way across No Man's Land or should he go alone? With German-speaking Anna by his side his chances were probably better, but so was the chance of him leading her to a firing squad. Could he even live with that possibility? He loved Anna just as much as he loved Rita, or was that because Anna was here and now, and Rita wasn't? In fact the odds were that his darling Rita might definitely be never. Had he known she was pregnant it would have swayed him heavily in her direction, but right now she was but a distant dream. It was a more practical thought that got him out of bed and over to the wash-stand for a wash and a cold-water shave. Now dressed he tapped on Anna's door.

'Who is it?'

'Me.'

He opened the door without invitation and went over to her bed. 'It's okay I'm not going to jump on you. I just wondered how you are, how you'd slept and stuff.'

'I think I maybe had two hours' sleep, but I'll come round.'

'I know you will. You're a most remarkable person. No wonder your dad was so proud of you.'

'How do you know he was proud of me?'

'I could see it in his eyes. Everything about him told me he was proud of his darling daughter.'

'Really? Is *your* father proud of you?'

'I think so, yes. You'd like my dad. Anyway, look, the reason I came here is that I noticed Sébastien has his own telephone.'

'Has he really?'

'Yes. I thought it might be a good idea if you telephoned the hospital to tell them what has happened to your dad and that you'll be taking more time off. They'll understand that and it'll give us some more room to manoeuvre without being missed.'

'And what are you supposed to be doing while I mourn my father?'

'I did tell you about bullshit, didn't I?'

'You did.'

'Then use some.'

Half an hour later Anna picked up Sébastien's telephone and asked the operator to put her through to a number in Mannheim. Two minutes

278

later she was talking to Dr Ingrid Lehmann.

'Doctor Lehmann this is Anna Kohler.'

'Ah, good morning, Nurse Kohler. I trust you had a pleasant break and will be joining us this morning?'

'I'm afraid I won't, Dr Lehmann. You see my father was killed during a cycle ride and I will need more time off.'

'Oh dear! Killed? How was he killed?'

'We were cycling past an army convoy as it was attacked by a British plane. One of the trucks exploded and killed my father. He was tending to wounded at the time, as was I.'

'Oh my God! Damned British murderers. Killing doctors. Were you injured?'

'I have a minor injury to my arm. I wonder if you might do me a favour and contact my father's work colleagues to tell them the news. It happened near the French border. The three of us were having a short bicycling holiday that turned into a nightmare.'

'Three of you? Oh, of course you have the patient Schmidt with you. How is he coping?'

'The attack affected him badly but he seems to be recovering. Do you have a bed for him if we could get him back to Mannheim?'

'Er, no we are very busy right now.'

Anna knew this would be the answer or she wouldn't have asked this question.

'I see. Look, I am staying with relatives. We can look after him if it makes things easier.'

'If you're sure?'

'I'm sure. I will contact you in a week if that's all right?'

'Yes, take all the time you like.'

Lehmann hadn't asked for a contact address which was remiss of her, or was she simply happy not to have the returning problem of Thomas Schmidt to cope with? Anna put the phone down with a slight burden having been lifted from her, but her father's death was still weighing heavy on her heart. It would be some time before she smiled again.

Tommy was standing beside her with his eyebrows raised in anticipation, having not understood a word of the telephone conversation.

'Well, they don't want you back and, they're not expecting me back for at least a week.'

'That gives us some breathing space,' said Tommy. 'Time to decide what to do.'

'What do you mean?'

'I mean do we carry on or not?'

'Thomas. I'm carrying on, even if you're not. I want to justify the pride you say my father had in me.'

'What? You'd go without me?'

'Yes.'

'No you're not.'

'Try and stop me.'

'I don't have to. We're going together. But I want you to get your mind right and your arm better before we go.'

He looked at her arm which had a new, clean bandage on it. 'Sébastien came into my room last night,' she explained.

'Did he now? I might have to have a word with Sébastien.'

'Between us we dressed my wound and even

put a few stitches in it. I'm amazed you didn't hear me crying out.'

'I heard something. To be honest I thought it was grief rather than pain.'

'No, that was definitely pain. He's a man of many talents is old Sébastien.'

Chapter 36

Pontefract. April 30th 1917

'Dad!'

No answer.

'Dad are you in the house?'

No answer.

'Come on, Dad. I'm in trouble. The baby's coming and I think I've broken my leg! Dad, I've fallen down the stairs!'

Rita's screaming had taken all of her strength. She was guessing it was around six o'clock. Her dad should be home about now. Then she remembered it was Friday evening which meant her dad would be in some pub and wouldn't be home for at least four hours. The labour pains came again. More acute this time. A worse pain than the one in her broken leg which was twisted beneath her. If only her Tommy was here.

'Tommy! Tommy Birch, I need your help!'

She'd gone to bed early when suddenly her waters broke and she decided to come downstairs and alert a neighbour to her plight. Mrs Lythe next door had said she'd help her out. Maybe ring for an ambulance or get the midwife round. She'd tripped over the hem of her nightie and fallen down the whole flight, ending up with her right leg twisted beneath her. The acute pain added to her contractions and told her it was broken. She was now sincerely hoping that Mrs Lythe could hear her screaming at the top of her voice.

'Mrs Lythe, please, I need help! Oh, please!'

No answer.

She was too far away from the wall to bang on it, besides she had nothing to bang with. Bloody hell! Broken leg and a baby on the way into the world and no one around to help her. What was going to happen to her?

The labour pains returned. She lay back on the stairs to make herself a bit more comfortable and the movement exacerbated the pain in her leg to the extent that she passed out. Her next labour pains woke her up. She was now crying in pain and fear and helplessness. Was she just going to die here? Her and her baby?

She could see through into the living room that was now only lit by the embers of a dying fire. This dismal room might well be the last sight she ever saw on this Earth. She might never see the sun again and she might never see her baby who would soon be fighting to get out. What do I do if the baby comes out and I can't do anything to help it? Do I just let it lie there until my father comes home drunk? And what if he does come home? What can that useless bastard do to help? Maybe wake up a few neighbours, that's what he could do. But will my baby survive such a horrible birth?

And she would never see her Tommy again. Oh, Tommy. If only you were here to help me. Now more than any time in her life did she want and need her lovely Tommy. Surely if he were alive he'd somehow feel her terrible distress and come to her rescue?

'Tommy, Tommy Birch I need you now! Please!'

She closed her eyes and waited for the pain of her next contraction. It would soon be here, fighting for supremacy above the pain of her leg. She was losing consciousness when she heard a voice through the fog of her mind.

'Oh my God, Rita!'

The voice came from above her. She opened her eyes and peered up at a dark figure looming over her in the gloom.

'Who are you?'

'It's me, Agnes.'

'Agnes?'

'Yes.'

All Rita could think to say was, 'Hello, Agnes. What are you doing here?'

'Well, I was thinking about our Tommy to be honest, and I just came. What's happened?'

'The baby's coming. I fell down the stairs and broke my leg.'

'Where's your dad?'

'Out.'

'And he's left you on your own?'

'What does it bloody look like?'

'Oh my God! How long between contractions?'

'I don't know. Not long. Aagh! Here's one now.'

'You need an ambulance.'

It was a minute of heavy, painful breathing

before Rita could answer. 'I don't think there's time for an ambulance. Mrs Lythe next door, she'll help me.'

'Next door, which side?'

Rita pointed to the wall in front of her.

'Right, I'll be back in a tick.'

She was indeed. Mrs Lythe appeared, her husband having been despatched to the police station on Station Road where they could use the telephone to organise an ambulance. Agnes and Mrs Lythe managed to carry Rita into the living room and laid her out on the hearth rug, taking great care not to disturb her broken leg. Mrs Lythe pulled the switch to ignite the gas mantle.

'Is that as light as it gets?' Agnes asked.

'It is,' said Mrs Lythe, not particularly liking Agnes's disparaging tone of voice. 'I suppose you've got electricity in Pontefract.'

'There are some candles in the cupboard,' said Rita sensing the animosity between the two women – just about the last thing she wanted right now.

'They might help us see better,' said Agnes. She took four candles from the cupboard and set them up on the hearth so they could light up the incoming infant.

'Do you have any clean towels, Rita?' asked Mrs Lythe.

'Bottom drawer over there.'

Agnes put the kettle on for some hot water and Mrs Lythe got the towels as Rita lay there, grateful that these two saviours had arrived, but still in excruciating pain.

'You let it all out, love,' said Mrs Lythe. 'Scream

the damned street down if you want to.'

Rita proceeded to scream the damned street down.

'Push,' said Agnes, holding a candle a bit nearer to Rita. 'I can see its head.'

'Bloody hell!' said Mrs Lythe. 'Don't set her nightie on fire.'

'I'm not. She needs to push.'

'Push? She'll go up in smoke if you set her nightie on fire.'

'Shut up, shut up, shut up will you!' screamed Rita, who'd just had enough of everything. 'You can stick that bloody candle up your arse for all I care!'

'I think she's talking to you,' Mrs Lythe said to Agnes.

Agnes scowled at Mrs Lythe, but withdrew the candle to a safer distance. Rita pushed, but pushing exacerbated the pain in her leg.

'One more big push, love, and it'll all be over,' said Mrs Lythe.

'I can't. It hurts too much.'

'Come on, push and scream, push and scream.'

Rita pushed and she screamed. Ernest Lythe knocked on the door and looked in. 'Is everything all right in there? Half the street's coming to their doors with all this racket.'

'Just bugger off, Ernest!' snapped his wife. 'And tell that lot to bugger off as well!'

'I've told the bobbies,' he said, 'they've sent for an ambulance.'

'It's definitely coming,' said Agnes. 'Push harder, Rita.'

Rita let out a blood-curdling scream and

pushed as hard as she could until she was almost passing out with pain.

'It's coming, it's coming, it's coming, it's ... it's a boy, Rita. It's a little boy!'

The two women gathered cushions from the chairs and put them behind Rita so she could sit up to receive her child who was crying lustily, wrapped in a towel, still attached to her by its umbilical cord. Ernest went off to tell the street it was a boy, which was far better than telling them to bugger off.

'Is he all right?' Rita asked. After all she'd just been through it would be a wonder if her child was still in one piece.

'Perfect,' said Mrs Lythe, checking the baby's fingers, toes and other important extremities, 'and he's got a good pair of lungs on him.'

'What about the cord?' asked Agnes.

'Leave that for the ambulance people,' said Mrs Lythe. 'What're you going to call him, love?'

'Benjamin Charles,' said Rita.

At nine o'clock the next morning Rita was in bed in Pontefract hospital with Benjamin Charles in a cot by her side. Her right leg was in plaster and she was slightly dazed by the pain-killing drug she'd been given. A nurse was standing over her.

'You're causing us something of a problem, Mrs Birch, what with you belonging in the postnatal maternity ward and this being an orthopaedic ward.'

'Sorry,' said Rita. 'To be honest I'm just glad to be anywhere. There was a time last night when...' It was a sentence she struggled to finish.

'Yes, I heard about last night. It must have been terrible for you.'

'It was a bit of an ordeal.'

'Lucky your mother-in-law popped in to visit you.'

'That wasn't luck, nurse. That was nothing short of a miracle.'

'It'll be visiting time in an hour. Do you want to do your hair or anything, or maybe stick a bit of make-up on?'

'Well, I'm not sure who'll be coming but I wouldn't mind a brush and a mirror, and some lipstick and a bit of rouge. I must look a proper sight.'

'Well, you do look a bit washed-out, but that's hardly unusual after all you've been through. How's the leg? Any pain?'

'Not too bad at the moment.'

She had three visitors, Agnes, Edith and Mrs Lythe. All of them had nothing but smiles for her.

'Charlie and Stanley'll come tonight,' Agnes told her.

Rita fixed her with a long stare. She'd been waiting for this moment. 'What made you come round last night, Agnes?'

'I er, I don't know really. I suppose I got to thinking you were very near your time and I wondered how you were getting on.'

'Nothing else?'

'How do you mean?'

'When I asked you what you were doing there you said you thought Tommy sent you.'

'Did I?'

'Yes, and I think he did send you. I mean, after all this time you not coming to see me and it gets to the very moment I actually *need* you and there you are, large as life, there to help me. That was more than just a coincidence, Agnes. I don't know what would have happened to me if you hadn't turned up. I was shouting my head off but no one could hear me, and yet something ... or *someone* ... caused you to come to me.'

'You mean our Tommy?'

'Yes, my Tommy.'

'Well, I must admit he was on me mind was the lad. I'd just put their tea out for them and I got to thinking you must be near your time and it set me wondering what sort of a dad our Tommy'd make, and then I thought he'd like me to come and see how you're getting on, because I didn't know, obviously.'

'So, Tommy being on your mind brought you to me?'

'Actually he did, yes. In fact I went out of the house without having any tea meself and without putting me coat and me headscarf on and got straight on a Featherstone bus. You know me, I never go out without me coat on. Charlie wondered where the devil I'd gone.'

Rita smiled at her and said, 'I thought so.'

Agnes smiled back and gave her no argument.

'Where was your father?' asked Mrs Lythe.

'Friday night he'll have been in some pub. Where is he now by the way?'

'No idea. He hadn't come home by the time the ambulance left with you. Me and Ernest went to bed after that.'

'So, when did you tell my dad?'

Agnes and Edith both looked at Mrs Lythe. 'Erm, me? Last night I didn't see him to tell him.'

'He'll have come in half cut and gone straight to bed,' said Rita. 'What about this morning?'

'Well, I knocked on the door but there was no reply. I expect he'll have gone off to work.'

'I expect he did,' said Rita. 'He's usually gone by the time I get up.'

'So, he doesn't know about what went on in his house while he was out guzzling beer?'

'And he doesn't know he's a granddad?' said Agnes.

Rita shrugged. 'How can he?'

'None of this would have happened if you'd been living with us,' Edith pointed out. 'We'd have looked after you properly.'

Agnes looked guilty and took Rita's hand. 'Look, Rita, I'm really sorry for what I said to you that night. It was uncalled for.'

'And I'm sorry for what I said to you.'

'What was that, love?'

'I believe I told you to stick a candle up your bottom.'

'I don't think you said bottom, Rita.'

'Okay, we'll call it quits then.'

'Call it what you like just as long as we're all friends again.'

'I do hope we are, Agnes.'

'And...?' said Edith, looking impatiently at her mother.

'Oh, and when you come out of here we'd all love it if you and the baby came back to live with us. You can go on about Tommy as much as you like, in fact, after last night's miracle I'm beginning to think he is still around, somewhere, and Charlie'll be proper chuffed you've called the lad after him. I'm quite chuffed meself.'

'I'd like to come back very much,' said Rita.

'About flipping time,' said Edith.

'Whoever tells my dad about this,' said Rita, 'I want you to go easy on him. He'll feel guilty enough without you banging on about what a useless bugger he is.'

'Point taken,' said Mrs Lythe. 'I expect it'll be me who tells him what's happened. He'll want to come and see you tonight, I would think.'

'I would think you're right, Mrs Lythe, and don't worry, *I'll* tell him what a useless bugger he is.'

'So long as someone does,' said Edith.

'He is what he is,' said Rita. 'He does his best, which isn't much, but it's all I can expect of him.'

Chapter 37

May 14th 1917

Rita was breastfeeding baby Benjamin when the knock came to the door. He was now two weeks old and thriving.

'I'll get it,' said Agnes.

It was a man in a suit holding a briefcase, a sight that made Agnes immediately uncomfortable. Men with suits and briefcases rarely arrived with good news. She assumed it would be something to do with Charlie – maybe Stuart Gooding's lawyer looking for help for his client.

'My husband's out,' she said, defensively.

'What? Oh no it's erm... I'm looking for a Mrs Rita Victoria Birch and I've been told by her father that she lives here.'

'What's it about?'

'It's a matter I need to discuss with her personally. Is she here?'

'Well she is, but she's feeding her baby right now.'

Rita, who now realised they were talking about her, appeared behind Agnes, carrying Benjamin.

'I'm Rita Victoria Birch.'

'Oh, good. I wonder if I might come in?'

'Depends,' said Agnes. 'Who are you?'

'My name is Beamish. I'm a solicitor representing the estate of George Miller.'

'George Miller? Is it good news or bad news?'

'News? Oh I see. Well, it isn't bad news.'

'In that case you can come in.'

Agnes and Rita stepped aside as he walked past them into the living room and stood there, obediently, as though awaiting further instructions from Agnes.

'Sit yourself down,' she said, her tone friendly now. Good news was a welcome visitor in this day and age.

'Thank you.'

'So, what's it about?'

'I think it's about me, Agnes,' said Rita. 'I can speak for myself.'

'Of course you can, love.'

'So,' said Rita. 'What's it about?'

'Well it's to do with the last will and testament of George Miller, formerly known as, erm, Müller.'

'What has that got to do with me? I wasn't related to Mr Miller.'

'No, apparently he doesn't have any relations – not in this country anyway. But I assume he was a friend of yours?'

Rita sensed a disapproving glance from Agnes. 'Yes, he was a friend,' she said, 'no more than that.'

'Well, as the late Mr Miller's solicitor, I'm here to inform you that you are the sole beneficiary of Mr Miller's estate.'

'What?' The women spoke in amazed unison.

'He left you his property, his business and all his other assets.'

'Me?'

'Yes.'

'He left me all his stuff? Why me?'

'Well, I drew the will up for him and when I asked him for the name of a beneficiary he at first mentioned a distant relative in Germany – a cousin he'd never met – and when I pointed out the difficulty this might present with us being at war with Germany he said he didn't know anyone in England well enough, then he came up with your name, Rita Victoria Birch. The address he gave me was the Yorkshire Bank on Ropergate. They gave me your father's address in Feather-stone, and he sent me here.'

Rita looked at Agnes and said, sternly, 'Agnes Birch, don't you dare read anything into this! I went to the pictures with him a couple of times, that's all.'

'I suspect that's more than anyone else did,' said Beamish.

'Sounds to me as if you knew him better than I did,' said Rita. 'Did you know he was German?'

'He wasn't German,' Beamish told her. 'His German roots were too distant for him to be anything other than English.'

'I wish someone could tell that to the people who killed him,' said Rita. 'It wasn't just Stuart Gooding, it was everyone who was there.'

'I agree with you, Mrs Birch. What happened to him was outrageous. He was a good man. Pontefract should be ashamed of what those people did.'

'To a fellow Englishman,' added Rita, 'who had done them no harm.'

'Quite.'

'So,' said Agnes, 'Rita owns a butcher's shop.'

'She does indeed,' said Beamish, 'plus quite a large amount of cash.' He looked inside a folder he'd taken from his briefcase. 'After taxes and other expenses, one thousand three hundred and forty-four pounds to be precise. That is before we deduct his funeral expenses ... with that not having taken place yet.'

'Good God!' said Agnes. 'That's more than five years' wages for my husband, and he's on good money.'

'The business is worth quite a lot as well,' said Beamish. 'Even if you can't sell it as a going concern Mr Miller owned the property outright. We've had it valued at six hundred and fifty pounds, added to which all the damage that was done is covered by insurance, of which you are also the sole beneficiary.'

'And he still hasn't been laid to rest?' said Rita. 'It's months since he died.'

'I know,' said Beamish. 'It's the unfortunate circumstances of his death that delayed his funeral.'

'So, who arranges that?' asked Agnes.

'Well, we were hoping Mrs Birch would.'

'I'd be pleased to,' said Rita, before Agnes could object. 'If he's left me all that money, it's the least I can do.'

'That's what I was going to say,' Agnes said.

'I wonder what Tommy'll say,' said Rita, 'when he comes home to find we're rich? It'll be a nice home-coming for him.'

'I think it might take a bit of explaining,' said Agnes.

'I think I'd like to use some of it to help Stuart with his appeal,' said Rita.

'That would be most unusual,' said Beamish. 'For the victim to indirectly pay for his killer's defence. I wonder what Mr Miller would think about that.'

'I think Mr Miller might agree with me,' said Rita. 'Had he not died he wouldn't have wished Stuart too much harm for getting caught up in a heat-of-the moment riot. He was a very decent man.'

'And Stuart's a very decent young man,' added Agnes, deciding it would do no harm to take Rita's side, despite her misgivings.

'Would you like me to put you in contact with Mr Gooding's solicitor?' Beamish asked.

'Please.'

Chapter 38

Pontefract. May 21st 1917

The knock on the door was quite timid. Rita answered it. 'Dad, what are you doing here? What's happened to you?'

Her father was in something of a state. His face was bruised, his right eye blackened, his lips swollen and his clothes torn. 'I'm having a bit of a bad time, love.'

'You'd better come in.'

'Thanks, love. I much appreciate it. Is Charlie in?'

'Everybody's in, Dad.'

She took him into the living room where he was greeted with looks of shock, even from Stanley.

'What's happened to you, Benny?' asked Charlie. 'Has somebody beaten you up?'

Benny's gaze dropped in embarrassment. Charlie looked at Stanley. 'Stanley, go upstairs for a bit while we talk to Mr Clayton.'

'Aw, Dad.'

'Stanley! Do as you're told.'

A disgruntled Stanley did as he was told and Benny was given a chair at the table. 'I got set upon,' he said.

'Why?' asked Rita. Many concerned people would have asked 'who by?' but Rita knew there was a 'why' involved here.

'Is it to do with the bookie's job, Dad?'

He looked up at her, amazed at her accurate perception. 'How do you know that? Who's been talkin' to yer?'

'Nobody's been talking to me, Dad. I just know what you're like.'

'Have you been taking bets and not placing 'em?' Charlie asked.

Benny nodded. 'I just do it now and again when I know the horse has got no chance.'

'And this "no chance horse" won, did it, Dad?'

'It did, love, and that's not the worst of it.'

'Go on.'

'The bloke who placed the bet's Arthur Wilmot.'

'What?' said Charlie. 'Arthur Wilmot who works at the Dog and Gun as a chucker-out?'

Benny nodded.

'Blimey! I've heard about him,' said Charlie. 'He's a right thug.'

'He had ten bob to win on Flying Duchess at fifty to one,' said Benny. 'It had no chance. I reckon the race were fixed.'

'But it won?'

'It did. I told him I didn't manage to get it on in time and I offered him his ten bob back. This is what happened.'

'Good God, Benny. Not got it on in time? No one's gonna believe that. He'll think you picked up his twenty-five quid, and he'll want it.'

'He does want it. He's been to the bookies and they gave him the elbow. They'll give me the elbow when they find out what I've done. But it's not them I'm worried about. They reckon he killed somebody once and got away with it.'

'Yes, I've heard that,' said Charlie. 'Nobody'd

296

come forward as a witness.'

'You should go to the police,' said Agnes.

'And tell 'em what? He's done nowt wrong. There's no law against laying a bet with a runner. It's the runner who's breaking the law, and that won't go in me favour with the police.'

'What's he said to you?' asked Rita.

'He says he wants his money by tonight or he'll start breaking me bones. And I believe him.'

'So do I,' said Charlie.

'Can't you have a word with him, Charlie?' asked Agnes. 'He won't dare lay a finger on you.'

'Agnes, that man won't be satisfied until he gets his money.'

'We should pay him then,' said Rita.

'What?' said her father. 'Where are you going to get twenty-five quid? It's two months' wages for me.'

Edith opened her mouth to explain but her mother nudged her in the ribs. It wasn't common knowledge that Rita had been left money by George Miller. Benny hadn't been told lest he constantly pester Rita for money.

'I've got some money put by,' Rita told him. 'We'll pay him and be done with it. Will he be in the Dog and Gun now?'

'I think so.'

'Well, I've got some money upstairs. I'll go and pay Mr Wilmot his money. Charlie, will you come with me?'

'I think I'd better do, Rita. I don't want you getting into trouble as well.'

'I won't. I want to see this bully's face when I tell him what I think of him!'

'Oh heck!' said Charlie, reaching for his coat. 'Get the money. I'll take you in the van.'

Ten minutes later, they were walking through the door of the Dog and Gun. It was one of Pontefract's less salubrious houses, catering mainly for the lower end of the social spectrum. Late-night fights were frequent and the likes of Arthur Wilmot were invaluable to the running of such an establishment.

There were just two rooms. A best room and a tap room. Charlie thought the tap room was the most likely place to find Wilmot. He was leaning against the bar, talking to a barmaid. Charlie pointed him out to her. She walked up to him. He turned and looked at her.

'By the heck! Have you just walked into the wrong place?'

'If this is the dump where that lowlife bully Arthur Wilmot works I've come to the right place!' snapped Rita.

'Hey, just watch who you're callin' a lowlife, yer mouthy bitch!'

His voice was loud enough to still all the conversation in the room.

'Why, what will you do? Will you beat me up like you beat my father up? He's half the size of you.'

A broad smile spread across Wilmot's face. He addressed himself to the room. 'Hey, I think this must be Benny Clayton's lass. Has he sent yer ter pay me in kind? Now let me see. That's twenty-five quid at ten bob a shag. That's fifty shags, but are yer worth ten bob?'

Charlie's fist flew past Rita's face and crunched

into Wilmot's nose, breaking it. Wilmot sank to the floor in pain with blood pouring down his shirt. Charlie leaned over him, grabbed him by the scruff of his neck and pulled him to his knees. 'She came to pay you your blood-money, you worthless piece of shit!'

Rita held out five white fivers and dropped them over his head. They fell to the floor, becoming soaked in his blood. Rita looked at the men in the room. 'There you are. You're all witnesses. Twenty-five pounds paid to the bully on the floor.' Wilmot looked up at her with hatred in his eyes. She met his gaze with hatred of her own.

'Let this be a lesson, Wilmot. The Birch family always pays its debts, whether we take it out of your nose or we pay what we owe. You might be good at chucking drunks out of this dump but you mess with the Birch family, you lose.'

As he drove her home, Charlie apologised. 'Sorry about the swearing back there.'

'No need. He is a worthless piece of shit. I didn't expect you to punch him, though.'

'Rita, bullies like him only understand a good punch on the nose. He won't be troubling your dad again.'

'Well, it certainly was a beauty. That punch would have flattened Jack Johnson.'

'Don't tell Agnes. In fact don't tell any of them.'

'I bet you're more frightened of Agnes than you are of Wilmot.'

'Maybe. You shouldn't keep that kind of money in your room, by the way.'

'Don't worry, nearly all the money's safe in the

bank. I drew some out to buy us a washing machine. There's a really good one out now with its own gas water-heater and a built-in mangle and everything. It's called a Maytag and it's from America. They had one on display in Pollard's window in town so I've ordered one.'

'Really? Does Agnes know?'

'No, I thought it'd be a nice surprise. Anyway, I'm still getting one despite what happened tonight.'

'I daren't ask you how much it's costing.'

'No, and I daren't tell you. How's the fist?'

Charlie looked at his grazed fist and shook his head. 'Hmm. How do I explain this?'

'Maybe you did it getting the van started. You always have trouble with that starting handle.'

'Genius.'

'Tommy would have called it bullshit.'

Chapter 39

May 22nd.
The road five miles east of Betschdorf
Tommy and Anna spent three weeks with Sébastien to allow Anna to properly recover from her injury and to mourn her father's death. It was also Sébastien's idea that in those three weeks the advancing Allied front would have moved several miles nearer to them. Tommy could see the logic in this. He was still weak from his former injuries and could also do with a bit of respite of his own.

The final act of mourning was to be the erection of Benjamin's memorial. It was raining steadily as a 4-ton German army truck pulled up alongside the huddled group standing at the side of the road beneath three black umbrellas. Parked nearby was a horse and trap, a four-seater Daimler motor car, two bicycles and a motor cycle. One of the group was a priest. The cab of the truck was open to the elements and the back had a canvas canopy, under which were twelve German soldiers. The saturated driver had been ordered to stop by his Oberleutnant, who had abandoned the damp front seat to travel in the back under cover. The driver put up his collar in a vain attempt to ward off the rain and rested his elbows on the steering wheel, awaiting further instructions. None of the roadside group turned to look at the vehicle. They had seen it coming and were apprehensive now that it had stopped. German soldiers were rarely helpful to French civilians. The officer jumped out and walked over to the group as the priest was reciting a Latin prayer for the dead. Some of the soldiers jumped out and followed him.

'Oh bugger!' muttered Tommy, under his breath.

Even the mildest confrontation with German soldiers could escalate into him and Anna being taken into custody, which could quickly escalate into them facing a firing squad. Anna was thinking much the same, only she was mentally composing what she might say to the officer if she was questioned. She had one or two things in her favour. The biggest was that she was German and that they were having a memorial service for her father who had given his life trying to save the lives of

301

German soldiers. Surely this would be enough, but it all depended on the mentality of the man who was questioning her. If he was anything like the lunatic German who had tried to shoot her dead it could get tricky. She avoided all eye-contact with him, but she was aware that women as pretty as she always attracted the attention of men whether they liked it or not. She moved forward a little to place Dr Lehmann between her and his eye-line and dropped her head in silent prayer.

'*Requiem aeternam dona ei, Domine,*' said the priest.

The officer stood respectfully at the back of the group waiting for the priest to finish. His men did likewise. Set in the verge beside the road was a black marble memorial stone with an inscription in French:

Docteur Benjamin Kohler 1870 à 1917 mort ici.
Un homme courageux.
Que Dieu ait pitié de son âme.

Using his very basic knowledge of French the officer translated this as meaning:

Dr Benjamin Kohler 1870 to 1917 died here.
A courageous man.
May God have mercy on his soul.

It was over three weeks since Benjamin's death, during which time Sébastien had organised a monument to be made to his friend and had arranged for his colleagues and friends in Mannheim to come and pay their last respects. There was no body to bury. Benjamin's remains had been scattered far and wide, along with six German soldiers. The Oberleutnant had heard about the incident but he hadn't known about a doctor being killed. Anna, Tommy and Sébastien, standing next to the priest, pretended to be unconcerned at the German's arrival. It was Dr Ingrid Lehmann who spoke to the officer, revealing herself to be as German as he was.

'He was a colleague from Mannheim. A fellow countryman of ours. Killed attending our wounded soldiers. We think he deserves a memorial.'

The junior officer, who was no more than twenty-one years old, stepped up to the memorial and saluted. Then he turned to the uneasy group and said, 'I apologise for disturbing your ceremony.'

They all breathed silent sighs of relief. The priest said, 'Thank you, my son,' which Anna and Tommy thought was a wonderfully patronising way to address an enemy officer who, along with his men, climbed back on board the truck, which moved away. Tommy winked at Anna as both their heart rates subsided. Benjamin's sister noticed the priest's glare following the truck as it drove off.

'My brother spoke highly of you,' she said, with her eyes on the vanishing truck.

'I only knew his voice in the confessional.'

'Perhaps I should take his place in your confessional from time to time.'

'You will be most welcome, my child. I hear confessions in the church of St Mathias in Mannheim every Wednesday and Saturday evening from six until seven-thirty.'

'It is a long journey,' she said. 'But I think it might well be good for my soul.'

'It would be good for many souls,' said the priest.

Chapter 40

May 23rd

The rain had gone from the day and it was a warm evening. The pale blue sky was fading into twilight and the three of them sat outside Sébastien's house on a wooden verandah overlooking the orchard. Their only light would soon be an old oil lamp hanging from the roof. Sébastien had supplied a couple of bottles of wine from a local vineyard, and it was going down well.

'I must say, I wouldn't mind bringing my family up in a place like this,' said Tommy. 'That's if I ever have a family to bring up. Warm climate, beautiful countryside, plenty of room for the children to play, no shortage of apples by the look of it. Bit different from Pontefract. Even the light's better here – all we have in Pontefract is coal, horse muck and fog. We haven't even got a rugby team – we have to make do with Featherstone Rovers.'

Anna was wishing he was including her in this family, but she knew her wish was forlorn and this made her even sadder. Tommy spotted her eyes glistening. He leaned over and took her hand as

Sébastien spoke.

'Ah, there will be many fine apples this year. In September a neighbour will pick them from the trees with the help of his wife and he will sell them in the market for a good price. I will get half of the proceeds. We have been doing this for twenty-one years since my dear wife passed away and every single franc I have saved in the town bank. I say this to you because you may be in need of money to smooth your path.'

'I have *some* money,' said Anna. 'But most of our money was destroyed, along with my father who kept it in a money belt. It was all in marks.'

'Then I will give you some francs,' said Sébastien. 'I really have no use for much money at my age.'

'You are a very kind man,' said Anna, 'and you are putting yourself in danger by helping us.'

'As a Frenchman it is the least I can do. We may not have the strength to fight the Germans but by gathering and passing on intelligence we can help the Allied forces in any way we can. Last year I sheltered a British airman in this house for three months until I passed him on to a resistance group who, I hope, helped him to get back to England.' He took a sip of his wine and added, 'In fact I would like to give you his details so that when you get to England you can find out if he managed to get home and let me know.'

'I imagine he'll be able to do that himself,' said Tommy.

'He would if he knew who I was or exactly where he was staying. He was brought to me in the middle of the night after crashing his flying

305

machine in a nearby field. He spent three months with me, mainly in my cellar. He only knew me as François, which is my middle name. I never told him my address and he didn't ask for it. That way he could never betray me. It is the way things are in these awful times.'

'But *we* might betray you if we were tortured,' Tommy pointed out.

'I would prefer you do betray, me, Thomas, rather than suffer a painful death. I am at an age where death does not frighten me.'

'Thomas would never betray you, Sébastien,' said Anna. 'He'd just give them a load of bullshit!'

Sébastien laughed. 'Ah, I have heard of the famous British bullshit – the curse of all German torturers.'

'Tommy's an expert,' said Anna.

'I am,' confirmed Tommy. 'I speak three languages – English, Yorkshire and bullshit.'

'And the people at the hospital thought you could not speak in any language,' said Sébastien.

'You don't know how hard that was,' said Tommy. 'I nearly slipped up quite a few times, which is why I don't want to push my luck by going back to Mannheim.'

'And Anna and her father joined you so they could be with Anna's mother in England. Yes, you have good reasons for doing what you are doing, and I wish you both success.'

He went quiet for a while, as if mulling over a problem. His lips moved in a silent discussion with himself. Tommy and Anna chose not to interrupt his thoughts. It was several minutes before he spoke again. He looked at Tommy and asked,

'Thomas, can you drive a motor car?'

'Well, I'm not an expert but I've driven a few army trucks.'

'Army trucks? That might be even better. The vehicle I am thinking about is an army vehicle.'

'I'm not sure what you're talking about,' said Tommy.

'Of course not. I am an old man, whose mind can only think about one thing at a time.'

'So,' asked Anna, 'what are you talking about?'

'I'm thinking about the tremendous difficulties you face between here and Nancy. Despite the loss of your dear father your road has been easy, but the next hundred miles will be quite different.'

'We're talking miles not kilometres?' said Tommy. 'Is that how far away we are?'

'It is,' said Sébastien. 'One hundred very dangerous miles. Especially for two people on bicycles, and one of you not speaking French – or any acceptable language for that matter. So, when you near the western front it will arouse suspicion and you will be handed over to the German Secret Service Police.'

'Are you telling us it's going to be impossible?'

Sébastien gave this question some considerable thought, then said, 'I'm saying that it will be extremely dangerous.'

'We're definitely going to give it a try,' said Anna. Tommy nodded his head in agreement, then asked, 'What's this about a car?'

Sébastien looked at her and smiled. 'I know where there is a stolen armoured vehicle. We do not have a resistance as such, but we do have an experienced thief in our group. He is a wild young fellow who is intent on driving it across enemy lines and perhaps selling it to the British. So far we have persuaded him not to be so foolish, but he insists he can do it.'

'I'm not sure about the British army buying it off him,' said Tommy. 'They're more likely just to take it off him.'

'I agree, but if you are with him, once the vehicle is across the line that will be his problem not yours.'

'I see,' said Tommy.

Anna's eyes were now shining with excitement. 'We could give him whatever money we have,' she said.

'I do not think your German marks will be any use over there,' said Sébastien, 'but my French francs will. The exchange rate is all over the place at the moment but I can give you four thousand francs.'

'What?' said Tommy. 'That's an awful lot of money.'

'Yes, and it will seem an awful lot of money to our impetuous friend, but it's really about one hundred of your pounds.'

'That's a year's army pay for me. Do you think he'll take us?'

'I'm sure he will. He has the vehicle, but we have the petrol to go in it.'

'Who's we?' asked Anna.

Sébastien smiled and touched his nose with a finger. Anna held up her hands in understanding.

'Does this vehicle have a gun?' asked Tommy.

'It has two machine guns, and I suppose that

you, being a soldier, will know how to fire them.'

'I'm not bad with a rifle,' said Tommy, 'but I'm not exactly an expert on machine guns. I can probably get them firing, though.'

'Probably get them firing eh? Well we must hope you never have to,' said Sébastien.

'If you could supply me with a decent rifle and some ammunition it'd be more than useful to get us out of any trouble.'

'I believe the vehicle can travel at thirty miles an hour, which should get you out of trouble quickly.'

'Well, it certainly sounds like a plan,' said Tommy, 'which is more than we have at the moment. I don't suppose your people could supply us with the safest route?'

'I think we can manage that.'

The next morning the three of them took a short journey on Sébastien's horse and trap to a nearby farm where the armoured car was being secreted.

'Our man's name is Louis,' Sébastien told them. 'He lives with his mother and younger brother. His father was killed at the beginning of the war by the Germans. They farm sugar beet along with a few chickens and six cows, but mainly sugar beet. Louis is something of a scoundrel, but likeable enough. His mother despairs of him and his ways and the quicker the armoured car goes the better, as far as she is concerned.'

'So he's planning on leaving his mother and brother to cope on their own?' said Tommy. 'I don't wonder she despairs of him.'

'His mother and brother run the farm with a

little outside help. Louis isn't interested. He takes after his father in many ways. Before the war he spent quite some time in prison for theft, but for the past three or four years the law doesn't seem quite so hard on him.'

'I take it he's what you call a black marketeer?' said Anna.

'Well I would call him a black and white marketeer. He acquires his goods mainly from crooked German quartermasters and he knows plenty of those.'

'Is that how he got the armoured car?'

'Oh no. That was straightforward opportunism. It was left unattended with the engine running. It was very careless, but the Germans think they are untouchable and that no one dare do anything to offend them. But Louis being Louis could not resist such a golden opportunity. He simply climbed into it and drove it back to his farm where he has a wonderful hiding place for such things. The Germans have searched everywhere for it, including here.'

Louis's mother's farm was a run-down affair, as were many places that had endured three years of war and subjugation. Tommy and Anna stayed on the trap as Sébastien knocked on the door. A young man opened it. Slim build, dark-haired, late twenties and pleasant enough judging by the smile of greeting he gave his elderly neighbour.

'He is rather nice looking,' commented Anna.

It was a comment that went unappreciated by Tommy. The two of them watched for Louis's reaction as Sébastien outlined the proposition.

Tommy guessed that Louis's next smile would come when Sébastien told him how much money he'd pay for his services. Sébastien turned and waved them to come and join him.

'This is Louis,' he said. 'I'm about to ask him to take you.'

Young Louis looked at Tommy with suspicion until Tommy spoke to him in English. He didn't understand a word Tommy was saying, but he recognised the accent. He grinned and held out a hand to Tommy, then he kissed Anna's hand in a manner that Tommy found slightly annoying. Sébastien noticed this.

'He likes to play the romantic Frenchman,' he murmured.

'Does he now?' murmured Tommy, taking an unreasonable dislike to Louis. There was a further discussion between Sébastien and Louis, with the young Frenchman showing a marked reluctance to agree with the old man's proposal. Then Sébastien took a thick wad of francs from his pocket and showed them to Louis, whose mood began to change. He looked from Sébastien to Tommy and Anna and then back. Sébastien said to them, 'He's not happy with outsiders knowing about the armoured car and his secret hideout. If word of it gets to the Germans he'll be shot.'

'Just tell him he can trust us with his secret as much as he can trust anyone,' said Tommy.

Sébastien relayed this to Louis, along with a second wad of money from another pocket. It was obviously too much of an offer for the Frenchman to refuse. He nodded, took all the money and

311

shook hands with Sébastien who said to Tommy and Anna, 'He will take you. I have told him that when you reach Allied lines you will vouch for him and persuade them to buy the armoured car, rather than just let them take it from him, and you will ask them to allow him to advance with them, so that he can return in safety.'

'I can definitely ask,' Tommy said. 'Can't guarantee anything though. I was only a corporal.'

'If I know anything about the army I think you'll find you're still a corporal,' said Sébastien, 'perhaps even still earning corporal's pay as an undercover agent of the king.'

'Now there's a thought,' said Tommy.

'Anyway Louis has agreed to show us the armoured car.'

With Sébastien doing the translating as they walked, the four of them went to a stack of square hay bales, ten feet high and twenty feet square.

'Why have you brought us to see a haystack?' said Anna.

Sébastien translated. Louis laughed out loud, walked over to the stack, grabbed what looked like a handful of hay and pulled. A door in the haystack swung open, ten feet wide by eight feet high.

'It's actually a large wooden shed, ingeniously encased in hay bales,' Sébastien explained. 'It was made by his father, who was a much bigger villain than Louis. Only a very select and patriotic few know of its existence, which has been the cause of many a mystery about large disappearing objects in this area. Louis once even stole my horse and trap but it was returned when his father realised where he'd got it from.'

'And the Germans have never taken a close look at it?' said Tommy.

Sébastien and Louis had a brief conversation, then Sébastien told Tommy, 'Louis said, "What you don't suspect; you don't investigate."'

'He's dead right there,' said Tommy, shaking his head in amazement. Odd bales of genuine hay scattered nearby seemed to add to its authenticity. He walked over to it and looked inside, then gasped with further amazement when he saw the whole interior of the haystack was taken up by an ugly-looking armoured car. It was a large vehicle made of riveted steel panels and four large steel wheels with solid rubber tyres. It had no windows, just an assortment of steel shutters which opened outwards on side hinges. On the top was a circular turret with the black barrels of a two guns poking out, one either side. The engine compartment was huge and would need to contain a very powerful motor to move this monster around. Two large headlamps glared at him from either side of an aggressive-looking radiator grille. The metal was unpainted, with the exception of two white-painted squares which provided the background for black Germanic crosses.

'Bloody hell!' said Tommy. 'I'm not sure I can drive that.'

'It apparently drives the same as a normal motor car,' Sébastien told him. 'But what that is, I have no idea.'

Louis went to one side, opened a small steel door and invited Tommy to look inside. There was just one seat for the driver, plus room behind for the gunner who could just about stand up with

313

his head in the turret to fire the guns through. Tommy's weapons training told him that the weapons were MG 08 heavy machine guns and he also knew that operating them was at least a two-man job – the second operator would be feeding the ammunition belt through.

'This gun's supposed to be a four-man job,' he said. 'Could be done by two at a pinch.'

'One man, one woman,' said Anna. 'You drive, Louis and I can work the gun.'

'Maybe I should let Louis drive,' Tommy said. 'I've had weapons training.'

'You know the weapon do you?'

'I do. It fires up to 500 rounds a minute with an effective range of up to two miles. There should be ammunition belts to go with it, with two hundred and fifty rounds on each belt.'

Sébastien translated this to Louis who climbed into the back, opened a metal box and brought out two ammunition belts. Then he stood up and took hold of a crank handle fitted just below the turret and began to wind it. As he did the turret began to turn. Tommy nodded that he understood. He also noticed that the top of Louis's head was almost touching the underside of turret, and the Frenchman was a few inches shorter than Tommy. He tapped the top of his own head and mimed, 'Hey! Change of plan. You're the gunner, I'm the driver.'

A further translation from Sébastien had Louis grinning his agreement, then talking at length.

'He says he too has had weapons training in the French army and he knows how to handle the gun.'

'Good for him.'

Tommy sat in the driver's seat. 'Any idea how it starts?' he asked Sébastien, who translated this to Louis.

The young Frenchman jumped out and produced a long starting handle from a side compartment. He went round to the front, threaded it into the engine and cranked with all his might. After several turns the engine coughed, then roared into deafening life, its pistons pounding out a roaring beat that echoed against every riveted panel.

Tommy worked out that the gearstick was a lever attached to the steering column and that there were only three gears he could find – two forward and one reverse. He depressed what he assumed was the clutch pedal and slammed the gearstick into what he hoped would be first gear, then he released the clutch for just long enough for him to find he was in reverse. He stuck the stick back into neutral and slammed his foot on the brake, coming to a halt with the back of the vehicle just inches away from the back of the hideout.

'Right, well that's reverse found,' he said to Sébastien. 'One of the others is bound to take me forward.'

'I sincerely hope so. Perhaps you should ask Louis?'

'I'll be here all day if I have to have all my questions translated. I'll figure it out.'

Tommy found another gear and repeated the exercise with the clutch. This time the car moved forward very slowly. He drove it out of the haystack onto a stone track that led to Louis's humble home. The steering was heavy and his stay in hospital had taken its toll on his strength to the extent that he was now thinking of asking Louis to drive, but the faster he went, the easier it became. He found the higher gear and arrived in front of the house where Louis's mother stood, stern-faced with her arms folded. He managed to put the gearstick into neutral and found a handbrake which took both hands to ratchet up.

He was breathing heavily when Sébastien, Louis and Anna came running up, grinning all over their faces. 'Well done, Thomas,' said Sébastien. 'I thought for a minute back there that you wouldn't able to drive it.'

'Sébastien, I'm knackered and I've only driven it fifty yards. I don't know what I'll be like after a hundred miles, with people shooting at me.'

'Apart from that, is it to your liking?'

'We'll have to fit a seat for Anna.'

Sébastien said something to Louis who replied and nodded as if to say it was no problem.

'Louis has a seat he can fit,' Sébastien told him.

'Do you know how much petrol it uses, or does it run on diesel?'

A short conversation in French ensued.

'It runs on petrol and Louis believes it will take one hundred litres to get to Nancy.'

'A hundred litres for a hundred miles?' Tommy's engineer's brain did a quick conversation to gallons. 'Blimey! That's not much more than five miles a gallon.'

'The tank holds one hundred and fifty litres, which is how much you will be given. We have a store that will supply this.'

'How much is in now?'

Another conversation in French then Louis took a long dipstick out of the side compartment, unscrewed the fuel cap and stuck it into the tank. He drew it out and spoke to Sébastien, who smiled.

'About enough to get back to the haystack.'

Louis's mother said something uncomplimentary to her son, who smiled broadly at her and handed her, what to Tommy, looked like all of the money Sébastien had given him. She looked at it in some surprise and called out to Sébastien.

'*Merci beaucoup*, Sébastien.'

'You must thank your son, not me. I gave the money to him.'

She murmured reluctant thanks to Louis who gave her a big hug.

'What a generous young man,' said Anna. 'Don't you think so, Thomas?'

'Absolutely,' said Tommy, with undisguised insincerity. He was now wondering how he and this handsome, generous young man would get on, both cooped up in the steel vehicle with the lovely Anna who thought Louis looked rather nice. He pushed his thoughts homewards, where they belonged. *'Get a grip, Tommy! You're married to Rita.'*

'You don't like him, do you?'

'I'm not sure I like this whole plan, Anna. It's all a bit gung ho. My plan would be to keep our heads down and sneak through the lines. This is exactly the opposite. We'll be out there for everyone to see. One shell could wipe us all out.'

Sébastien had overheard him. 'I agree with you to a certain extent, Thomas, but the secret of this method is speed. If you can travel at thirty miles an hour you'll be as fast as anything out there. A fast moving target. One minute you're there, the next you're gone. Bullet proof as well. Motor cars and motor cycles will be no problem to you. You ignore them and drive on like the Germans they think you are, as if you have an important military objective. Louis knows these roads well. He will take you on a route that's maybe one hundred and twenty miles, but away from most of the big guns. He plans on being over the lines within four or five hours of setting off. On foot or bicycle it might take four days of danger. You biggest danger will come from the British at the end of your journey.'

'I suggest we travel at night,' said Tommy.

'Louis agrees with you. Tomorrow night there is a good moon and the weather should be clear.' He added something in French to Anna, which made her blush slightly but she nodded her agreement.

Sébastien went into the house with Louis and his mother. Tommy asked her what he'd said. She looked up at him, wondering whether or not to tell him.

'He thinks you are jealous of Louis. He told me to give you no cause to be jealous. Are you jealous?'

'I'm a married man,' said Tommy. 'I've no right to be jealous.'

'That wasn't an answer.'

Chapter 41

Betschdorf, Eastern France. Sunday May 27th 1917. 10 pm

The day's fine weather had turned into a clear, starlit night with the countryside illuminated by a three-quarter moon. Sébastien had stocked them up with provisions for a week despite Louis being confident they could get across the lines easily by dawn. He had also roped the three bicycles to the back, including Benjamin's which he had recovered, just in case they were needed. The fuel tank was full and the engine serviced by Louis, who had many talents, except those required in the farming of sugar beet – or farming anything for that matter. His mother had come with them to the haystack and, as the evening wore on to their departure time of eleven o'clock, she became more and more tearful. As her son made to climb aboard the vehicle she grabbed him in a bear hug and seemed disinclined to ever let him go.

'You are my son,' she told him. 'And I worry that I will never see you again.'

Louis drew himself away from her and kissed her on the cheek. 'Maman,' he said, 'do not fear for me. I will always come back to torment you.' He looked over her shoulder at Sébastien. 'How long do you think before the British arrive in Betschdorf?'

'One month,' said Sébastien, who hadn't a clue really.

'There you are, Maman. One month and I will be back with the money I get from selling the car.'

'Do not annoy the British officers,' she warned. 'You have a talent for annoying those in authority. If there's a problem just give them the car.'

'Maman, I will charm the money from their pockets and their bowler hats off their heads.'

'And the clothes off their women?'

'He will be charming nothing off me,' Anna said, to Tommy's amusement.

Louis held his mother's tearful face between his palms. 'Maman, there is not a girl in the world I will ever love as much as I love you. I will be back in one month.'

'Is there no end to his charm?' murmured Anna to Tommy, after translating Louis's words.

'It'd never work in Pontefract,' said Tommy.

'Maybe not on your wife?'

'Doubt it,' said Tommy, but he wasn't at all sure and, just for a moment, he wondered if some Pontefract charmer might be hanging around his Rita. It was an uncomfortable moment. All these bloody charmers making eyes at his women.

Louis took out the starting handle and started up the engine. All three of them climbed on board. Parked within the haystack it was even darker inside the car. There was no interior lighting, no instruments to record speed or fuel level, everything was educated guesswork.

Suddenly there was light. Tommy turned round to see that Louis had lit a small paraffin lamp.

'If you smell petrol fumes you must tell me and I will kill the lamp ... before it kills us.' He added the last bit with an illuminated smile, mainly for Anna's benefit. He was doing nothing to endear himself to Tommy and Tommy was beginning to think this was deliberate. If so, Tommy had a whole armoury of ways to annoy Louis.

He put the engine into bottom gear and drove outside. He and Louis opened the tiny side windows and waved goodbye to the pair outside as Tommy put his foot on the accelerator and drove away.

Anna sat beside him in a tractor seat that Louis had bolted to the floor; Louis sat behind them on a cushion, resting his back on the side of the vehicle. He began giving directions in French to Anna, at least that's what Tommy assumed, as Anna was directing him where to go.

'He says we are going to take a cross-country route, avoiding all major towns and military installations.'

'He knows them all, does he?'

Anna and Louis exchanged a few words in French than Anna said, 'Yes, he does. He has travelled these roads many times. He says he will know them better than the Germans do. We are currently north east of Nancy, which is about four miles due west of the front line. He intends us approaching the front line from the south east as the line angles south eastwards making it nearer to us the further south we go. Do you understand?'

'Not entirely, but I see some logic in it so long as we don't go too far south.'

'I will tell him that.'

321

Anna and Louis had a long conversation which seemed to be little about their direction of travel but Tommy concentrated on his driving which was difficult in this cumbersome vehicle with very heavy steering. Tommy was often using the full width of the road to keep travelling in a more-or-less straight line. He was grateful not to have met any oncoming traffic.

They had travelled perhaps five miles and through many twists and turns before they came across a man on a bicycle heading their way. He abandoned his machine and flung himself onto the grass verge as they lumbered over his bicycle and drove on. Louis called out an apology in French through the rear window only to be rewarded with a shaking fist.

'I know him,' he said to Anna. 'He is a friend of my family and he will be drunk. I will buy him a new bicycle when I return.'

Anna translated this to Tommy who said, 'I couldn't really avoid his bike. He more or less threw it in front of me. He was terrified of us.'

'That's probably a good thing,' Anna said.

'How are we doing for direction?'

'According to Louis we are heading for a place called Truchtersheim but we do not go straight through it, we go past it using side roads. I think it's about twenty or so kilometres from here.'

'It's all very quiet,' commented Tommy. 'I hope it stays quiet.'

As he spoke the moon disappeared behind a heavy cloud cloaking the whole countryside in darkness. Up until then visibility had been diffi-cult but possible in the bright moonlight. Now the light had gone. Tommy stopped the car. Louis said something in French.

'Apparently there is a switch on the dashboard that works the lights,' Anna translated.

'Now he tells me.'

'He was hoping not to use them. Less conspicuous that way – and I agree with him.'

'Do you now?'

Tommy ran his hand along the dashboard until he felt a switch. He flicked it on and the two headlamps gave out a dull glow, lighting the road for perhaps ten yards in front.

'Better than nothing I suppose,' said Tommy.

Louis spoke again to Anna.

'Apparently they are powered by a thing called a dynamo. The faster the engine goes the brighter they get.'

With the gear in neutral Tommy depressed the accelerator. As the engine roared the lights flared, lighting up the road for a good hundred yards in front. It also lit up a squad of German soldiers marching towards them.

'What the hell are they doing out here at this time of night?' Tommy wondered. 'Some sort of night manoeuvres?'

Anna said, 'More to the point, what are we going to d–?'

Her last word was drowned by the rattle of the machine gun as Louis blazed away at the unsuspecting Germans. The bullet-belt was already threaded into the gun. Anna took hold of it and guided it through as previously instructed by Tommy who had his foot on the accelerator, keeping the scene brightly illuminated until the last of the Germans fell to the ground.

'Jesus!' Tommy said. 'We've started something now.' The three of them stared at the scene of carnage they had just created. Not one of the bodies was moving.

'I should get out and take a look at them,' said Anna.

'Some of them may be still alive.'

'Anna,' said Tommy. 'We're at war with them. It's our job to kill them before they kill us.'

'I know but–'

'But nothing. We have to drive on and leave them.'

'You mean drive over them?'

'I'm sorry but I can't go round them and there's no room for a three-point turn, not in this thing anyway.' Louis was tapping Tommy on the shoulder urging him to move on, and shouting instructions.

'I assume he agrees with me,' Tommy said.

'Yes,' she said reluctantly. 'I'm not going to watch this.'

Tommy put his foot hard down and drove straight over several German bodies, possibly ending the lives of men just wounded. He would never know. For the next few miles he felt a sickness in his stomach. Eventually he stopped, got out and threw up at the side of the road. After he had finished he looked up to see that both Louis and Anna had done the same. Without a word to one another they all boarded the vehicle and continued on their journey.

Eventually their headlights illuminated a sign pointing right and saying Truchtersheim 2km.

Louis told him to turn left, then right a short way down that road.

'I think we need to get as far away from here as possible as soon as possible,' he said to Anna, who relayed his words to Tommy who nodded his head vigorously. In the heat of battle he'd seen many enemy fall, but never before had he been a party to the killing of so many unsuspecting men. It was almost like murder.

'There is a small place called Lutzelhouse about thirty kilometres from here,' said Louis. 'I think we should head in that direction.'

Anna relayed his words and Tommy just followed Louis's directions as they came, trying his best to get as much speed out of the vehicle as possible. The headlights made driving a little easier, or it did until the dynamo gave up the ghost and left them travelling by moonlight once again.

'I think this is safer,' said Louis.

'But not as easy,' said Tommy.

They were now an hour and maybe thirty kilometres from the scene of the shooting. It was half past one in the morning when they saw a manned roadblock ahead of them. Tommy peered through the glassless opening that served as a windscreen. Without headlights they were probably as invisible to the soldiers as the soldiers were to them. There was a lowered single bar barrier and a small hut to one side.

'There will be three or four men in the hut,' said Louis. 'And they may have been alerted about the shooting back there.'

'Maybe we should try a different way,' said Tommy.

'I doubt if it will make any difference. All the roads will have roadblocks. We're going to have to blast our way through all of them until we get to the front.'

Louis's words were translated by Anna but Tommy looked at the Frenchman when he said, 'Did you anticipate this from the start?'

When the question was passed on, Louis gave a Gallic shrug and said, 'Yes. There was never going to be any other way.'

'Bloody hell! Did Sébastien know?'

'He did. If you two had been on bicycles when you came across the soldiers you would be arrested by now and handed over to the Secret Service. Then you would have been shot. The Secret Service are very prompt in such matters.

'I suggest Thomas drives on, slow down as he gets near, wait until they come out of the hut, then he puts his foot down when I start shooting.'

Tommy drove until he was maybe ten yards from the road block, then stopped. No one came out of the hut for several seconds and Tommy was beginning to think the roadblock was unmanned when a single soldier came out and shouted something in German. Louis opened the lid in the turret and shouted back, also in German.

'Wir haben Aufträge für Sie, lassen Sie uns über.'

'We have orders for you to let us through.'

It was a prepared speech for which he had perfected the words and accent. The soldier asked him for his papers and was given a torrent of well-rehearsed German obscenities by Louis. By this time two more soldiers had appeared. One of them shouted equally vehement obscenities back at Louis who suddenly opened up with a gun and cut all three of them down. The 250-round bullet belt was barely a quarter used. Once again Anna helped feed it through. Louis then turned his fire on the hut just in case there was another man in there. He then urged Tommy to drive on but Tommy pulled on the handbrake and got out, lifted up the wooden barrier, drove the car through, then got out and lowered it again.

He got back in and said to Anna, 'Anyone in a road vehicle would just blast the soldiers, smash through the barrier and drive on. With it not being broken they'll think we're on foot and they'll be searching for us in the local area, when we'll be thirty miles away.' She translated this to Louis who grinned and gave Tommy a slap on the back. Tommy drove on, hitting what seemed like forty miles an hour after less than a minute. No one spoke until Tommy needed to take a turning.

'Right here to Lutzelhouse,' said Anna who was feeling sickened by her active part in the shootings. Tommy noticed this.

'You did well, Anna,' he said. 'If it's any consolation I know how you feel, but what we did was necessary.'

'Was it?' said Anna, unconvinced.

'Yes. This is war, Anna.'

'We can go straight through there,' said Louis. 'There is an epidemic there and no Germans are occupying the town.'

'What sort of epidemic?' Anna asked him.

'I don't know. Some sort of flu I think.'

'Probably Spanish flu,' said Anna. 'It must be a bad epidemic to be scaring off the Germans.'

327

'Well, we won't catch it, we're just driving through.'

They drove past sleeping buildings with shuttered windows. Occasionally someone whose flu-ridden sleep had been disturbed by the approaching mechanical monster came to a window to stare down at it. They would sneer at the Germanic crosses and go back to their beds cursing the Hun who wouldn't even let them nurse their aching bodies in peace, having no doubt brought the flu here from Germany. But they'd had word that the Germans were losing this stupid war they'd started and it wouldn't be long before the French were liberated.

'Where next?' asked Tommy, as the last of the houses disappeared behind them.

'Baccarat, I think.'

'How far?'

'Forty kilometres.'

'One hour at this speed ... given no roadblocks. How far from there to Nancy?'

'About fifty kilometres but only thirty-five to the front. We will meet a lot of opposition in that time.'

'Maybe we should ditch the car and go on foot,' suggested Anna.

'How?' asked Louis. 'The country is heavy with German troops. An armoured car is the only way.' He said it scornfully which annoyed Anna.

'I think Anna has a point,' Tommy said. 'We can't drive this through heavy artillery. It might be bullet proof but it's not shell proof.'

'I am not saying it will be easy,' said Louis. 'I am simply saying it is the only way. We may get through, we may be killed. We will be running a gauntlet. It is the way of war. You risk nothing, you win nothing.'

As usual the conversation was translated by Anna with a heavy slant towards her side of the argument, but Tommy didn't need a slant. He was on Anna's side anyway – no matter what side she took.

'How many roadblocks between here and Baccarat do you think?' he asked.

'I would guess at one, possibly two,' said Louis.

'What time does it get light?'

'About six o'clock.'

Tommy looked at his pocket watch by the light of the paraffin lamp. 'It's now quarter past two. We could be home and dry by then.'

'More likely dead,' said Anna, without translating this to Louis.

'I think we should bludgeon our way to Baccarat and see how things pan out,' Tommy said.

'Pan out? How am I supposed to translate that?'

'It just means ... see how things turn out. Try him with that.'

Anna tried Louis with that. He just shrugged, as he often did. 'He's not happy,' she said.

'He's dead set on selling the car to the British.'

'Will they buy it off him?'

'I'd like to think they would, but I honestly doubt it.'

Louis was right. There was only one roadblock on the way to Baccarat. This time Tommy didn't slow down. He went for it at high speed and Louis opened fire at the hut from a range of two hundred yards before anyone came out. No one did come out. This time Tommy drove straight through the barrier, having made up his mind to ditch the car when they got near Baccarat. If Louis wanted to carry on without them, so be it. He didn't need them.

Tommy estimated that they were no more than three miles away from Baccarat when they found themselves driving through a dense wood. Without explaining why, he spun the steering wheel to the right and drove the vehicle up a steep bank and into the trees. Anna said nothing. She knew what was happening and she approved. Louis shouted in French but Tommy ignored him and carried on driving until the car was well and truly obscured from the road. He switched off the engine and turned to face Louis, but he was talking to Anna.

'Louis tells us that we now need to cross a river and that the only bridge he knows about is the one in Baccarat, which is a fairly big town. To take this thing through after what we've done back on the road will be suicide. Do you agree?'

'I do.'

'Then tell him please.'

Anna repeated Tommy's words to Louis who scowled at first, then thought about it and reluctantly agreed with the sense of it.

'At first light the three of us ride straight through the town on the bikes,' Tommy said. 'Ask him if he has any francs.'

Louis had francs to the equivalent of twenty-two British pounds and Anna had the equivalent of twenty pounds in marks, so between them they were more than solvent should the need arise. They taught Tommy a few phrases in French just

330

in case a German asked him any questions. Louis taught him the Gallic shrug, much to Anna's amusement. His dodgy French accent wouldn't be picked up by Germans, and Anna and Louis would take care of all conversations with the French.

Just after dawn they were cycling across La Meurthe, the river that divided the town into east and west districts. They stopped at an early morning patisserie to buy cakes, pastries, croissants and orange juice. Ten minutes later they were stopped at a roadblock at the western edge of the town. It was Anna's native German that convinced the guard that they were simply a German girl and her two French cousins on their way to visit relatives in the neighbouring village of Badménil. The guard pointed his rifle at Tommy and said something in German to him. Tommy shrugged and said, *Je suis désolé. Je ne vous comprends pas.*'

'They do not understand our language,' said Anna to the guard. 'I am trying to teach them, but it is not easy.'

'This is a very dangerous part of the world,' said the guard. 'Badménil is very near the front line.'

'They know, they live here,' Anna said smiling, 'and I believe it is no more dangerous in Badménil.'

'British shells can reach there.'

Anna reached into her bag and took out her identification papers. 'As you can see, I am a nurse from Mannheim hospital. Our relative in Badménil is ill, which is why I travelled here. Are the shells actually dropping on Badménil?'

The guard said nothing. He felt he was on the

cusp of betraying a military secret to a civilian.

'Do you have orders to stop us travelling there?' Anna asked him.

The guard shook his head, raised the barrier and waved them through. They all cycled through in silence and didn't speak until they were well out of earshot. Anna related her conversation with the guard in both French and English.

'Anna, that was a stroke of genius,' Tommy said.

'Really? I thought it was just bullshit.'

'Anna. That was bullshit of the highest order.'

'I don't know about that. I'm guessing he should have asked for all our identification papers. I assume Louis has his, but yours are from the hospital.'

'Oops!'

'I know. We'll have to go back to you being a mentally damaged German.'

'Agreed. It's a good scam though. I wonder how near to the front we can get, pretending we're visiting a sick relative?'

'Well,' said Anna, 'I imagine there are plenty of locals living very near to the front line unless the Germans have moved them all out.'

Anna translated this to Louis who told her, 'The people are still there. They have nowhere else to go.'

'Not too sure about that,' said Tommy. 'I've been on the other side and the civilians were all evacuated, apart from essential personnel and there weren't too many of them. So we're three innocent civilians, until it all gets too hot.'

'Then what?' Anna asked.

'Then we play it by ear ... can you translate that to Louis?'

'I think so.'

They had just passed through Badménil when Tommy raised a hand to stop them all.

'What is it?' Anna asked.

'Can you hear that?'

They all listened. In the distance was the sound of heavy guns, brought in on a westerly wind.

'How far away do you think they are?' Anna asked Louis.

'Who knows? Maybe ten kilometres ... maybe fifteen.'

Anna translated this to Tommy who converted it to the miles he understood better. 'Six to ten miles. We could be there in under an hour. The trouble is, what lies between here and there? We're on back roads here but we're bound to run into heavy German military soon. They're not going to let us ride our bikes right up to the front line.'

Louis suggested they climb to the crest of a nearby hill and take a good look at what lay ahead. They abandoned their cycles in a hedge and spent ten breathless minutes hill-climbing. The view was extensive and panoramic. The horizon was clouded with smoke, within which they saw flashes of fire and heard loud explosions.

'I'd put that lot no more than five miles away,' Tommy said. 'Five miles between us and our ticket to Blighty.' He looked at Louis and said to Anna. 'Ask him if he really wants to come with us. I mean, if he hasn't got the armoured car to sell he might not see any advantage.'

Anna spoke to Louis who was distracted by something he saw halfway down the hill. He was pointing at it and asking what it was. Tommy followed his pointing finger and saw what looked like a large metal object standing in a field, perhaps half a mile away.

'What is that?' Louis was asking.

Tommy was equally curious and began scrambling down the hill, followed by the other two. As he approached the object it became clearer until he could identify it.

'It's a tank,' he said.

'What's a tank?' asked Anna.

'It's like an armoured car, only bigger and on tracks. And if I'm not mistaken that's a British tank.' He looked at Anna. 'Surely we haven't crossed over to the British side without noticing?'

'I doubt it,' she said, looking to her left. He followed her gaze and saw a German military convoy travelling along a road which would have taken it past the three of them had they not decided to climb the hill. They all dropped to the ground to make themselves less conspicuous. The convoy went on its way and Tommy got to his feet, once again looking at the tank. It was shielded from the road by dense bushes and Tommy wondered if this had been done purposely. If it was a British tank, maybe there was a British crew inside. The thought excited him. A British tank that had somehow sneaked behind enemy lines.

'How do you know it's British?' asked Anna.

'Not sure. I've never actually seen a German tank, but that looks very much like some British tanks we had attached to our regiment. I don't think the German tanks look much like ours. That's got no German markings on it and the German army do like painting black crosses on everything.'

The three of them advanced warily on the tank. It was a huge, threatening vehicle, ten feet high and twenty-five feet long, parallelogram in shape, made of heavy, riveted steel with curved edges and with a metal track running all the way around it from top to bottom. A large, powerful-looking gun poked out of the side on which was written the word LUSITANIA.

'It must be British,' said Tommy. 'Why would the Germans write that on the side of a tank?'

'Lusitania? What does it mean?' Anna asked.

'It's the name of a British passenger ship a German U-boat sank a couple of years ago. A lot of Americans were on board and were drowned. According to your father it's what really brought the Americans into the war.'

Anna translated all this to Louis who said he'd be happy to cross the line with them, provided they went in the tank.

'I think we'd better take a closer look at it first,' said Tommy. 'There might not be anyone in it, or they might be Germans.'

'Not if it's a British tank, surely.'

'I'm not sure, Anna.'

'I think it's worth a try. Louis is right. It's our best way of getting across the line.'

'I can't argue with that.'

'If they're Germans we'll just have to bullshit out way out of trouble.'

Tommy grinned. 'I can't argue with that either.

You're the expert bullshitter here.'

'Flatterer,' said Anna.

Tommy held a finger to his lips to tell them both to keep quiet as they got nearer. They stood right at the tank's side and listened for voices from within. Nothing, apart from a noise that Tommy whispered was either a mechanical sound he couldn't identify, or somebody snoring. As silently as he could he clambered up to the top where there was a turret with an open hatch. He was about to shout down in English when he realised French was much safer. He climbed back down and asked Anna to climb up and shout down in French. If a German answered she could speak in German and if the voice was English he would speak to them. All possibilities catered for.

'What if he's French?'

'The French don't have any tanks.'

'Right.'

Anna climbed up on to the tank, closely followed by Tommy and Louis. The hatch was wide open. She crept towards it and called down, softly at first, *'Bonjour.'*

'Louder,' whispered Tommy.

Louis muscled them aside and shouted, *'Bonjour. Quelqu'un est là-bas?'*

'Anybody down there?'

A voice said, *'Wer sind Sie?'*

'He's German,' whispered Anna. 'He wants to know who we are.'

'Tell him we're friends,' said Tommy, 'and ask him to come out.'

'Wir sind Freunde. Können Sie rauskommen?'

A worried voice said, *'Sie sind Deutsche Armee?'* *'Are you German army?'*

Anna translated to Tommy. 'He wants to know if we're German army. He sounds a bit worried if we are.'

'Tell him we're civilians.'

'Nein, wir sind Zivilisten,' said Anna.

A thought struck Tommy. 'Ask him if he's a deserter. Tell him we're still friends if he is.'

'Sind sie ein Deserteur?'

Silence.

'Wir sind immer noch Freunde, wenn so.'

Anna translated Tommy's exact words. There was a silence from below, then a young man popped his head out of the hatch and looked around at them. He was no more than twenty-one years old with a filthy face and wearing a German cap that looked much like a British sailor's cap flat on his head only without the sailor's jauntyness. In fact there was nothing at all jaunty about this young man. He held up both hands to indicate he wasn't armed.

'Ask him how many of them are there?' said Tommy.

Anna did as requested.

'Nurich.'

'Just him.'

'Ask him–'

Anna stopped Tommy's next question with a raised hand. 'Just let me have a conversation with him.'

A two-minute conversation ensued, with Anna constantly nodding her understanding, and even looking sympathetic at times. They stopped talking and both looked at Tommy who was getting impatient.

'His name is Dieter,' Anna told him. 'He stole the tank after the British crew were all killed or had abandoned the tank. It was stopped in a crater in No Man's Land.'

'Who killed them?'

'He just found three dead and he managed to drive the tank away.'

'Where are the dead men?'

She pointed beyond the front of the tank... 'Over there, somewhere.'

Tommy walked over to where she was pointing and saw three British soldiers lying in a depression in the ground. He called Anna across to ascertain that they were dead. She confirmed this.

'I wonder what happened to the others,' Tommy said, so that Dieter could hear him and reply, 'What others?'

'A tank like this carries a crew of eight. I wonder why they abandoned it?'

'No ammunition,' said Dieter. 'None inside.'

'You understand English?' said Tommy.

'A little.'

'We should bury them,' said Tommy, 'and mark their graves.' To Dieter he said, 'Do you have a shovel in the tank?'

Dieter didn't understand. Tommy mimed using a shovel, then pointed to the tank.

'*Nein.*'

Tommy looked around him. There was a broken stone wall nearby. 'We could bury them under that stone,' he suggested. They all looked reluctant.

'Look, they're three men who died fighting for

what we all believe in. We can't just leave them to rot.' He took the dog tags off each man and went to fetch a stone. Dieter joined him and, shamed into it, so did Anna and Louis. It took them an hour to bury the British tank crew under the stones.

The German then found two short sticks and, using a length of cable he fashioned a small cross that he stuck on top of the stone grave. All four of them gathered around it as Anna said a prayer in English.

'Eternal rest grant unto them Oh Lord,

And let perpetual light shine upon them,

May they rest in peace...'

The prayer was completed by four Amens and a sign of the cross from Anna. Tommy walked back to the tank.

'So it still drives,' he said.

'Apparently,' said Anna. 'Dieter was in No Man's Land with heavy fire from all sides. People dropping dead all around him. The fighting all got too much for him. He saw the tank with smoke coming from the hatch. He thinks someone had thrown a grenade in. He climbed inside and drove it here, which is where he's been for two days without anyone missing him. Without the tank for protection he'd be dead. It still works reasonably well. It seems the Germans are heavily outgunned and outnumbered and he's scared of being killed by his own side for desertion and by the British for being an enemy driving a British tank.'

'Do we believe this?'

'Thomas, what difference does it make if we don't? It's still a tank and he's a driver.'

'He could drive us straight into German hands.'

'Tommy, he's shaking all over. The man's terrified. He's suffering from bomb shock. We had a lot of it in the hospital.'

'It just seems too good to be true. Ask him how far away are the British lines?'

Dieter told her they were about five miles away from No Man's Land which was about two hundred metres across.

'How fast can the tank go at top speed?'

The German told Anna he could get to No Man's land in one hour at top speed.

'I could walk it faster than that,' Anna commented.

'Tanks can only travel at walking pace,' said Tommy. 'Will he do it if we guarantee him safety at the other side? You can tell him I'm a British soldier.'

Anna spoke to Dieter for a few seconds, until Dieter spoke to Tommy in heavily accented English. 'You are English soldier?'

'I am.'

'Where is your uniform?'

'It was blown off me by a German mine. Where did you learn English?'

'I learn English at university.'

'Which university?'

'Leeds. Will I be safe in England?'

'You will be in a prison camp until the war is over, but you will be safe enough. I can request special treatment for you.'

It wasn't a lie. He could request it, but his request would be ignored. No point telling Dieter that. Tommy paused before asking the big question. 'Dieter, are you willing to drive us all to No Man's Land and over to the British side?'

As Dieter gave this careful thought Tommy asked another question. 'Are there many tanks in the area?'

'No. The German army has none in this area. My tank was damaged at the Somme, which is where many of our tanks are. I was sent to be an infantry soldier.'

'So, what about taking us?'

'A look of determination formed on Dieter's dirty face. 'I will do it,' he said, 'but we must wait until night when the shooting stops.'

'We could do with some sleep before we go,' Tommy said. 'I haven't had a decent night's sleep for ages. Have we all got our sleeping bags?' He was looking at Louis.

Anna translated, Louis patted his rucksack.

'We will need a white flag,' said Anna.

'There is French flag inside,' said Dieter. 'There are French over the lines as well as British.'

Anna translated. 'All the better,' laughed Tommy. Louis laughed as well. He didn't know what he was laughing at except that things seemed to be going their way. When Anna explained things to him he rubbed his hands, saying that he would get much more selling the tank than he would an armoured car. Anna chose not to mention this to Tommy.

'Okay, Dieter,' said Tommy. 'You can go back to sleep inside your tank, we'll kip down here for a few hours. Do you want anything to eat first?'

Dieter said he was hungry so they all tucked into the food they'd bought in Baccarat. Tommy

341

slept for ten straight hours and woke up re-freshed, in the late afternoon. The other two were still asleep. Dieter was sitting on the top track, smoking. He had a rifle across his knees. Still in his sleeping bag Tommy eyed it, suspiciously.

'You planning on shooting us, Dieter?'

'No, I am guarding you. You have all been sleeping very well. I wish I can sleep as well, but I have a lot of worry.'

'So do we. But when it gets dark it will all be over in an hour or so – one way or another.'

'It is this one way or another that troubles me.'

'If there aren't any other tanks that can harm us?'

'The Germans have many big guns.'

'Yes, I've seen them. Big cumbersome things. If we are moving they will struggle to get a good bead on us.' He mimed what this meant.

Dieter nodded. 'I will drive as fast as I can but the ground is not good. Many holes made by shells and bombs.'

Tommy got to his feet and patted the steel tracks. 'These tracks will take us over that lot, surely.'

'Surely they will,' said Dieter, who had a nervous tic in the left side of his face. He wasn't one of life's heroes, Tommy concluded. It was to be hoped he didn't crack up completely before they got to No Man's Land. Not a good place to be stranded in a tank flying a union jack. He decided to ask for driving lessons just in case the worst happened. He woke up Louis and Anna, explaining what he wanted, then he told Dieter who agreed to give them all the rudiments of what made the tank move forwards, backwards and slew sideways. They spent an hours learning these things without actually starting the engine. Then Dieter showed Louis how to fire the guns, something Tommy and Anna sincerely hoped would not be necessary, and finally, he showed them how to start up the engine.

It was six o'clock in the evening when he drove it back up the hill and pointed to a landmark church steeple in the distant fading light, almost obscured by the fading smoke of battle. Then he took out a compass and took a reading. 'We drive to that church. We do not take any roads, we just drive through fields and fences and walls on a bearing of two-seven-eight degrees,' he said. 'If any buildings get in our way we go around them and continue on two-seven-eight degrees. That will take us to the nearest point in the line. I will drive at the top speed, there will be guns shooting at us. Many small bullets will hit us and do no harm. We must hope we are too fast for the big guns to hit us. I suggest we do not raise the French flag until we are in No Man's Land. That way the Germans will not be sure who we are.'

'Will that take us into the French or the British?' Anna asked him.

'I am not sure. French I think.'

'Do you not have a German flag?' Tommy asked. 'That would confuse them even more.'

'Why would an English tank carry a German flag?'

'Subterfuge,' said Tommy.

'Then I will look in the locker,' said Dieter.

Five minutes later he emerged holding a flag

343

which he stretched out at arm's length. It had three horizontal stripes in black white and red.

'It is old Prussian flag,' Dieter said.

'Near enough to confuse them,' said Tommy. Anna agreed as did Louis who could see many francs coming his way. He said something to Anna in French.

'He wants you to confirm that the tank is all his once we get across. Not yours and not the Germans'.'

'All his,' said Tommy. 'Although he might have been better off trying to sell it to the French. The British won't take too kindly to buying back a tank that was stolen from them.'

Anna confirmed to Louis that the tank was his to sell. He grinned broadly and said something to her.

'He says he can drive it,' she told Tommy.

'He may well get the chance if Dieter lets us down.'

'Talking of Dieter, I think you should take charge of the rifle,' she said.

'Don't you trust him?'

'Thomas, he's German soldier.'

Tommy called out to Dieter to give him the rifle as Dieter would be busy driving with no time to be shooting anyone. Dieter, who hadn't let the weapon out of his possession since Tommy first saw him with it, held onto it tighter.

'*Nein. Darf nicht lassen Sie mein Gewehr.*'

Tommy looked at Anna and asked. 'What's he saying?'

'He says he must not let go of his gun.'

Tommy turned to Dieter. 'That's what our officers tell us in the army. Dieter, we are not army officers. We are your friends. You must trust us.'

Dieter now spoke English. His voice was wavering, uncertainly. 'I must keep it,' he said. 'I must not give you my gun.'

'Why, don't you trust us?'

There was a challenge in Tommy's voice which caused a manic light to appear in Dieter's eyes. His nervous tic got worse. He pointed the gun at Tommy and screamed in German. *'Sie wollen mich fangen!'*

'Careful, Tommy,' said Anna. 'He thinks we've been sent to get him.'

'Dieter, I'm English,' said Tommy. 'Why would I want to get you?'

Dieter marched up to him and stabbed the rifle in his chest. 'Hey!' protested Tommy, holding his hands aloft. 'Just watch it. That bloody thing might go off!'

Louis had picked up a heavy stone and was circling around the back of Dieter. Tommy, with his hands in the air, had his eyes on the two of them. Between them they might be the death of him but he daren't say anything to warn Louis off, lest it spook the man pointing the gun at him.

'Dieter,' said Anna, calmly. 'You're not yourself. All the fighting has made you behave badly. Okay, you can keep the gun, just put it down. We're here to take you to safety.'

Tommy was nodding his agreement. Louis was closing in on Dieter from behind. 'She's right, Dieter,' Tommy said. 'Just put the gun down and we'll all get off. One hour and we'll all be safe.'

Dieter's crazed look grew worse. 'You say they

345

will put me in prison.'

'Not prison – a prisoner of war camp in England, away from all the fighting, among your own people. It will only be for a short time and you will be treated well. The war will be over soon and you can go home to your family.'

'I do not believe your lies. You are here to take me to be shot.'

Dieter's rifle was pointing at Tommy's chest as Louis's arm swung down and the stone in his hand hit the back of Dieter's head. The gun fired and a bullet hit Tommy, going straight through him and out of his back. He dropped to the ground. Louis grabbed the rifle from Dieter's unconscious hand as Anna knelt beside Tommy.

'Is he dead?' Louis asked, not showing too much concern.

'If he is you caused his death, you idiot! The man was pointing his gun at him.'

'I know and I thought he was going to pull the trigger.'

'He *did* pull the trigger!'

Tommy opened his eyes and looked up at Anna. 'Is it bad?' he croaked.

She opened his shirt to reveal a wound just to the right side of his stomach. 'It's not too bad,' she lied, 'but we need to get you to a hospital. I can give you morphine for the pain.'

'Give me plenty,' said Tommy. 'It hurts like hell.'

Anna injected a full syringe of morphine into his arm and watched, tearfully, as he drifted into unconsciousness. Louis was standing over the unconscious Dieter, pointing the gun at him. 'I should shoot him,' he said. 'Then you and I can take the tank over the lines.'

'Oh yes, and what about Thomas?'

'Anna. Look at him, he's had it. You did what you could for him and he's about to die a painless death.'

She shook her head. 'Not if he gets proper medical attention.'

'How are we supposed to get that without giving ourselves up? They will shoot all three of us. I'm sorry but Thomas is a dead man. He is in no pain. We must leave him. You and I will take the tank. It's our only chance. We could be good together.'

'Good together? You idiot! You killed my Thomas!'

Anna suddenly hurled herself at Louis, screaming German profanities and slapping him hard across the face several times, punching him in the mouth and splitting his lip. He pushed her hands away. She fell to the ground in a sobbing heap, resting her head against Tommy's chest. Tommy was still breathing, although his chest was saturated in blood, much of which he was now transferring to Anna. Louis felt he had to say more.

'Anna, this is ridiculous. What the hell do you want me to do?'

She looked up at him with blazing eyes. Her voice was shrill and angry. 'First I need to stop the bleeding and dress his wound, then we put Thomas in the tank and then you drive us to the line. I suggest you get that damned thing started up.'

Louis fingered his swelling lip then he pointed at Dieter, lying unconscious on the ground.

'What about him?'

Without sparing Dieter a glance she said. 'What about him?'

'Will he die?'

'I hope so.'

Shaking his head in exasperation and without another word, Louis climbed into the tank as Anna eased Tommy onto his side to see if the bullet had gone clean through. It had, which was good in a way, but she knew the exit wound would be much bigger than the entrance wound. What she didn't know was what damage had been done to his internal organs, his lungs, possibly his heart. Louis was probably right, Thomas would soon be dead. Even if he wasn't, how could he possibly survive the severity of the flight across No Man's Land? The shells, the bullets, the bombs; being hurled from side to side within the claustrophobic steel box as it battled its way through barbed wire and bounced up and down the myriad shell craters and across dozens of trenches. Tommy was a badly wounded man with a nasty hole right through his body. She herself might not survive such a journey and she was fit and well. The very thought had her in floods of tears. She took a calming breath, opened her bag and took out her medical supplies. The colour had drained from Tommy's handsome face, his breathing was slight and she knew he'd lost a lot of blood. She had seen many men die in comfortable hospital beds from wounds such as this. How could he possibly survive what she had in store for him?

'Oh my darling Thomas, please do not die. Not now.'

Chapter 42

Pontefract. Monday 28th May 1917

'By heck, Rita. This washing machine's brilliant. I've done a week's washing in an hour. All I've got to do now is put it through the mangle and hang it out. After that I'm a lady of leisure ... are you all right, love?'

Rita was clasping a hand to her stomach, gasping for breath and squeezing her eyes together in an effort to make a sudden pain go away. She was sitting with her broken leg resting on a footstool.

'What is it?' Agnes asked her. They were at home alone and getting on quite well. Everyone else was either at school or work. 'Is it your leg?'

'No. I feel as if I've just been shot in the stomach.'

'Oh, I had pain like that after Stanley was born. It comes from nowhere. It's your body's way of telling you to stop messing it about, that's what the doctor told me, and you messed your body about quite a lot when Benjamin was born.'

'True,' said Rita. 'I suppose I'm entitled to a few aches and pains, but this felt different.' She touched her stomach, gingerly, saying, 'I've got a pain exactly here. It wouldn't surprise me if I've got a bruise – and a pain in my back as if something had gone right through me.'

She undid her cardigan, unbuttoned her blouse

and pointed to the spot. 'Here, can you see a bruise?'

'No, nothing.' Agnes touched the spot.

'Ouch!'

'Could be something to do with breast feeding, or maybe even some knock-on effect from your leg. It does happen. How's the leg doing by the way?'

'Well, I'm managing on one crutch now, so it's coming along.'

'Good girl. I'll make you a cup of tea. That'll take the pain away.'

Rita called after her. 'Agnes...'

'What?'

'I know you think this is stupid, but I think this has something to do with Tommy.'

'Why?'

'I don't know.'

'Why would our Tommy want to hurt you?'

'I don't think he does want to hurt me. Maybe someone's hurt him.' She smiled. 'If they have, it means he's definitely alive.'

'I'll make that cup of tea,' said Agnes. 'Have you decided what to do with your new-found wealth?'

'I'm putting the money in the Yorkshire Bank. Mr Gibson's advised me on a way to invest it safely at a good interest rate. I've been advised to put the shop up for sale as a going concern. The estate agent knows a chain of butchers who might buy it. When Tommy comes home we'll buy a nice house. Blimey, Agnes, I wish this pain'd go away. Tommy Birch, if this is you, I'd like you to stop it, please!'

This amused Agnes. 'He was a bugger for playing tricks was our Tommy.'

'I don't think this is a trick, Agnes. I think Tommy might be in pain.'

'Good, if it means he's still alive.'

'I hear that Stuart's been granted an appeal. It'll be heard in London next month.'

'Are you going?'

'I feel I should, but it's too much of a journey with this flipping leg.'

'Perhaps that's as well, love. It might be a bit upsetting for you if he gets turned down and you two hundred miles from home and having to get yourself back. How much is this barrister costing?'

'Well he's not the one who defended him last time. This man's supposed to be very good at appeals.'

'How much?'

'About two hundred pounds.'

'Good grief! That's more than a year's wages for some.'

'Less if it's over quickly.'

'More if it's not. If young Stuart gets off with life he owes it to you.'

'No he doesn't, he owes it to George Miller. That should give him something to think about when he's doing his time.'

'I can see what our Tommy sees in you. There's a lot more to you than a pretty face.'

Rita smiled at this rare compliment from her mother-in-law. 'You said that as though you believe he's still alive.'

'Well, it suits me better that way. Helps me to cope.'

'I think I'll go to bed after this cup of tea. I feel very tired all of a sudden.'

'Maybe you should see the doctor, love.'

Rita yawned. 'If it's still painful tomorrow I will. I hope Tommy's all right. I pray for him you know.'

'So do I, Rita. Every night. I pray for all of you.'

'I didn't know you were religious.'

'I'm just a mother.'

Rita had prised herself to her feet and was on her way to bed, helped by a single crutch, when Charlie came home early. His face was red-eyed and drawn and he looked to have been crying. He sat down and buried his face in his hands. Agnes put a hand on his shoulder. Rita limped back into the room, equally concerned. Agnes spoke to him.

'Charlie, what's wrong?'

'Every bloody thing.'

'Is it the job?'

He shook his head, then he looked up at her. 'It's young Stuart. He's gone and hanged himself in prison! The lad's dead and it's my bloody fault! If I hadn't opened my big mouth he'd still be alive ... and so would that butcher feller.'

The two women stood by as he wept. Then Rita placed a hand on his shoulder.

'Charlie,' she said, 'you're no more to blame than I am. I told you and you told Stuart. Should I be crying as well? I feel sad for the boy but I feel sadder for George and I definitely caused him to get killed by opening my big mouth.'

'To me,' said Charlie. 'You opened your mouth to me and I'm family. It was something that should have been kept in the family.'

'You couldn't have seen what was to come, love,' said Agnes. 'There's none of us expected that.'

'Certainly not me, or I'd have warned George,' said Rita. 'If we put our minds to it we could probably blame any number of people. We could blame whoever started the riot outside his shop for a start. That's what caused it, not you.'

'If we're going to blame anyone,' said Agnes, 'we should be blaming whoever's supposed to be guarding kids like that in prison. A lad who'd been sentenced to death's got to be a likely candidate for suicide. It's not the first time it's happened in Armley jail.'

'Charlie,' said Rita, gently, 'the only person blaming you for this is you. I doubt if Stuart's mother even blames you.'

'Do you know who I blame?' said Charlie, suddenly. 'I blame that bloody judge. He sentenced the lad to death when he knew there'd be an appeal that'd leave the proper sentencing to someone else. Young Stuart's barrister told me that.'

'The barrister I got for Stuart's appeal said he had an excellent chance of a reprieve,' said Rita. 'So, you're right, Charlie. The trial judge should never have sentenced Stuart to death. It's his fault and someone should tell him.'

'I think I might be the one to do that,' said Charlie. 'I was the lad's boss, it's most probably my duty. I'll write to him and I'll send a copy to the papers. That'll bloody learn him.'

He sat there for a while, nodding to himself, then he took out his pipe, filled it with tobacco and began his ritual of lighting it as he mentally composed his letter. Agnes glanced at Rita and winked. All was well with the Birch family once more.

Chapter 43

Night had fallen and it was time to move off. Dieter was still unconscious and an unconcerned Anna said he would most probably die without regaining consciousness, his head injury was so bad. Her love for Tommy far outweighed her nurse's concern for the injured man who had all but killed him.

The interior of the tank was on two levels: a higher level with two seats for the driver and his mate and a lower level for the crew. The lower level was an intricacy of fuel lines and storage racks for shells. These racks were all empty, telling of the heavy action the tank had seen just before it was abandoned. It was built for a crew of eight, which meant there was room to lay Tommy down full length on the steel floor. Anna and Louis had brought him through a side door in the wall of the tank.

Anna looked around to see if there was anything soft he could lie on. She folded up her coat and placed it under his head then looked around for anything else.

'Surely Dieter found something comfortable to sleep on.'

'I could try and wake him up and ask him,' said

Louis, in a vain effort to raise a smile from her. But joking about a dying man didn't impress Anna one bit. Her sole concern was for her Thomas.

'Shut up, Louis.'

In the gloom Anna pointed to a greatcoat hanging from a hook at the end of the very narrow walkway that ran beside the empty shell racks.

'What's that?'

A chastened Louis gave it to her. She laid it beside Tommy and they moved him onto it. It provided a thin layer of warmth and softness between him and the cold steel floor.

'Anything else?' she asked. 'Where did Dieter get the flag from?'

Louis found the locker from which Dieter had got the flag. Inside were several more coats, a blanket, a rifle, some steel helmets and gas masks. They used the coats to give Tommy more padding between him and the steel floor, and the blanket to cover him up. He was still under sedation, hopefully feeling no pain, but he was hardly breathing and his heart rate had slowed right down. She had stopped the bleeding and had dressed his wounds front and back. It was all she could do for him. She knew that without proper treatment he would die within a few hours. She said a silent prayer that she could get him that treatment in time. She wasn't the only woman praying for Tommy at that particular moment. The Almighty was being inundated with earnest supplications for Tommy's wellbeing from both Pontefract and France.

Louis started up the massive engine as Anna stared down at Tommy. Using a heavy metal shell box she had formed a narrow passage between it and the tank wall the same width as Tommy's shoulders and wedged him into it so he wasn't going to roll around much. Louis found a switch that turned on electric interior lights, making him whoop with triumph and raising a thin smile from Anna. She needed light to look after Tommy. She knelt at his head with a palm at either side. Louis, sitting way above them, called out, 'We are rolling, hold on.'

The whole interior roared with violent sound as the tank moved off down the hill. Tommy's eyes flickered, which was a good sign to Anna. Louis looked at the compass he'd taken from Dieter and set the tank on a westerly heading of two-seven-eight.

It was the only tank for miles and was displaying a Germanic flag from its flagstaff. The night cloaked it from most eyes but the noise it made would draw much attention. Hopefully the flag would allay any suspicions. It would certainly do no harm. Above Anna was a gun that would send a six-pound shell two miles. Only there weren't any six pound shells on board. In fact there was no ammunition for the two Lewis guns or the Hotchkiss machine guns. The tank was a formidable weapon of war when fully armed but right now it was as lethal as Sébastien's horse and trap and, at four miles an hour, almost a sitting target.

Louis had now reached the bottom of the hill and was driving straight through the hedge that had shielded the tank from the road. Maintaining a westerly heading it knocked down two substantial stone walls, one at either side of the road

and headed out to what looked like open countryside. Louis now found a headlight switch that lit
his way for at least two hundred yards – just grass-
land with an occasional bush and small tree,
nothing that could be called an obstacle. He was
enjoying himself as the prospect of selling a whole
tank loomed larger with every yard he travelled.
He looked at his pocket watch, which read 10:15.
In a couple of hours he'd be involved in financial
negotiations with the British or the French for
recovering one of their very expensive tanks. He
would prefer to deal with the British who were
known to be a reasonable race – reasonable to the
point of gullible, and Louis found gullibility to be
a most endearing trait in his customers.

In the dim interior light Anna looked down at
Tommy. With all the noise she couldn't hear his
breathing and with all the sudden and jerky movement and vibration around her she couldn't
distinguish his pulse or check that his eyes might
flicker now and again. She just prayed that he was
alive and still would be when they got him into
British medical hands. She looked down at this
man she loved, not knowing if he was alive or
dead. With her tears dripping onto his face she
kissed him on his forehead to test his body for
warmth, but there was too much heat in the tank's
interior for a dead man's body to cool down.

After a while she felt like screaming at Louis to
stop and switch the engine off so that she could
check for Tommy's life signs, but she knew she
mustn't do that. Louis was their lifeline to free-
dom. If her lover was alive, the quicker they got to
their destination the better. She spoke to Tommy

but he couldn't reply. In all her life she had never felt so desperate, so bereft, so helpless.

'Please be alive, my Thomas.'

And so it went on for an hour until Louis called out, 'I think we are crossing into No Man's Land. You need to fly the British flag.'

Battery Commander Captain Harry Waltham wiped the lenses of his binoculars, which were pretty useless when there were no flares up above. The enemy guns were a quarter of a mile away and his own battery just to the side of him. They'd been exchanging fire for some time beneath the illumination of flares. Someone nearby shouted a warning. 'Gas, gas, gas!'

Another flare lit up the smoke pouring from a gas shell and heading towards the British lines on the breeze. Waltham donned his gas mask after calling out for the whole unit to do likewise. Most of them didn't need telling. They'd seen soldiers suffering from mustard gas poisoning: great mustard-coloured blisters, blind eyes stuck together, throats closing, fighting for breath, choking to the most horrible of deaths. A vile way to fight a war. But no war is pleasant.

Machine guns rattled like cackling geese, heavy guns boomed, the smell of gunpowder heavy in the air, as was the smell of death. Men were taking cover in trenches and shell craters, faces pressed into the earth as death zipped and whined over their heads. One man, completely terrified by the noise and violence of the war all around him, had defecated in his trousers and, in his misery and confusion, had failed to put on his gas mask. There wasn't much glory in most deaths in this war and his would be a most inglorious one. Others were crying out after being hit; horses neighing for the same reasons; some being shot to take them out of their misery. Waltham hated that. Killing horses. He hated the fact that horses had been brought into the war. This wasn't their war. Back home he was a member of the Quorn and owned two beautiful hunters. No way would he ever have brought them to such a man-made hellhole.

He was on his knees still looking through his binoculars. A bullet ricocheted off his helmet knocking him backwards, but just before he fell he saw something approaching. He peered towards the German lines and called out to a sergeant.

'Sarn't. Is that what I think it is?'

'A tank, sir.'

Both voices muffled by gas masks.

'They haven't got any tanks here.'

'That's definitely a tank, sir. In fact it's a British tank ... a Mark Four, sir.'

'We haven't got any Mark Fours in this area. They're all further up the line. Could be a Hun driving it.'

'Sir. It's heading straight for us, sir.'

'Have the howitzer take its undercarriage out, sarn't. If it's one of ours I'll apologise.'

'Sir.'

The tank was only twenty yards away when the howitzer shell exploded beneath it and no more than ten yards away when it slewed to a halt with one of its tracks destroyed.

'It's flying a British flag, sir,' said the sergeant.

'The Hun have plenty of them, sarn't.'

'Do you want me to drop a grenade in the hatch, sir?'

'Erm, no. We'd better see what comes out of the hatch before we do anything.'

Enemy shells were now bouncing off the tank, encouraging Waltham in the belief that it was indeed a British tank. All British eyes were on the hatch which had been flipped open. A head appeared, lots of blonde hair, then ducked back down to avoid passing shells. A hand appeared waving a white flag, followed by the blonde head once more.

'Bloody hell, sarn't! Is that a woman?'

'Looks like it to me, sir.'

'What the hell's a woman doing in a tank on the front line?'

'Beats me, sir.'

'Well, I'd better take a look. Try and cover me, sarn't.'

'I'll do my best, sir.'

Using the tank as a shield against incoming fire the officer darted towards the tank, climbed on top of it and dropped through the hatch with a pistol at the ready. Anna glanced up from tending Tommy and said, calmly, *'Bonsoir, monsieur.'*

'Evening,' said Waltham.

'And you are English, good.'

'What did you expect?'

'French or English. We were not sure. I prefer the English.'

'Good, you prefer me, then. I don't wish to be rude but might I ask what you're doing with one of our tanks...?'

The watching sergeant was calling his officer a stupid bugger for taking such a risk, but he heard no shots being fired inside the tank. He looked at a couple of gunners lying on the ground nearby and said, 'Do your best to cover me, lads. I'm going after the daft bugger.'

'Sarge.'

Inside the tank the officer was talking to Anna who was pointing down at Tommy and explaining the situation as best she could. Her face was smeared with grease, dirt, tears and Tommy's blood. The walls of the tank were reverberating from the engine and shaking as enemy bullets hit the sides. A tank buster shell came straight through the inch-thick steel, missed Waltham by inches and ricocheted around inside until it was spent, miraculously not hitting anyone. Waltham didn't flinch.

'They only come right through if they hit at a ninety degree angle,' he assured her. 'Not many will do that, most just bounce off.'

'We need to get Tommy to hospital. He's a corporal in your army.'

'Is he alive? He's not looking too good to me.'

'Yes. I've just checked him. I have dressed his wounds but he needs further attention straight away.'

'Well, we have a mobile medical unit here but we need to get him to a Casualty Clearing Station by the sound of it. That's about three miles back over pretty rough country.'

'We have just driven a tank over very rough country.'

'Yes. I appreciate that. Oh, here's my sergeant. He can give us a hand to get Corporal Birch out of here. Is he unconscious or sedated?'

'A bit of both.'

'They need gas masks, sir,' said the sergeant, who was wearing one. 'Another one's just gone off.'

'Damn these bloody Hun.'

'I think we have some in a locker,' said Anna. 'If Thomas is sent to England I would like to go with him. My mother lives there. She is English. My father was a doctor who was killed during our journey from Mannheim to here.'

'Bloody hell!'

'I think that describes our journey,' said Anna.

'I would have described it as an impossible journey. Who's idea was it to embark upon such madness?'

'Mine I think. Tommy and my father fully agreed with me.'

The bullets and shells hitting the tank side seemed to be increasing. Louis was standing under the hatch wondering whether or not to climb out.

'I think we need to get out of here, sir,' said the sergeant.

'Of course. I was a bit distracted listening to her story, fascinating don't you think, sergeant?'

'I'm a bit distracted by all that stuff hitting this tank ... sir.'

'Okay. It's tally ho and away. We're only a few yards from our trenches. We should scramble out quickly and use the tank to shield us from enemy fire.' He said this to Anna, who relayed his advice to Louis who was already climbing out of the hatch. Anna shouted after him in French.

'You might have helped us get Thomas out!' Then to Waltham she said, 'He's hoping to sell the tank back to the British army.'

The captain and the sergeant laughed out loud. Anna didn't need this laughter explaining to her, although Louis wouldn't be amused. Waltham took a quick look out of the hatch then ducked back down as shells whistled over him.

'I think your French friend made it to the trenches,' he said, 'but it might be a bit tricky hoisting Corporal Birch out of the hatch under fire. Any ideas, sarn't?'

'There's a small side door in the tank wall,' said Anna, 'back there.'

The sergeant went to take a look. 'Door here, sir.'

'On the sheltered side?'

'Erm...' The sergeant took a couple of seconds to get his bearings. 'Yes, sir. With us being slewed almost sideways on to the enemy we should have plenty of cover behind it if we go out this way.'

'Tradesman's entrance it is then,' said Waltham, 'or tradesman's exit in our case. Once they get their masks on, sergeant, get the door open then give me a hand with Tommy.' He looked at Anna. 'Can you manage the trip on your own? Er ... I didn't get your name.'

'Anna ... I'll come along with you if that's all right.'

'Won't let him out of your sight eh?'

'Something like that.'

'Excellent. Well, if you can get the gas masks on

yourself and Tommy we'll deliver you both to the mobile medics. They'll make the arrangements to get you to the Clearing Station.'

'Thank you.'

'Well, Anna, it looks like your impossible journey was a success. Congratulations!'

Anna looked down at Tommy and said, 'It's not over yet.'

Chapter 44

Pontefract. Monday 4th June 1917. 6.15 pm
'I suppose you've heard,' said Agnes as Charlie came in from work. He'd been out checking on a gang working overtime. Part of his management duties.

'Heard what?'

'About Florence Gooding.'

'What about her?'

'I thought you might have heard at work. Mrs Morley came round to tell me. She's hung herself.'

'Oh no.'

'Oh yes, Charlie, and do you know what? I blame meself for all this for kicking off at Rita like I did. That's what set it all off. That butcher was as good a man as anyone round here.'

'Nay, Agnes. Let's not go into all that blame business again. It seems to me that it was everyone's fault and no one's fault.'

'She'd lost both her boys. She had nothing to

live for. She tied one end of her clothes line round her neck and the other to the bedstead in her bedroom, then she opened the window and jumped out. She made a right mess of herself in more ways than one. It was a milkman who found her, this morning.'

'Oh my God!' said Charlie. 'I bet she was an awful sight.'

'When Lily Morley heard she went straight round there. You know what she's like for not wanting to miss anything.'

'I do.'

'Poor Florence was still hanging there. Lily said it was really horrible. The milkman was so sickened he couldn't finish his round. He threw up in her yard. How bad have things got to get to make you do such a thing? I mean I feel dreadful about our Tommy, but at least I've still got Edith and Stanley and you ... and Rita and young Benjamin, now that I've come to me senses. Florence had no one left.'

'She'll have wanted to join her boys,' said Charlie.

'Well, she's done that all right,' said Agnes. 'We must hope they're all together – choose where they all are.'

'I sometimes wonder who's having it worse in this damned war,' said Charlie, 'us or the ones fighting it. At least when you're out there fighting you have some sort of control over whether you live or die, but us left back here have got no control. All we get's a letter in a brown envelope and we're expected to carry on regardless.'

'I'll make the tea,' said Agnes. 'It's poached

eggs on toast.'

'You're a good woman, Agnes. Never let anyone tell you different.'

The Birch family had finished their evening meal when the knock came on the door. It had been a quiet meal, due to the news about Florence Gooding. Everyone around the table knew what it was like to lose someone to the war.

It was an official knock, three loud raps. Charlie looked round at his family as if to confirm that they were all there. They were. So if it was bad news it couldn't be the worst news. He'd had enough worst news to last him a lifetime. He went to the door. On the step stood two officers from the KOYLI, in dress uniform. The single crown on his epaulette identified one of them as a major; the other officer was a lieutenant. It was the major who spoke.

'Am I addressing Sergeant Charles Birch DCM?'

'Not any more. You're addressing Charlie Birch building manager for Scurfield's Builders.'

The major smiled. 'Ah, the very man we want. May we come in?'

Charlie stood back and let them through as he called out to his family, 'Attention! KOYLI officers coming through.' Only Stanley stood up and saluted. The officers returned his salute.

'Sit down, gentlemen,' said Agnes. 'I do hope you've brought us some good news for a change.'

'We have indeed, madam.'

Rita was nursing young Benjamin on her knee. 'Is it about my Tommy?' she blurted. It was the only good news she was interested in.

'If you mean Corporal Thomas Birch MM, then it is.'

Rita clasped a hand to her mouth. Eyes wide, almost fainting with anticipation.

'Spit it out, sir,' said Charlie. 'It's our lad you're talking about. Is he alive or dead? We only want to hear about him being ali–'

The major interrupted him. 'He's alive.'

Rita screamed so loud she had everyone wondering if she was hurt in any way. 'He's alive! My Tommy's alive!'

'Where ... w ... where is he?' asked Charlie. He was scarcely able to get the words out.

'He's in a hospital in Kent with a wound he sustained escaping from Germany.'

'He escaped from Germany?'

'He did, yes.'

'But he got blown up in France, what was he doing in Germany?'

'Apparently, he was in a German hospital, pretending to be a German soldier who had lost his power of speech after being blown up by a mine.'

'Blown up by a mine?' said Charlie. 'We knew about that but we were told it had blown him to bits.'

'He was quite badly injured but all in one piece. We don't know the full story yet but it all sounds quite miraculous from beginning to end.'

Agnes had clasped her hand to her mouth in shock. 'Honestly? Is ... is ... is he alive?'

'Alive but wounded – expected to make a full recovery, I hasten to add.'

'Was he badly hurt?'

'I believe he was, but he's definitely recovering.'

'How do we get there?' asked Charlie.

'We have arranged rail passes for you all. I understand you were told he was killed in action.'

'We were, sir, yes ... nine months ago.'

'The army apologises for that. It's very rare we make such a mistake but it seems his survival was something of a miracle.'

'But he's definitely alive is he?' said Charlie. 'And he's been behind enemy lines all the time.'

'Your son's story is quite remarkable, Sergeant Birch.'

'He's a remarkable lad,' said Charlie. Then to his family he said, 'Right you lot. Tomorrow we're off to see our Tommy.' He took hold of Agnes and danced her round the room singing at the top of his out-of-tune voice. Agnes and Edith sang as well. Stanley ran outside and raced up and down the street shouting at the top of his voice.

'Our Tommy's coming home, he's alive!'

People came to doors to listen to the boy. They looked down the street at the Birch house and saw Agnes emerge with Charlie holding onto her waist and Edith holding onto his, dancing the conga up the street. They were more amazed when the two officers joined on the end of the conga line. Not to be outdone the neighbours joined the line as Charlie took it out onto the main road, then back down the street.

It all broke up outside the house as Charlie stood on his top step and addressed the gathered neighbours at the top of his substantial voice. 'These two KOYLI officers have just come to tell us that our Tommy's alive and in a hospital down in Kent. We're going down to see him tomorrow.'

'If you like you can travel overnight and get there first thing in the morning,' said the major.

'Did you hear that?' shouted Charlie. 'We can go tonight and by the heck we damn well will!'

'Three cheers for Tommy Birch,' someone shouted. They were on their fourth rousing cheer as the family and the officers went inside.

'I'm not sure we should have been seen dancing the conga in the street in dress uniform,' said the major.

'He's one of your own, come back from the dead, sir. I think it's most appropriate behaviour,' said Charlie who couldn't wipe the broad smile off his face. 'You should have heard what they marched to when the Koylis paraded through Pontefract.'

'Ah, yes. I was there myself. I believe that chant was about you, was it, sergeant?'

'I believe it might have been, sir. I still have the bullet hole to prove it.'

'Don't you dare show him it, Charlie Birch,' said Agnes.

'Thank you, madam. I'm prepared to take his word for it.'

Charlie's grin was plastered permanently to his face. 'Right everybody,' he said, 'just pack enough for two nights. Stanley, change into something clean and wash that muck off yer face.'

To the major he said, 'Would it be in order if I wore me KOYLI beret and me medals?'

'Absolutely. I would insist on it.'

'I want to do my lad proud when we get there. I assume it's a military hospital is it?'

'It is,' said the major. 'It's called Orchard Hospital. It's a military convalescent hospital in Dartford. They took him there due to its proximity to the English Channel he'd just crossed. Once we get the train times I'll arrange transport from the station to the hospital.'

'Convalescent?' said Agnes. 'Did you hear that, Charlie? If he's convalescing it means he's getting better.'

'Yes, I heard that, love. By heck I can't wait to get down there. How long will it take?'

'I don't know for certain. We can get you from here to Leeds Station, then you'll have to change in London for the Kent train. We've brought rail passes with us. You'll need five will you?'

'Six, there's baby Benjamin as well,' said Edith. 'He's Tommy's son.'

'I doubt if the infant will need a pass.'

'Tommy doesn't know about him yet,' said Rita.

'Oh,' said the major, 'I suspect he won't know about his Military Medal either. If you have it here you might want to take it with you.'

Charlie had tears in his eyes when he took the major's hand and shook it vigorously. 'By heck, sir, I'm so bloody happy I could bust!'

He looked at Agnes who was standing at the window, looking out in silence with one hand clutched over her mouth.

'What's up, love?' said Charlie, who knew that pose.

'I don't know. I got to thinking about poor Florence hanging there, and here we all are, dancing around with our Tommy being alive.'

He put an arm around her. 'It's like I said, love. You're a good woman with a big heart, but Florence is with her boys now and there's nothing we can do about it. This war stinks, love, and it looks like we're going to get out of it without losing anyone. That's all we need to think about.'

The junior officer was looking at Rita who was numb with shock, clinging onto her baby with tears streaming down her face. 'Are you all right, madam?' he asked.

'She never gave up on Tommy,' explained Edith. 'She always knew he was alive. Never had any doubts did you, Rita love?'

Rita smiled through her tears and kissed her baby. This was the day she'd been waiting for and she couldn't stop crying. Why was that? Was it true? Was she really going to get her Tommy back?

At seven-thirty the following morning they were picked up at the Dartford Railway Station by an army troop transporter pulled by two horses, and taken to Orchard Hospital where Charlie went to reception.

'I know it's very early for visiting time but we're here to visit my son, Thomas Birch.'

The receptionist smiled. 'Ah, the Birch family. We're all expecting you. I'll get someone to show you to ward 16 which is up on the first floor.'

'We have suitcases. Can we leave them here?'

'Yes, just pass them over, I'll keep an eye on them for you.'

'Thank you.'

A young porter appeared and led the group up a staircase, through a door and into a corridor.

'Ward 16 is the door at the end on the right. Mr Birch is in the first bed on the right. I know, I brought him up here,' he added. 'Hey, he's a good bloke for a Yorkshireman.'

'We're all good blokes, yer cheeky beggar!'

The young porter laughed, ran forward and opened the door for them. They were about to troop through when Charlie put up a halting hand. 'I think we should let Rita go in first with young Benjamin. We'll give them five minutes alone then we'll go in.'

Agnes was about to argue when he stayed her with a warning glance. Rita looked at them all. It would have been her preference to go in on her own, so she wasn't going to protest.

'Can you manage with Benjamin?' Charlie asked her.

'If Tommy's through that door I can manage anything, Charlie.'

'Of course you can.'

He held the door open for her. With a crutch under her right armpit and holding Benjamin in her left arm she went in and looked to her right. There was someone in the bed but she couldn't see a face. She went nearer. Whoever it was had his face half covered by a sheet and was fast asleep.

'Tommy?'

No movement.

She placed Benjamin on the bed and, reaching out with her free hand, she pulled the sheet away from his face and squealed with delight. It was Tommy, her Tommy. It was his lovely face. A lot paler than she remembered, and he was snoring gently.

She leaned her crutch against the bed and kissed the side of his face, whispering in his ear, 'Wake up, sleepy head,' as she had so many times in the past.

He opened his eyes. Her face was an inch from his. He blinked away the sleep and asked, 'Who is it?'

'Me.'

'Who's me?'

'Rita Victoria Birch.'

'Rita, it's you!'

He sat up and opened his arms to her. They hugged for a full minute, then he saw young Benjamin. He drew away from Rita and looked from him to her. She was smiling and crying at the same time.

'Who's that?'

'That's Benjamin, he's our son.'

'What? You're joking!'

'He's six weeks old. He's our son.'

'I didn't know we'd got a son.'

'Well, you do now. This is Benjamin Charles Birch.'

Tommy was now overwhelmed with happiness. He looked from Benjamin to Rita and back. The pain from his wound was numbed by his euphoria as he asked for another hug. Rita obliged. Tommy looked over her shoulder and asked, 'Whose is that crutch on the bed?'

'It's mine. I broke my leg.'

'Did you?'

'Yes.'

'Oh, Rita just come here and kiss me.'

She sat beside him, leaning into him and kissing him passionately. It was what she'd been waiting for and praying for. Him as well.

'The army told us you were dead, Tommy, but I never believed it.'

'Oh no, I was never dead.' He looked at Benjamin. 'This is my son is he? What's his name?'

'I've just told you. Benjamin ... Benjamin Charles.'

'Benjamin Charles. Wow! How did this happen?'

'What? How do you think, Tommy? He was conceived on your last home leave. You can remember that far back can you?'

'Bits of it. I took a nasty knock back in September.'

'It was quite a memorable occasion.'

'Was it? Oh yeah, I remember now. My last night home. You were wearing...' He scrunched his face up, trying to remember.

'I wasn't wearing anything, Tommy.'

'Oh, right. Oh, yes, I definitely remember now. So that's when we made Benjamin Birch is it?'

'It is.'

'By heck! We did a good job. Look at him.'

'Yeah, he's a great kid.'

'Rita, I wouldn't mind doing it again right now. I've thought about it so often. I want you right now.'

She laughed. 'Tommy Birch! Behave yourself. This is a hospital full of people. All the family's through that door.'

'Are they? How've you got on with them?'

'Fine, we got on fine.'

'My God, Rita! I thought I'd never see you again. I've had a right old time getting back.'

'So I hear. Oh Tommy, it's so good to have you back. I do love you so much. How are you?'

'Well considering I had a bullet go right through me I'm not doing so bad.'

'Right through you?'

'Yes.'

A thought struck her.

'When?'

'About a week ago I think.'

'Could it have been last Monday?'

'Erm... Let me think. Is it Monday today?'

'Tuesday.'

'I lose track of days, but yes it was Monday. We'd been travelling on our bikes since the previous night which was erm ... Sunday, so it was definitely a Monday.'

'And the bullet went right through you ... where exactly?' She thought for a second and said, 'No, no ... let me guess.'

Rita pointed to the spot on her own body where she'd had the pain the night Dieter shot Tommy. He unbuttoned his pyjamas and showed her his dressing which covered the exact same spot.

'How did you know that?'

'I'm guessing that you got shot in the evening a week ago today.'

'That's right. I'd say about six o'clockish. This German guy, he was supposed to be on our side but he suddenly went crazy and shot me.'

'I felt your pain, Tommy. Your mother was with me, she'll tell you. It was the same night Dad came home upset because Stuart Gooding had hanged himself.'

'Young Stuart Gooding? Oh no! Why would he

do that?'

'Oh, it's another story, but it was definitely last Monday. Your dad came home an hour early, all upset about Stuart. Hang on – that would make it about five, and that was an hour before you say you were shot. Maybe I've got it wrong.'

'Not really – Germany's an hour ahead of us in time, Rita.'

Tommy took her in his arms again and kissed her. 'I hope it wasn't as bad as the pain I felt. I thought I was a goner.'

A doctor appeared beside the bed. 'Ah, I take it you're his wife?'

'I'd better be. He keeps kissing me.'

'I don't blame him. Your husband's had a lucky escape from death, in fact I believe he's had a few lucky escapes from death over the past few months.'

She prised herself off the bed, picked up her crutch and asked the doctor, 'How did he survive with a bullet straight through him? I mean it's not as though it went straight through his shoulder or anything, it went through his stomach.'

'Well, not quite. It actually went clean through his gall bladder. Absolute miracle really. Judging from the size of the bullet-hole it was no more than seven millimetres in diameter. It made a mess of his gall bladder, which we've now taken out, and went through his body, front to back, slightly off-centre, which meant it completely missed his spine. It did break a rib but that'll mend easily enough, so all he's lost is his gall bladder, which he won't miss one bit.' He looked down at Tommy and addressed his next words to him.

'You know, Tommy, many of your comrades, with much lesser wounds than yours, died of infection rather than the wound itself but you miraculously avoided all infection. You're a lucky man in so many ways. It must have been really painful though.'

'It did sting a bit but I had a wonderful nurse with me,' said Tommy. 'She gave me morphine, straight away.'

'A wonderful nurse?' said Rita. 'Oh yes. I bet she was young and beautiful.'

'She's standing right behind you,' said Tommy. 'Rita, this is Anna. She saved my life many times, sometimes putting her own life in danger. Her father was killed helping me to escape so I'm greatly indebted to them both.'

Rita turned to see that Anna was indeed quite beautiful, standing there in her English nurse's uniform. She took her hand and said, 'Thank you, Anna. Tommy is my life. This is his son, Benjamin.'

'He's a beautiful child, takes after his mother.'

'Hey, he looks the spitting image of me!' said Tommy.

'Was he always this conceited?' asked Anna, doing her best to conceal her jealousy of Rita.

'Always,' said Rita, looking into Anna's eyes to try and detect something as the nurse glanced down at Tommy. Yes, it was there. This nurse loved her Tommy. Why was that a surprise?

'Do you work here now?'

'Yes, I accompanied Thomas here from Germany and when I told them I was a Red Cross nurse experienced in military injuries they gave me a job on a temporary basis. My mother is English and she lives quite near, so it comes in handy.'

'So, you'll be nursing Tommy while he's here?'

'No, I am on a different ward.' Anna saw the relief on Rita's face. 'And I believe he should be ready for transfer to his home town very shortly, so you'll have him all to yourself.'

All to myself. He's my husband. Why shouldn't I have him all to myself? Have I been sharing him with you? I think you and I ought to have words, madam. And I might need to have words with Tommy once he's better.

Tommy watched this exchange between the two women he loved and felt bereft at the prospect of losing Anna. He looked up at her, she caught his eye, he looked back down. It was a brief exchange of glances that told Rita all she needed to know. She placed Benjamin in the bed beside his father who put his arm around him and smiled.

'Blimey. I never knew about this one. My boy eh?'

'There's something else you didn't know about, son.'

The voice came from behind Anna. It was Charlie, accompanied by Agnes, Edith and Stanley, who was holding a packet of grapes he'd half eaten himself. He gave them to his brother, then he stood there hoping for a hug. Tommy obliged.

'This is my family,' Tommy told Anna. 'Family, this is Anna. She's German and she saved my life many times over there.'

Rita couldn't resist this. 'Fancy her being German and saving Tommy's life,' she said, looking at Agnes, pointedly.

Agnes looked away from Rita as they all murmured their thanks to Anna who left the happy group, knowing that Thomas wasn't *her* Thomas any more. She couldn't compete with his beautiful wife and son, much less his family. She gave a bleak smile, left them all to their family joy and went out into the hospital garden for a weep.

A familiar figure was heading her way up the path. He saw her and waved. 'Anna, I was hoping I would see you here.' He spotted she'd been crying. 'Oh dear, have I arrived at an inopportune moment?'

'Erm no, I er, I'm sorry I never got your name.'

'Harry ... Harry Waltham. I wondered if I should come in uniform as you might recognise me easier. Bit hairy the last time we met, what? I heard they'd given you a job here. Your hospital people asked me for a reference, would you believe? My name was on the pass at the Clearing Station which accompanied Corporal Birch all the way here. Grief! I only knew you for an hour at the most, but I didn't tell them that. Told them you were a skilled and dedicated professional. Anyway I got a seven-day leave and I thought I'd look you up. See how you two were going on. I assume you're a couple are you?'

'I do not know what you mean.'

'I mean is he your boyfriend? You took care of him with so much love and affection back there that I assumed it to be the case. How is he? Did he er, did he make it?'

'Yes, he survived.'

'So, happy ever after for you two eh?'

'Not for me. Thomas is married. He is in there

now with his wife and family. He has a young baby son he did not know about.'

'Good Lord! Am I right in thinking this is bad news for you?'

She looked at him. He was in his late twenties, quite handsome, dashing almost, with a moustache and dark, glossy hair. Most unlike Tommy whose hair was always untidy.

'Perhaps I might take you out for a spot of breakfast somewhere? Are you allowed off the premises?'

'I do not know.'

'If they haven't told you they can't fault you for it. I have a roadster parked down the way, why don't we go out for a spin? There a café about five minutes away.'

'I don't suppose they'd miss me for half an hour.'

'Jolly good. Do you smoke?'

'No.'

'Mind if I do?'

'Not at all.'

His manner was breezy and immensely friendly. She also knew him to be a brave and resourceful man. They approached the car which was an open-top four seater roadster, bright shiny blue with red spokes in the wheels and huge brass headlamps. It looked brand new.

'Is this yours?'

'Oh no. I just rented it from a local garage. I have one very much like it though, so you don't have to worry about whether I know how to drive it or not.'

As she got into the car she asked him, 'Where do you live, Harry?'

'I live near a town called Melton Mowbray. It's way north of here, over a hundred miles away.'

He got out the starting handle and cranked the engine to life. She looked at the cut of his suit and the quality of his shoes. 'Are you a rich man?'

'Do I need to be rich to take a charming young lady out to breakfast?'

'I think you are rich.'

'Okay, if I need to be rich I will pretend to be rich, so long as you pay for the breakfast.'

This made Anna laugh. Tommy had made her laugh as well. During breakfast she told him chapter and verse about her time with Tommy in the hospital and the journey to the British front line. He was most attentive, fascinated by her story. He sat back and lit a cigarette.

'And now you're heartbroken that his wife's turned up.'

She gave a slight nod.

'Well, Anna, if there was something I could do to fix your broken heart I would.'

'You are a kind man.'

'I might be a man who is taking advantage of a beautiful woman with a broken heart.'

'You are buying me breakfast, you are not taking advantage of me.'

'I thought you were paying.'

'I'm a penniless nurse.'

'In that case I would like to buy you dinner sometime.'

'Why is that? Do I look as if I am starving?'

'Anna, when I asked if you and Tommy were a couple I was sincerely hoping you'd say no. My only reason in coming here today was to find

381

that out.'

'You mean you want *us* to be a couple? I hardly know you except you are a British Army officer.'

'If I tell you what I am it might put you off me.'

'Give me a try.'

He gave it some thought before he answered. 'Well, I'm what we English call an aristocrat. My father is a baronet. I live in a tiny hovel called Waltham House. It's got seventy-three rooms and is set in a thousand acres of mainly farmland. There you are. You can walk away from me right now. In my favour I might add that I am not heir to the family throne, just the younger son of a noble lord. I got a half-baked second at Oxford that was barely enough to get me into Sandhurst, but I'm quite good at soldiering and will probably rise to colonel or maybe even brigadier given a following wind.'

'So, you are rich.'

'I got a few quid when grandpa died eight years ago but I mainly exist on my army pay. I might get a few more quid when the old man pops off but he's only fifty-two so that's a long time off. My older brother will get the house and the land and the title, although I do own a small lodge on the land which I use now and again.'

'So, are you a sir or an earl or anything?'

'Well, I'm an honourable, for what good it does me. At fancy functions I'm announced as the Honourable Captain Henry Waltham MC.'

'You've got an MC?'

'Yes, it's what they give officers with no sense of self-preservation. Had I been a corporal I'd have got an MM like Tommy.'

'Tommy's got a bravery medal? He didn't tell me.'

'It was awarded posthumously. He wouldn't have known. He'll know now he's been resurrected.'

Agnes was the first to give her son a hug, to the extent that Charlie thought she might be smothering the life out of him, just when they'd got him back.

'Mam,' he said. 'It's lovely to see you but I've got a bullet-hole in me and it's a bit tender.'

'Put him down, Agnes,' said Charlie. 'Leave some for us.'

Hugs for Edith and Charlie followed, with Charlie burying his face in his son's shoulder until he'd wiped away the tears on Tommy's pyjamas. Tommy tried to ease the situation by asking his dad, 'What else was it that I didn't know about, Dad?'

'Ah, it's this.' Charlie took a box out of his pocket and from the box he took a medal with a red, white and blue ribbon attached. He pinned the medal onto his son's pyjamas, stood back and saluted him.

Tommy was looking down at it, trying to see what it was.

'It's the Military Medal,' said Charlie. 'You were awarded it posthumously, son. For bravery in the field – that's what it says on the medal.'

'Wow! They gave me a gong. I hope I don't have to give it back now I'm alive again.'

'No chance of that, lad. You won it fair and square at the first battle of the Somme, July 1st 1916 when you saved an officer's life.'

'Lieutenant Peter Walker,' said Stanley. 'He wrote us a letter, didn't he, Dad?'

'He did that, son. Thought the world of you did Lieutenant Walker.'

'He was a good officer,' said Tommy. 'Civil engineer in civvy street.'

'Well, we have his address in England so we can let him know you're back.'

'That's if he's still alive.'

'You're alive, lad, and you won't be going back. No matter how long this war lasts. It's over for you.'

'Really?'

'Really. You took a German bullet and sustained a major wound that entitles you to a full time Blighty ticket, *and* you took a bomb blast that nearly blew you to kingdom come. I'm gonna get you invalided out, Tommy, and if I have my way you won't be going back down that pit.'

'Oh yeah, what do I do for a living, Dad?'

'Site engineer, lad. Scurfield's branching out into road building. You know all about setting-out and using them surveying instruments, you should be able to apply all your learning to being a site engineer with fresh air in your lungs and the sun on your face.'

'Sun ... Pontefract?'

'All right, fresh air then.'

Tommy looked at his mother. 'Mam, Rita told me something really strange just now. It was last Monday evening that I got shot – about six o'clock German time, five o'clock English time.' He pointed to the dressing on his stomach wound. 'The bullet went in here and came out of my back. Does that ring any bells?'

Agnes frowned at him. 'How do you mean?'

'I mean what were you doing at that time last Monday?'

Agnes shrugged and looked at Rita who raised her eyebrows in encouragement and pointed to her own stomach, saying, 'It was just before Charlie came home all upset about young Stuart.'

'What? Oh yes!' said Agnes. 'I remember now... Oh no, I don't believe this!'

'Come on, Agnes, you were there,' said Rita. 'Just tell them what happened to me.'

Agnes looked round at the others and said, 'Well, Rita got this real nasty pain at exactly that same time and at the same part of her body, front and back.' She indicated where, using both hands. 'Same as where Tommy was shot. She said at the time it was something to do with Tommy, but I didn't believe her. You felt really tired after that, didn't you? You were going to go to bed and then Charlie came home early.'

'I was tired as well,' said Tommy. 'Anna gave me a morphine shot.'

'Oh my God!' said Agnes. 'Rita was living your life.'

'She was nearly living my death. I'm glad for Rita's sake that I pulled through.'

'Nobody believed me when I said Tommy wasn't dead,' said Rita.

'No, we didn't, love,' said Charlie. 'Good God! Is this true?'

'It is, Charlie, yes.'

'Well, from now on I'll believe every damned thing Rita says.'

'I believe Tommy's going to do as you say and become a site engineer for Jack Scurfield,' said Rita.

'I definitely believe that,' said Charlie.

They all laughed, but Tommy didn't think it was such a bad idea. The chat went on for an hour or so and Rita thought it would do no harm to allow the family some alone time with Tommy so she decided to hobble outside for a stroll. She was happy, her Tommy was back and he wouldn't be going to war again. She was just on her way out of the door when she met Anna coming in.

'Hello, Anna.'

'Hello, Rita. Have you broken your leg?'

'I have, yes.'

'It must be awkward looking after a baby.'

'I get a lot of help from Tommy's family.'

'How is he? Happy I hope.'

'Happy and sad I think.'

'Oh? Why would he be sad?'

'He's a bit of a charmer, isn't he?' said Rita.

'Yes, he's a very charming man. I like him a lot.'

'Yeah, all the girls like my Tommy, and with him being away from his home for so long I did wonder how he was coping without me.'

'He missed you very much.'

Rita studied the German nurse as she posed her next question in her mind. She could think of no other, way than to come right out with it.

'I fell in love with Tommy the day I met him. How long did it take you to fall in love with him, Anna?'

Anna turned her face away from the question. Rita reached out and gently turned it back. 'You

386

did fall in love with him, didn't you?'

Anna saw no reason to deny her feelings for Tommy. 'Of course I did.'

'Of course you did,' said Rita, without a hint of malice.

'In fact I still love him.'

'I know. Did you come to work here because you wanted him to come to you instead of me?'

'No, I am working here for the reason I told you. But if he had chosen me I would have been overjoyed and you would have been sad. But I cannot have him because he loves you. He always told me that.'

'Did he ever tell you he loved you?'

'He told me he could not love me because he loved you. He has you,' she said, 'and now he has baby Benjamin who is such a beautiful child. When he leaves here I will never see him again and my heart will be broken.'

'You loved him enough to save his life, almost at the cost of your own, and now I am rewarding you by taking him away from you. You must hate me.'

'I do not hate you. I always knew if he got back to England he would come to you.'

'And yet you helped him.'

'I helped him because I wanted him to be happy. You may not believe this but when he was shot and I thought he would die I was as sad for you as I was for me. It was a strange and terrible feeling that I never wish to experience again. Love can be so cruel.'

'Anna, I believe you, and I promise you that I will make him happy.'

'It will please me for him to be happy, but I will never again meet anyone like him. I think you know that.'

'Anna, I do know that. Now that you are living in England you can come and visit us if you like.'

'Rita, if I come to visit you I will try to steal him from you.'

Rita smiled at this woman whom she was growing to like. 'In that case I withdraw my invitation, but I thank you so much for bringing Tommy back to me. By the way, I know that Tommy will have fallen in love with you. He couldn't have helped himself.'

When Rita got back to the ward Agnes, Edith and Stanley were still in happy conversation with Tommy. Charlie was standing out in the corridor, in earnest discussion with a doctor.

'Who's Charlie talking to?' Rita asked Edith, who grinned, as did they all.

'Well, Dad might be staying on for a few days,' she said. 'Apparently the Koylis told the hospital all about his bullet in the bum story and they've offered to take it out.'

'I didn't realise it was still in.'

'Oh yes – and it's been giving him bother for years. Always will if he doesn't have it removed. He's often talked about it but never got round to it. Now's his opportunity.'

Stanley called out, 'Hey, they've got an operation that can get rid of a pain-in-the-arse.'

'I should keep quiet about that if I were you, Stanley,' said Edith, 'otherwise they might get rid of you.'

Rita looked at them both and smiled. The Birch family were back together and in full swing. *Her* family.

Chapter 45

Pontefract. Friday 1st November 1918

It was seventeen months since Tommy got back. Seventeen happy months which now saw young Benjamin Charles toddling around their new house, Tommy's wounds had fully healed and he was working for Scurfield's as a site engineer – a job he much preferred to working underground. He was twenty-three years old, he had a beautiful son, he had colour in his cheeks, four pounds a week in his wage packet and a certificate to say he was now a qualified civil engineer. Rita was as beautiful as ever and their love was as deep as ever it had been. He was getting ready for work when she called out to him from her bed.

'Tommy, I wonder if you could take Benjamin to your mam's today? I'm not feeling so good. I could do with a day in bed to be honest.'

'Not so good? Why, what's the matter, love?'

Rita coughed and said, 'Oh, I don't know. I've got a bit of a cold, aches and pains. I could hardly sleep last night and you know what I'm like if I don't sleep properly.'

'Hey, you just stay where you are, love. Do you want me to make you some breakfast?'

'No, just a cup of tea and there's some aspirins

in the cupboard. You can take him in the van, can't you?'

'Yeah, sure.'

After breakfast Tommy took his eighteen-month-old son out to the firm's van, similar to the one his dad had, and looked back at the house they'd bought with George Miller's money. He knew his mother thought there was more to Rita's friendship with the dead butcher than Rita admitted, but Tommy believed his wife had remained faithful to him, even after being told he was dead, and even if she hadn't, he had no room to complain, after what he'd got up to with Anna. There was no point in him refusing George's largesse out of petty principle. The money was in their account and George was dead. There was no one to give it back to.

It was a fine three-bedroom detached house in a desirable area on the edge of Pontefract and it had cost a large chunk of the money George had left Rita. It even had one of the few telephones in Pontefract, supplied by Scurfield's Builders, with Tommy being management.

Tommy thought about the hovel she had always lived in and how she aspired to better things. Well this was better, no doubt about that, and Rita deserved it, no doubt about that either. There was no mortgage on it; they could live comfortably on Tommy's wage; the war was coming to an end, and Jack Scurfield had big expansion plans for when peacetime came; plans that included Tommy and his dad.

He looked at his son and knew that the only cloud on his horizon was Anna who was now married to the very army officer who had helped him over the lines last year. He had no right to be jealous, but he was. He had loved Anna as much as he loved Rita and now she was married to someone else. It was a strange, emotional confusion that he was struggling with, especially as he had to keep it to himself.

He had been invited to the wedding which was a society affair and, to rub salt into his wounds, Tommy would have had to hire a morning suit to watch a woman he loved getting married. It was an invitation he politely turned down, assuming Anna would understand. God help him if Rita ever managed to read his mind – and he couldn't put that past her. He took Benjamin into his father's house and called out for his mother.

'What is it, Tommy? Your dad's just left. Hello, little cheeky face.'

Benjamin said something like 'lo ganma,' which amused Agnes.

'Rita's not so good. She's having a day in bed. Would you mind looking after Benjamin?'

'Not at all. What's wrong with her?'

'She's got a cold. Aches and pains. Couldn't sleep properly last night. A day in bed and she'll be as right as rain tomorrow most probably.'

'It's not flu is it? There's a lot of it about, and it can be very nasty.'

'I don't think so.'

'Is she coughing? Has she got a temperature?'

'She's coughing a bit but I don't know about her temperature.'

'I think I'll take a walk round with Benjamin. If she needs to see the doctor I'll send him.'

A nasty thought struck Tommy. 'Mam, that flu's killing people. You don't think she's got that, do you?'

'Of course I don't, but it's always better to be safe than sorry. If she does need a doctor he can give her something for it. I'll take a look at her myself first.'

Tommy worked until mid-afternoon then he called in the yard to say he was going home early to see if his wife was okay. When he got there Agnes was downstairs, looking worried. Benjamin was playing with a toy train on the floor.

'She's not good, Tommy. The doctor's been and given her something and he's calling back later this afternoon.'

Tommy went upstairs to find Rita holding her throat and fighting for breath. 'I can't breathe properly, Tommy,' she croaked. 'Can you get the doctor back?'

Tommy rushed back downstairs. 'Mam, I'm going for the doctor. She can hardly breathe. I think she's got it, Mam. I think she's got this flu!'

He ran out of the house and jumped into his van, returning ten minutes later with the doctor who had cancelled his appointments in order to attend to Rita. When they got into the bedroom she was choking, her skin was turning blue and there was bloody froth coming from her nose and mouth.

'Her lungs have filled with fluid,' said the doctor. 'We need to get her to the hospital for them to drain it.'

'Can't you do it here?'

'I'm afraid I can't, no. I believe you have a

392

telephone. I need to get an ambulance.'

'Yes, it's in the hall.'

Rita held out her hand for Tommy to hold. He did so, crying now with fear for his wife's life. Then she stopped choking and her face grew calm. Her eyes turned to him. Her mouth was moving as if in speech but he couldn't hear anything. He put his ear to her mouth, just in time to hear her murmur, 'Goodbye, my darling.'

Her eyes were partially open but the light had gone out from behind them. Tommy stared at her, looking for movement, listening for her breathing. He took her shoulder and shook her gently.

'Rita, Rita, wake up, love.'

Nothing.

'Rita, come back to me, love. Don't leave me.'

He wasn't at all prepared for the worst, but he knew it had happened. He turned to Agnes who was ashen-faced. 'This isn't right, Mam. She only had a cold this morning. She can't be dead. She can't, Mam!'

The doctor came back up and surveyed the scene before taking Rita's pulse. He then put a stethoscope to her chest and listened for her beating heart as Tommy and his mother looked on in shocked silence. Then he looked up at them and shook his head.

'She's gone, I'm afraid. I'm terribly sorry.'

Tommy dropped to his knees by the side of the bed they had shared as man and wife the previous night. 'But she can't have gone so quickly. She was all right this morning.'

'It's a deadly virus,' said the doctor. 'It often happens very quickly. I will need to keep an eye on the others in your family, Mrs Birch, including Benjamin.'

Agnes said nothing. She was too shocked to speak.

Epilogue

St Joseph's Church, Pontefract. Monday November 11th 1918

On that memorable day in the streets of Pontefract – in fact in every road and street in every village and town and city in Britain and throughout all the Allied countries of the world – there were massive and jubilant celebrations. Flags hung from almost every window and lamp post; bunting was strung across roads; people danced and sang in the streets. Strangers kissed strangers, buses and charabancs took crowds of cheering people on tours of the streets. It had been announced at five o'clock that morning that the Germans had surrendered and that the Armistice would be signed at eleven o'clock. Such was the stupidity of the war that in the six intervening hours the fighting continued and 3,000 men died.

In St Joseph's Church there was nothing to celebrate. It was Rita's funeral service. Her coffin was carried in by Tommy, Charlie, and two men from the undertakers. As soon as they lowered it onto the bier in front of the altar a KOYLI bugler at the back of the church began to play 'The Last Post'. It was an intensely dramatic and moving sound

394

that drew tears from every eye in the church.

The whole congregation, following the lead of Tommy and his father, got to their feet out of respect and stood to damp-eyed attention. When the bugler had finished, the congregation sat down and the church organ began to play a muted 'No Tears In Heaven' as Charlie walked up to the lectern that had been placed on the altar steps. He took out a sheet of paper from his pocket and laid it in front of him. The church was packed full of Rita's friends, family and work colleagues. The Birch family was on the front row along with Rita's father who had declined an invitation to do the eulogy for his daughter.

'I'm no good wi' words, me. Most likely mek a fool of meself.'

Charlie cleared his throat, looked at his pocket watch and, with the organ playing in the background, he said, 'Well, according to my watch this is the eleventh hour of the eleventh day of the eleventh month, and I believe this is the very minute that the war ends.'

'Thanks be to God,' said Father Mulvaney, standing next to him.

'Amen,' said the congregation.

The organ played on as Charlie continued: 'The war still isn't over for those of us who are yet to be stricken with this dreadful illness which seems to be killing more of us than the Kaiser. It's said to have come from the mud and gore of the trenches over there. I asked for "The Last Post" to be played because if that's the case then Rita was a victim of this war as much as any of our armed forces.

'Rita, my daughter-in-law, was a most wonderful young woman. She was the only child of Benny Clayton who is too grief-stricken to speak today. Rita's husband, my son Tommy, is too grief-stricken to speak at all. A year ago last September we had word from the army that Tommy had been killed in France. It was confirmed by two officers who came to visit us, and in a letter from Tommy's senior officer. That day was the worst day of our lives. He'd been blown up by a massive mine and there was nothing left of him to bury ... or so we were told. Of course with such notification we all knew he was lost to us forever and we mourned him. The army even presented him with a posthumous bravery medal which he rightly deserved after what he did at the first battle of the Somme – Military Medal he got. Everyone knew he was dead. Everyone except Rita. You see, Rita knew he was alive and she drove us mad telling us – and we drove her mad not believing her.'

Charlie looked down at his son. 'And Rita was right of course. There he is, large as life, just as Rita always said he was.' Charlie injected some force into his next words which he spoke slowly, and deliberately: 'You see Rita never once believed him to be dead! Not for one single minute in all the many months he was gone from us did she think he was lost to her! She told us countless times, until one day I told her shut up about it and learn to accept that he's gone. I bitterly regret that. She even told Father Mulvaney here.' The priest nodded his head in concurrence, remembering that day when Rita had been to see him.

'Yes, she did indeed. In this very church.'

'So,' said Charlie, challengingly, 'how did she know he was alive?' He threw up his hands in bewilderment. 'I can only guess, but I think my guess is near to the truth. You see, when people love each other as fiercely as our Tommy and Rita did, they just ... well, they just feel each other's existence in this world. They even feel each other's pain.' He leaned forward with a hand on each side of the lectern. 'Now listen to this – when our Tommy got shot on his way home from Germany Rita felt his pain. She felt the bullet go in and she felt it go out at the exact time our Tommy was shot. I'd never have believed it, but my wife was there when it happened, weren't you, Agnes?'

'I was,' called out Agnes. 'I was with her. Five o'clock on that same Monday. She screamed out like someone had just shot her, and she thought it was something to do with Tommy. She said it might mean that Tommy was hurting but if he was hurting he had to be alive. I'm not sure I believed a word of it until Tommy mentioned it to me.

'And I'll tell you something else. On the night baby Benjamin was born, Rita fell down the stairs in her dad's house. Well, I reckon it was about that time that I got to thinking about our Tommy. Right out of the blue. I thought about how our Tommy'd want me to go see Rita who I hadn't seen since we had that daft falling out, which was my fault. I admit that now.'

Tommy looked at his mother. He knew nothing about the falling out. The family had kept that to themselves on Charlie's orders. Agnes continued:

'That thought I had about Tommy wanting me to go see her was so strong – so strong that I went straight out of the house and got on a Feather-stone bus without even putting me coat or me headscarf on. When I got there she was lying in a heap at the bottom of the stairs with a broken leg, her baby was coming and there was no one around to help her. Broken leg, baby on the way and not a soul to help her. Can you imagine that? Not a single soul to help her.'

Many heads were shaking in the congregation.

'And then I turn up right out of the blue. If our Tommy hadn't managed to get into my thoughts, well ... I just don't want to think about what would have happened. It was a bloody miracle ... sorry, Father.' With a wave of his hand the priest dismissed her apology as unnecessary.

'I got Mrs Lythe round from next door and we delivered the baby between us, mostly by candle light.'

'That's right,' called out Mrs Lythe. 'You were worried that I might set fire to her and you were giving me so much advice about where to put the candles that Rita lost her temper with you.'

'Well, women having babies do lose their temper a bit,' said Agnes.

'That's right. She told you where you could stick the candle.'

The congregation roared with laughter, which completely baffled Tommy, who was confused by the whole story. Charlie held up his hands to restore order and continued:

'Well, we're all laughing, and Rita wouldn't have wanted it any other way, but our Tommy's sitting there, stricken dumb with grief. But I'm here to tell you, son, that your Rita's not in that coffin.

Never in a million years is she in that box. A magical woman like that'd never let herself get stuck in a wooden box. What's left of her might be in there but her spirit and her soul and her love is all around you. That's why we've just had laughter. She'll never leave my son, and she'll never leave her Benjamin.'

The focus of Tommy's mute gaze transferred itself from somewhere in the middle distance up to his dad. Since minutes after Rita's death he hadn't said a word. Charlie looked down at Tommy who was now looking back at him. 'That's right, son. You mark my words. Can you not feel her presence?'

Tommy frowned and gave a slight, uncertain nod.

'Believe me, son, that girl's here in this church all right, but she's not in that coffin. She's out here with you and she'll always be with you. Never forget that, Tommy Birch. Never forget that, my son.'

As Charlie stepped down from the altar a few in the congregation picked up on the tune now being played on the organ and began to sing 'Abide With Me'. Almost at once everyone was singing the hymn that Benny had chosen. It was his only contribution to the ceremony but it turned out to be a rousing one.

It was a cold, dull day, appropriate for the occasion. As hordes of people over newly-freed Europe celebrated the armistice, Rita Birch was laid to rest. To avoid crowding the graveyard she was buried in the company of her family and her closest friends only.

Tommy stood between his father and mother, who both had their arms around him. Tommy remained silent as he stared, dry-eyed, at the lowering coffin. He had no tears left to shed. After the blessing, Father Mulvaney invited people to throw handfuls of earth onto the coffin. Many did, including all the Birch family except Tommy, but including one man who looked to have come on his own.

'Is that Benny Clayton?' asked Agnes.

'It is,' said Charlie.

'He's looking better than he did the last time we saw him. We should ask him back to the house.'

'I'll ask him,' said Edith. She went round to the other side of the grave and spoke to Benny who looked to be nodding his acceptance of the invitation. Then he pointed to a woman standing nearby, also on her own. Edith went over to her.

'Who's that?' Agnes asked. 'Mutton dressed as lamb.'

'Don't be like that, Agnes,' murmured Charlie. 'Remember where we are.'

'It's Rita's mam,' said Mrs Lythe, who was standing with them.

'Isn't she the one who ran off with the coalman?'

'She is.'

'It looks like she'll be coming to the house as well,' said Charlie, 'so you be nice to her, and no talking about coalmen!'

Benny joined them on the way back to the house. His wife seemed to be making her own way, having fallen into conversation with other mourners. Tommy hadn't moved. His father called out to him.

'We'll leave you with Rita, Tommy. Don't be too long, lad.'

Tommy said nothing. Charlie left him to it. Edith glanced back over her shoulder and gave a smile of recognition.

'What are you smiling at, Edith?' Charlie asked her.

'Nothing. I just want our Tommy to be happy that's all.'

'Well he won't be happy for quite some time. He won't find another Rita in a hurry, that's for sure. I'm just glad we got him back in one piece. He's going to need some looking after. We must all do our best for him.'

'I am, Dad.'

Tommy stood there, alone with Rita at last. Dark thoughts swirled through his head. Thoughts about her saying, 'Goodbye my darling,' to him. That meant she knew she was dying. Bloody hell! What was that like? One minute she had a bit of a cold and the next minute she knew she was dying. He should have taken her straight to the hospital that morning. But his dad had said you don't take someone to hospital with only a cold.

He was now having memories of being in the trenches. Missing pieces of his mental jigsaw fell into place – not all of them, just some. He remembered the young German's face after he'd shot him dead, point-blank. The lad had a look of shock and indignation on his face, as if Tommy had no right to shoot him; he remembered stumbling across

No Man's Land carrying the officer on his back; he remembered being shot in the leg and a fleeting moment soon afterwards when he was lying naked on barbed wire. It was the briefest of memories but it was there in stark reality. It was a memory of him being an inch away from a death he knew was coming for certain. He was hearing nothing, feeling nothing and seeing only smoke and sky above him and, in that moment, wondering if he was on the way to heaven or somewhere a lot warmer. It was a two-second picture, now imprinted forever in his memory. He remembered the firing squad and he remembered his fine German boots and Dieter shooting him and once again thinking that he was dead. Blurred and brief memories of being in the tank in a lot of pain and Anna's voice, talking to him. Telling him she loved him and please do not die, Thomas. Then he remembered that Anna was married and the additional heartache that information had caused him.

'Hello, Thomas.'

He wasn't certain if the voice was an echo of his thoughts or coming from behind him. He turned, slowly, and spoke his first word for a week. She was wearing a wide-brimmed black hat and a long black coat and she looked quite beautiful.

'Anna.'

'Yes?'

'You look ... er, you look very er, very nice.'

'Thank you.'

'Erm, er ... what are you doing here?'

'Edith wrote to me and told me what had happened, so I came to offer my condolences.'

The mention of his sister had him regaining

some composure.

'Edith has your address has she?'

'Yes, we exchanged addresses back at the hospital where I met you all. It is how I invited you to my wedding.'

'Of course. Congratulations. Sorry I couldn't come.'

'I was glad you didn't. I might not have gone through with it.'

She studied his bereaved face. A face that had been so handsome, even in Mannheim hospital after his massive injury. Now it was pale and drawn with deep unhappiness.

'You deserve to be happy, Anna.'

'So do you, Thomas.'

He closed his eyes, wondering just how he felt about her being here, this woman he had loved just as much as he loved Rita. But his mind was clouded with confusion. All he could come out with was banal small talk.

'Do you er, do you still work at the hospital?'

'I do, yes. I enjoy working there. Oh, Sébastien's airman got back to England all right.'

'His airman?'

'Yes, the one he hid in his cellar.'

'Oh yes, I remember. There's so much I've forgotten.'

'I hope you haven't forgotten me.'

'What? No, of course not.'

'When we were there I got his address from Sébastien and wrote to him. He's going over to France to pay the dear old gentleman a visit.'

'Sébastien will like that. Yes, I remember Sébastien.'

'Do you remember Louis?'

'The mad Frenchman who drove the tank? I do, yes.'

'He got back home all right.'

'Oh, good.'

He remembered having mixed feelings about Louis, but he wasn't sure why. 'Did he manage to sell the tank?'

'I don't think so.'

'So it was all for nothing.'

'He saved our lives and got us over the line. I wouldn't call that nothing.'

'He did, yes. If you ever write to him you must thank him from me. I still remember what your father did for us. He was a very good man.'

'When the French heard about everything he'd done during the war they awarded him a post-humous Légion d'Honneur. I believe Sébastien had something to do with this. He got one too.'

'There were a lot of brave people helping us back then, especially your father.'

'My mother didn't know he had been killed until I got back. I was the one who told her.'

'Oh no. That must have been hard for you. How is she?'

'She took it quite badly. Still does. She won't be out celebrating today. I'll be taking her to visit Father's monument. You could come with us.'

'That's very kind of you but I don't want to leave Rita. I intend to visit her every day and talk to her.'

Anna gave a slow nod and said, 'She was lucky to have you, Thomas.'

There was a silence between them as Tommy

looked back at the grave, then Anna said, 'Are you going to be all right?'

'Oh, I don't know. Rita dying like that was worse than me being blown up, worse than being shot. Worse than anything I've ever known. I don't know how to live with it.'

'But I know you will learn to live with it.'

'How do you know?'

'I know, because my Harry was killed.'

Tommy didn't know what to say at first, so used was he to receiving sympathy that he wasn't really ready to give it out.

'Oh ... no,' he said eventually. 'In er, in France?'

'Germany actually.'

'Germany?'

'Yes, he was shot three weeks ago by a machine gun, and he died instantly.'

Tommy gave a shudder at a memory and said, 'I remember the machine guns. They killed so many of us ... so many of my friends were just shot and killed by faceless people who didn't even know they'd killed anyone. They were just pulling a trigger and firing into dust and smoke. Mind you, we did the same.'

'They brought Harry's body back for burial,' Anna told him, tears in her eyes now as she looked down. 'Laid him to rest in the family plot on the Waltham Estate.'

'Oh yes, he was some sort of nobleman wasn't he?'

Anna smiled. 'Not really. He'd have laughed had you called him a nobleman. You and he would have become great friends I'm sure.'

'He won an MC didn't he? I suspect he was a

very brave man.'

'He was, but he didn't think he was very brave. He used to say he simply had no sense of self-preservation. I thought he was joking but he has been recommended for another medal for the action that killed him. Apparently he was being very brave and very stupid. It's a posthumous one of course – a DCM, whatever that is.'

'Distinguished Conduct Medal.'

'I'd much rather have Harry.'

'Look, I'm er ... I'm really sorry, Anna. It does me no good at all to know that you're unhappy as well.'

'I loved him, Thomas, but it was never as strong as the love I had for you. I will never know such love again.'

He turned and looked at her. 'Anna, I can't love you today. I have nothing inside me to give you.'

'I know that, Thomas. You have suffered a great loss.'

'You loved Harry?'

'I did. He was a wonderful man, just as your Rita was a wonderful woman. I met her you know, at the hospital in Kent. She asked me how long it took me to fall in love with you.'

'How did she know you had?'

'I do not know. How did she know you were still alive?'

'Beats me,' said Tommy, 'but she never wavered from that belief all the time I was away. You say Edith wrote to you. Did she erm ... did she know about us?'

'I think she might have guessed. Rita knew, maybe she told Edith. If it's any consolation, Rita did not hate me. She understood that I would fall in love with you, as did she.'

Tommy was now convinced that Edith had set this meeting up, but he couldn't see what harm she'd done. Seeing Anna was certainly doing him no harm. At least he was talking again.

'Were you in the church?' he asked.

'I was at the back. It was most unusual ... and quite entertaining.'

'We're an unusual family. That thing about Rita falling down the stairs and Mam coming to the rescue was a story I didn't know about.'

'And yet, according to your mother, it was you who somehow sent her there to help Rita.'

'So she says. I can't explain my part in that. Maybe if I try to remember where I was and what I was doing at the time Benjamin was born I could make sense of it.'

'I imagine you'll have been with me. What day was he born?' Anna asked.

'April 30th.'

She stared at him, as if he should know the significance of that date.

'What?' Tommy said.

'April 30th. And I don't suppose he was born around six o'clock in the evening?'

'That's exactly when he was born. I was told that much at least.'

'Thomas, that is precisely the day and time father was killed.'

'Really? Was it that same day?'

'Yes. April 30th. A daughter does not forget the day her father dies. My father, Benjamin, left this world at the same time as your son Benjamin entered it.'

'No.'

'Yes,' she said. 'Whose idea was it to call him Benjamin?'

'Rita's I suppose – it's her dad's name. His name's Benjamin Charles after his two granddads. Well, everyone calls her dad Benny, but I imagine his proper name's Benjamin. So, at that time something in me told my mother to go and visit Rita, did it?'

'I do not know,' Anna said. 'You tell me.'

'Well, around that time my only thought was to get you out of danger.'

'Me being your loved one.'

'Yes.'

'But I was not your *only* loved one who was in danger at that time.'

'What? Well obviously not, but I didn't know about Rita being in danger.'

'You called me Rita back then, so she was on your mind in a moment of crisis.'

'Did I?'

'Yes, twice.'

'Well, she was often on my mind.'

Anna smiled and said, '"There are more things in heaven and earth, Horatio, than are dreamt of in your philosophy."'

'What does that mean?'

'Oh, I was quoting your William Shakespeare's *Hamlet*.'

'You know Shakespeare?'

'Not personally.'

Tommy smiled as he remembered she had a similar sense of humour to Rita. 'Okay,' he said, 'what does it mean?'

'It means we don't have to understand everything that goes on around us.'

'We certainly don't if I had anything to do with my mother going to see Rita.'

'Thomas, were it not for you I'd have been blown up, and what would have happened to Rita and your son if your mother had not arrived to help?'

'You mean...? It's all a very, erm, I don't know ... very spiritual is this, Anna.'

'Thomas, despite having been told you were officially dead your wife knew that you were alive, without questioning how she knew this. It seems to me that she was a spiritual person. I'm guessing she called for your help and you gave it without knowing.'

Anna kissed him on his cheek and stood back, facing him, with the gloomy graveyard and her black mourning clothes in stark contrast to her beautiful face, her sparkling blonde hair and her beguiling smile. She was offering him a last vision of herself which, she hoped, would be indelibly imprinted on his mind.

'My darling man,' she said. Her voice was just audible above the wind murmuring through the trees above their heads. 'I will leave you with your grieving right now, but I want you to know that I am forever yours if you need me.'

Then, she turned and walked away with no backward glance, just a soul full of sorrow for her lover.

And a heart full of hope for herself.

Acknowledgments

To my old pal, Malcolm Roberts, for donating an amusing anecdote to my story and to his wife, Rita, for donating her name. And to another pal, Dennis Birch, who donated his surname to my book without knowing he'd done it.

The publishers hope that this book has given you enjoyable reading. Large Print Books are especially designed to be as easy to see and hold as possible. If you wish a complete list of our books please ask at your local library or write directly to:

Magna Large Print Books
Magna House, Long Preston,
Skipton, North Yorkshire.
BD23 4ND

This Large Print Book for the partially sighted, who cannot read normal print, is published under the auspices of

THE ULVERSCROFT FOUNDATION

THE ULVERSCROFT FOUNDATION

... we hope that you have enjoyed this Large Print Book. Please think for a moment about those people who have worse eyesight problems than you ... and are unable to even read or enjoy Large Print, without great difficulty.

You can help them by sending a donation, large or small to:

**The Ulverscroft Foundation,
1, The Green, Bradgate Road,
Anstey, Leicestershire, LE7 7FU,
England.**
or request a copy of our brochure for more details.

The Foundation will use all your help to assist those people who are handicapped by various sight problems and need special attention.

Thank you very much for your help.